CW01499196

Table of Contents

Introduction

Although Sir Arthur Conan Doyle's Sherlock Holmes canon, beginning with the 1887 publication of *A Study in Scarlet*, creates a vivid physical and mental portrait of the consulting detective, adaptations even during the author's lifetime have embellished the details of his more than 80 stories. Illustrator Sidney Paget made clothing choices, such as the deerstalker, that Conan Doyle never described and drew Holmes as more attractive than the author likely intended. When actor William Gillette immortalized Holmes on stage and later on screen in the first feature-length film about the Great Detective, Holmes not only became sexier, but his emotions also received a romantic overhaul. By the conclusion of *Sherlock Holmes* (1916), the title character acquired a love interest and was ready for marriage. Since then, the creative minds behind filmic adaptations have chosen to mold one or more aspects of Sherlock Holmes's identity into the way they imagine—or want—Holmes to be. Fans, too, are involved in the identity-creation process; through fan fiction, videos, and art, for example, they match their creative endeavors to the Sherlock Holmes in their "head canon."

Nearly 130 years after the introduction of Sherlock Holmes to readers, the Great Detective's identity is being questioned, deconstructed, and reconstructed more than ever. In this book alone, the authors analyze not only who Sherlock Holmes is or has become, but why and how his identity has been formed in a specific way. The essays cover Sherlock Holmes and other familiar characters as they are presented in adaptations released since 2009: the films *Sherlock Holmes* (2009), *Sherlock Holmes: A Game of Shadows* (2011), and *Mr. Holmes* (2015), and television series *Sherlock* (2010–present), which receives the most emphasis in this book, and *Elementary* (2012–present). A range of fan responses to these filmic texts also is discussed in depth, including feminist criticism of female characters' roles and identities, Johnlock (the sexual relationship between John Watson and Sherlock Holmes) as a way of reading the characters' identities, and the interpretation of on-location filming and fan responses to news leaked from the *Sherlock* set, which helps to create a fan-specific identity for popular television characters. Such a range of analyses illustrates the continuing popularity of Sherlock Holmes and the passion with which adaptors—whether officially sanctioned by film or television production companies or unofficially but popularly shared among fan communities—define him in new ways to better appreciate him as Other, learn from his experiences, or personally relate to him.

Many adaptations for film or television since 2009 emphasize the unique way Sherlock Holmes thinks as a way to understand who he really is. His identity—whether referring to a public persona or his deeply personal self—often is determined by the way he processes information. Some stories take audiences inside Sherlock's mind, via mind palace (*Sherlock*) or Holmesvision (the Guy Ritchie–directed *Sherlock Holmes* film series). Other adaptations (such as *Mr. Holmes*) question who Holmes would be without his brilliant mind. Yet even this most obvious method of categorizing Holmes can lead different adaptors to different conclusions. In *Sherlock*, the title character self-identifies as a "high-functioning sociopath," yet he defies medical diagnostic definitions. His mind is often described as like a machine (particularly a computer), yet recent adaptations reveal the emotional man behind the logical deductions. Who is Holmes of the magnificent mind—and who would he be if he no longer were perceived as brilliant? Several authors explore the man behind the deductive process to examine Sherlock Holmes's true identity.

Although Holmes is still considered machine-like—at least in the beginning of several adaptations—his emotions are revealed and dissected nearly as often as the consulting detective unravels clues and deduces crime scenes. Television adaptations *Sherlock* and *Elementary* chronicle Sherlock Holmes's emotional development through episodic explorations of his relationship with Watson (John or Joan, respectively) and struggles with personal demons, ranging from drug use/abuse to archenemy Moriarty. On film, an elderly *Mr. Holmes* also struggles with his emotions as he unravels his last case—the one that led him to Sussex and a retirement of studying bees.

Holmes's identity is often forged by cultural expectations. Whereas canon stories are most often set within the latter years of the Victorian (1837–1901) or in the Edwardian (1901–1910) era, even canon-era adaptors took creative license with their presentation of Sherlock Holmes. More than a century later, adaptors who seek to re-create canon's now-historic setting must introduce a Sherlock Holmes who meets audience expectations of Victorian Holmes while appealing to a 21st-century audience. What is "masculine" or "normal" in one time and place may be interpreted very differently within a different cultural context—and cultural contexts may make Holmes seem even more Other than expected to audiences from a differing culture. As several contributors note, the Sherlock Holmes of canon-era adaptations is often a challenge to portray in historically accurate terms while also offering something new to audiences.

Films *Sherlock Holmes, Sherlock Holmes: A Game of Shadows,* and *Mr. Holmes* and the special *Sherlock* episode "The Abominable Bride" align Holmes with a now-historic time period but also modernize the character's identity.

The critical lenses of narrative theory, religious symbolism, and psychoanalysis also can help viewers and readers clarify Holmes's identity, especially as portrayed either within a specific *Sherlock* episode or across the whole series. An in-depth look at dialogue, set dressing, and filming techniques lead to insightful deductions about Sherlock's character development.

Other contributors analyze Sherlock Holmes's behavior and the influences on him from childhood to adulthood. Although John Watson is a powerful influence in many adaptations (especially in the *Sherlock Holmes* films and *Sherlock*), he is not the only factor in determining how and why Holmes will act and how the public perceives him. He may be motivated by stress (including Post-Traumatic Stress Disorder) as much as love or the desire to solve a puzzle. He absorbs information about himself from others, especially those with whom he compares himself, whether brother Mycroft or nemesis Moriarty. Sherlock Holmes may perceive himself most clearly when he sees himself through the eyes of others.

Each Sherlock Holmes—in canon or adaptation—must be a clearly understandable character whose private or public identity allows the audience to relate or be attracted to him. Adaptations released to the public since 2009 also must contend with so many familiar versions of Sherlock Holmes that have come before (e.g., the popular Jeremy Brett–starring Granada television series in the late 20th century), as well as tough competition from concurrent cinematic or television rivals for audience attention. Newer iterations of Sherlock Holmes must be recognizable as the Conan Doyle character but unique in the way Holmes is appealing to audiences. He must remain familiar but reveal something new about himself and allow audiences to be surprised.

"Who is Sherlock Holmes?" is a viable question, even after more than a century of adaptations and character analysis. The answers suggested by contributors to this book provide innovative ways to consider beloved characters from Conan Doyle's canon and may reflect who we are—as audiences or individual fans—as much as they unravel the continuing mystery of Sherlock Holmes. Analyses in the following essays indicate how surprising new identities for Sherlock Holmes have been created or maintained by illustrators, scriptwriters, directors, costume designers, set designers, actors, and fans or interpreted through the critical lenses of art, religion, or psychology. From contemporaries of Conan Doyle like Paget and Gillette to the teams producing 21st-century Sherlock Holmes films and television series to fans who develop their own interpretations based on what they observe on screen or in person, a wealth of creativity goes into the development of Sherlock Holmes's identity.

From Paget to Screen
A (Re)Vision of Sherlock Holmes for the 21st Century

CLARE DOUGLASS LITTLE

Sir Arthur Conan Doyle frequently portrays Sherlock Holmes's efforts to educate John Watson on the power of visual details to reveal identity and the importance of not just seeing but *noticing*. Such an exchange occurs in "A Case of Identity" following the departure of a distressed Miss Sutherland and her tale of the mysteriously disappeared Mr. Hosmer Angel:

> "You appeared to read a good deal upon her which was quite invisible to me," I remarked.
> "Not invisible, but unnoticed, Watson. You did not know where to look, and so you missed all that was important. I can never bring you to realise the importance of sleeves, the suggestiveness of thumb-nails, or the great issues that may hang from a boot-lace. Now, what did you gather from that woman's appearance? Describe it" [Conan Doyle, *The Original Illustrated Sherlock Holmes* 47].

Holmes emphasizes the value of going beyond merely seeing to critically "reading" the individuals involved in each new case. In this way, Holmes, and so Watson and the audience he represents, gains a fuller understanding of the characters' motives and identities. If the surface (the visual details) reveals so much and typically proves essential for solving each case, then the artists who provide the audience with representations of these visual indicators have great power and responsibility.

How an artist visually adapts the textual descriptions Conan Doyle provides through Holmes's instructive demonstrations limits and highlights what the viewer notices and so understands. Visual realizations of the text represent a retelling of the stories filtered through the lens of the editor-artist. The most well-known illustrator of the Holmes stories, Sidney Paget, and, more recently, the director of the blockbuster *Sherlock Holmes* movies, Guy Ritchie, demonstrate the importance of these visual elements and, through countless artistic choices, dictate what details must be more than just seen but, as Holmes explains, noticed for the audience to more fully understand the stories and their characters' identities. At times, this results in illustrations in which Paget either leaves out or embellishes certain textual details to guide readers in noticing (or occasionally not noticing) those elements that suit Victorian sensibilities. Though the creative team members behind Ritchie's film adaptations distance themselves from Paget's iconic illustrations, they often include similar details and ultimately reinforce aspects of Paget's creative decisions in their effort to direct what viewers should *notice* in the visual experience of Holmes and his adventures.

Illustrated stories characterized much of the Victorian period, as readers expected image and text to go hand in hand in serialized stories and novels. Much has been written about the history of illustrated fiction, which highlights the complex dynamic of text and image in the same space and points to the power of the illustrator to visually rewrite the story itself. However, in the case of Paget's illustrations, he had the added responsibility of capturing certain visual details key to solving cases. Unlike most other novel and story illustrations that simply reflect plot and general character descriptions, Paget's illustrations generally allow the reader-viewer to participate in the investigation by trying to follow Holmes's instruction and explanation of the case. While this does not mean Paget captures every last detail Holmes lists when describing a character, it does mean illustrations *generally* follow Conan Doyle's descriptions. For example, the prose details of Miss Sutherland's dress largely do match Paget's illustrations of her, with feathered hat and dark jacket sporting plush "at the neck and sleeves," details Watson lists in answer to Holmes demand to "[d]escribe it." Those minute details Holmes provides to highlight what Watson missed, like "[t]he double line a little above the wrist" indicating her frequent use of a typewriter, certainly *could* be there, even if the viewer cannot make it out (Conan Doyle, *The Original Illustrated Sherlock Holmes* 47). The fact that the illustration, lacking some of the details Holmes notes, reflects Watson's observations in this instance solidifies that connection between the reader and Watson, both of whom Holmes instructs in the art of noticing. In Paget's work for Conan Doyle, the experience of trying to notice the details he does include in each image suggests, as Christophe Gelly points out in "Sir Arthur Conan Doyle's Sherlock Holmes Stories: Crime and Mystery from the Text to the Illustrations," that "[i]llustrations here appear as clues among others" and "that they also enrich the text in a peculiar way and fail to be merely 'illustrative' in a restrictive sense" (108). This view of Paget's illustrations indicates they do, in fact, generally support and enhance readers' experience of Conan Doyle's stories.

Although Gelly does highlight moments when Paget resists aspects of Conan Doyle's gritty, even violent, content, he points to this as further evidence of Paget's efforts to capture and respect Victorian sensibilities, making him a sort of product and protector of his time. As an example, Gelly refers to Conan Doyle's "The Adventure of the Silver Blaze" and the image of John Straker's dead body, which does not show the extent of Straker's wounds as described in the text, suggesting Paget's efforts to minimize the violence of his murder and the graphic nature of the scene (118–119). Paget further deviates from Conan Doyle's stories by minimizing evidence of Holmes's character flaws, straying from Conan Doyle's original description of the detective. When a disguise includes a prop related to Victorian moral depravity, Paget leaves it out of the illustration. His image of Holmes in "The Man with the Twisted Lip" shows Holmes disguised as a thin old man but lacking the opium pipe Conan Doyle gives him.

In the absence of such strict social mores, how do artists of the 21st century take a product of the 19th century and create a period piece for a modern audience? Do they make use of Paget's details when making their own stylistic choices? How do these choices shape the way contemporary viewers, who may never have read the original stories, let alone seen the illustrations that accompanied them, understand Conan Doyle's stories and the identities of his characters? Following Holmes's lesson for Watson and striving to truly notice, to carefully compare and analyze iconic visual elements in the Paget-illustrated *Adventures of Sherlock Holmes* and Guy Ritchie's *Sherlock Holmes* (2009) and *Sherlock Holmes: A Game of Shadows* (2011) reveals intriguing similarities between Paget and the filmmakers' artistic visions.

Taking Holmes from Page and Screen

To many viewers, the bare-chested, brawling Holmes (Robert Downey, Jr.) of Ritchie's *Sherlock Holmes* seems a far cry from the tweed-wearing, ratiocinating Holmes of the original stories. However, if, as Gelly suggests, Paget visually tempered some content and Holmes's more questionable traits and activities, then the Holmes appearing on screen in *Sherlock Holmes* and *Sherlock Holmes: A Game of Shadows* may not be as great a leap from the original stories as many critics presume. In an interview for *IndieLondon*, Ritchie suggests that he and *Sherlock Holmes* writer-producer Lionel Wigram believed this to be true. When asked about leaving behind iconic Holmesian symbols like the deerstalker hat, Ritchie replies, "Lionel and I made a decision early on that if we were going to do this we'd have to dust off Sherlock Holmes and create what we thought to be, to some degree, an authentic Conan Doyle version of Sherlock Holmes that wasn't contaminated with previous symbols, so we could have a fresh take on Sherlock Holmes" (Carnavale). Wigram reinforces this approach in his interview with the *Londonist*'s Matt Brown. When describing his experience rereading Conan Doyle, Wigram says, "When I read him, I saw a very different character to the one portrayed more commonly. I think primarily, I saw somebody ... a character who was a great deal more modern and more accessible." Wigram describes the flawed, complex character of Holmes as being quite modern and refers to Conan Doyle's references to Holmes's boxing days and knowledge of a martial arts form called baritsu as a sort of justification for the intense action of the film: "So here we have a character who has all these modern complications to his character, but also we can portray as an action hero without compromising the integrity of the original stories." Jenny Beavan, the film's costume designer, contrasts her image of Sherlock to those of Paget's illustrations and Basil Rathbone's previous film incarnations: "[I]n fact, we weren't taking any liberates [sic.] at all—we were simply doing our version. The other was never Conan Doyle's version; he never described any of that clothing. From [a sartorial] point of view, if you actually read the stories, it's [the clothing] very all over the place" (Ryan). The resulting films show a frequently manic, disheveled, fighting, drinking Holmes that may actually reflect elements of Conan Doyle's stories either downplayed or left out of the Paget illustrations.

One of the most notable ways Paget, at times, deviates from Conan Doyle's textual descriptions relates to Holmes's physical appearance, something Conan Doyle himself noted when he stated that Holmes "was a more beaky-nosed, hawk-faced man, approaching more to the Red Indian type, than the artist represented him," though he does go on to say how much Paget's illustrations "please[d]" him (Conan Doyle, "A Gaudy Death"). Paget's illustrations often show a less angular-featured Holmes than the textual description of Holmes first given readers in *A Study in Scarlet*:

> His very person and appearance were such as to strike the attention of the most casual observer. In height he was rather over six feet, and so excessively lean that he seemed to be considerably taller. His eyes were sharp and piercing, save during those intervals of torpor to which I have alluded; and his thin, hawk-like nose gave his whole expression an air of alertness and decision. His chin, too, had the prominence and squareness which mark the man of determination [Conan Doyle, *A Study in Scarlet* 10].

Paget's version of Holmes, supposedly inspired by the appearance of his brother Walter (Klinefelter 15, Redmond 85), was not so far from the text version as to alienate readers or the author, despite its variations and frequent lack of the dramatic nose and profile Conan Doyle describes. While the moviemakers verbally align themselves more with the original stories than with Paget's illustrations, they may actually have followed in Paget's footsteps in several ways, including in the image of the detective and their similar willingness to take creative liberties.

Some film critics note the dramatic deviation from previous images of Holmes in print and film as evident in Ritchie's use of a more conventionally handsome detective in the form of Robert Downey, Jr. While Downey, Jr., certainly lacks the traditionally slender build and aquiline features of previous Holmes incarnations, the image of a more physically appealing Holmes can, in fact, be found in Paget's illustrations. Whether as a result of inconsistencies in Paget's style or, as Walter Klinefelter suggests, likely influenced by the fact that at least six different engravers created the prints of Paget's drawings, certain images do show a more attractive Holmes. "A Scandal in Bohemia" and "A Case of Identity" showcase what Klinefelter describes as a "cloyingly handsome" Holmes, one later contrasted with the "downright unhandsome Holmes" appearing in "The Naval Treaty," in which a balding, almost gaunt Holmes reflects on the beauty of a rose (17–18). This "cloyingly handsome" Holmes, the Holmes seen, interestingly, in "A Scandal in Bohemia," the story focusing on Irene Adler, and "A Case of Identity," another story featuring a young woman, appears in Ritchie's films. Pulling out the Holmes from these stories certainly plays up the potential for a romantic Holmes. While certainly serving the filmmakers' desire to emphasize, or perhaps create, the character's sex appeal and so draw in audiences, the use of a physically attractive Holmes may not be as dramatic a deviation from Holmes portraiture as one might think.

While, as Ritchie, Wigram, and Beavan point out, the deerstalker remains absent in the films, certain, more subtle characteristics of the Holmes Paget depicted do carry over to the screen. For example, the image of Holmes deep in thought with fingers touching appears in the movies and frequently in Paget's illustrations, though not always in Conan Doyle's accompanying text. At least seven times, Paget shows Holmes with fingers crossed or peaked together as he appears in some degree of reverie or mental engagement; two of these images appear in one story alone: "A Scandal in Bohemia"—a case posing a particular challenge, given the craftiness of Irene Adler. Similarly, when facing the supposedly supernatural villain in *Sherlock Holmes*, Holmes hears the news of Blackwood's (Mark Strong) having survived being hanged with a piqued mind and corresponding peaked fingers. In *A Game of Shadows*, Holmes sits, seemingly half asleep, with the fingertips of his index fingers touching and the rest of his fingers interlaced, as he and Watson roll by wagon into a gypsy camp. His pose in the scene, besides generally calling to mind this visual trope of Paget's images, possesses similarities to his position in "A Case of Identity" when Watson enters to find him "half asleep, with his long, thin form curled up in the recesses of his armchair" (Conan Doyle, *The Original Illustrated Sherlock Holmes* 48).

However, despite the filmmakers' assessment of their film being truer to the stories than Paget's illustrations and previous film versions, certain of Paget's stylistic deviations actually seem to be reinforced by the Ritchie movies. For example, an illustration Gelly uses as further evidence of Paget's mild censoring of Conan Doyle's content could be taken right out of the

Sherlock Holmes films. Gelly refers to an illustration from "The Solitary Cyclist" in which Holmes fights with Mr. Woodley in a pub, describing "the characters ... as look[ing] stiff and unnatural ... so that it looks as if we were faced with a technical drawing dealing with a particular wrestling figure and not an actual fight" (120). The illustration, like the image of Arthur Holder preparing to strike Sir George Burnwell in "The Adventure of the Beryl Coronet," lacks a certain realistic quality, with its men seeming posed or as if play acting, much like the stylized violence of Ritchie's movies and the slow motion, special effect-laden, highly choreographed fight scenes that the filmmakers termed "Holmes Vision" (or "Holmesvision") for the movies. This device shows Holmes mentally walking through the steps he will take to defeat his adversaries before the actual fight takes place. Robert Downey, Jr., captures the feel of Holmes Vision when he cites Ritchie's instructions to "try a take where I was punching through peanut butter" (BJSprecher). The stilted, technical, almost freeze-frame style of the movie sequence matches the technical nature of the drawings perfectly.

Common Visual Themes

In many ways, the movies seem to overtly emphasize their connection to Conan Doyle and Paget's *Strand Magazine* publications. The frequent appearance of illustrated newspapers in the movies represents an intriguing visual trope that is not only period appropriate but seemingly a nod to the original illustrated, serialized works. Actual newspaper titles, including *The Penny Illustrated Paper and Illustrated Times* and *The Daily Graphic: An Illustrated Newspaper*, appear in the films at least six times. Certainly this detail adds realism and authenticity to the scenes and shows how people of the era got their news, but it also highlights the stories' origins, something emphasized all the more in the opening and closing of each movie. The first scene of *Sherlock Holmes* ends with a frozen shot of Lestrade (Eddie Marsan) and Watson (Jude Law) facing viewers while Holmes covers his face at the moment he is photographed for a newspaper. Oddly, this "photograph" morphs into a sketch featured on the front page of *The Penny Illustrated Paper and Illustrated Times* with the heading "Scotland Yard Catches Killer!" and a smaller subheading "Sherlock Holmes Aides Police," ultimately transforming the whole scene into a printed newspaper page. This device features in the ending of both movies, as images of characters freeze and become graphic illustrations during the closing credits. While the creative minds behind the movie distance themselves from the early visual symbols of Holmes in certain respects, in many ways they either overtly or subtly solidify their roots and connection to the earliest visualizations of Holmes and Conan Doyle's world.

More explicit similarities between Paget's illustrations and elements of the films exist as well, particularly in tone and color as well as in certain iconic images carried over to the screen. A certain soft or hazy-edged style characterizes many of Paget's illustrations and certainly seems to have been carried over into the movies. Warren Scheidman, in a 1983 issue of *Baker Street Miscellanea*, says of Paget's illustrations, "The lines drift into the text, sometimes like smoke, clouds, dreams, or thoughts, often in physical conjunction with the words they illustrate" (qtd. in Redmond 87). Indeed, a high percentage of Paget's illustrations lack defined borders. This blending of borders between text and image represents the interdependency of print and illustration media in the serial context and reflects the multi-sensory reading-seeing experience. In certain illustrations, this hazy effect functions on a more literal level to emphasize the actual smokiness of the setting, typically when Holmes smokes his pipe, a frequent pastime:

> Nearly always there was a thick haze of pungent blue smoke contributing considerably to a lowering of the visibility in the Baker Street sitting room whenever Holmes was on the premises, and this haze continued to become denser and denser as more and more smoke billowed upward in puffs from his pipe, or cigar, or cigarette, until the atmosphere inside often was much foggier than it ever became outside in Baker Street [Klinefelter 23–24].

The amount Holmes smokes correlates to the challenge of the case, and the question at the heart of "The Red-Headed League" proves to be "quite a three pipe problem" (Conan Doyle, *The Original Illustrated Sherlock Holmes* 33). In this sense, the cloud of smoke represents Holmes's mental "haziness" while figuring out the answer. An image of Holmes with "pipe still between his lips," surrounded by "a dense tobacco haze," captures both his practice of contemplative smoking and the darkly shadowed, borderless style of many Paget illustrations. The movie-version Holmes also smokes a pipe, and, while perhaps not as essential in helping the detective solve cases, the pipe does become associated with his working through cases at times, as when he isolates himself to mentally discover Blackwood's plan.

Scenes from the movies use this hazy style, both in literal smokiness and its overall muted, drained tone. A. O. Scott, in his rather critical review of the movie, describes this quality when he writes that "like its predecessor 'Sherlock Holmes: A Game of Shadows' confects a smoky, overcast Victorian world." While the general dinginess of scenes works to capture an industrialized London, it also, like Paget's illustrations, reflects the layered mysteries and intrigue in which Holmes and Watson are immersed. Scenes drained of color, almost monochromatic at times, add to this illusion, which also conveys a sepia, antique quality adding to the historical feel of the movies. Holmes's dusty rooms and the typically smog-filled city scenes in *Sherlock Holmes*, as well as the smoky street scenes and fog-fringed gypsy camp and mountain landscape scenes in *A Game of Shadows*, exemplify the general haziness of the movies.

The plot of *A Game of Shadows* lends itself to particular use of this device, as Moriarty's (Jared Harris) acquisition of a massive amount of arms and a munitions factory leads to frequent gunfire and even cannon explosions toward the end of the film. One of the most dramatic sequences featuring special effects, an almost monochromatic color scheme, and a great amount of smoke caused by gun-/cannon fire occurs when Holmes, Watson, Madam Simza (Noomi Rapace), and other gypsy companions run from the factory and Moriarty's well-armed men. Though exaggerated and more violent in form, this movie device, like the smoke-filled, hazy-edged style of many Paget illustrations, reflects the tense desperation as characters struggle to find their way out of a dangerous problem, either literally or figuratively. Furthermore, this effect of haze and shadow in the illustrations and on screen seems to echo Holmes's ever-shifting identity in taking on one new role or disguise after another.

The complete transformation of Holmes in disguise also appears in both illustration and film. Paget depicts a Holmes so masterful at disguising his true identity that he appears to become a different person entirely. His whole body seems to change in dimension, and his facial features retain little to none of their natural traits, as can be seen, for example, when he disguises himself as "an amiable and simple-minded Nonconformist clergyman" in "A Scandal in Bohemia" (Conan Doyle, *The Original Illustrated Sherlock Holmes* 20) and an Italian priest unrecognized by Watson in "The Adventure of the Final Problem" (Conan Doyle, *The Original Illustrated Sherlock Holmes* 333–334). Not all of the movie detective's disguises work as convincingly as Paget's complete re-vision of Holmes's appearance, as few viewers likely fail to discern Holmes beneath the stereotypical "Chinaman" costume in an early scene of *Sherlock Holmes*. However, his disguise as a drunken beggar, reminiscent of Conan Doyle's "drunken-looking groom" as illustrated in "A Scandal in Bohemia" (Conan Doyle, *The Original Illustrated Sherlock Holmes* 17), proves quite effective, and he only seems to improve his craft in the sequel. In two instances from *A Game of Shadows*, an equivalent to Paget's utter obfuscation of Holmes's identity occurs when Holmes camouflages himself to blend in completely with his surroundings, first in his own rooms when Watson comes to visit and, much later, when he hides in Watson's study to leave a clue that he did not die with Moriarty. These costumes rely more on setting than facial transformation, but they have the same impact on the deceived and amazed viewer as Paget's interpretation of Holmes's disguises.

Women and The Woman

In a similar way, the movies' depiction of certain characters does not stray as far from Paget's images as the filmmakers' supposedly more modern sensibilities would suggest. Both Paget's and the films' portrayal of women proves to be rather complicated. As Gelly points out, the original illustrations remain true to Conan Doyle's "recurring pattern" of Holmes having to save a young woman (109): "Sidney Paget indeed faithfully conveys that feature, reminiscent of the eighteenth century theme of 'virtue in distress,' through a depiction of women as submissive, docile, and mostly helpless, as their postures suggest" (110). Women visit Holmes for help in numerous illustrations, but poses more explicitly conveying feminine vulnerability appear in "The Man with the Twisted Lip," as a "Lascar scoundrel" pushes Mrs. St. Clair (Conan Doyle, *The Original Illustrated Sherlock Holmes* 84–85); in "The Adventure of the Copper Beeches," when a terrified Miss Hunter braces against the suspicious Mr. Rucastle; and in multiple images of a distressed Miss Stapleton in *The Hound of the Baskervilles*, to name a few. Irene Adler, "*the* woman" (Conan Doyle, *The Original Illustrated Sherlock Holmes* 11), represents an intriguing character to study in this comparison, as in Conan Doyle's stories she represents an exceptionally shrewd and self-determined woman for the period. One might expect her to be even more autonomous and empowered in a movie made in the 21st century. Although so she is, to some extent, she still finds herself controlled by men and limited in certain ways, as her emotional attachment to Holmes makes her vulnerable in her efforts to protect him. Adler (Rachel McAdams) shows her greatest physical strength in *Sherlock Holmes* when she fights Blackwood's henchmen and expertly dismantles the poison-bomb before running off with a piece of the machine. However, she does so at the command of Moriarty, who takes advantage of her feelings for Holmes to control her. Moriarty presumably kills her early in the sequel, in which she seems much weaker in mind and body.

Adler is, of course, the woman who comes closest to achieving an equality with men in both Paget's illustration and on screen. In addition to her craftiness, she gains an external sign of her "masculine" fortitude through her manner of dressing. Adler's menswear-inspired costume in *Sherlock Holmes* certainly gives her the range of movement needed for action scenes while also distinguishing her from the stereotypical Victorian woman. (Madam Simza in *A Game of Shadows* wears long skirts but fights and rides horses unrestrained; her masculine physicality and menswear-inspired hat and coat take her female clothes in stride and make her seem all the more capable and empowered for being unhindered by them.) Paget also gives Adler this distinction, even more overtly, in his illustration for "A Scandal in Bohemia" in which Adler, disguised as a man, greets Holmes after he returns home from her house. In typical Paget style, she seems to completely take on a new identity and appears unrecognizable to readers and Holmes, pointing to her gift for disguise and a mental prowess on par with Holmes. In a way, this affords her greater freedom than other women and places her on a level with the male hero, perhaps as effectively as her adapted character on screen.

In comparison with the women of Paget's illustrations, female characters on screen do appear more independent, particularly in their physicality, but this cannot be said of all the women in the films, and even those possessing a more "masculine" physical strength become vulnerable because of their "feminine" emotions and romantic or filial attachments. While women in the films generally seem more independent than the women of Victorian literature and certainly of Paget's illustrations, they also have their vulnerabilities, typically linked with their emotional attachments to male characters. Mary Watson (Kelly Reilly) skillfully holds a gun on a villain disguised as a soldier, and Madam Simza shows little fear and great skill with knives when being attacked by a Cossack in *A Game of Shadows*. Yet Mary Watson and Madam Simza are motivated by their feelings for men, a husband and a brother, respectively, that put them in mortal jeopardy multiple times. Of course, the ever faithful, if a bit anxious Mrs. Hudson (Geraldine James) continues to serve Holmes, only revealing her concern and discontent in pleas for help expressed to Watson. While the women certainly appear more active and involved in the movies, in many ways they suffer from the same romantic limitations and gendered expectations repeatedly depicted in the original stories and Paget's illustrations.

Villains and Moriarty

Presumably influenced by the popularly accepted "sciences" of phrenology and physiognomy, Conan Doyle frequently describes villains as appearing like criminals, not just acting like them (Gelly 110), as in his description of Moriarty, whose "face protrudes forward, and is for ever slowly oscillating from side to side in a curiously reptilian fashion" (Conan Doyle, *The Original Illustrated Sherlock Holmes* 331). However, Paget frequently seems to have resisted a simple, straightforward inner-outer correlation of character. Take, for example, Dr. Grimesby Roylott, the villainous stepfather in "The Adventure of the Speckled Band," whom Conan Doyle describes as having a face "burned yellow with the sun, and marked with every evil passion ... while his deep-set, bile-shot eyes, and his high thin fleshless nose, gave him somewhat the resemblance to a fierce old bird of prey" (Conan Doyle, *The Original Illustrated Sherlock Holmes* 114). The corresponding image of Watson and Holmes's first introduction to the man does show a seemingly enraged figure, but here, and certainly in the last illustration of the story, which depicts Dr. Grimesby Roylott frozen in death, his evil nature is not necessarily written on his face, as Conan Doyle would suggest.

The ultimate, most challenging of Holmes's nemeses also defies this expectation to an extent. The outward appearance of Moriarty on screen in *A Game of Shadows*, like the Moriarty of Paget's illustrations, does not necessarily match the vile nature it hides. Of course, this only adds to his effectiveness as a villain, as he, a respected ex-professor of mathematics, seems quite the gentleman in many ways, making him all the more despicable given his heartless and destructive intentions. Certainly, the large illustration of Moriarty accompanying his description in "The Adventure of the Final Problem" shows a rather gaunt individual, with the "deeply sunken" eyes and "ascetic-looking" appearance Conan Doyle describes (Conan Doyle, *The Original Illustrated Sherlock Holmes* 331). However, lacking the "reptilian" movement ascribed to him by Conan Doyle, the man's appearance, while perhaps suspicious with its shadows and deep-set lines, does not fully convey his evil nature or intent, particularly when compared to images of Holmes. In fact, if a gaunt appearance indicates moral depravity, then the illustrated Holmes himself could be accused of the same at times, appearing with similarly angular features in his less flattering images, as in the aforementioned picture of Holmes reflecting on a rose in "The Adventure of the Naval Treaty." This becomes especially clear when readers examine the image that follows Moriarty's portrait, in which Holmes and Moriarty, who bear a striking resemblance, appear together. Paget does not provide a visual key to the villain's character; instead, he makes Moriarty and Holmes look similarly haggard and weary, perhaps to demonstrate their equal strength as adversaries. Likewise, the filmmakers do not provide viewers with a two-dimensional character who wears his villainy on his sleeve. While the Moriarty of Paget's illustrations resists easy categorization by appearing to double Holmes, the Moriarty of *A Game of Shadows* instead wears the mask of respectability, as, unlike the Moriarty of Conan Doyle's story, the Moriarty on screen continues to hold his position as Professor, even signing copies of his mathematical treatise while on tour. The movie Moriarty may not physically echo Holmes as he does in the text, but the respect his cinematic façade earns him among the general public works to mask his malicious actions and intent. These depictions of Moriarty may use different tactics, but, ultimately, they work to complicate the villain's identity for readers and viewers, just as it is complicated for Holmes himself.

A continued faithfulness to a visual detail largely attributable to Paget rather than Conan Doyle lies in the depiction of the final confrontation between Holmes and Moriarty. In "The Adventure of the Final Problem," readers rely on Watson's description of what must have occurred between Moriarty and Holmes at the falls of Reichenbach, as Watson does not actually see the scene play out: "An examination by experts leaves little doubt that a personal contest between the two men ended, as it could hardly fail to end in such a situation, in their reeling over, locked in each other's arms" (Conan Doyle, *The Original Illustrated Sherlock Holmes* 339). The precise manner of their posture in this image remains unclear, as it relies on conjecture given the likely outcome. Nevertheless, Paget depicts this moment with Holmes embracing Moriarty, who, interestingly, has one arm raised, pinioned in a rather awkward position. While the setting gets some adjustment in *A Game of Shadows*' movie version of this scene, Moriarty also appears with his arm trapped in a similar pose. Both versions could suggest that Moriarty makes an aggressive movement toward Holmes at the moment when Holmes grabs him, but this is not clear in the text, which just as easily could describe the men with interlocked arms or Moriarty with arms pinned to his sides. Additionally, just as in Paget's illustration, viewers see this dramatic moment before Holmes and Moriarty fall from Watson's perspective, driving home the emotional loss of Holmes's connection with Watson (and so to the audience).

Certainly, Paget's iconic images of Holmes and his adventures do not define Ritchie's 21st-century adaptations. However, the similarity of visual devices and elements between the illustrations and films legitimizes Paget's artistic choices for the Victorian *and* the modern audience. Despite their claims to the contrary, the filmmakers of *Sherlock Holmes* and *Sherlock Holmes: A Game of Shadows* use visual icons similar to Paget's. Although this could suggest a subconscious influence of Paget's illustrations on the design of the films, it definitely points to the insightfulness of Paget's visual interpretation of Conan Doyle's text and Paget's desire to make a Holmes that fits Victorian times. The fact that modern moviemakers, supposedly on their own creative path, make so many similar choices reflects the strength of Paget's visual devices and the details he chose to help viewers not just see, but notice, characters' struggles and identities.

WORKS CITED

BJSprecher. "Robert Downey, Jr. Explains Guy Ritchie's '*Holmes* Vision.'" REELZChannel. 26 Dec. 2009. Web. 27 Feb. 2016.

Brown, Matt. "Interview: Lionel Wigram, Producer and Writer for the Sherlock Holmes Movie—Part 2." *Londonist.* 24 Dec. 2009. Web. 21 Jan. 2016.

Carnevale, Rob. "Sherlock Holmes—Guy Ritchie Interview." *IndieLondon.* n.d. Web. 22 Jan. 2016.

Conan Doyle, Arthur. "A Gaudy Death: Conan Doyle Tells the True Story of Sherlock Holmes." Interview. *Tit-Bits. The Conan Doyle Encyclopedia.* 15 Dec. 1900. Web. 27 Feb. 2016.

_____. *The Original Illustrated Sherlock Holmes.* New York: Castle Books, 1976. Print.

_____. *A Study in Scarlet. Sherlock Holmes: The Complete Novels and Stories—Volume 1.* New York: Bantam, 1986. 1–103. Print.

Gelly, Christophe. "Sir Arthur Conan Doyle's Sherlock Holmes Stories: Crime and Mystery from the Text to the Illustrations." *Cahiers Victoriens & Édouardiens* 73 (2011): 107–129. Proquest. Web. 10 Dec. 2015.

Klinefelter, Walter. *Sherlock Holmes in Portrait and Profile*. Syracuse: Syracuse University Press, 1963. Print.

Redmond, Christopher. *Sherlock Holmes Handbook*. Toronto: Dundurn Press, 2009. Print.

Ryan, Mike. "Sherlock Holmes's Costume Designer on the Case of the Missing Deerstalker Hat." *Vanity Fair*. 23 Dec. 2009. Web. 22 Jan. 2016.

Scott, A. O. "Holmes and Watson: But Is There Mystery?" *New York Times*. 15 Dec. 2011. Web. 25 Jan. 2016.

Sherlock Holmes. Dir. Guy Ritchie. Perf. Robert Downey, Jr., Jude Law. Warner Bros., 2009. Blu-ray.

Sherlock Holmes: A Game of Shadows. Dir. Guy Ritchie. Perf. Robert Downey, Jr., Jude Law. Warner Bros., 2011. Blu-ray.

Modernizing Victorian Sherlock Holmes for *Mr. Holmes* and the BBC's *Sherlock* Special

LYNNETTE PORTER

When Sir Arthur Conan Doyle wrote the Sherlock Holmes stories, he described the Great Detective's physical appearance and personality but left the rest of his Victorian persona to the imagination of readers. After all, Conan Doyle wrote for his contemporaries, and they would have a good idea of what a man of Holmes's profession (no matter how unique) and social status would likely wear or do and what aspects of his personality or appearance were out of the ordinary. More recent fans of Sherlock Holmes, however, have often built their expectations of Victorian Holmes's appearance or attitude at least as much from the earliest visual adaptations of the character as from Conan Doyle's prose.

Sidney Paget, whose *Strand Magazine* illustrations adapt Conan Doyle's text, sometimes took creative license in translating the author's prose descriptions into specific images—such as Holmes wearing a deerstalker cap or an Inverness cape. In fact, as *Smithsonian* writer Sarah C. Rich notes, in 1891, Paget "gave Sherlock a deerstalker hat and an Inverness cape, and the look was forevermore a must for distinguished detectives—so much so that while the deerstalker was originally meant to be worn by hunters …, the hat now connotes detective work, even without a detective's head inside it."

Paget's style of illustrating Holmes's physical appearance, including facial expressions, ultimately created a more handsome consulting detective than Conan Doyle describes as a tall, thin, hawk-nosed man. Similarly, actor/writer William Gillette helped determine how Holmes should look in 20th- or 21st-century television or film adaptations when he brought the Great Detective to life first on stage and then in the 1916 film, *Sherlock Holmes*. Like Paget,

Gillette shows Holmes wearing the deerstalker and Inverness cape when he does field work, such as tracking down Moriarty's gang. However, the attractive actor made more extensive changes to the character; he also turned Holmes into a romantic leading man who falls in love by the end of the play or film. Today the popularized image of Victorian Holmes likely owes at least as much to Paget or Gillette (especially since the 1916 film adaptation was found, restored, and released on disc in 2015) as to Conan Doyle.

Especially in the 21st century, current viewers of television or film adaptations likely outnumber readers of the original works, despite their continuing popularity. Digital natives typically watch visuals or prefer digitized information more often than reading books, even e-books. As Mark Prensky, in "Digital Natives, Digital Immigrants," explains, those who have grown up with digital technology (which means a large portion of the audience who watches films or television series on any platform) "prefer their graphics *before* their text" and "thrive on instant gratification" (2). This audience may not take time to read canon stories or even to look closely at two-dimensional illustrations. They prefer a faster way to digest a story—such as a television episode or a film. The shift in popularity from paper to electronic texts and prose to visuals adds even more weight to the power of Paget's 19th- to 20th-century illustrations and Gillette's 20th-century cinematic adaptation, simply because these visual texts may be faster and easier for adaptors to access online and use as source materials when they create their own Sherlock Holmes adaptations for digital natives. Several web sites carry these images, and an online search readily produces video clips or drawings of Sherlock Holmes as adapted by Paget or Gillette. Added to this popular visual Victorian "identity" for Holmes, created during Conan Doyle's lifetime and reflecting adaptations by his contemporaries, are more recent promotional photographs of characters from films or television series that illustrate Victorian Sherlock Holmes in, for example, *Mr. Holmes* (2015) or the *Sherlock* special, "The Abominable Bride" (2016). All these images provide compelling visual evidence for modern audiences that Victorian Sherlock Holmes should look or dress a certain way in order to be "authentic," but that presumed authenticity relies at least as much on popular perception as history or literary canon.

Thus, the "modernized" Victorian Holmes in television or film adaptations needs to provide a bridge between the past and present, as well as between prose and cinematic texts. The challenge for 21st-century adaptations of Victorian Holmes is to meet initial audience expectations (i.e., to hook viewers and receive high ratings or lucrative box office receipts) while finding a novel way of subverting audience expectations as a way of offering new insights into the character (i.e., to create a memorable story that stands out from other similarly set adaptations). Modernized adaptations of Victorian Holmes must be both comfortingly familiar but surprisingly unique.

The public has a wealth of television or film footage of Victorian Holmes from past successful adaptations, including but not limited to Jeremy Brett's portrayal in the Granada television series *Sherlock Holmes/The Adventures of Sherlock Holmes* (1984–1994) and the Guy Ritchie-directed *Sherlock Holmes* (2009) and *Sherlock Holmes: A Game of Shadows* (2011) film franchise starring Robert Downey, Jr. Victorian adaptations *Mr. Holmes* and "The Abominable Bride" may be compared with adaptations released only a few years prior as well as with beloved earlier adaptations, such as Brett's, that have survived the test of pop-culture time.

What makes these latter adaptations unique as objects of analysis is that they were filmed and released within a few months of each other and designed to compete in an era filled with adaptations of Sherlock Holmes. Filming for *Mr. Holmes* took place in mid–2014, with *Sherlock* being filmed in early 2015; *Mr. Holmes* was released in mid–2015, with *Sherlock* arriving simultaneously on television in the U.K. and U.S. on January 1, 2016, followed a few days later by an international theatrical release. Promotional images were also released online and in print publications around the same time, allowing these projects to be easily compared. Their coincidental similar development and release time also brought up the question (again) of how many adaptations of Sherlock Holmes could be sustained in the market. Yet, when box office receipts were tallied, both *Mr. Holmes* and *Sherlock* proved to be lucrative projects. "The Abominable Bride," for example, earned more than $38 million in international box office receipts ("The Abominable Bride [2016] Financial Information"); *Mr. Holmes* brought in more than $28 million ("Mr. Holmes [2015] Financial Information"). These adaptations successfully sold their versions of Victorian Holmes to international audiences who apparently cannot get enough of the Great Detective.

Even more important is that both of these latter Victorian era-themed projects require audiences to suspend disbelief even more than is typical when viewers watch a filmed fiction. *Mr. Holmes* requires audiences to accept an elderly Holmes (Ian McKellen) still clinging to his heyday in the Victorian era but trying to correct continuing misconceptions about his popular identity forged during his prime. Holmes has not been previously portrayed in physical and mental decline (during the 1940s), and the strength of images of Holmes during the early 20th century only reinforces the significance and persistence of his vibrant public persona.

The BBC's *Sherlock* had a very different problem, although this younger Victorian Holmes, played by Benedict Cumberbatch, also must convince audiences to accept a very different portrayal than they are accustomed to (or comfortable with) seeing. Television viewers who have wholeheartedly accepted the modern-era Sherlock—including a presentation of the John Watson-Sherlock Holmes relationship that regularly teases the two may be more than good friends—may have greater difficulty accepting the duo in an overtly sexually repressed era. Fans of the modernized series also may not want to accept a character portrayal appropriate for the Victorian era but not as brash or flamboyant as they are accustomed to seeing. Typically, when Holmes and Watson are introduced as Victorian characters and a production employs actors to portray them as such (as Downey and Law were for the Victorian-themed film franchise), audiences generally suspend disbelief and accept these actors playing these roles within a Victorian setting. The "leap of faith" is much greater for *Sherlock* audiences who, since 2010, have grown fond of Cumberbatch and Martin Freeman portraying Sherlock and John as modern men and best friends dealing with 21st-century expectations of what a male-male friendship is or should be. To see these actors playing a Victorian version of their characters set in a time period with more rigid gender expectations and social mores regarding sex could be jarring, at least, and possibly off-putting.

Although the obstacles to having audiences accept either aged, mentally failing Holmes or modern Sherlock transplanted into 19th-century London were far greater than those posed to other Sherlock Holmes adaptations set in the Victorian era, both *Mr. Holmes* and "The Abominable Bride" managed to present an audience-accepted Victorian identity for Sherlock Holmes as a result of meeting audience expectations for Holmes's exterior (e.g., his clothing or mannerisms) while providing surprising new insights into Holmes's interior (e.g., his self-perception and the image he chooses to present to the world at large).

Creating Holmes's Victorian "Exterior"

Mr. Holmes and "The Abominable Bride" attempted to be faithful to the past while presenting an intriguingly new adaptation through costume, setting, and dialogue. The pre-release "teaser" images emphasize the familiar Victorian stylistic influence. The movie poster for *Mr. Holmes* shows McKellen as a man in his sixties (Sherlock Holmes's age during the flashback sequences to 1919) who matured and developed his sense of style during the Victorian era. He wears a long frock coat and a top hat, one hand rather arrogantly placed on his hip, the other resting on a fashionable walking stick. This pose is typical of Victorian photographic portraits in which the subject is standing. A Victorian photograph collection, such as one presented online by professional photographer Leif Norman, illustrates this style. For example, a photograph captioned "Victorian man in top hat and walking cane," by pioneering portrait photographer J. F. Langhans, features the frequently used pose appropriated for the *Mr. Holmes* poster. In both the promotional poster and the Victorian-era photograph, the formally attired gentleman stands facing the camera, leaning on a walking stick. This Victorian-appropriate image establishes the essence of Sherlock Holmes in *Mr. Holmes*, even in scenes set in 1947, when Holmes is 93 and beginning to decline. The man pictured in the poster is the one with whom the decades-older Holmes is obsessed throughout the film and is the image that attracts audiences to yet another Sherlock Holmes movie.

McKellen based his interpretation of Holmes first on his character's appearance—makeup and costume. "There was no problem with Sherlock Holmes once we got the look right," the actor explained during a promotional interview, noting that he felt the same way when the look for another iconic character, Gandalf from *The Lord of the Rings* and *The Hobbit* trilogies, had been established before filming began. "Once we got the look, once I looked in the mirror and saw, 'Oh! There he is,' it was then very easy to, with imagination, say, 'The man who looks like that talks like this. The man who talks like this walks like this.' It's, sort of, in the DNA" (Billington). In the poster, McKellen's Holmes exudes confidence, an image that helps the audience believe in this version of the classic detective. Holmes's Victorian-inspired formal attire signals to movie audiences that, although this Holmes may be far older than they are accustomed to seeing him, he nonetheless is the Sherlock Holmes of canon stories and many television or film adaptations set in that period. He is a familiar presence, in part because of the way in which his costume supports his personality and provides some expected markers of Victorian style, such as a frock coat and walking stick.

In promotional materials for special episode "The Abominable Bride," Cumberbatch has to be even more convincing as a Victorian gentleman, because *Sherlock* as a series has been modernized to the 21st century. Indeed, for many fans, Sherlock, with his knowledge of 21st century-digital technology, no longer seems possible to imagine within the Victorian era. When the special was announced, many fans worried that the late 19th-century setting would be too great a deviation from the other episodes, especially for those fans who want a plausible explanation for the time and culture shift. Series co-creator Steven Moffat explains that, after he and Mark Gatiss discussed logical reasons for the shift, such as a Victorian house party or dream sequence, they later decided not to provide any explanation. Moffat adds that "We never bother to explain why Sherlock Holmes and Dr. Watson are in the modern world in the normal series; why should we bother explaining now that we're back in Victorian times?" (Clark). He reminds fans that "when we first did *Sherlock*, [the] press asked how can Sherlock possibly survive in a world with an iPhone? and when doing the Victorian, the press came in and said how can he do this without his iPhone?" Even in the Victorian setting, Moffat assured fans in July 2015, "It's very much the show you know. It's *Sherlock* as you know it, but in the correct era" (Hibberd).

To promote the *Sherlock* special, the first two official photographs and the trailer released at San Diego Comic-Con show Sherlock Holmes and John Watson in Victorian garb. One of the most interesting early still images is a portrait of Holmes and Watson that closely resembles a Victorian-era portrait modernized in color. Although photographic portraits had become more common by the late 1800s, formal studio portraits are, as Judith Williamson indicates, "a record, a kind of proof that the traditional landmarks of life have been reached" (239). The subjects' expression is usually solemn as they look directly at the lens; their attitude matches their formal attire and denotes a special, serious occasion, such as a wedding, the commemoration of the family unit, or a professional achievement. True to Victorian photography, an official photo released by the BBC via Twitter in early July 2015 (BBC One) captures a sedate Holmes; the empty background suggests a studio portrait, as would be typical of formal Victorian portrait photography, not one taken "at home" on the 221B Baker Street set. Unlike Victorian portraits, an elaborate backdrop is missing, and the lone "prop" is a far more comfortable chair than the straight-backed type favored in many turn-of-the-century portraits.

In the BBC's photograph, Holmes sits, legs crossed, in that comfy leather chair and sternly looks toward the camera. He wears a three-piece suit, and his crisply starched shirt collar can be seen above the high-buttoned waistcoat—costume markers indicating the Victorian period. His dark hair is carefully slicked back. His attire, hairstyle, and sterner-than-usual expression align him with viewers' expectations of the Victorian era, and his position in the chair suggests that he is the photograph's focal point.

John Watson's pose is far more casual than Holmes.' Watson sits on the chair's arm and casually crosses his ankles, one hand defiantly on his hip as he looks toward the camera. The most striking physical difference between *Sherlock*'s Victorian Watson and 21st century John is a handlebar mustache, making him appear similar to Paget's illustrations of the good doctor. Watson's self-assured, "take no guff from Holmes" attitude, however, is far closer to his 21st- century characterization and aligns this version of John Watson more closely with 21st-century expectations of "buddy movies" than to less overtly emotional Victorian images of male friends. Along with the use of color photography, Watson's attitude and position leaning toward Holmes while casually perching on the chair's arm suggest that the John-Sherlock relationship from the 21st century has survived the trip to the past, and the friendship may seem more closely "buddy" than Victorian "platonic." This is a portrait of two men who are comfortable around each other and easily share personal space.

This image of Holmes and Watson includes status markers typical of Victorian portraits, such as "appropriate symbols of wealth or the person's occupation" (National Portrait Gallery). The leather chair and the subjects' fashionable formal attire attest to their being successful. Holmes also assumes a serious "thinking pose," with his left hand to his face, index and middle fingers pointed toward his temple, as if pointing out that his mind should be a focal point. Perhaps this subtle reminder of Holmes's brilliance is also a marker of being the world's only consulting detective. Holmes's and Watson's positions in relation to each other signal equality in their partnership. Although Holmes is photographed in the "power" position of being in the chair—typically a portrait's focus—Holmes and Watson share the frame equally. Watson is "taller" because he is leaning against the chair's arm; he also is "first" when the photograph is "read" from left to right. Although the Victorian-style portrait and attire are historically and comfortably accurate to turn modern John and Sherlock into Victorian gentlemen, the pose, attitude, and use of color also signal to viewers that the characters they know and love will work well within the Victorian setting.

Dealing with the Deerstalker

The stereotypical Victorian image of Sherlock Holmes requires him to wear a deerstalker and a long cape, as he does in many adaptations. Both the officially-sanctioned statue of Holmes standing near Baker Street, one of only two statues in England representing great literary characters, and the Sherlock Holmes statue in Edinburgh portray Holmes in this now-familiar (if not canon-specific) attire. According to Sherlockian website The Victorian Web, the deerstalker and cape have become key components of "Holmes's unforgettable trademark" (Diniejko). Conan Doyle only mentions that Holmes wears "his ear-flapped travelling cap" in "The Adventure of the Silver Blaze," the story in which Paget, with four illustrations showing the deerstalker being worn during this adventure, indelibly altered readers' and future audiences' expectations of Holmes's appearance.

The persistence of such a powerful image is dealt with humorously in *Mr. Holmes.* In a flashback scene detailing Holmes's final case, a music teacher does not believe that the real Sherlock Holmes is visiting her studio as part of an investigation. After all, he does not look like the illustrations accompanying published stories of his early cases, and she wants proof of his identity. Believing the public image presented by popular media is a constant problem for the people who come in contact with Holmes—they expect him to look or behave in the way presented by a magazine illustrator or in John Watson's stories, what Holmes terms "penny dreadfuls with elevated prose."

In *Mr. Holmes* and the *Sherlock* special, the title character addresses the issue of the deerstalker as a reflection of audience expectations but does so in a way that refutes the legitimacy of this stereotypical depiction. In *Mr. Holmes*, Sherlock Holmes is not a character, but a real man who has had movies made about his cases. When the now-older Great Detective queues to watch a movie supposedly about his last case, based on Watson's published account of it, no one recognizes him. The on-screen version of Holmes wears a long coat, lights a Meerschaum pipe at the conclusion of a case, dons his deerstalker, and walks off into the London fog. Holmes is amused as well as appalled by this fictitious depiction.

The persistent deerstalker follows him even to Japan. An important side story involves Holmes trying to stave off memory loss by visiting this post–World War II nation to track down an elusive plant that his host, Mr. Umezaki (Hiroyuki Sanada), assures him will help restore his mental faculties. Shortly after his arrival, Holmes learns that Mr. Umezaki's mother is surprised by his appearance. She is disappointed that he did not bring the deerstalker. Holmes explains that his image was largely created by the "embellishment of the illustrator." He never wore a deerstalker, and he prefers a cigar to a pipe.

The deerstalker assumes a more accepted presence in Holmes's wardrobe in the *Sherlock* special than in previous modern-day episodes. In "The Reichenbach Fall," for instance, Sherlock asks John to explain the "ear hat" that has been given to him and refuses to wear the confounding cap. By the time he has returned from the "dead" and a two-year hiatus dismantling Jim Moriarty's criminal network, Sherlock more graciously assumes his role as London's celebrity detective as portrayed by the press. His media-created public persona and many of his fans sometimes wear a deerstalker. At the conclusion of "The Empty Hearse," John says that Sherlock enjoys "being Sherlock Holmes" for the public, as the consulting detective prepares to step outside 221B to face reporters eager to interview him now that he has returned. Sherlock dons the deerstalker as part of his preparation to look the "part" that the public expects him to play.

Although the BBC's first-released photograph of Victorian Holmes in "The Abominable Bride" shows him wearing a top hat, the famous deerstalker is prominently featured in the *Sherlock* trailers. One released in late October 2015 even shows Watson shoving the deerstalker at Holmes and admonishing him to "Just wear the damn hat! You're Sherlock Holmes!" ("Sherlock: The Abominable Bride Trailer #2"). Watson knows that the public expects Holmes to look like the image depicted in their magazine exploits, and even Watson has come to expect that the brilliant detective is associated with this specific piece of attire. In "The Abominable Bride," Watson's insistence on Holmes wearing the deerstalker is partially a result of his arrival at Baker Street to find his friend in a stupor from the seven percent solution he has taken. Watson's anger at Holmes's indulgence, and then urgency at going out to solve a case (which has put Watson's wife Mary in danger), likely fuels the fixation with the deerstalker. To Watson, the Sherlock Holmes on which he (and the audience) can rely wears the deerstalker while following clues on a case.

Sherlock and Mr. Holmes rely on such a familiar image as the deerstalker to serve as a centerpiece for discussions about the differences between public and private personas. Whether tackling expectations of Victorian Sherlock Holmes specifically or, more generally, the difference between media hype and reality, both adaptations and actors portraying Holmes address "being Victorian" first through their costumes.

Making Sherlock Holmes's Victorian "Interior" Match Modern Audiences' Expectations of a Victorian Character

For a filmic adaptation to be successful with a setting in, as Moffat terms it, the "correct era" of the canon stories, Victorian Holmes—whether played by McKellen or Cumberbatch—must fit current-day audiences' understanding of what it means to be Victorian. The performance must determine the degree to which Holmes in an adaptation released in the mid–2010s can acceptably deviate from Victorian norms; the portrayal must suit modern audiences' taste in entertainment but still be believable in relation to the canon. For example, Sherlock owes much of its popularity to the "bromance" or teasing of Johnlock (i.e., a sexual or romantic relationship between Sherlock Holmes and John Watson). Conan Doyle's canon depicts much less of a "buddy" friendship, and Holmes is not interested in sex. The Victorian-set adaptation must be able to address these disparate interpretations of the Holmes-Watson friendship. In Mr. Holmes, the aged detective must still resemble his younger self, even if the plot is mainly about Holmes's coming to terms with his increasing memory loss.

Constructing Holmes's 1940s' "Interior" Identity

The title character of Mr. Holmes is not at all as modern as the BBC's Sherlock, even when both are "being Victorian." A complication to an aged Holmes's Victorian image is that Mr. Holmes's "present-day" scenes in spring and summer 1947 are set nearly 30 years later than the flashback sequences taking place just after World War I, and neither setting can accurately be termed Victorian by time period. Yet even in these settings, Holmes remains decidedly Victorian in manner and resonates Victorian styles in dress, helping the audience to connect him with the much younger Holmes of the Conan Doyle stories and many other Victorian-set adaptations. For example, when

Holmes travels to post-war Japan in 1947, he dresses formally, with a hat and three-piece suit, complete with a pocket watch—decidedly a Victorian-influenced fashion. McKellen matches Holmes's demeanor to his formal, traditional attire.

Jeffrey Hatcher's screenplay also makes the 1919 Holmes closer to audiences' expectations of the Victorian canon version. Hatcher explains that "by flashing back to 1919 we are reminded of the period of the classic Holmes/Watson thrillers." Producer Ian Canning praised costume designer Martin Childs for creating a "life timeline for Holmes which brings consistency between the different time periods of the film…. The older Holmes gets, the older his world gets; the furniture, the house, the surroundings age as much as he does" ("Mr. Holmes—Movie Production Notes"). Holmes feels most comfortable in the country cottage where he has retired. Upon returning from abroad, he visibly relaxes the closer he gets to home. After first visiting his bees, he escapes to his study, filled with mementos of his London life and cozily helping him hold onto as much of that time as possible. His books, magnifying glass, and equipment for a few experiments fill his study, a room which illustrates to audiences that which means most to Holmes from his life as a consulting detective.

In this adaptation, Holmes also must deal with differing cultural expectations of a hero. Whereas modern audiences are much more aware of and comfortable with morally ambiguous heroes, the Sherlock Holmes of the Victorian era is often expected to be more traditionally heroic than modern-day characters, even though Moffat reminds audiences that Conan Doyle's "hero isn't exactly, well, heroic" (xi). Although Conan Doyle wrote Holmes as a man more interested in solving puzzles than bettering society by solving crimes, the popularized Victorian Holmes of the recent Ritchie-directed film series is an action hero who frequently does whatever it takes to fight evil-doers. Holmes, in canon or adaptation, often forces audiences to struggle with what it means to be a hero appropriate to their time.

In *Mr. Holmes*, the title character is portrayed as a real man whose image takes on a more heroic life of its own. Watson's version of Holmes is that he is a hero, and information about the detective's last case is revised by Watson and published to ensure that the public continues to see Holmes that way, even if the reality is that Holmes fails his last client, becomes depressed, and eventually exiles himself to Sussex. Watson's story becomes the basis of the film that Holmes later sees in a cinema; the on-screen depiction is flawlessly heroic.

Decades later, Holmes confides in his housekeeper's son, Roger (Milo Parker), that he became estranged from Watson because of this case—it hurts Holmes unbearably that his friend could not see him as anything less than heroic and attempted to make him feel better about his failure by, in effect, lying to the public and hiding any evidence that might make him remember the facts. Before his death, Holmes feels compelled to correct Watson's interpretation of his last case and set the record straight. If he had enough time, audiences suspect that Holmes would, as he tells his Japanese host, "correct the million misconceptions created by [Watson's] imaginative license."

Although Holmes grieves that no one ever truly knows him, he nonetheless begins to allow his housekeeper Mrs. Munro (Laura Linney) and Roger to see him as an increasingly fragile, socially incompetent man once famous for his great mind and logical deductions. One critic compliments McKellen that his Holmes is a "stern, seldom-smiling protagonist," a portrayal that allows audiences to "get a better understanding of the characteristics that make the great man tick and make many others wince." The review, entitled "At Last, the Real 'Mr. Holmes' Shows Up," identifies McKellen's performance as one of the few in recent memory that is "true to the original character" (Toppman).

This Holmes can be prickly and thinks first of being pragmatic and only later of expressing sentiment. When Roger is attacked by wasps and Holmes finds the boy's unconscious body, the old man's immediate response is to return to the cottage to call an ambulance and explain what has happened. Logically, Holmes calls for help as soon as possible, but, unfortunately, he bypasses Mrs. Munro, who overhears his conversation and hysterically runs to her son. She angrily confronts Holmes, saying that he should have come to her because she is Roger's mother. She accuses Holmes of being unfeeling. Only when faced with Mrs. Munro's tirade does Holmes's stoic façade crack. He admits that he does care very much about Roger, and eventually he and Mrs. Munro share a hospital vigil, even clasping hands, as they await news about the boy. McKellen's older Holmes has grudgingly learned to show his emotions in front of others, but he still prefers logic over social conventions. As long as Holmes retains at least part of the personality described by Conan Doyle, audiences accept the idea that he mellows with age.

Sherlock's Victorian Soul in "The Abominable Bride"

Victorian Holmes, according to Moffat, is still recognizable as the Sherlock audiences know by his personality traits, although the Victorian version is less abrasive. "[Sherlock] has the manners of the Victorian gentleman, which he doesn't have in the modern version. So he is a lot less brattish when he's back then…. I would say this Sherlock is a little more polished, and he operates like a Victorian gentleman instead of a posh, rude man, which he does in the modern" (Fowler).

In an early *Sherlock* review, one critic highlights the distinctive traits that separate Conan Doyle's detective from his 21st-century counterpart:

> The Sherlock Holmes of the books is often detached and unemotional, but it's always clear that he cares about Watson…. The worst of his antisocial tendencies—shooting indoors and playing his violin in the early hours—stem from caring more about getting his mind to work to its best, than he does about social conventions. However, Sherlock Holmes in Steven Moffat and Mark Gatiss' *Sherlock* at times feels genuinely nasty [Stringer].

Similarly, in discussing the forthcoming *Sherlock* special and modern Sherlock's personality shift toward the Victorian, another critic reminds viewers that

> [i]n Conan Doyle's original stories Holmes is very much a Victorian gentleman. While the emotionlessness and blunt speech that make up Benedict Cumberbatch's Holmes certainly find their bases in the original canon, the original Holmes usually only insults the people he's dealing with after they've insulted him first. If Holmes thinks somebody is an idiot, the only person who ever usually knows it is Watson [Libbey].

Thus, as expected from the canon, and in contrast with Cumberbatch's depiction of 21st-century Sherlock, Victorian Holmes in the *Sherlock* special must act differently, in accordance with audience expectations of a Victorian gentleman, while still retaining at least a recognizable connection to the personality of his 21st-century counterpart. The "interior" must match the era-appropriate exterior.

The clip released for San Diego Comic-Con hints at such a personality shift and prepares fans for the then-still-months-away special. In the teaser, Mrs. Hudson (Una Stubbs) dutifully opens the door as Sherlock Holmes and John Watson alight from a carriage. John follows in Sherlock's wake and carries gruesome evidence pertaining to their latest case. A servant boy carries the rest of the baggage. Holmes looks like the detective from Paget's drawings. He wears a long coat and a deerstalker and holds a pipe. Holmes, in this Victorian adaptation, seems aloof and entitled as he allows Watson and the child to carry the baggage and expects Mrs. Hudson to wait upon him.

Once inside, the trio finds fault with Watson's published stories and the illustrator's depiction of them. Each is disgruntled with the way he or she is portrayed to the public, giving viewers the impression that the characters do not feel that they so easily mesh with Victorian social conventions or audience expectations of Victorian characters. The dialogue also sets up the conceit that if Victorian John, Sherlock, and Mrs. Hudson act out of character in this setting, especially within the sanctuary of 221 Baker Street, they are being true to themselves, not to the preconceptions of illustrators, authors, or viewers. In accordance with the previously mentioned comment that canon Holmes confides only in Watson, presumably behind closed doors, this Victorian Sherlock complains under his breath that, among Watson's stories, he barely makes an appearance in "the one with the dog" (i.e., *The Hound of the Baskervilles*). The comment suggests a bit of vanity, and possibly hurt feelings, at not being the star of that story.

Although Mrs. Hudson seems to conform to the role of housekeeper, she complains to Watson that she is far too subservient in his stories and barely says a word. When he explains that this is her "function in the narrative," she protests being a mere "plot device" to bring clients to Holmes. For his part, Watson bemoans the fact that the illustrator portrays him as having a mustache, thus forcing him to conform to public expectations that he sport one in real life, despite his aversion to it. (*Sherlock* fans likely recall news of Freeman detesting the mustache required for "The Empty Hearse" [Mellor].) The *meta* commentary in "The Abominable Bride" is meant to provide a wink-wink insider joke to fans of the modern-set series and to suggest that, despite being transported to a Victorian setting, *Sherlock*'s characters are very much 21st-century people dressed, as expected, in Victorian clothing but retaining their modern sensibilities. This *meta* commentary provides the bridge between *Sherlock* present and past, as well as makes this adapted version of Victorian Holmes acceptable to modern audiences. The not-really-Victorian gender relationships also create the necessary twist to make this adaptation stand out from others.

The Victorian setting of "The Abominable Bride" becomes increasingly *meta* when the plot shifts from the Victorian era to modern day, the plot twist being that 21st-century Sherlock is playing out a Victorian murder mystery in his mind palace. The "Victorian holiday special" is not really Victorian, and whatever dissonance in the setting or characterization viewers may perceive from "authentic" Victorian-set stories can be blamed on Sherlock's subconscious understanding of what it means to be Victorian. Thus, although the Victorian Holmes and Watson solving a mystery within Sherlock's mind palace differ in personality from the "real" modern characters, they also take time for a heart-to-heart conversation during a stakeout that reinforces the "bromantic" aspects of the modern series. Watson expresses his concern for Holmes, who does not have a wife and seems singularly alone. Similar to a scene in the modern-set "A Study in Pink," Holmes explains that he is not interested in an intimate relationship with anyone. His actions, however, indicate that he relies on Watson to help him battle his demons, and his friend sees aspects of Holmes's behavior that are revealed to no one else. "Victorian" Holmes and Watson in "The Abominable Bride" are a compromise—more Victorian than their modern counterparts played by the same actors, but "Victorian" only in the sense that they are "authentic" to viewers who have learned about the Victorian era from popular television series or films.

"Keeping up appearances" and "being Sherlock Holmes" require a great deal of energy and dedication to maintaining an image that the public expects. According to *Mr. Holmes* and the *Sherlock* special, the public's misconceptions about Victorian Holmes can be "blamed" on author John Watson or the unnamed illustrator, who established readers' expectations of what a Victorian consulting detective should wear or how he should act. Such expectations are often difficult to meet, although deviating too far can cause the public to reject an unexpected version of Holmes. In the most recent period-piece adaptations, even Sherlock Holmes expresses his discomfort with the Victorian public identity created for him and, especially in *Mr. Holmes*, with the loneliness that results from not even his closest friend truly knowing or accepting who he is. Like Sherlock Holmes in these adaptations, modern adapters must deal with audience expectations of Victorian Holmes, even if he has become an illusion made more elusive over time.

Works Cited

"The Abominable Bride." *Sherlock*. Writ. Mark Gatiss. Dir. Douglas Mackinnon. BBC Entertainment, 2016. DVD.

"The Abominable Bride (2016) Financial Information." TheNumbers.com. 2016. Web. 9 Mar. 2016.

BBC One. Twitter. 8 July 2015. Web. 8 July 2015.

Billington, Alex. "Interview: An Afternoon Chat with Ian McKellen from 'Mr. Holmes.'" FirstShowing.net. 17 July 2015. Web. 2 Sep. 2015.

Clark, Noelene. "*Sherlock* Creator Would Be Down for a *Doctor Who* Crossover." *Entertainment Weekly*. 9 July 2015. Web. 14 Aug. 2015.

Conan Doyle, Sir Arthur. "The Adventure of the Silver Blaze." *The Strand Magazine* 2, 1. Stanford Continuing Studies. Feb. 2007. Web. 3 Sep. 2015.

Diniejko, Andrzej. "Sidney Paget, the Artist Who Illustrated the Sherlock Holmes Stories." The Victorian Web. 28 Nov. 2013. Web. 3 Sep. 2015.

"The Empty Hearse." *Sherlock: Season Three*. Writ. Steven Moffat. Dir. Jeremy Lovering. BBC Home Entertainment, 2013. DVD.

Fowler, Matt. "Sherlock 'Less Rude' in Upcoming Victorian Special." IGN.com. 2 Aug. 2015. Web. 19 Aug. 2015.

Hibberd, James. "*Sherlock* Releases First Preview of Victorian-era Special." *Entertainment Weekly*. 9 July 2015. Web. 14 Aug. 2015.

Libbey, Dirk. "How Sherlock's Character Will Be Different in the Upcoming Special." CinemaBlend. 2 Aug. 2015. Web. 19 Aug. 2015.

Mellor, Louise. "Sherlock Series 3: Things We Learned from the Special Edition DVDs." Den of Geek. 28 Nov. 2014. Web. 3 Sep. 2015.

Mr. Holmes. Dir. Bill Condon. Perf. Ian McKellen. Miramax, 2015. Film.

Moffat, Steven. "Introduction." *A Study in Scarlet*. Croydon: BBC Books, 2011. Print.

"Mr. Holmes—Movie Production Notes." *Cinema Review*. 2015. Web. 3 Sep. 2015.

"Mr. Holmes (2015) Financial Information." TheNumbers.com. 2015. Web. 9 Mar. 2016.

National Portrait Gallery. "Portrait Photography: From the Victorians to the Present Day." n.d. Web. 31 Oct. 2015.

Norman, Leif. "Victorian and Vintage Photography." Leifnorman.net. 31 Oct. 2011. Web. 31 Oct. 2015.

PBS. "A First Look at the *Sherlock* Special." YouTube. 9 July 2015. Web. 2 Sep. 2015.

Prensky, Mark. "Digital Natives, Digital Immigrants, Part 1." MarkPrensky.com. 2001. Web. 9 Mar. 2016.

"The Reichenbach Fall." *Sherlock: Season Two*. Writ. Steve Thompson. Dir. Toby Haynes. BBC Home Entertainment, 2011. DVD.

Rich, Sarah C. "The Deerstalker: Where Sherlock Holmes' Popular Image Came From." *Smithsonian.* 26 July 2012. Web. 9 Mar. 2016.

Sherlock Holmes. Dir. Arthur Berthelet. Perf. William Gillette. Flicker Alley, 2015. DVD.

"Sherlock: The Abominable Bride Trailer #2." YouTube. 25 Oct. 2015. Web. 9 Mar. 2016.

Stringer, David. "Sherlock Holmes vs. Sherlock." Den of Geek. 22 Jan. 2012. Web. 19 Aug. 2015.

Toppman, Lawrence. "At Last, the Real 'Mr. Holmes' Shows Up." *Charlotte Observer.* 16 July 2015. Web. 3 Sep. 2015.

Williamson, Judith. "Family, Education, Photography." Ed. Nicholas B. Dirks, Geoff Eley, and Sherry B. Ortner. *Culture/Power/History: A Reader in Contemporary Social Theory.* Princeton: Princeton University Press, 1994. 236–244. Print.

"I made me"
Narrative Construction of Identity in Sherlock's "The Abominable Bride"

FELECIA MCDUFFIE

"The Abominable Bride," like the entire BBC series *Sherlock* of which it is a part, tells a story about the power of stories. In this special episode, Sherlock Holmes (Benedict Cumberbatch) tells himself a story as a way to solve the mystery of Moriarty's (Andrew Scott) ostensible resurrection from the dead. The complex narrative he creates has just as much to do with his own resurrection. Sherlock, through his narrative, reconstructs his own story and recreates his personal identity in the face of the threat of imminent death. Contrary to much publicity and intentional misdirection by series creators Steven Moffat and Mark Gatiss, "The Abominable Bride" takes up directly where the events of "His Last Vow" left off. After killing Charles Augustus Magnussen (Lars Mikkelsen), Sherlock is "sentenced" to a likely suicide mission in Eastern Europe. In the plane, Mycroft (Mark Gatiss) informs Sherlock of Moriarty's reappearance. The events of "The Abominable Bride" take place during Sherlock's brief flight, which returns him to London to battle the threat.

On the plane, Sherlock, drugged to the gills, retreats to his mind palace and creates a complex piece of theater reconstructing his past and creating a way into his future. He later claims that he took drugs to facilitate his ability to solve the puzzle of Moriarty's return. Mycroft's counterclaim that his brother was high before he got on the plane, however, seems a much more plausible interpretation of events. Sherlock enters the plane facing death, either from the suicide mission on which he is embarked or from a suicidal overdose to avoid that fate. Either way, the detective story he tells himself to solve the *deus ex machina* reappearance of his arch-nemesis becomes deeply entangled with the more important story of his own life and self-understanding.

33

Who is Sherlock Holmes? Who was he? Who can he become? The series raises these questions for the audience as well as for the characters. The writers organize the explorations of Sherlock's identity around one clearly-stated and overarching question. Sherlock Holmes is a great man, but will he ever become a good one? "The Abominable Bride" can be analyzed through the lens of the theory that people create their identities through narrative. Norbert Meuter defines narrative as "a self-organizing structure that mediates meaning and time" (34). People create their identities by structuring and assigning meanings to past events, including their own choices and actions, in order to understand themselves, evaluate their choices and relationships, and develop as moral beings. An examination of Sherlock's identity formation through traditional components of narratives such as theme, genre, narrative voice, setting, and character sheds light on the part "The Abominable Bride" plays in the overall trajectory of Sherlock Holmes from great man to good man.

Narrative Construction of Identity

What is personal identity? What makes a person *a* person, a unique individual, one self and not another? Theories of personal identity litter the fields of philosophy, psychology, sociology, and literary criticism. One of the most intriguing of those theories holds that a *self* is the stories that it tells about itself and the stories it accepts about itself. In particular, a person gains *identity* (i.e., a coherent, individual self that exists through time) by combining the raw material of experience, sensation, memories, and self-reflection into a coherent narrative that has meaning and moral coherence (i.e., theme and plot). The classical formulation of this theory comes from French philosopher Paul Ricoeur, who said that "narrative constructs the identity of the character, what can be called his or her narrative identity, in constructing that of the story told. It is the identity of the story that makes the identity of the character" (Ricoeur, *Oneself as Another,* 147–148, qtd. in Dauenhauer and Pellauer). This theory reflects Ricoeur's view that "there is no self-understanding that is not mediated by signs, symbols, and texts; in the final analysis self-understanding coincides with the interpretation given to these mediating terms" (Ricoeur, "On Interpretation," in *From Text to Action*, 15, qtd. in Dauenhauer and Pellauer).

Theorists of narrative identity formation make additional points relevant to *Sherlock*. No one totally controls his or her own story. A person's narrative identity develops in relationship to contingent events and interactions with other people. Stories form in the interactions among characters who seem to have minds of their own. Even the hero of a tale is, at best, the co-author of a story that cannot be totally controlled (see Klepper 38). Moffat drew attention to Sherlock's need (and that of the narrative itself) for interactions with others in a *BBC Breakfast* appearance. Moriarty, he said, "makes Sherlock a hero. Because you have an amoral character, Sherlock Holmes, so you want something for him to respond to that turns him into the hero he's destined to be" (Moffat). Within the narrative of "The Abominable Bride," Sherlock comes to terms with the need to hold himself to a higher moral standard because, against the odds, it seems that he is going to live after all. He needs to become a better man because, as he has Victorian-John tell him, the other people in his life need him to be better.

Theme: Recreation of Identity in the Face of Death

In a crucial central scene in "The Abominable Bride," Sherlock probes some closely interrelated questions about his identity. As the playwright of his own theatrical production, playwright-Sherlock sets the scene: a greenhouse in the dead of night, a man-to-man conversation with his best friend. Sherlock has John Watson ask him a series of questions. "Why are you always alone?" "Why do you *need* to be alone?" "What made you this way?" These questions are thematically central to this episode, and the answers to them are essential to the development of the overall "great to good" story arc of the series. This scene takes place literally at the center of the episode (at approximately minute 42) and is linked through verbal and visual references to similar themes in a strikingly similar scene in "The Hounds of Baskerville" (at approximately minute 42). In both scenes, Sherlock grapples with his self-understanding and the balance of emotion and reason in his life. Both these scenes use identical language to refer to Sherlock's understanding of himself as a "brain without a heart," a thinking machine. "All emotion is abhorrent to me," he says before the fireplace of the inn near Baskerville and in the greenhouse at Lady Carmichael's estate. "It is the grit in a sensitive instrument," he insists, "the crack in the lens." "The Hounds of Baskerville" presents this as his own narrative about himself. Sherlock vehemently denies that he has friends, spitting out the word as if the concept offends him. He only later tries to mend fences by telling John Watson that he considers him his *only* friend.

In "The Abominable Bride," Sherlock grapples with similar issues but begins to distance himself from the narrated self-identity of "The Hounds of Baskerville." Victorian-Sherlock readily "concedes" that Victorian-John is his friend, not bothering to deny that relationship. Sherlock as the creator and narrative voice of the scene has John remind him that the "Hounds of Baskerville" characterization of Sherlock as emotionless belongs to the persona that John created for public consumption. Sherlock then has Victorian-John in the greenhouse scene rewrite the narrative about the possibilities. "You are a living, breathing man," he tells himself through John. "You've lived a life. You have a past. You are flesh and blood. You have feelings." He has John ask him to explain what made Sherlock "like this," unable to fully lay claim to relationships or deal with emotions. Sherlock replies, "Oh, Watson, nothing made me. I made me."

In the opening of the special episode, the writers chose to replay a series of scenes from the first three seasons of the show under the familiar guise of "last seen on *Sherlock*." Then onto the screen comes the word "alternatively" and the date begins to roll back until it stops on 1895. This shift might be taken at first to herald the beginning of a light-hearted one-off, an exercise by the fanboy-writers who wanted to place their characters into their original Victorian setting for old time's sake. The narrative and its purpose, however, turn out to be more subtle: a reimagining of the past by Sherlock, for Sherlock. Narrative identity theorists would agree with Sherlock's statement "I made me" and also point out that he can remake himself. Sherlock weaves many scenes, settings, props, and dialogue into the melodramatic piece of theater he creates in his mind palace that have no direct relevance to the historic case under investigation. In the face of an unexpected chance at life, he re-creates his past and, in the process, re-creates his own identity and the possibilities for his future.

Genres: You're in Deep, Sherlock

Culture has a profound influence on life stories, because the narrative possibilities of self-formation depend in part on the narrative forms that a particular culture provides. As one theorist of narrative identity puts it, culture provides "a menu of themes, images, and plots for the psychosocial construction of narrative identity" (McAdams 2). Every culture has "biography generators," narrative forms and conventions into which people can pour the incidents of their lives to make sense of them, reflect on them, and judge them. These biography generators vary with time and culture, with forms as varied as the vision quest stories of Native American tradition, the "happily ever after" template of some fairy tales, or the years-long conversations of classical psychoanalysis parodied in some of Woody Allen's movies. "The Abominable Bride" explicitly references many story genres, including detective fiction, ghost stories, Victorian melodrama, fairy tales, and blog entries. Two more implicit story genres are also directly relevant to "The Abominable Bride": morality play and psychodrama.

G.K. Chesterton, who wrote both theology and detective stories, saw the latter as "modern morality tales" (Ahlquist). Sherlock, like all great detectives, seeks the truth, the vindication of good over evil, and justice for victims as well as perpetrators. "The Abominable Bride" goes beyond this obvious connection to some closer ties to the actual morality plays of the late Middle Ages and Renaissance. This episode of *Sherlock* ventures into much deeper waters than the simple exploration of good and evil of a typical detective story. It bears some resemblances to actual morality plays of the English theatrical tradition as it follows the adventures of Sherlock, an unlikely Everyman, in his confrontations with reason, passion, death, sin, and the devil. Morality plays were vivid things, staged with elaborate sets and peopled with "angels and devils, priests, doctors" (Warren). They explored the "perpetual struggle between Good and Evil for the possession of the human soul, often in the person of a character called 'Everyman,' in the light of the inevitability of death" (Macklin). These spiritual dramas showed people how to live in the face of temptation and the prospect of death and judgment. The later morality plays in England, influenced by the humanists, also portrayed the battle between reason and passion in each individual. For the humanists, the ideal person was one "in whom reason and passion existed in proper balance" (Brown 29). As the paradigmatic scene in the greenhouse demonstrates, Sherlock must find the balance between reason and passion in order to grow and thrive. The episode also reflects the older preoccupations of the "moralities" with death, sin, and the devil. In one sense, of course, all narratives are morality plays. Ricoeur argued that all narratives are "explorations in the realm of good and evil" because they explore "morally paradigmatic situations" (qtd. in Meuter 43). Death, sin, confession, and the Devil pervade the haunted atmosphere of "The Abominable Bride."

The episode reflects the longstanding Christian spiritual tradition of *memento mori*, which played a central role in the spiritual practice of *ars moriendi*, the art of preparing for death. Depictions of skulls and skeletons reminded Christians that death and judgment were always on their horizon and that viewers should (always) be in the process of evaluating their moral lives in light of that fact. Shakespeare drew on this tradition in *Hamlet* in the gravedigger scene and in Hamlet's contemplation of the jester's skull (see Jacobs 104). The skull resting on the mantelpiece of the modern 221B Baker Street and the skull painting on the wall always hinted at this theme. Skulls are particularly important symbols in the *ars moriendi* tradition, because they are "the most persistent reminder of death for the living" and a "key transit point between life and death" (San Juan 960–961).

In "The Abominable Bride," Death comes ever closer, and the *memento mori* multiply. The imagery, setting, and plot concern death on several levels. On the surface, any "murder mystery" deals with death. Sherlock works his way through the mystery of Moriarty's ambiguous death through the older case of a murderous ghost. This level of the narrative gives the viewer corpses aplenty in morgues and streets and country houses. At a deeper level, and consistent with the themes of morality plays, Sherlock contemplates his own death. The narrative at the end of "His Last Vow" pointed toward his death, within six months or so, on his Eastern European mission. "The Abominable Bride," as an addition or alternative, raises the possibility that Sherlock has courted a quicker death through a drug overdose. Whichever reading one adopts, at the beginning of "The Abominable Bride" death is very much on Sherlock's mind.

In his self-created theater, Sherlock confesses and repents of some of his previous moral failings and attempts to resist the temptations of the Devil/Moriarty to despair and death. The theme of repentance and confession relates to a controversial and often misunderstood aspect of the episode. The "brides" in the de-sanctified church dress in purple robes with peaked hoods that cover all of the face except for the eyes. While some condemned these as "Ku Klux Klan" robes, a more consistent interpretation within the story is that they reference the penitential robes or tunics and *capirotes* (pointed hoods) worn in Holy Week processions by Catholic groups in Spain. This costume goes back to the Middle Ages and still serves the same dual purpose: it marks a person as a penitent while also masking identity from public scrutiny (Hafiz, McGahan). Although the color of the robes varies by time period and group, the purple chosen by the brides is the liturgical color recognized by many branches of Christianity as signifying repentance and mortification (Morrisroe). The robes and the church mark out this scene as an arena of penitence. Sherlock confronts and repents of his mistreatment of the women in his life and, by extension, of his mistreatment of the emotional and feminine aspects of his own character.

Sherlock's repeated references to his need to go "deep" into his own mind call attention to another important narrative genre in "The Abominable Bride": psychoanalysis. Sherlock's dismissive reference in the greenhouse scene to the "Viennese alienist" has the opposite effect of dismissal. It brings Freud into the narrative and his overarching ideas that dreams and psychoanalysis are alike acts of narrative interpretation that deal with memories, emotions, and past guilt. Analysis and dreams alike are psychodramas. In dreams, the subconscious knits together symbolic narratives to deal with events and the emotions they evoke. In psychoanalysis, the patient and analyst create a shared narrative, interpreting dreams, associations, and the patient's own stories to bring forward elements from the forgotten or repressed past into the patient's conscious life-narrative.

Three elements of the greenhouse scene are relevant to this genre. First, Victorian-Sherlock spooks like a frightened horse when John attempts to talk about emotions and relationships. His reaction suggests Freudian ideas of repressed sexuality as well as repressed childhood memories. Second, Narrator-Sherlock has his character refer to Freud as an "alienist," a now-archaic term that is most often used to refer to psychologists who testify in criminal matters ("Alienist"). This draws attention to the possibility of feelings of guilt. Third, just at the point Sherlock insists to John that "I made me," they hear the howling of a dog. Sherlock responds to the sound by crying out the name Redbeard. Although audiences have puzzled over the mystery of Redbeard's identity over several years and several episodes, it remains a mystery. The term *Redbeard* connects to several scenes that probe Sherlock's relationship to emotion and identity, including the scene in "The Hounds of Baskerville" by the fireplace. In that scene, Sherlock says *"cherchez la chien,"* translated as "find the dog." Whatever Redbeard signifies, the name seems close to the heart of Sherlock's struggles. What is certain, and what is connected to the psychodrama Sherlock creates in "The Abominable Bride," is that whoever or whatever Redbeard literally signifies, it is a potent symbol of a formative past trauma, a wound that has not healed, a part of the story that has created his identity. Some "ghost" from his past haunts him, and the many interrelated references throughout the episode to death, ghosts, guilt, and memory suggest that the story Sherlock tells himself must eventually deal with the ghosts that he has made for himself.

Haunting by ghosts and digging into the graves of a buried past recall Freud's ideas about repression and the return of the repressed. The song of the wronged bride, Emelia Ricoletti (Natasha O'Keeffe), repeats the refrain "do not forget me." Sherlock goes deep into his mind palace in this episode, and it turns out to be both a rewarding and dangerous journey. The settings he chooses for his psychodrama—the morgue, the church, and the maze—hint at the fact that his explorations have turned to the products of his own unconscious. Freud's essential idea is that organic instincts play a powerful but repressed part in human life and development. According to one of Freud's theories, two fundamental instincts or drives war beneath the surface of all mental life. The desire for the excitement and connection of *eros* (libido) as well as the desire for the calm and disconnection of *thanatos* (death, destruction) are deeply embedded in the depths of the unconscious (Thurschwell 88–89; also see Razinsky). According to Victorian-Moriarty, dead is "the new sexy," and its siren song calls to Sherlock throughout the episode.

In the depths of the morgue, early in "The Abominable Bride," Sherlock hints at the war between these deeply buried drives of the id and his own ego and superego. In contrast to their original meeting, Sherlock imagines his first meeting with John in a morgue that is underground, dark, lit only dimly by gas fire. Also, unlike their first meeting, Sherlock is actually engaged in beating a corpse and leaves to attend a hanging. The *memento mori* multiply.

When he and John return to the morgue to examine the body of Emelia Rico-letti, Sherlock asserts reason against the fears and superstitions of Anderson (Jonathan Aris) and Lestrade (Rupert Graves). The subconscious, however, intrudes with the bloody red "You" painted on the walls by the obviously dead bride. Faced with his inability to rationally account for the anomaly, Sherlock's narrative breaks down. The "you" recalls his own shaky whisper of "you" in "The Hounds of Baskerville" when he hallucinates a vision of Moriarty, a death mask dragged up from the depths of his repressed fears. Shaken, Victorian-Sherlock leaves the scene.

As narrator, he then has Victorian-John make some observations about the corpse to Molly (Louise Brealey). Voice dripping sarcasm, she notes how observant John is "now that Daddy's gone." John replies, "I am observant in some ways, just as Holmes is quite blind in others." That Sherlock-as-narrator uses the terms *Daddy* and *blind* for himself invites further Freudian interpretation. *Daddy* is the Freudian father and represents the superego, the internalization of the demand by the parental figure that the child conform to the rules of culture and received standards. *Daddy* punishes transgressions, especially those motivated by the id, with guilt and neuroses. In this case, as subsequent scenes make clear, the *Daddy* that Sherlock has internalized is not his own father, but Mycroft, specifically Sherlock's perception of Mycroft's demands and the standards of rationality that he has made part of his self-concept. Immediately after this scene in the morgue, when confronted with his inability to formulate a theory of the case, he tells John that "these are deep waters, and I shall have to go deeper still." In the scene after that, with the larger-than-life Mycroft at the Diogenes Club, Sherlock assures John that he need not worry about the obese Mycroft's heart, because "there is only a large cavity where that organ should reside." Mycroft replies that "it's a family trait," and Sherlock accepts that characterization. Although Sherlock tries to assert his independence from Mycroft at every turn, he struggles with the integration of his own life-narrative against the dominance of *Daddy*.

One of Sherlock's problems, in his journey of "great to good," lies in his continuing inability to finally embrace and integrate the impulses of the id, especially *eros*, into his personality. Sherlock is not Mycroft, and his attempts to best Mycroft at his own game or to rebel against Mycroft's narrative of him have, thus far, been unsuccessful. Narrator-Sherlock expresses his fears about his failure through Victorian-Mycroft, who mocks Sherlock's life as "reason toppled by melodrama; your life in a nutshell." Sherlock's life was "toppled" by his melodramatic killing of Magnussen, his impulsive desire to save what he loves. As Moffat pointed out in an interview, Sherlock is not Mycroft (Cornet). They are different at their core. Sherlock has a poet's heart. He is still the boy who wanted to be a pirate and instead became a detective. In order to become a man, an integrated adult personality, Sherlock must accept *eros* as well as his poetic streak. A refusal to do so leaves him vulnerable to the other great impulse of the id, *thanatos*.

In medieval morality plays, Death was a fear and a warning. He represented the end of the opportunity for repentance and further good deeds in life and the threshold to God's judgment. In terms of Sherlock's psychodrama, death is more complex. In Freudian terms, death is both the inevitable human end and an object of desire. As a counter-drive to *eros*, it represents the seductive call of oblivion, "the ultimate release of tension," "the ultimate experience of stasis and complete calm" (Thurschwell 88). The part of *thanatos* in Sherlock's psyche is played by Moriarty. Sherlock summons him in "The Abominable Bride" by taking cocaine. When Sherlock tells Moriarty/Death that "[y]ou chose to come here," Moriarty reminds Sherlock that he himself knows "that's not quite true." Sherlock-as-narrator created and cast the scene. He has summoned Death, whether through his murder of Magnussen or drug overdose.

Morality play and psychodrama meet in John Watson's demand immediately after the scene with "Death," when the Victorian-Sherlock wakes up from his drug-induced vision. Victorian-John demands that he "hold himself to a higher standard," that he turn away from death to fulfill his duties to the people that he loves. This requires that he integrate the parts of his psyche that he has tried to deny into the narrative of the "good man" of John's "idiot stories." This reintegration requires that he go "deep" again, into the depths of a de-sanctified church. Mary (Amanda Abbington) insists that the church is "the heart of it all." It is the heart not only of the conspiracy but represents the heart that Sherlock is trying to reintegrate. In this scene, Sherlock confronts his failures in his relationships with the women in his life. He also, by implication, confesses his sins against the "feminine" side of his own character, the half of himself that has been at war with the other, the "patronized and disregarded" aspects of himself, the emotions that he has denied. In order to become not just great but good, this is a war he must lose if he is to live instead of die.

In terms of Sherlock's moral and spiritual growth, this is a way station on the journey. The scenes at the "Hounds of Baskerville" fireplace and "The Abominable Bride" greenhouse connect to another suggestive place of deep exploration yet to come. Sherlock at one point imagines himself, unsuccessfully, looking for truth by digging up (and jumping into) the grave of Emelia Ricoletti. Dream-Mycroft agrees to the project, saying *"cherchez la femme."* This connects, of course, to the *"cherchez la chien"* of "The Hounds of Baskerville" and implies that Sherlock has more digging yet to do.

Narrative Voice: Poetry or Truth?

Near the beginning of the episode, Detective Inspector Lestrade dramatically describes the appearance of the bride, "face white as death, mouth like a crimson wound." Victorian-Sherlock asks whether that description is "poetry or truth." Sherlock stubbornly clings to his self-understanding as an intellect trying to find the truth, solving mysteries through empirical evidence and reason. In forming this long-standing narrative identity, he thinks he has turned away from childish things, from the romantic impulses that led him to want to be a pirate as a child. Mycroft understands, better than Sherlock does himself, that his detective-persona also has unacknowledged romance embedded in it. Sherlock doesn't want to be a forensic scientist; he wants to be St. George.

In "The Abominable Bride," this repressed poetic streak returns in force, influencing Sherlock's narrative voice and the recreation of his identity. A life worth living for Sherlock, a character worth developing, requires poetry and drama, perhaps even melodrama. Theories of narrative identity development assume the ability of the self to change, diverge, and choose one version of the self over another (see, for instance, Klepper 7). Ironically, they realize that "identity" (being one self and not another) carries a considerable amount of "play" within it: that a self can choose among narratives and that the narrative does not have to be "true" to be chosen and formative.

Sherlock-as-narrator chooses poetry over truth, chooses it even over the protestations of Sherlock-as-character. Why does Sherlock choose the particular set of events he selects for his little piece of theater? Many events and settings seem peripheral to the case of the murderous bride. He could have taken up the case at any point in relation to the space/time of his actual life, since he creates the theater. He chooses to begin with a strong misreading of his own history at the point he meets John Watson. Any story "begins with the selection of a contingent event: something happens marking a beginning … [it is] a dynamic process in which the selectivity of each event is passed on to the next one" (Meuter 36). Sherlock, in his mind palace on the plane, begins to read John's blog and weaves it into both levels of his narrative: the analysis of Moriarty's return through the bride case and his self-examination and confession. That very fact should tip off viewers to the fact that the Moriarty case is only one level and of lesser importance. There is actually no need to go back to what Sherlock clearly sees as the inciting incident of this part of his life and its most significant relationship. He focuses on John on the battlefield, but the scene he imagines is different in significant ways. In "A Study in Pink," John dreams of the battlefield as a confusion of gunfire and explosions. Sherlock imagines John as a heroic figure, treating the wounded under difficult conditions. John is his moral compass as Sherlock tries to find his way from what he suspects or fears he is—an addict and a failure—to what he hopes he can be: the "gentleman hero," the person who can hold himself to a higher standard for the people who need him. Irene Adler once mocked Sherlock by saying that his "higher power" is himself. That is almost, but not quite true. Sherlock has come to believe in the people who care about him and, in turn, the hope that he can reinvent himself in the image of the person in whom they believe.

The question of the interrelationship between truth and poetry returns toward the end of the episode. Sherlock-as-narrator has Moriarty ask, "What do you want, Sherlock?" Although the Sherlock-character immediately says that he wants truth, he has his mirror-image-Moriarty reply that "truth's boring." Through his own narrative voice, Sherlock slowly comes to terms with choosing a new identity, an identity quite different from that of his older brother. As Moffat said in an interview, Mycroft "hasn't got the heart of a poet, which is what Sherlock has, really.... There's tremendous *romance* in Sherlock Holmes. He *needs* to be fighting crime and fighting bad guys" (Cornet).

Setting: The Stage Is Set, the Curtain Rises

Every story has a setting, a particular location in time and space. Narrator-Sherlock presents his decision to set his "play" in 1895 as necessitated by the facts of the Victorian Ricoletti case. His own past, however, becomes just as much a part of the "play" as the case at hand, thus killing two birds with one stone. Sherlock's identity formation connects much more closely with space than with time, the space being 221B. Although most biographical genres are based on a time-trajectory, Martin Klepper suggests the intriguing idea that currently the most significant biography generators of the modern West "are organized as [virtual spaces] such as social networks, personal home pages, dating sites and chatrooms. One does not tell a story, one organizes a space" (20). The "curtain" cannot rise on Sherlock's psychodrama except in Baker Street, and it returns full circle to Baker Street at the end. The prince and the princess live happily ever after or, at least, John and Sherlock end up in front of the fire, talking.

Sherlock's mind palace, the heart of the psychodrama, combines features of time and space in a way that particularly lend themselves to the creation of narrative identity. Creating a coherent life story requires that memories be interpreted and incorporated into a coherent narrative. Because memory is actually more spatial than temporal, especially for Sherlock with his particular technique for storing memories in spatial locations, memories can be restructured, reinterpreted, revisited, and assigned new meanings. In fact, the purpose of such re-visitation is to "experience and manage the reversibility of meaning" (Meuter 36).

In dreams as well as in Sherlock's dream-like drug visions, re-presentation of the past is spatialized through symbols, locations, and structures. The sets and locations of "The Abominable Bride" are noticeably darker than those in the rest of the series, gesturing symbolically to death, repression, and the unconscious. This gloomy atmosphere pervades the obvious locations like the morgue, the church at night, the greenhouse at night, and the labyrinthine maze at the Carmichael estate. Even 221B is darker, a fact Mrs. Hudson (Una Stubbs) complains about at the beginning of the episode and which John blames on the illustrator. Symbols of death have also multiplied in Victorian-221B. The head of the dismembered country squire comes into the episode early via hatbox and later shows up turned into a skull. It cozies up to the skull from modern 221B, both now perched together on the desk. The John Pinkerton skull print of modern 221B gives way to an even more explicit *memento mori,* a print of Charles Allan Gilbert's drawing *All Is Vanity.*

Characters: People, People, People—Can't Keep Anything Shiny

If a person's ability to reinterpret the past and create a new self-understanding is the positive side of narrative creation identity, the shadow side of narrative creation occurs when other people try to impose stories and roles that box a person into the confines of a static and inauthentic persona. What happens when the characters in such static narratives rebel against the roles assigned to them? "The Abominable Bride" has fun with the idea of this rebellion in Mrs. Hudson's critique of her role in John's stories and in the unexpected sassiness of John's maid. Even Victorian-Moriarty rebels against Sherlock's characterization of him as the "Napoleon of Crime" and insists that only Sherlock himself keeps that distorted figure alive.

Sherlock's growth requires the realization that people are not entirely classifiable into the roles and functions he wishes to assign them, and that applies equally to the narratives he has applied to himself. Mrs. Hudson is not (just or ever) his housekeeper; Molly and Janine (Yasmine Akram) were never there just to serve his needs and whims. They are people he has wronged; they are full human beings with voices he has not heeded or respected. He must also break out of his self-imposed narratives, as little brother, as sociopath, as the man without a heart. As much as Sherlock may have presented himself early in the series as a Cartesian rational ego who exists in only the most tangential and unwilling relationships to either his own body or the people around him, the cracks in that façade started showing from the beginning. Sherlock's actions and his plot trajectory long ago belied his self-understanding as a brain without a heart. As "The Abominable Bride" shows, his self-understanding has not quite caught up with the plot.

In the scene of confrontation between Sherlock and Moriarty, Moriarty notes that much of the dust on the mantelpiece comes from the skins of people and says, "People, people, people. Can't keep anything shiny." The reference to dust is another *memento mori*, a reference to the phrase "earth to earth, ashes to ashes, dust to dust" which was part of the burial service of the 1662 *Book of Common Prayer* and was derived from Genesis 3:19: "for dust thou art, and unto dust shalt thou return." Being involved with people means, for Sherlock, that he cannot exist simply as an intellect, staying uninvolved and keeping everything "shiny" away from the mess of embodiment and relationships. Caring for others, as he has found to his cost, leads to loss and pain and death. In "The Abominable Bride," he presents several narrative identity choices to himself. He can still strive to become like his mind-Mycroft, the ever-superior and rational man without feelings. He can still become Moriarty, the amoral man without a soul.

Conclusion: A Somewhat Shorter Exile Than We'd Imagined

In "The Abominable Bride," Sherlock goes down into the depths, into the grave, even into hell. Will he be resurrected, recreated to live a new life? The iconic scene at the Reichenbach Falls suggests an affirmative answer, and that answer relates to Sherlock's hat. The deerstalker hat appears periodically in *Sherlock,* an always ambiguous marker of Sherlock's identity. In "The Hounds of Baskerville," Dr. Frankland (Clive Mantle) tells Sherlock that he recognized him when he first saw him in Baskerville, but that he "thought you'd be wearing your hat, though." Sherlock replies, "That wasn't my hat." The hat serves as a synecdoche for the narrative identities imposed from the outside, identities that have little to do with the real human person that is Sherlock Holmes. The "iconic" deerstalker was, in fact, never mentioned in Conan Doyle's stories but was added by illustrator Sidney Paget, then worn by actor William Gillette in Broadway plays starting in 1899 (Terjesen 99). After that, "[s]tick a deerstalker on a melon and it is instantly recognizable as Sherlock Holmes," as one journalist has pointed out (Segal 60, qtd. in Rixon 169). At times, Sherlock despairs of ever shedding the straightjacket of other people's narrative constructions of his identity. Even Victorian-John insists at one point, "You're Sherlock Holmes. Wear the damned hat" ("The Abominable Bride").

The hat-wearing Sherlock Holmes, however, is the man without a heart, the "unsavory companion of dubious morals," the addict, the man unworthy of the love of his friends. In the confrontation at the Falls, Sherlock almost gives in to the call of death, the guilt over his weaknesses, the temptation to "lie back and lose." Then Victorian-John appears, the voice calling Sherlock to live up to a higher standard. The real Sherlock, the wounded heart at the "heart" of the puzzle, takes a leap of faith and decides to live. He throws away the deerstalker and with it his old narrative. Then he takes a leap of faith and throws himself toward the future.

WORKS CITED

"The Abominable Bride." *Sherlock*. Writ. Mark Gatiss, Steven Moffat. Dir. Douglas Mackinnon. BBC, 2016. Television.

Ahlquist, Dale. "Detective Stories." The American Chesterton Society. n.d. Web. 28 Feb. 2016.

"Alienist." *Findlaw Legal Dictionary*. n.d. Web. 6 Jan. 2016.

The Book of Common Prayer. 1662. Cambridge: John Baskerville, 1762. Web. 11 Mar. 2016.

Brown, Dorothy H. *Christian Humanism in the Late English Morality Plays*. Gainesville: University of Florida Press, 1999. Print.

Cornet, Roth. "Sherlock Spoiler Alert! Steven Moffat, Benedict Cumberbatch, & Martin Freeman on the Surprises, Big Changes, and Bigger Return, in Sherlock Season 3." IGN.com. 3 Feb. 2014. Web. 14 Jan. 2016.

Dauenhauer, Bernard, and David Pellauer. "Paul Ricoeur." *The Stanford Encyclopedia of Philosophy*. Summer 2014 Edition. Ed. Edward N. Zalta. n.d. Web. 12 Jan. 2016.

Gilbert, Charles Allan. *All Is Vanity*. 1892. Drawing.

Hafiz, Yasmine. "Penitents Observe Holy Week in Seville, Spain with Processions and Robes." Huffington Post Online. 14 Apr. 2014. Web. 12 Mar. 2016.

"His Last Vow." *Sherlock: Season Three*. Writ. Steven Moffat. Dir. Nick Hurran. BBC Worldwide, 2014. DVD.

"The Hounds of Baskerville." *Sherlock: Season Two*. Writ. Mark Gatiss. Dir. Paul McGuigan. BBC Worldwide, 2012. DVD.

Jacobs, Henry E. "Shakespeare, Revenge Tragedy, and the Ideology of the Memento Mori." *Shakespeare Studies* 21 (1993): 96–108. Print.

Klepper, Martin. "Introduction." In *Rethinking Narrative Identity: Persona and Perspective*. Ed. Claudia Holler and Martin Klepper. Studies in Narrative 17. Series editor Michael Bamberg. Amsterdam: John Benjamins, 2013. 1–31. Print.

Macklin, Susan. "Mysteries and Morality Plays." *Continuum Encyclopedia of British Literature*. Ed. Steven R. Serafin and Valeria Grosvenor Myer. New York: Continuum, 2003. 699–702. Ebscohost. Web. 12 Feb. 2016.

McAdams, Dan P. "Moral Personality, Generativity, and the Redemptive Self." Notre Dame Symposium on Personality and Moral Character, October 12–14, 2006, Center for Ethical Education. n.d. Web. 12 Jan. 2016.

McGahan, Florence. "Confraternities of Penitents." *The Catholic Encyclopedia, Vol. 11*. New York: Robert Appleton, 1911. Web. 27 Feb. 2016.

Meuter, Norbert. "Identity and Empathy: On the Correlation of Narrativity and Morality." In *Rethinking Narrative Identity: Persona and Perspective*. Ed. Claudia Holler and Martin Klepper. Studies in Narrative 17. Series editor Michael Bamberg. Amsterdam: John Benjamins, 2013. 33–48. Print.

Moffat, Steven. Interview. *BBC Breakfast.* "Steven Moffat and Sue Vertue Talk About Sherlock (BBC Breakfast)." YouTube. 17 May 2011. Web. 14 Jan. 2016.

Morrisroe, Patrick. "Liturgical Colours." *The Catholic Encyclopedia, Vol. 4.* New York: Robert Appleton, 1908. Web. 27 Feb. 2016.

Razinsky, Liran. "Driving Death Away: Freud's Theory of the Death Drive." *Freud, Psychoanalysis and Death.* Chapter 7. Cambridge: Cambridge University Press, 2013. Print.

Rixon, Paul, *"Sherlock*: Critical Reception by the Media." *Sherlock and Transmedia Fandom: Essays on the BBC Series.* Ed. Louisa Ellen Stein and Kristina Busse. Jefferson, NC: McFarland, 2012. 165–178. Print.

San Juan, Rose Marie. "The Turn of the Skull: Andreas Vesalius and the Early Modern *Memento Mori.*" *Art History* 35, no. 5 (Nov. 2012): 958–975. Print.

Segal, Victoria. "Critic's Choice." *Sunday Times, Culture* 1 Aug. 2010: 60. Print.

Terjesen, Andrew. "Was It Morally Wrong to Kill Off Sherlock Holmes?" *The Philosophy of Sherlock Holmes.* Ed. David Baggett and Philip Tallon. Lexington: University Press of Kentucky, 2012. 93–108. Print.

Thurschwell, Pamela. "Freud's Maps of the Mind." *Sigmund Freud.* Chapter 5. Routledge Critical Thinkers. Abingdon-on-Thames: Taylor & Francis, 2000. Print.

Warren, Kate Mary. "Moralities." *The Catholic Encyclopedia, Vol. 10.* New York: Robert Appleton, 1911. Web. 24 Feb. 2016.

Inside the Mind of Sherlock Holmes

Lynnette Porter

What makes the Great Detective great? Critics and scholars have often praised Sherlock Holmes's mind as what separates him from those around him, explaining that "[h]is chief supremacy lies in the way he makes use of his intelligence to the core, and only that eminent quality distinguishes him from the other investigators," both within the Sherlock Holmes canon and among other fictional detectives (Kayalvizhi 142). In an essay published in *Genius on Television,* Carol-Ann Farkas reiterates that "the appeal of Holmes has always been that he is not meant to be *like* us. Holmes is meant to be the embodiment of flawless, logical problem-solving, of ratiocination, of decryption, of character that takes on something of the fantastical: encyclopedic, arcane knowledge, a seemingly-eidetic memory, indifference or even aversion to the distraction of emotional response, and drug use which calms his overpowered mind" (162–163). Unsurprisingly for a genius, in canon and adaptations, Holmes creates his own unique job title, the consulting detective, and devotes his full attention to attaining and accessing knowledge useful to this career.

Early in Arthur Conan Doyle's first Sherlock Holmes novel, *A Study in Scarlet,* Holmes seems very pleased with himself when he professes, first to readers of the article he has written and then, in person, to John Watson, that "all life is a great chain, the nature of which is known whenever we are shown a single link of it" (Conan Doyle, *A Study in Scarlet* 23). Holmes's analysis of causal relationships leads him to the development of the Science of Deduction. According to Holmes, facility with it "can only be acquired by long and patient study" (23), although even a lifetime may not be long enough to achieve perfection. Holmes devotes much of his adult life to the study of deduction and the application of scientific principles to his logical, objective method of solving puzzles. He even provides a creative metaphor to explain his thought processes.

Holmes defines his "attic theory" of how the brain stores information: "a man's brain originally is like a little empty attic, and you have to stock it with such furniture as you choose…. It is a mistake to think that that little room has elastic walls and can distend to any extent…. It is of the highest importance, therefore, not to have useless facts elbowing out the useful ones" (Conan Doyle, *A Study in Scarlet* 17–18). Whether in canon, television adaptations *Sherlock* and *Elementary*, or film adaptations *Sherlock Holmes, Sherlock Holmes: A Game of Shadows,* and *Mr. Holmes,* Sherlock Holmes carefully monitors the contents of his mind and shares with audiences his unique way of processing information. In canon, as well as in these adaptations, Holmes is defined by the way his brain has been trained to work. Understanding the mind of Sherlock Holmes is key to knowing how Holmes thinks of himself and the ways that everyone else—from friends and family to the general public—perceives him.

The canon term *brain attic* has been translated into similar terms for television audiences and introduced in the early episodes. *Elementary* prefers *mind attic*. In the second episode, Holmes (Jonny Lee Miller) explains to Watson (Lucy Liu) that his mind can be represented by the empty glass he lifts from a convenient table at an outdoor café he and Watson are passing. Holmes next appropriates a carafe of gold liquid and fills the glass halfway with what he illustrates as "golden" thoughts that should be retained. When Holmes finally pours water to fill the glass to its brim, the combined liquid is diluted, the golden thoughts intermixed with "drivel" ("While You Were Sleeping"). Holmes does not want his thoughts to thus be polluted with meaningless "nattering." (Nevertheless, in this series, Holmes is a recovering heroin addict who, by the end of Season Four, has a relapse, a situation that might lead at least some viewers to wonder if Holmes's mind has not been negatively affected by his addiction and whether "nattering" is the least of his mental concerns.) Despite this contradiction, which also occurs in canon through morphine or cocaine use (e.g., *The Sign of Four*), and, in some *Sherlock* episodes (e.g., "A Scandal in Belgravia," "The Abominable Bride"), allusions to Sherlock's occasional fall from sobriety, Holmes is still primarily thought of as being very particular about what goes into his mind. Of all the many ways that Sherlock Holmes's identity is developed, the most prevalent way of categorizing or identifying him is through the way that he thinks and his success in deducing what most people never could (his brother Mycroft being a notable exception).

The Sherlock Holmes of *Elementary,* just like canon Holmes, indicates that the brain/mind has a fixed amount of space that must be carefully utilized. When writing about "Sherlock Holmes and the Infamous Brain Attic,"

Maria Konnikova, however, presents the more modern, scientific description of this brain attic, which

> can be broken down, roughly speaking, into two components: structure and contents. The attic's structure is how our mind works: how it takes in [and processes] information. How it sorts it and stores it for the future. How it may choose to integrate it or not with contents that are already in the attic space. Unlike a physical attic, the structure of the brain attic isn't altogether fixed. It can expand, albeit not indefinitely, or it can contract, depending on how we use it.

In *Sherlock,* for example, Sherlock's mind palace—a term that automatically implies more space—seems to be in a process of continual expansion. In "The Hounds of Baskerville," John Watson (Martin Freeman) describes to a Baskerville scientist what Sherlock (Benedict Cumberbatch) means when he demands that they leave him alone so that he can go into his mind palace. John explains the mind-palace memory technique to the scientist (and the audience). The scientist queries "but he said it's a palace?" John replies, "Well, he would, wouldn't he?" John, well aware of Sherlock's ego, suggests that only the consulting detective would have a palace-sized mind.

Viewers realize by Season Three that Sherlock needs such a large mental home where all the characters inside his head can live. Instead of *brain attic,* the mind palace refers to more than a simple storage space that can expand as new data is acquired or contract as data is lost. *Sherlock* employs the "mind palace" as a method of actively interacting with data and making it human. He visually expands the real-world definition into a technique used by *Sherlock*'s writers to illustrate Sherlock's humanization and the resulting changes to his thought processes. Throughout the first three seasons' episodes, viewers see increasingly elaborate depictions of Sherlock's mind at work, culminating in Season Three with ever more-detailed visits inside Sherlock's mind palace, where the audience, like Sherlock, can see and hear how the consulting detective solves puzzles and makes decisions. Especially in the follow-on special episode, "The Abominable Bride," which is a continuation of or epilogue to "His Last Vow," Sherlock's mind palace has been expanded far behind the "memory technique" real-world definition that it initially referenced in Season Two. Mycroft rebuffs Sherlock's concept of his mind palace, in which the consulting detective retreats to solve a Victorian-era murder mystery and, along the way, envisions his and his Victorian counterpart's relationship with John Watson. Mycroft explains once again the accurate definition of the mind-palace memory technique, but Sherlock insists that Mycroft does not understand the way Sherlock's mind—or mind palace—works. John backs him up, confirming that he has witnessed Sherlock going into a sort of trance as he goes deeper into his mind. By "The Abominable Bride," Sherlock's mind palace is not only a place with increasingly rich visualizations of plot elements and character interactions, but it is the setting for nearly an entire 90-minute episode. The expansion of the mind palace has become a defining feature of the BBC's Sherlock Holmes and a key way for viewers to understand the way that Sherlock constructs his self-identity and deals with the way that others perceive him.

Whereas *Mr. Holmes* also builds a story primarily around the way that Sherlock Holmes (Ian McKellen) thinks and how his thought processes relate to a case many decades old, the aging Holmes has a far different problem with his mental "space." His brain attic is contracting, providing the plot device for this story, as Holmes tries in vain to find a way to keep track of so many items that seem to disappear or have new hiding places. Although no term is specifically coined for Holmes's mind, the *brain attic* term introduced by Conan Doyle seems most applicable, especially because Holmes is often seen retreating into his attic study in his Sussex cottage, his "*sanctum sanctorum*" as he defines it to his young protégé Roger Munro (Milo Parker).

No matter what it is called, in canon and the adaptations discussed in this chapter, Sherlock Holmes's brain and his thinking process distinguish him from other characters and often make him the object of awe. His mental capacity and brilliance in deducing information thus become most important to Holmes's self-identity and the identity promoted even by those who should know him best. If or when Holmes's mind is compromised, the audience and the character struggle to redefine Sherlock Holmes's identity.

Hero-Worshipping Sherlock's Brain

Canon encourages audiences to admire and, as much as possible, understand Holmes's mental processes. Readers identify with John Watson, who, particularly at the beginning of his and Holmes's adventures, frequently praises Holmes's brilliance. That does not mean that, as the stories progress throughout the years of their friendship, Watson overlooks his friend's flaws. Nevertheless, for the most part, Watson is Holmes's cheerleader and continues to believe that his friend's spectacular brain can solve almost any puzzle with relative ease. By the conclusion of their first adventure, *A Study in Scarlet*, Watson has seen Holmes in action and been impressed by his deductions to the extent that he is distressed when Scotland Yard detectives, not Holmes, receive credit in the newspaper for solving a series of murders. He decides to—and does—write and publish Holmes's adventures, by which the Great Detective can receive his due. Watsons (and audiences) have been following suit and believing in Holmes's brainwork ever since.

In *Elementary*, especially during the first season, Holmes astounds Watson by the way his mind works. He can mentally write a book several chapters long and ask if she wants to hear the latest chapter aloud. He watches several televisions simultaneously and immediately repeats dialogue verbatim ("Pilot"). Throughout the series, Holmes keeps copious notes and charts during cases that illustrate the diverse data he is recombining in his head. Such illustrations reinforce to audiences that Holmes is a unique thinker and uses far more of his mental capacity than does his audience. These scenes also show Watson appreciating that, beyond the Science of Deduction, Holmes's brain does far more than most people's.

Yet even Watson, who becomes Holmes's dear friend, in canon and adaptation, sometimes considers the way Holmes's mind works to be alien and "machine" like. At least once in canon (and again in *Sherlock*), Watson compares Holmes to a machine: "He was ... the most perfect reasoning and observing machine the world has seen" (Conan Doyle, "A Scandal in Bohemia" 1). In this Conan Doyle story, the comment is benign—Holmes's mind works with machine precision, and, during a Victorian age filled with emerging mechanical technologies, that comment was meant as more of a compliment than readers might perceive it nowadays. Even in that description, however, Watson is reporting Holmes's cold, scientific mind. He apparently can deal with Holmes's personality, although Stamford, who first introduces the pair, tells Watson that Holmes is too scientific (i.e., emotionless, precise) for his taste (Conan Doyle, *A Study in Scarlet* 8).

When *Sherlock*'s John calls Sherlock a machine, he does so not in print but to his face, and angrily at that. He accuses Sherlock of having no feelings for their landlady and dear friend Mrs. Hudson, who reportedly is dying. As part of his plan to confront Moriarty, Sherlock needs John out of the way and has set up the story of Mrs. Hudson's (Una Stubbs) impending demise as a way to distract John. In his indignation that Sherlock refuses to accompany him to Mrs. Hudson's side, John splutters, "You machine!" ("The Reichenbach Fall"). It is decidedly not a compliment. Soon after John delivers such a dramatic putdown by calling Sherlock a machine within hours of his apparent death, he regrets his words. In the aftermath of Sherlock's fall from St. Bart's roof, John stands at Sherlock's grave and chokes out his apology: "You were the most human human being" ("The Reichenbach Fall"). Even John struggles with Sherlock's public identity, that of the emotionless, logical machine, and the fallible man who is his friend. Sherlock, who also struggles with this dichotomy, relies on John to decide which identity is "real."

Perhaps that is one reason why, in "The Abominable Bride," the modern-day Sherlock "watching" Victorian Holmes and Watson investigate a series of murders revisits what must have been a disturbing, if necessary, confrontation with John before Sherlock's fall ("The Reichenbach Fall"). Victorian Watson explains to Holmes that, although he writes about the machine-like, unfeeling consulting detective as a character, he knows that this depiction is only a façade. His friend, the real Holmes, is a flesh-and-blood man ("The

Abominable Bride"). At this point in *Sherlock*, the humanization of Sherlock Holmes is viewed through Sherlock's thought processes. His "conductor of light" (as he dubs John in "The Hounds of Baskerville") tells him, in Victorian guise, that he is a man worthy of love, not a cold-hearted machine. Nevertheless, in a discussion with Mycroft, John, and Mary Watson (Amanda Abbington) outside the mind palace, Sherlock once again refers to his "hard drive" (brain). Sherlock's ongoing self-comparison to a machine even infiltrates the Victorian setting within the mind palace. He and Mycroft both refer to the "virus" that can corrupt the data, a term outside a Victorian's vocabulary—and an indication that, even in the increasingly humanized, emotion-filled mind palace, Sherlock struggles with the dichotomy of being perceived as a man or a machine. In Sherlock's mind, by "The Abominable Bride," *machine* has become a derogatory term, not the ideal that he wants to emulate in Season One.

Sherlock Holmes critic Bran Nicol is more complimentary in his assessment of Holmes-as-machine. He has argued that the BBC's Sherlock Holmes virtually impersonates a computer (Nicol, qtd. in Boer 10) by terming his brain his "hard drive" ("The Great Game"). Nicol even suggests that Sherlock's emotions equate to computer viruses: "a threat to the functioning of the machine" (qtd. in Boer 10). Perhaps Nicol is right within the context of both "The Reichenbach Fall" and "His Last Vow." In both episodes, Sherlock sacrifices himself to save his friends, especially John. The "virus" of emotion leads Sherlock to give up everything—including possibly his friends' acceptance and understanding when they see the results of his dire actions (i.e., faking his death or accepting a suicide mission, respectively, in these episodes). As a result, Sherlock-as-machine suffers—the machine has difficulty functioning as efficiently on his own now that he feels so much emotion for his closest friends.

"The Abominable Bride" takes the concept of emotion as a virus one step further. This episode reveals that the virus corrupting Sherlock's hard drive is Moriarty—or at least he visually represents Sherlock's self-doubt and vulnerability. Moriarty exclaims joyfully that he "keeps [Sherlock] down," while on screen he physically overcomes Sherlock on the precipice by the Reichenbach Falls and contains him by placing a foot on his chest. Sherlock by himself cannot overcome his fear that he may be lesser than Moriarty or a victim of Moriarty's "evil," which is expressed in this episode and "His Last Vow" as trying to undermine Sherlock's positive actions and to sanction Sherlock giving up on life. In his mind palace as well as in his waking world, Sherlock relies on John Watson to "save" him from himself and to view him as a real person, even if he is flawed, rather than a perfect machine. In "The Abominable Bride," Victorian Watson holds a gun on Moriarty until he stands away from Holmes on the ledge by the falls. Then he forces Moriarty to his knees and kicks him into the falls. Sherlock, in this series, needs John to destroy not only the virus in the hard drive but to insist on Sherlock's humanity.

Although *Sherlock* relies on John's ability to hero-worship Sherlock, even while complaining about or condemning his shortcomings, Watson's tendency to hero-worship Holmes's brain and thought processes, if not all of his actions or words, creates problems for Holmes that are analyzed in depth in other adaptations. *Mr. Holmes* shows the most extreme results of Watson's (and likely the audience's) hero worship. Because Watson (Colin Starkey) cannot bear the thought that Holmes (Ian McKellen) has failed a client and reacted badly, and Holmes's Boswell worries about his friend's continuing depression, he publishes a final story about what turns out to be Holmes's last case. He portrays Holmes as a hero, changing the case details to reflect this narrative, which becomes part of the myth, in print and on film, surrounding the Great Detective. Like Watson, the public believes that Holmes's brilliance means that he never fails to solve a case. Holmes, however, knows the truth about the case that caused him to leave his profession and retire to the country. He also realizes that the truth is in danger of being lost forever if his failing memory cannot help him write down the details before he dies. Sadly, Holmes grows estranged from Watson because of this final case and Watson's inability to see Holmes as anything less than a hero. Holmes always regrets that even his closest friend did not truly know him.

Knowing Sherlock Holmes, whether in *Sherlock* or *Mr. Holmes,* requires understanding the consulting detective's unique thought processes, as well as his human foibles. Whereas Holmes explains that Watson always took care to keep Holmes's private life private, for example, by giving the fictionalized detective an address across the street of where he actually lived, Watson also never understands the real Holmes, who is moody about his failed case and unable to articulate why it depresses him. Instead, Watson relies on the style of fiction that he has always published, in which Holmes is always a hero. At least in *Sherlock*'s "The Abominable Bride," John Watson acknowledges that Sherlock Holmes is very human, even if that may not always be the way he describes the successful consulting detective, whether in a 21st-century blog or a 19th-century *Strand* story.

Holmesvision in the Sherlock Holmes *Film Series*

Because, like Watson, audiences tend to believe in the unique power of Sherlock Holmes's mind, every filmic adaptation must find a way to make Holmes's internal thought process not only external but technologically innovative and visually interesting. Among adaptations' visualizations of Holmes's mind, two stand out as technically superior: the Guy Ritchie-directed *Sherlock*

Holmes film series and *Sherlock*. They employ sophisticated, innovative uses of filming technologies. (In contrast, *Mr. Holmes* deals with Holmes's memories through the well-known and often-used flashback, and *Elementary*, like canon, most often relies on Holmes's dialogue to explain his thoughts.)

To distinguish itself from other adaptations' simpler methods of illustrating Holmes's mental landscape, the *Sherlock Holmes* movie franchise developed and promoted Holmesvision to attract and entertain audiences. Holmesvision shows the audience what Holmes is thinking as he plans moves at lightning speed and considers many cause-effect relationships before choosing the most advantageous way to act. On screen, Holmes's consideration of possible actions and likely outcomes is shown in slow motion before the real action (i.e., Holmes's decision) is played in fast motion. Although a Holmesvision scene may take several minutes of screen time to show the array of potential cause-effect sequences, audiences understand that Holmes's consideration of all these possibilities takes less than a second.

Holmesvision distinguishes the way this Sherlock Holmes thinks from the other Holmeses in the adaptations discussed in this chapter by predicting, not deducing information. Typically, Holmes deduces how a crime took place or what someone did—actions that occurred in the past. The actions might be as mundane as what a person ate for breakfast, because crumbs are still evident on clothing. Nevertheless, Holmes understands what has happened by deducing facts from the evidence. The *Sherlock Holmes* films' use of Holmesvision implies that Holmes can predict the future, based on his analysis of the way an opponent will react to a given stimulus. Thus, if Holmes throws a handkerchief in a fighter's face during a bare-knuckle brawl, he anticipates the punches and kicks he must throw to incapacitate his foe, and he knows exactly the moves that his opponent will make (*Sherlock Holmes*). Holmesvision makes Holmes a superb strategist who predicts or correctly anticipates future actions, based on his knowledge of his opponent and, specifically, the way he fights. This insight into the way Holmes's mind works presents a different adaptation of the Great Detective's mental capabilities and his uses of them.

Holmesvision even shows how Holmes sees no possible positive outcome when he contemplates how to contain Moriarty (Jared Harris) and save his own life as the two grapple against a low wall above the Reichenbach Falls (*Sherlock Holmes: A Game of Shadows*). The realization that Holmes can only "win" this struggle if both he and Moriarty tumble into the falls is heartbreaking for the audience. The scene is made more emotional when Watson (Jude Law) arrives, only to helplessly watch Holmes and Moriarty fall together to their apparent deaths. The camera cuts from Watson's horrified expression to Holmes's gazing one more time at his friend before closing his eyes, ensuring that Watson is the last thing he sees. The audience's access to Holmesvision ends when Holmes's eyes close. The way this scene is filmed emphasizes not Holmes's sacrificial decision as a final illustration of "machine" logic but his emotional reaction to severing himself from Watson. Once again, in adaptation, Holmes-as-fact-analyzing-machine is shown as less important to understand than Holmes's very human emotion. In the adaptations discussed in this chapter, emotion becomes the focus of climactic scenes.

Although Holmesvision celebrates film technology as a way to illustrate Holmes's mental processes, the actor's depiction of Holmes is often sentimental or emotional in scenes with Watson. Yet even in a buddy film series, the "science" or "technology" of Holmes's brainwork is necessary to a successful cinematic depiction of Sherlock Holmes.

A Trip Inside Sherlock's Mind Palace

As David Sidore notes in *Genius on Television*, television geniuses are often portrayed as Other because of the way they think, and *Sherlock*'s Sherlock Holmes is an excellent example. He seems to have an eidetic memory, which, Sidore emphasizes, "is something scientists have never confirmed in adults, [and] just being able to recall lots of facts does not make one brilliant. What matters is what one can do with the information" (14). Thus, a genius portrayed in a television adaptation must be able to "recognize what information is relevant, place it into context, ... and see the bigger picture" (15), all which Sherlock illustrates in the series' mind-palace sequences.

Beginning with the first episode of *Sherlock* ("A Study in Pink"), visual overlays depict the way that Sherlock thinks at lightning speed and mentally pictures everything from the fastest route to run across London to, as the mind-palace scenes become more elaborate, whole conversations with people who advise Sherlock while he makes a decision (e.g., "His Last Vow"). The simplest illustrations occur during the first season. When Sherlock directs John to a shortcut to intersect a potential murderer, a GPS-styled image appears over the scene to indicate how Sherlock thinks of a better route and the speed at which he and John can complete it ("A Study in Pink"). Unlike Holmesvision, which forms the basis of an entire scene and is not simply an overlay of one image atop another, Sherlock's thoughts are viewed as taking place at the same time that he and John are running. The simultaneously shown images, one overlaying another, represent Sherlock's multitasking in this scene—running and being aware of his current surroundings while mentally plotting the most efficient route to intercept a potential criminal ("A Study in Pink").

During the Season Two episode "The Hounds of Baskerville," the visual overlays become a more elaborate focal point of an entire Sherlock-centric scene. Sherlock demands that John and a Baskerville scientist leave him alone in a lab so that he can think. John sardonically explains to the perplexed scientist that Sherlock has to be alone to spend time in his mind palace. This is the first time the term has been used to describe where Sherlock "goes" when he seems lost in contemplation for hours at a time. During the previous episode, "A Scandal in Belgravia," Sherlock "returns" after a long stay inside his mind. He immediately calls for John, only for Irene Adler (Lara Pulver) to tell him that John left the flat hours ago. (A similar scene occurs in "The Abominable Bride," when Holmes speaks to Watson, but Inspector Lestrade [Rupert Graves] points out the empty chair and reminds Holmes that Watson is married and moved out months ago.) In "A Scandal in Belgravia," Adler also explains that John told her that Sherlock sometimes stays within his mind for hours at a time. She finds Sherlock's mental processes, including his ability to tune out everything in favor of his thoughts, quite the sexual turn on. John, who deals with Sherlock daily, accepts his "absences" but sometimes complains that Sherlock does not even know if he is gone for long periods of time. John once went to New Zealand for more than a week, and Sherlock did not even realize he was gone ("A Scandal in Belgravia").

In "The Hounds of Baskerville," audiences receive more than a description of the intensity of Sherlock's thinking. They see Sherlock physically move his hands to shove words or images out of the way; the data in Sherlock's mind is once again overlaying the "regular" image of Sherlock sitting on a stool in a quiet lab. The scene is a visual brainstorm—Sherlock thinks of every association for "hound," including an image of Elvis Presley, a photo of a wolfhound, and an acronym for an old research organization. When he sorts data and finally makes a connection among disparate images and facts, he knows who is behind the terrifying mystery taking place in the moors around Baskerville. The Eureka moment involves the deduction being visually emphasized as words on screen over Sherlock's wide-eyed return to "reality." Sidore explains that this moment of euphoria is key for audiences to appreciate and even come to like a television genius: "[s]uch moments of enlightenment offer one of television's favorite spectacles of genius … the moment when the genius stares off into space and the light goes on in his or her eyes, letting the audience know that he or she has connected the dots and can now see the truth" (15). Although in "The Hounds of Baskerville" the audience also sees what Sherlock is thinking and how he considers, disregards, and eventually links relevant data leading to the Eureka moment, they also see Sherlock's face as his eyes fly open and he exclaims "oh" upon making the connection. The audience has been invited to better understand and appreciate Sherlock's genius by seeing how his mind works—not just the resulting euphoric moment.

In Season Three, audiences are finally granted full access into Sherlock's mind palace for increasingly long scenes. There is no need for a close-up of Sherlock's face during the Eureka moment because the audience sees and hears everything that is going on in Sherlock's mind and follows Sherlock's interaction with data, including seeing and hearing how he finally makes an important deduction. Viewers accompany the character through his thinking process.

The rooms within Sherlock's mind palace have been designed according to a traditional mental construct. In *Smithsonian*, Sarah Zielinski summarizes the mind palace construct, as reportedly invented by the Greek poet Simonides of Ceos, as a building such as a house. In this version, "every room is home to a specific item … to remember. To take advantage of the mind's ability to hold onto visual memories, it often helps to embellish the item being stored…. When those memories need to be recalled, [the person] can walk through the building, … seeing and remembering each item" (Zielinski, "The Secrets of Sherlock's Mind Palace"). *Sherlock* employs this model for the many rooms in Sherlock's mind palace, which are filled with the people who can provide him a specialized perspective (e.g., Molly Hooper's [Louise Brealey] medical knowledge; Mycroft's [Mark Gatiss] ability to chide or bully Sherlock into concentrating on logic). Even Redbeard, Sherlock's beloved childhood pet, is housed within a room of the mind palace and obligingly runs to find his master when he needs emotional nurturing.

All of these rooms do not quite fit together, however, making it unlikely that Sherlock's memory palace is a real place. Instead, each room fits its occupants or the types of discussions that need to take place. When Mycroft takes Sherlock through the logical deductions required to understand the Mayfly man's one-night relationships with a series of women, the brothers badger each other within the study of an expensive manor, its shelves lined with books. Sherlock needs knowledge outside his realm of personal experience, and so he turns not only to his older brother but to the one person who is smarter than he is and willing to goad him into solving the case ("The Sign of Three"). When Sherlock has been shot and needs to understand in which direction to fall so that he is more likely to survive, he envisions Molly, who understands medicine but also conducts autopsies to determine cause of death. She wears a lab coat as a visual reminder of her medical status ("His Last Vow"). After Sherlock is declared dead and surgeons have given up reviving him, "mind-palace" Sherlock sits with Moriarty (Andrew Scott) in a dungeon. Moriarty promises Sherlock that he will like being dead, but poor John will be left alone with his wife (who shot Sherlock) and will cry "buckets and buckets" upon Sherlock's death ("His Last Vow"). Motivated to save John from sorrow and a possibly dangerous Sherlock-less future, Sherlock drags himself from the dungeon and, one stair at a time, up a winding staircase— back to life, reality, and John. The likelihood of such rooms existing, much less in a logical arrangement, within the same home is highly remote.

Although most people construct their mind palace based on a real place that is easy for them to visualize, the mind palace does not have to be based in reality. University of Alberta researcher Jeremy Caplan and colleagues "had a group of people develop a palace using the conventional method, with a real building they knew. A second group explored a virtual building on a computer screen for five minutes and were instructed to place their memories inside that structure. When tested on their memories, the two groups of participants performed equally well at memorizing a list of unrelated words" (Zielinski).

Not surprisingly, Sherlock does not take the easy way of constructing a mind palace built on a frequently visited structure. Instead, he builds the structure around familiar people and situations that he needs to encounter in each room. He also does more than retrieve information; he truly interacts with it. He learns from the characters in his mind and often takes comfort from them. In this way, Sherlock *is* his mind palace. It is an extension of himself and his complete personality. In the mind palace, he is not fragmented into a public or a private persona or someone who shields his emotions. His mind palace reveals that, contrary to earlier visualizations from the series, Sherlock is not a computer or another type of machine, but an emotion-filled man with a rich inner life.

The mind palace also illustrates Sherlock's journey from being a great man to a good one, as Detective Inspector Lestrade suggests in the first episode ("A Study in Pink"), or the gradual change from Sherlock's notion that "alone protects me" to John's assertion that "friends protect friends" ("The Reichenbach Fall"). As Sherlock increasingly comes to value and emotionally interact with his friends in the real world, his mind palace includes people in addition to inhuman data.

As a symbol, the mind palace works far better than would the brain attic introduced in canon. "The key insight from the brain attic is that you're only going to be able to remember something, and you can only really say you know it, if you can access it when you need it" (Konnikova, qtd. in Zielinski). The mind palace is more beneficial because it allows information to be organized in a certain way for easier retrieval. No people—only data—inhabit the brain attic, whereas Sherlock's data increasingly takes the form of a well-known person who states the relevant data stored in Sherlock's mind. Although it is his mind—and he is obviously is the one to store or retrieve the data—Sherlock now relies on his mental representations of people he knows well to tell him what to do or to provide the emotional catalyst (e.g., unconditional love from Redbeard, goading from Moriarty) for the decision he must make.

The mind-palace scenes in "The Sign of Three" and "His Last Vow" exemplify the modern scientific idea that the brain's mental capacity can be expanded. Unlike earlier seasons' depictions of single images or text, the Season Three version of the mind palace involves entire scenes showing elaborately furnished rooms. Like Holmesvision, the fully illustrated mind palace requires the audience's full attention and more than an overlay of iconic words or drawings to indicate the multi-dimensionality of Sherlock's mind and the increasing richness of that inner life (now that John has been successfully socializing Sherlock for years).

Viewers know that Mycroft claims to be smarter than Sherlock, and his younger brother does not dispute that claim ("The Empty Hearse"); however, Mycroft's thought processes are never shown. Thus, it may be surprising that Sherlock's most fearsome enemy, Charles Augustus Magnussen (Lars Mikkelsen), also has a version of the mind palace, one that is depicted on screen. Magnussen's mind vaults allow him to visually retrieve pertinent information, which is illustrated on screen as computer files. Appledore, his home, is not where he stores his most important information (for control and potential blackmail of powerful people)—it is his mind.

Whereas Sherlock's data in his mind palace is visual and interacts with him, Magnussen's is human-free, most often shown as scrolling text, which makes him seem truly like an unfeeling machine. Even when he views "film" of John in a bonfire from which Sherlock frantically works to save him, Magnussen is simply watching a "video" file in his mind palace ("His Last Vow). Nowhere does he consult "an imaginary friend" for advice. He stores computer-like mental files for "visual" retrieval. When he visits his mind vault, viewers only see him accessing data to view. Seeing the computer-like representation of Magnussen's mind reminds viewers just how far Sherlock has come since Seasons One and Two, when his thoughts were similarly displayed as computer data. As revealed in Season Three, Sherlock's inner life is full of emotion—from crazed Moriarty to comforting Redbeard.

In contrast, Magnussen's mind is emotionless and purely business oriented. Magnussen's identity is so closely tied to his mind vaults that Sherlock feels he must shoot Magnussen in the head to destroy the information stored within them. To Sherlock, this is a "logical" action. The aftershock, however, prompts his emotional meltdown. The brilliant man who has survived a treacherous mission to dismantle Moriarty's criminal network nonetheless sees himself as a child in the latest, most emotion-based version of his mind palace. After he kills Magnussen, the camera focuses on Sherlock as a terrified boy, facing the authorities who will determine his fate ("His Last Vow"). The audience sees Sherlock as he sees himself.

Far from the cool, data-processing mind illustrated during the first two seasons, third-season Sherlock recognizes the value of friendship and love, even if he is still behind in his emotional development. According to Sidore, most television geniuses "view most people as less than human, [and] not caring about them is the price they pay in order to have their profound abilities" (24). Although this is true of Sherlock at the beginning of the series, the shift in the way he thinks about people as far more than data is evident in the changed depiction of the mind palace frequently visited during Season Three. Instead, the price he pays by the end of Season Three—loss of freedom, reputation, and The Work on his own terms—must be paid *because* he thinks with his heart rather than his computer-like brain.

Sherlock's self-perception at this stage is that, emotionally, he is more child than man when it comes to understanding and expressing emotions. Not only does he appear as a frightened child after killing Magnussen, but the concept of Sherlock the Child has been introduced during "The Sign of Three," especially when Sherlock tells newly married John and Mary Watson that they no longer need him, because they soon will have a real baby. In this scene, Sherlock verbalizes what audiences already know—he has learned about emotions and begun to give them equal weight with logic, as illustrated in the mind-palace scenes, as a result of his continuing interaction with John Watson. By the conclusion of Season Three, Sherlock not only is identified by his mind but—to viewers at least—the emotions his mind palace reveals. He is beginning to "grow up" emotionally, and his self-image is reflected in an elaborate representations of Sherlock's mind.

The next episode, "The Abominable Bride," shows the consequences of becoming an adult, as well as Sherlock's need to hold on to his friendship with John Watson, despite being sent on a suicide mission to Eastern Europe following Magnussen's murder. Almost every scene takes place within Sherlock's mind palace, although viewers are not alerted to that fact until midway through the special episode. As Sherlock goes ever deeper into his mind, aided by a potent drug cocktail, he envisions that a Victorian version of himself, accompanied by a mustached Victorian John Watson, are solving the mysterious murders seemingly committed by a dead woman, Emelia Ricoletti (Natasha O'Keeffe). Only later does the audience—along with modern-day John, Mary, and Mycroft—learn that Sherlock investigates and solves this cold case in order to help him determine if Moriarty is really dead and, if so, how he seemed to show up simultaneously on every media screen in the U.K. to ask "Did you miss me?" The resulting answer—Moriarty is indeed dead, but someone obviously is carrying on his work—is left to subsequent episodes' plots.

The most important aspect of this episode is its "insider" perspective of Sherlock and his relationships. Sherlock admits that he often finds it helpful to see himself as John sees him, especially because he seems cleverer that way. (Throughout the mind-palace scenes in this episode, Mary and Mycroft remind Sherlock that he is not as smart as his older brother; during a carriage ride, even Watson comments on the younger Holmes's defensiveness about his intellect and deduces that they must be on their way to visit Holmes the elder.) This dialogue provides a great deal of insight into the way that Sherlock perceives himself, and his self-identity is explored visually through the extended mind-palace scenes in "The Abominable Bride." Perhaps drugs seem necessary so that Sherlock can escape the confines of logical thought and explore his most deeply hidden emotions, which are excavated in the Victorian story-within-a-story.

Victorian Sherlock seems to live the ideal life he wants to live, or believes he once had, with John. Although Victorian Watson, like his modern counterpart, is married to Mary, the Victorian man has no qualms about leaving his wife for hours or days at a time so that he can accompany Sherlock on adventures. As in contemporary London, Victorian Watson often is Holmes's emotional as well as physical caretaker, as well as his sounding board and companion. During a stakeout, for example, Watson broaches the topic of Holmes's isolation. He gently tells his friend that, although he publishes stories in which Holmes is machine like, he believes that Holmes undoubtedly has had "a life" and "experiences." He worries that Holmes lives alone, despite the consulting detective's protests—as in "A Study in Pink"—that relationships with women are not his area. The conveniently timed arrival of the mysterious murdering bride interrupts their conversation, but Holmes makes his point without words throughout this episode—he would rather spend time with John than anyone else and is not looking for female companionship (or any kind of substitute for John). Later, when Holmes takes a little more than the typical seven percent solution and lies in a stupor in his Baker Street sitting room, a livid Watson barges in, demanding to know what he has taken. He reminds Holmes of his promise not to experiment with (then legal) sub stances during a case and threatens to empty the cocaine solution out the window. Watson's concern for Holmes's emotional and physical well-being is palpable throughout the Victorian story.

Throughout this mind-palace episode in particular, Sherlock subconsciously acknowledges how much he relies on John, the only person Sherlock trusts to keep him safe. "The Abominable Bride" also illustrates just how deeply Sherlock values sentiment, something which he sneeringly proclaims he detests in previous episodes. By 2016, Sherlock's mind palace is the key to understanding this adaptation of the Great Detective—and his emotions, not his logical deductions, reveal Sherlock Holmes's true identity.

Holmes and Memory Loss

All adapted Sherlock Holmeses define their identity by their mental capacity and derive their social/professional roles from their superiority to other human minds. For example, during Season One, *Sherlock*'s consulting detective incredulously asks his colleagues "What must it be like in those funny little brains of yours?" ("A Study in Pink"). *Elementary*'s Sherlock Holmes also recognizes his intellectual difference from everyone around him, although he expresses a greater emotional reaction to his Otherness: Seeing a puzzle in everything "has its costs" because puzzles are everywhere, and "once you start looking, it's impossible to stop." People, with "all the deceits and delusions that inform everything they do, tend to be the most fascinating puzzles of all." When Joan Watson suggests his is a lonely lifestyle—to study people from a distance instead of connecting with them—Holmes replies, "As I said, it has its costs" ("The Rat Race"). Given modern adaptations' focus on Sherlock Holmes's Otherness, what happens when Holmes loses his memory or (as will be discussed in the next section) suffers from senility or dementia?

Author/editor Ashley Lynn Carlson notes that, in an internet age, people especially value ever-faster access to information, but they also fear that reliance on the web is causing them to lose their ability (or need) to remember; she emphasizes that "the accessibility of information via the internet has created anxiety that human memory may become obsolete" (54–55). Fan fiction is one way that fans—many who are intense internet users—deal with the fear of memory loss, whether their own or a loved one's. To explore this fear, some fans turn to fiction to consider the ramifications of such a loss.

Fan fiction writers who choose to explore answers to the question of what a memory-deprived Holmes would be like typically emphasize Sherlock Holmes's difficulty in dealing with change in his mental status and search for creative solutions to his memory loss or physical "disconnect" between his mind and body. Many stories involve Johnlock—the sexual partnership of John Watson and Sherlock Holmes—and are set within the world of the BBC's *Sherlock*. Fan fiction writers often pose questions such as these: What would Sherlock do if he could not remember John? What does Sherlock intuitively know about John, even if he cannot recall why John is so important to him?

Memory loss accounts for only a tiny percentage of all the Sherlock TV-related stories available in Archive of Our Own, the largest online repository of fan fiction. A search of "Sherlock, memory loss" yields 318 (292 in English) of 79,640 stories, as of January 2016. This is a tiny percentage of *Sherlock* fiction, perhaps because this trope is often difficult to do realistically or even because even hurt/comfort fans do not choose a mentally impaired Sherlock as a source of entertainment.

Stories relating to Sherlock's memory loss most often are about amnesia, leading to Johnlock when Sherlock sees John without the lens of his previous preconceptions or fears. John, faced with losing the Sherlock he knows, finally recognizes that his feelings are love. The hurt-comfort premise leads most often to Johnlock and Sherlock's recovery—resulting in an improved Sherlock whose identity can incorporate his brilliance as well as his love for John.

In such stories, which are romantic if not medically realistic, John "fixes" Sherlock—not only curing his amnesia but his sole focus on The Work. Genius, in some stories, can be modified so that Sherlock can have a "normal" love relationship while still being smarter than everyone else. The need to normalize Sherlock and make him more emotionally relatable to fans is evident in the plot summaries. Statements like "Sherlock loses his memory. John has to fix him." (ThatGirlFromHobbiton and whitchry9) or "Sherlock loses his memory and rediscovers his relationship with John" (sevenpercent) alert readers to a happy ending with a new, brilliant-yet-simultaneously-more-normal Sherlock. Such stories manipulate the characters from *Sherlock* to make Holmes more lovable, romantic, and affectionate. The "missing" part of his identity is supplied by these fan-authors.

In the "Ink Your Name Across My Heart" series, Sherlock deals with permanent memory loss. The author, prettyvk, summarizes Sherlock's logic in the story's synopsis: "The metaphor is imperfect but still workable. If my long-term memory is a hard drive, then my short-term memory is RAM. The hard drive became read-only following the illness. New data is stored in RAM and can be used while I remain awake. Going to sleep—'turning off'—wipes the RAM, returning the system to what it was prior to the illness." Like other academic and fan fiction writers, prettyvk describes Sherlock's brain as a computer—just as the character does in the television series. She then allows him to find a way around the damaged section of the hard drive, as well as develop additional coping mechanisms to "reboot" his life when he repeatedly awakens with memory loss. This story eventually shows Sherlock trying to reorganize his mind palace to help him recall the most important information in his life—or to help him re-create a basic understanding of himself. He follows a thread to guide him through his mind palace to the piano, where notes about new information he has been able to retain is displayed. He discovers that he can acquire new knowledge by teaching his brain how to circumvent part of the damaged "hard drive." Nevertheless, Sherlock will never be cured

This popular series (2467 kudos by January 2016) incorporates elements from popular memory loss-themed films. Like Drew Barrymore's long-term memory-damaged character, Lucy, in *50 First Dates*, Sherlock in this story cannot retain long-term memories. He is frequently amazed by John's love and evidence of their long-term relationship.

To remind himself of the most important facts he must remember, Sherlock periodically gets a tattoo so that he can always access the information key to his understanding of his identity and lifestyle. Like *Memento's* Leonard (Guy Pearce), Sherlock trusts the statements he instructs a tattoo artist to inscribe on his body. Unlike Leonard, Sherlock does not lie when he writes these notes to himself. (Leonard knows that he will not remember the origin of the tattoo, only that he carved the message onto his body. Sometimes he tells himself lies to make himself accept his plan of action or to forgive his past misdeeds.) Sherlock's first tattoo, which he reads in the mirror every time he awakens, is "I was diagnosed with anterograde amnesia." Sherlock's most important note, on his chest, is "I told John I love him."

Although hurt-comfort Johnlock stories usually end by reaffirming the friends'/couples'/husbands' bond, in this story Sherlock also must come to accept his mental limitations and re-evaluate his self-identity. He deals with the frustrations of memory loss and the repeated surprise after awakening to a mirror image of an increasingly older man in a marriage/relationship he does not remember.

Holmes and Senility or Dementia

Beyond the late-era Conan Doyle stories or the casting of middle-aged actors to play Holmes, the character seldom has been portrayed as an older man, much less one who is slowly losing his mind as a result of senility or dementia. Perhaps because Holmes is defined primarily by his mental prowess, readers or audiences may not want to consider the beloved character in such a way. A small percentage of fan-written stories and a few mainstream adaptations nonetheless have postulated how Holmes might react or what he might be like if his mind failed him.

In the Archive of Our Own collection of Sherlock Holmes stories, only 33 (31 in English; January 2016) deal with Sherlock Holmes and dementia or specifically Alzheimer's disease. However, Sherlock is not usually the one with diminishing mental capacity, perhaps because fans have greater difficulty in accepting this character without his identity-defining brilliance. Thus, in most stories, Sherlock's parents, an elderly John Watson or Mycroft Holmes, Jim Moriarty (cared for by partner Sebastian Moran), or Irene Adler provide the angst while Sherlock deals with the loss of someone close to him. Nevertheless, in a few notable stories, not only Sherlock, but also the fan-author, has trouble accepting a mentally diminishing consulting detective. In one story, Sherlock even chooses assisted suicide rather than allowing himself to lose his mental acuity. Creating a "happy ending" or a "fix-it fic" from an Alzheimer's plotline seems unrealistic for these fan-authors.

One mainstream adaptation took a different approach, using Holmes as a source of dark humor. A "politically incorrect" episode of British television show *That Mitchell and Webb Look* features a skit in which elderly Holmes, confined to a nursing home, is the focus of "deeply unsubtle jokes about incontinence, memory loss, and difficulty with identifying close acquaintances" (Christime). The source of the humor is that the once-brilliant Sherlock Holmes has lost that which has made him uniquely special, rendering him a clumsy, foolish figure. The success of this television series often relies on shocking the audience and treating cultural icons less than reverently; Holmes, in this context, is just another icon to be spoofed.

A more subtle and sensitive approach to studying Holmes struggling with advanced age and memory problems is the focus of Mitch Cullin's novel, *A Slight Trick of the Mind*, and the film adapted from it, *Mr. Holmes*. In both, Holmes is presented as a real man immortalized through Watson's stories and the films made of them. The truth about Holmes's life is often couched in Watson's misinformation or misdirection, either to give Holmes privacy or to make him seem more heroic than he is. In both the print and film versions of this story, Holmes retires (or rather exiles himself) to Sussex after a case in which he does not understand human emotion and ends up horribly failing his client's family. Watson, however, rewrites history so that Holmes's adoring public continues to think of him as solving every case brilliantly.

The problem of distinguishing between fiction and reality is exacerbated when Holmes becomes forgetful. Following the instructions of his physician, he inks dots in a diary when he realizes he has forgotten something; the pages increasingly are filled with ever larger dots. On his starched, white shirt cuffs, he writes the names of those who are important to him so that he does not forget who they are when he talks with them; he casually checks his "crib sheet" while he straightens his cuffs.

Beyond the immediately pragmatic approach to dealing with memory loss, Holmes tries to apply the scientific method to find the cause of his forgetfulness. In "A Medical Perspective on the Adventures of Sherlock Holmes," James Reed emphasizes canon Holmes's reliance on science. In *Mr. Holmes*, this belief in science helps him diagnose (and, he hopes, treat or cure) his insipient dementia. As in the canon stories, Holmes relies on deductive reasoning to draw conclusions from the effect (e.g., a murder, or, in *Mr. Holmes*, increasing forgetfulness) to the cause (e.g., the murderer with a specific motive, or, in *Mr. Holmes*, a treatable mental malady) to a likely course of action (e.g., apprehension and conviction of the murderer, or in *Mr. Holmes*, improvement or at least retention of memory). Yet the Science of Deduction, although often compared to the medical process of diagnosis, is not always effective in the practice of medicine. Reed concludes that

> comparing Holmesian deduction to the process of diagnosis is an oversimplification. Very rarely does diagnosis of disease consist of a simple trail of logic from problem to solution. The facts of the presenting complaint are clearly important, but, at a more abstract level, elements of the experience of the doctor (the "gut feeling") come into play. One could imagine Holmes being very dismissive of such "fancies" [80].

Furthermore, diagnostic "clues" are often unique to a patient, and other mitigating medical factors may make the kind of direct effect-to-cause-to-action relationship so often found in Holmes stories far less likely in real medicine. Whereas a "Holmesian problem is proved or disproved by the train of logic alone," Reed notes that "the route to the diagnosis could appear logical, but still be incorrect" (80). Thus, in *Mr. Holmes*, elderly Holmes conducts scientific research into the properties of several other potential remedies for his Swiss-cheesed memory before concluding that the prickly ash, found in Japan, may stem memory loss. When his ingestion of the plant as a food or tea additive does not produce the results he would like, Holmes turns the plant into a liquid form that he can inject.

This experimentation on himself harkens to the first Sherlock Holmes story, *A Study in Scarlet*, in which Stamford explains to John Watson that Holmes might experiment on his friends, if he thought it would help him gain knowledge, but he would be just as likely to experiment on himself (Conan Doyle, *A Study in Scarlet* 8). However, in *Mr. Holmes*, the experiments with prickly ash, in whatever form, do not stem Holmes's dementia. As Reed explains, "there are cases in which there is no 'solution'" (80) to be derived from logical deduction. Holmes's decreasing mental capabilities evident in *Mr. Holmes*, what today might be called Alzheimer's disease, to date have no long-term effective treatment, much less a cure. Far less was known about the disease during the late 1940s, the time in which 93-year-old Holmes lives. The inevitability of loss—especially of his ability to remember and think clearly—is, to Holmes, most difficult to accept. Nevertheless, by the end of the film, he is depicted as finding some measure of peace by memorializing his dear departed (Mrs. Hudson, John, Mycroft) and allowing his housekeeper and her young son to take over some of his beekeeping responsibilities. Holmes may not be cured of dementia, but he has accepted the diagnosis and begun to rely on his newest friends to assist him with daily life.

The Final Problem

All these adaptations conclude what Conan Doyle illustrates in canon: Sherlock Holmes needs to become involved with other people (in canon and the *Sherlock Holmes* movie series, primarily John Watson; in adaptations like *Sherlock*, *Elementary*, and *Mr. Holmes*, the circle of friends greatly expands). The "final problem" in Holmes's life is not his ability to store and access data, but to open his mind to the possibility of being vulnerable around his friends and accepting the help of those who love him. Unlike Nicol, who has equated emotion to a virus contaminating Sherlock's hard drive of a brain, the adaptations discussed in this chapter conclude that emotion is ultimately what saves Sherlock Holmes. The mind may begin to inaccurately deduce facts and produce a faulty conclusion, and memory fails—the human brain is not a perfect machine but a humanly imperfect, aging organ. Whether he is brilliant or fallible ultimately is not what keeps his dearest friends close. It is simply Holmes himself.

Perhaps when Holmes begins to redefine his self-identity to equally value "friend" as much as "consulting detective" or "logical thinker," he becomes more human and even more admirable as a character. His identity does not have to be "diminished" to "normalize" him, but his mental capacity can be accepted and appreciated as only one aspect of his complex persona. Holmes can still be different from readers and other characters without being seen as only a machine. Sherlock Holmes, in canon and these modern adaptations, is worth knowing as both brilliant *and* human—not one *or* the Other.

Works Cited

Boer, Dieneke. "Inspector Gadget: *The Technologically Advanced Afterlife of Sherlock Holmes*." Unpublished Master's thesis. Leiden University, 2015.

Carlson, Ashley Lynn. "The Human Hard Drive: Memory, Intelligence and the Internet Age." In *Genius on Television: Essays on Small Screen Depictions of Big Minds* (Ed. Ashley Lynn Carlson). Jefferson, NC: McFarland, 2015. 49–58. Print.

Christime, Tom. "Far from Elementary: Mitchell and Webb, Sherlock Holmes and Dementia." Dementia.stir.ac.uk. 16 July 2014. Web. 16 Sep. 2015. doi: 10.1348/000712607X224469.

Conan Doyle, Arthur. "A Scandal in Bohemia." *The Adventures of Sherlock Holmes* (1–28). London: BBC Books, 2011. Print.

_____. *A Study in Scarlet*. London: BBC Books, 2011. Print.

Cullin, Mitch. *A Slight Trick of the Mind*. New York City. Knopf Doubleday, 2006. Print.

"The Empty Hearse." *Sherlock*. Writ. Mark Gatiss. Dir. Jeremy Lovering. BBC, 2014. DVD.

Farkas, Carol-Ann. "What's the Difference? Pathologizing Genius and Neurodiversity in Popular Television Series." In *Genius on Television: Essays on Small Screen Depictions of Big Minds* (Ed. Ashley Lynn Carlson). Jefferson, NC: McFarland, 2015. 156–174. Print.

50 First Dates. Dir. Peter Segal. Perf. Adam Sandler, Drew Barrymore. Columbia Pictures, 2004. DVD.

"The Great Game." *Sherlock*. Writ. Mark Gatiss. Dir. Paul McGuigan. BBC, 2010. DVD.

"His Last Vow." *Sherlock*. Writ. Steven Moffat. Dir. Nick Hurran. BBC, 2014. DVD.

"The Hounds of Baskerville." *Sherlock*. Writ. Mark Gatiss. Dir. Paul McGuigan. BBC, 2012. DVD.

Kayalvizhi, A. "Cerebral Analysis of Sherlock Holmes in Detection." *Language in India* 12, no. 4 (Apr. 2012): 142–158. Print.

Konnikova, Maria. "Sherlock Holmes and the Infamous Brain Attic." BoingBoing.net. 14 Jan. 2013. Web. 16 Sep. 2015.

Memento. Dir. Christopher Nolan. Perf. Guy Pearce, Carrie-Anne Moss. Newmarket, 2000. DVD.

Mr. Holmes. Dir. Bill Condon. Perf. Ian McKellen. Miramax, 2015. DVD.

"Pilot." *Elementary.* Writ. Robert Doherty. Dir. Michael Cuesta. CBS Television Studios, 2012. DVD.

prettyvk. "Ink Your Name Across My Heart." Archive of Our Own. 6 Dec. 2013. Web. 10 Oct. 2015.

"The Rat Race." *Elementary.* Writ. Craig Sweeny. Dir. Rosemary Rodriguez. CBS Television Studios, 2012. DVD.

Reed, James. "A Medical Perspective on the Adventures of Sherlock Holmes." *Medical Humanities* 27 (2001): 76–81. Print.

"The Reichenbach Fall." *Sherlock.* Writ. Stephen Thompson. Dir. Toby Haynes. BBC, 2012. DVD.

"A Scandal in Belgravia." *Sherlock.* Writ. Steven Moffat. Dir. Paul McGuigan. BBC, 2012. DVD.

sevenpercent. "Time Forgotten." Archive of Our Own. 6 Jan. 2013. Web. 11 Oct. 2015.

Sherlock Holmes. Dir. Guy Ritchie. Perf. Robert Downey, Jr., Jude Law, Rachel McAdams. Warner Bros., 2009. DVD.

Sherlock Holmes: A Game of Shadows. Dir. Guy Ritchie. Perf. Robert Downey, Jr., Jude Law, Jared Harris. Warner Bros., 2011. DVD.

Sidore, David. "'Spectacularly Ignorant': The Conflicted Representation of Genius." In *Genius on Television: Essays on Small Screen Depictions of Big Minds* (Ed. Ashley Lynn Carlson). Jefferson, NC: McFarland, 2015. 12–31. Print.

"The Sign of Three." *Sherlock.* Writ. Stephen Thompson, Steven Moffat, Mark Gatiss. Dir. Colm McCarthy. BBC, 2014. DVD.

"A Study in Pink." *Sherlock.* Writ. Steven Moffat. Dir. Paul McGuigan. BBC, 2010. DVD.

ThatGirlFromHobbiton, and whitchry9. "Memory Error: Troubleshooting Sherlock." Archive of Our Own. 25 Dec. 2012. Web. 11 Oct. 2015.

"While You Were Sleeping." *Elementary.* Writ. Robert Doherty. Dir. John David Coles. CBS Television Studios, 2012. DVD.

Zielinski, Sarah. "The Secrets of Sherlock's Mind Palace." *Smithsonian.* 3 Feb. 2014. Web. 16 Sep. 2015.

It's Traumatic Stress, My Dear Watson

A Clinical Conceptualization of Sherlock

JENNIFER DONDERO *and*
SABRINA J. PIPPIN

Stress is an everyday occurrence in all aspects of life. Whether it is family drama, inability to get good health insurance, concern over student loans, or the frustration from sitting in rush hour traffic, stress is unavoidable. Our world is stressful as well, and people seem increasingly aware that corruption and human suffering are all around. Consequently, most laypersons have a general idea of what constitutes stress, likely from personal experiences that evoke feelings of anxiety, dread, or perhaps exhaustion. For most people, stress is transitory and rarely leads to chronic disruption in general functioning. For some, however, chronic stress can begin to upset environmental and emotional equilibrium.

In addition to the many direct ways people may process and mitigate the effects of personal or global stressors, such as psychotherapy or improved self-care, popular media offer real examples of healthy cognitive coping. From the self-help movement to television programs like *Intervention* (2005-present) to guided meditation channels on YouTube, we live in a world with unprecedented access to resources that can help better our lives. It is easy to dismiss a television program such as the BBC's *Sherlock* (2010-present) as a legitimate delivery system for better understanding the nature of chronic stress, but humans have consistently demonstrated that observational learning often leads to cumulative evolution, where mass consumption of modeled behavior may be passed down at a societal level (Boyd and Richardson 152).

In other words, societal learning is often the byproduct of ubiquitous cultural narratives. Although this phenomenon typically expresses itself as a trend or a piece of media that "goes viral," it is becoming increasingly common to see popular television characters model challenging, emotionally-resonant issues that invite opportunities for adaptive learning. Popular LGBTQ characters (e.g., Kurt Hummel from *Glee,* Sophia Burset from *Orange Is the New Black*) have had an impact on cultural narratives, which have helped LGBTQ persons cope in actual life. The character portrayals of the two protagonists featured in *Sherlock* often emphasize their mental health, in particular how these characters experience and respond to stress.

From the outset, *Sherlock* revolves around characters who experience stress in heightened frequency and duration, to the point both Sherlock Holmes (Benedict Cumberbatch) and Dr. John Watson (Martin Freeman) exhibit symptoms of Post-Traumatic Stress Disorder (PTSD) per the *Diagnostic and Statistical Manual of Mental Disorders* (American Psychiatric Association 271), the primary diagnostic tool used by mental health practitioners. The protagonists on *Sherlock* are particularly compelling, as they are vulnerable to intrapsychic and environmental stress but are largely able to manage their stress while accomplishing tasks that are far outside the boundaries of what most would consider a "normal" day.

Observing characters who are able to overcome obstacles, cope with extraordinary stress, and maintain interesting relationships are important factors when viewers choose a show to watch and in which to become emotionally and intellectually invested. In addition to the high production value and general excellence in acting and writing, the incredible popularity of *Sherlock* may reflect the audience's preoccupation with stress and the emotional resonance many viewers experience when watching flawed heroes who are often mentally unstable and socially inept. The overwhelmingly positive response to *Sherlock* suggests audiences empathize with Sherlock and John as they grapple with personal and professional struggles and slowly develop healthier ways of managing clinically significant stress.

Stress and Sherlock Holmes:
Lessons Learned in Childhood

More so than previous incarnations of Sherlock Holmes, the most recent version from the BBC is depicted as somebody who experiences frequent, if not constant, disruptive stress. The presence of stress can be seen in Sherlock's environment, as evidenced by his work as a consulting detective, which often encourages him to willingly and regularly put himself in mortal danger in pursuit of criminals. In the first episode, Sherlock sneaks away to meet with serial killer and taxi driver Jeff Hope (Phil Davis) and then participates in a "game" that involves the possible ingestion of fatal poison ("A Study in Pink"). Viewers learn that this sort of behavior is a pattern for Sherlock, who pursues and creates opportunities to insert himself in the midst of deadly chaos in each subsequent episode of *Sherlock*.

Sherlock's preferred interpersonal relationships are also informed by stressors, most notably his propensity to be drawn to persons, such as love interest and rival Irene Adler (Lara Pulver) or arch nemesis Mr. James Moriarty (Andrew Scott), both of whom are likely to induce stress through criminal actions that put Sherlock in immediate danger. Despite this, it is worth noting Adler and Moriarty are the only two characters Sherlock allows himself to openly admire without self-consciousness or internal conflict about whether they are worthy of his attention.

This is in significant contrast to characters like John or Detective Inspector Lestrade (Rupert Graves), whose personal value to Sherlock only becomes apparent over time. Sherlock usually antagonizes less intelligent people, even those with whom he lives and works. Particularly during the first two seasons of *Sherlock*, Sherlock thinks nothing of letting John know that he is intellectually inferior or casually insulting medical examiner Molly Hooper (Louise Brealey) by telling her, for example, that her mouth looks too small without lipstick ("A Study in Pink").

The stress present in Sherlock's relationships is often caused or encouraged by Sherlock himself. Overt emotional expression is especially challenging for him and sometimes makes him uncomfortable to the point of immobility, as evidenced by his catatonic reactions to the rush of emotion that occurs when John asks him to be the best man at his wedding ("The Sign of Three"). Sherlock eventually delivers a moving best man's speech, but only after many social missteps and emotional turmoil.

This difficulty relating to others may be because Sherlock experiences a tremendous amount of intrapsychic stress (i.e., stress related to individual processes within one's mind). Any glimpse inside Sherlock's head shows that it is overcrowded with stimuli, to the point where he must "delete" information to focus on what he considers important, such as when he reveals to John he has long since "deleted" the basic properties of the solar system in favor of information pertinent to his investigative pursuits. He is also prone to boredom and acts out behaviorally when he does not have something with which to busy himself, most notably when John finds Sherlock carelessly firing a gun at their apartment wall ("The Great Game"). However, Sherlock is capable of sophisticated cognitive coping in times of extreme stress; he does not have an equally sophisticated "mind palace" to sort and make sense of emotions.

While it is convenient to conceptualize intellectual stagnation and dismissal of social niceties as the byproduct of a brilliant mind, it is quite possible

Sherlock never learned to effectively manage his intrapsychic stress and keeps busy or lashes out at others to avoid addressing it. As Perry and Szalavitz note, maladaptive interpersonal functioning is often repeated because the human brain is a highly use-dependent organism that develops patterns of behavior based on experience (239). It is the reason one might take the same route to work every day or why someone as brilliant as Sherlock may develop habits and behaviors that allow him to avoid processing emotions. Consequently, Sherlock seeks out interpersonal interactions where he feels comfortable and secure. His interest in playing "the game" with Adler or Moriarty, for example, creates a situation where he feels confident and exhilarated because he is in his element. Both Adler and Moriarty are like Sherlock in that they value intrigue and intellect over personal warmth. By contrast, Sherlock experiences confusion and anxiety when he sincerely wants to please or reassure someone, such as when he attempts to perform best man duties for John's wedding, despite his obvious limitations in understanding how to plan a bachelor party or give a toast.

Consider the conversation Sherlock has with his brother, Mycroft (Mark Gatiss), before he re-enters society after faking his death. Mycroft asks Sherlock if he has thought of how his closest friend John will react after learning he has been alive since his supposed death two years prior ("The Empty Hearse"). Sherlock proceeds to brush off the conversation. When he reveals himself to John, he chooses an approach that seems insensitive to John's feelings. Sherlock disguises himself as a waiter and makes awkward jokes about John's appearance ("The Empty Hearse"). After John physically attacks him, Sherlock seems to relax and engage in easy conversation with John. This type of interpersonal pattern where one is more comfortable with a familiar conflict than an unfamiliar moment of sincerity may be analogous to an emotionally undeveloped, delinquent youth who constantly argues with authority because he does not feel comfortable having an "adult" conversation about his strong feelings.

The level of stress displayed by Sherlock is a clinically significant and character-defining trait. Cumberbatch's Sherlock does not simply experience stress; the nature of his character is shaped by stress, which has a profound impact on his functioning. One might argue that Mycroft is under just as much duress in his role as a secretive government operative, but he seems to manage his daily functioning better. At a critical point of character development for the Holmes brothers, Mycroft explains to Sherlock the reason for his aloofness: "Caring is not an advantage." Instead, according to Mycroft, caring about others is ultimately an unhelpful liability ("A Scandal in Belgravia"). Mycroft's implication is that Sherlock struggles because he cares about others and experiences profound distress at his inability to manage those feelings or even reconcile their existence.

Understanding what makes Sherlock's stress diagnostically unique requires examining it through a psychological lens, as his clinical presentation is subtler than John's, who displays more traditional symptoms of PTSD and whose pathology can be clearly traced to an earlier traumatic event (i.e., combat). The DSM-5 identifies several criteria for PTSD, including experiencing an event or events where one is significantly distressed or responds with helplessness and horror, re-experiencing the event in the form of nightmares or intrusive thinking, avoidant behaviors, and hypervigilance (American Psychiatric Association 271–274). Sherlock meets all of these criteria, as he is objectively a person under stress and often experiences extreme distress in response to that stress, perhaps more so than he would like to admit.

For example, Sherlock's terrified reaction to the supposedly spectral hound in "The Hounds of Baskerville" demonstrates that his emotional world can be rattled, despite his best efforts to minimize his feelings. Since meeting John, Sherlock has become increasingly sensitive to his emotional needs and those of others, which has considerably heightened his stress, because interpersonal stress is generally more challenging for Sherlock than environmental stress. There is also evidence Sherlock experiences intrusive thinking when under duress or hypervigilance. For instance, he is frequently overwhelmed with sensory information during high-pressure situations, which *Sherlock* depicts in the form of free-floating words representing Sherlock's thoughts or by having him retreat within his "mind palace," which he seems to view as an impenetrable and discrete location within himself ("The Hounds of Baskerville").

Sherlock often copes with stress by engaging in avoidant behavior, such as his history of illicit drug use and his propensity toward regressing into childlike behavior like sulking. Although he may be doing these things because he is bored, his reaction to intrapsychic stress suggests he simply does not function well when left with only himself for company and tries to create environmental or even interpersonal stress, which may be easier for him to handle. The previously mentioned incident in which Sherlock discharges John's firearm indoors and then argues with his landlady, Martha Hudson ("The Great Game"), illustrates obviously dangerous behavior, but also demonstrates his inability to tolerate mental isolation. Even Sherlock's self-diagnosis of "sociopath" can be seen as an easy excuse to remove emotional reflection and interpersonal responsibility from his self-concept. As Perry and Szalavitz note, a true sociopath does not have the capacity to experience compassion (116–117). Sherlock is genuinely, albeit rarely, deeply concerned on behalf of others, particularly John, which somewhat negates the idea that his attitudes and behavior can be attributed to a sociopathic personality.

Instead, Sherlock presents more like somebody who has experienced complex or developmental trauma, rather than having trauma symptomology emerge from a single event or situation. Developmental trauma is characterized by stressful events, usually beginning in childhood or adolescence when significant cognitive, emotional, and social learning takes place (Silva and Kessler 32–33). The third season of *Sherlock* offers a wealth of evidence suggesting Sherlock likely endured several distressful circumstances for sustained periods of time during his formative years. He felt like an "idiot" for a significant portion of his upbringing, a point which was regularly reinforced by his more intelligent older brother Mycroft ("The Empty Hearse"). The Holmes parents, while well meaning, are not as emotionally or intellectually sophisticated as either of their children ("The Sign of Three," "His Last Vow"), likely making it difficult for them to meet their children's emotional or social needs. Children who do not feel emotional or mental attunement to their caregivers are much more likely to develop interpersonal and social difficulties, in addition to experiencing increased levels of stress (Siegel 73–74). This may have been an especially stressful dynamic for Sherlock, as he grew up with a great capacity for fantasy and imaginative play, as evidenced by his fanciful childhood wish to be a pirate when he grew up ("His Last Vow").

Finally, Sherlock also carries significant losses from his childhood, most notably the death of his dog, Redbeard. While Sherlock is trapped in a near-death state after being shot by John's wife, assassin Mary Morstan (Amanda Abbington), viewers see Sherlock imagine himself as a child playing with Redbeard and telling him to never go away ("His Last Vow"). This suggests a strong attachment between Sherlock and Redbeard, which is significant when considering Sherlock has trouble freely giving that kind of affection to humans. It is common for children who experience complex or developmental trauma to make emotional attachments with animals easier than with people, because animal behavior and emotional reciprocity are easy to understand and do not require the kind of trust and complexity found in human interaction (Dietz, Davis, and Pennings 667). Incidentally, the safe bond that can be created between a child and a dog is cited as one of the primary reasons why canine therapy is efficacious with children who have experienced traumatic stress (Dietz, Davis, and Pennings 678–679). These factors indicate that Sherlock was likely an emotionally sensitive, highly intelligent child with few outlets to process his feelings in a way that formed secure attachments. The most secure attachment he experienced as a child may have been to his dog, which was "put down" ("His Last Vow"). Invariably, attachment patterns during development affect the ability to form healthy relational attachments later in life. If Sherlock indeed spent a significant portion of his childhood feeling isolated and then processing a major emotional loss or losses, those could certainly carry over to how he approaches relationships as an adult.

Siegel suggests emotionally sensitive children who experience insecure attachments in childhood are more likely to later display problems with behavioral control, affect regulation and emotion identification, and substance abuse (84–87). Feeling marginalized and/or isolated during childhood can also lead to difficulties achieving developmental milestones like autonomy or identity formation, both of which are integral to making adaptive independent decisions and having a strong sense of self in relation to others (Corey 70–71). If Sherlock encountered difficulties with these areas of psychosocial development, it may explain why he often presents similarly to persons with Autism Spectrum Disorder or Reactive Attachment Disorder, both of which are characterized by deficits in social interaction, limited emotional responsiveness to others, and periods of sudden moodiness or irritability (American Psychiatric Association 50–51, 265–266).

Stress and John: Healing Self and Others

John assists Sherlock in coping with his stress while dealing with his own significant stress. At the beginning of the series, John suffers from psychosomatic symptoms (i.e., difficulties walking and a tremor in his hand) due to an incident in the war in Afghanistan ("A Study in Pink"). After meeting Sherlock, John seems to "forget" about his psychosomatic symptoms. During a conversation with Mycroft, John does not exhibit these psychosomatic symptoms while speaking of his relationship with Sherlock. In a time of severe distress, however, John regains his psychosomatic symptoms, such as difficulties walking, as evidenced by reliving trauma when he sees Sherlock upon his seeming return from the dead ("The Empty Hearse").

The healthy aspects of the John-Sherlock relationship seem to have mitigated the cognitive distortions that can be seen in various formats. John experiences false schemas regarding himself in the form of needing acceptance from Sherlock for validation of his own being. Additionally, during times of increased stress, he experiences psychosomatic symptoms such as needing a cane for walking assistance when his service in the military is discussed ("A Study in Pink"). Part of the allure of his relationship with Sherlock is the thrill of excitement he gets from successfully managing high-pressure situations. The two have shared multitudes of high-pressure situations that keep their relationship in homeostasis. During these times of intense stress, their friendship is renewed time and time again. For example, John is put in danger of being burned alive at the Guy Fawkes Day bonfire celebration without knowledge of the reason for his abduction. This traumatic, near-death experience leads to a small mend in his now-estranged relationship with Sherlock after he rescues him ("The Empty Hearse"). This event becomes another turning point in John's complex trauma history. During the third season's premiere episode, their friendship, along with trust, is renewed only when the two are presented with a life-and-death situation: a bomb set to explode within seconds ("The Empty Hearse"). When the two are not presented with stress and excitement, however, their homeostasis is threatened, and both individuals become uncomfortable and distrusting.

After first meeting Sherlock, John continues to reach out and explore similarly exciting relationships, such as his marriage to Mary Morstan ("The Sign of Three"). Whereas he is initially infatuated with Mary, he is unsure from where the attraction stems. Throughout the beginning of the third season, John is privy to brief instances of Mary's secret and exciting attributes from her past life, such as Mary identifying the necessity of covering up Sherlock's supposed death, as evident in the need for a "conspirator" during his absence and the understanding of the code sent to her after Watson's abduction ("The Empty Hearse"). As the third season continues, John becomes increasingly aware of the thrilling life that his wife experienced as a spy ("His Last Vow"). He has found sexual and romantic allure in someone who is essentially a female version of Sherlock. Mary is smart, witty, and secretive, all traits that are present in the allure that John finds within his friendship with Sherlock. By marrying Mary, John is agreeing to a day-to-day personal life filled with danger, thrill, and excitement. This allows John's stress to be maintained consistently through his work with Sherlock along with his personal life with Mary and their unborn child.

In instances where stress is present, John tends to deal with his stress levels primarily through his emotions, along with many vocal tones and forms of body language. This can be seen when John sees Sherlock for the first time after Sherlock's supposed death ("The Empty Hearse"). During this episode, John displays a low voice in moments of intense anger and quick speech during moments of extreme frustration, in addition to frowning and physically fighting with Sherlock ("The Empty Hearse").

To help manage stress levels such as these displayed by John, other characters offer ways of coping with stress. Characters such as Mrs. Hudson serve as an emotional sounding board, a stress-relief persona, and a motherly figure for both John and Sherlock. Sherlock, especially, profoundly feels her motherly influence, because Mrs. Hudson likely has a more realistic idea of what Sherlock needs and wants from a parental figure. John's mother is not mentioned in the series, and Mrs. Hudson fills that gap by providing motherly guidance to John after he quarrels with Sherlock. When Sherlock criticizes Mrs. Hudson, John instructs him to "go apologize," so as not to hurt Mrs. Hudson's feelings ("A Scandal in Belgravia").

John is also cognizant of the emotional toll Mrs. Hudson experiences due to her relationships with both John and Sherlock. When Mrs. Hudson is kidnapped and held at gunpoint by CIA agents invading 221B, John is aware that, after the event, she may need a vacation to ensure that her emotional and physical well-being is intact ("A Scandal in Belgravia"). When John grieves Sherlock's apparent death, Mrs. Hudson seems to both comfort John and take the place of Sherlock with her witty banter ("The Empty Hearse"). These scenes demonstrate how much *Sherlock*'s characters are aware of and responsive to each other's stress.

John requires an abundance of approval and interpersonal support from Sherlock and offers a tremendous amount of social support in return. John views himself through Sherlock. Therefore, when the public and the media turn on Sherlock ("The Reichenbach Fall"), John gets upset. When others criticize Sherlock, there is an assumption that John is viewed poorly as well. At times John acts similarly to a dog protecting his master. Even Moriarty reflects on this dog-owner relationship when he mentions to Sherlock that John is similar to a pet that Sherlock gets sentimental about, similar to his childhood dog, Redbeard ("The Great Game"). Watson also follows behind Sherlock or, when individuals threaten Sherlock, stands in front in order defend or protect his friend. For most people, such close association to Sherlock may result in literal and figurative ruin. However, John's synergy with Sherlock ultimately mitigates the presence of stress, because John understands that the two together make up a more functional person than each is separately. The two individuals complement each other and are able to bring the best out of each other, as well as challenge each other in order to completely understand the dangerous situations that they encounter. As a result of their friendship, John is able to better understand himself, and Sherlock allows himself to be more vulnerable with others.

John's response to Sherlock's (later revealed to be faked) suicide ("The Empty Hearse") indicates the grieving process is a trauma experience for John and has a profound effect on him ("The Reichenbach Fall"), as if his soul has been crushed. While most persons are expected to experience transitory sorrow, anger, or confusion following the death of a loved one, John's grieving period is prolonged enough that it may be closer to Complicated Bereavement (i.e., a stress-related disorder recognized in the DSM-5 and centered on traumatic loss). The extent of John's grief is evidenced in many of his behaviors and even in his personal appearance. For example, he attempts to "cover up" by growing a mustache. This mustache symbolizes John attempting to age himself and cover up his emotions during his time of grieving over the loss of his friendship with Sherlock. Even when Sherlock returns to John's life, John retains the mustache in defiance of the distrust from his friend. Only when John becomes ready to embark on the thrilling experience of marrying Mary and reentering the world of crime solving with Sherlock does he shave ("The Empty Hearse").

To complicate viewers' understanding of John's stress, he is introduced in "A Study in Pink" by displaying features of clinical PTSD (American Psychiatric Association 271). The development of PTSD stems from difficulties that soldiers experience after returning from war (Creamer et al. 160–165).

John has frequently observed traumatic events, including battle and his friend's "suicide." Throughout the series, John experiences many additional symptoms of PTSD, such as increased sleep deprivation, negative mood (i.e., a person's reported emotional state), and negative affect (i.e., a person's observed emotional state). Further, lack of concentration and pleasure in normal activities are particularly compromised for John during periods of stress related to Sherlock's alleged death, and alcohol consumption increases for John during this time as well, which is considered to be a maladaptive and avoidant long-term coping skill. These examples suggest that while John has a history of stress-induced symptomology, he is most profoundly affected by stress as it relates to his relationship with Sherlock.

Intrusive thinking and imagery are also a hallmark of PTSD. While John presents with classic examples of intrusive thinking (e.g., nightmares), his everyday life often includes intrusive communication. For instance, he is inundated with reporters and public personnel requesting information about Sherlock and his demise. More frequently, the cases that the two solve involve excitement, distress, and internal and external stressors; their detective work is often covered by the press. This consistency of having the duo's exploits brought into public communication such as emails, web pages, print newspapers, and newscasts underscores John's persistent sources of excitement (or stress). The intrusiveness of communication styles in *Sherlock* can even be seen in the literal words that appear on screen during Sherlock's deductions or incoming texts to either John or Sherlock. John may complain about the barrage of text messages he receives from Sherlock, but these are also reminders John lives in a world of heightened arousal, and his insistence on maintaining a blog of Sherlock's exploits suggests he seeks out continued feedback from others.

One scene depicting high levels of stress and John's physical reaction to such distress is set during one of the most important evenings of his life. He attempts to propose to Mary, but he is unable to process thoughts or words properly. His stress level increases as he experiences the trauma of seeing Sherlock, who has apparently returned from the dead and shows up just when John is about to propose. All of the symptoms and signs of PTSD are evident in John's response to Sherlock's return. He becomes angry, flustered, and unable to speak rationally. Additionally, John presents with signs mirroring the beginning of a panic attack (i.e., labored breathing, hunched over posture) brewing the moment that John sees Sherlock.

Before Sherlock returns to John's life, John maintains the symptoms of PTSD. There is an indication that between the time that Sherlock leaves and returns to John's side, trauma-focused therapy is sought out for his PTSD symptoms. During a scene at his wedding, John eludes to "therapy, it helps" ("The Sign of Three"). He does not seem to retain any skills learned in therapy, however, as he does not go through the necessary stages of grief (i.e., denial, anger) and attempts to use a "band aid" fix in regards to understanding and processing his grief. John may be expected to require individual counseling therapy services in the future to deal with the complex trauma that he has experienced in both his personal and professional life, including Mary shooting Sherlock, leading to revelations about her past as an assassin; Sherlock's murder of Charles Augustus Magnussen (Lars Mikkelsen) in front of John; and Sherlock's (aborted) exile ("His Last Vow").

Throughout the series, even when John has not had a trauma of this magnitude, he engages in a form of narrative therapy by "journaling" in his blog in order to release the anxiety present in his life. By writing a blog, he is able to relive his trauma in a setting in which he is comfortable and where he is entirely in control of the story. The people who follow John's blog offer positive acknowledgment of his writing skill and exciting life as Sherlock's partner. John's blog offers him a form of control over his life experiences and creates a situation where others look up to him or seek his approval (through their posts in response to his blog entries), similar to his own relationship with Sherlock. This is similar to narrative therapy. It is based on the theory that people need to author their own stories in order to process and understand life events and relationships (Morris 1). In the series, John learns to take authorship of intrusive forms of communication (e.g., constant texts from Sherlock, unwanted media attentions) by starting his blog, which may serve as a way of processing his previous trauma. Utilizing this therapeutic technique, John is able to delineate his frequent stressors and take more ownership of how he and Sherlock are perceived by the public.

Sherlock describes the past as "ghosts … the shadows that define our every sunny day" ("The Abominable Bride"), which is a rather poetic way to say one is haunted by an accumulation of distressing experiences that continue to be part of daily life. Fortunately, Sherlock and John seem to help each other confront the true nature of the other's stress due to the uniquely supportive nature of their relationship, which is likely a large part of *Sherlock*'s appeal to a mass audience. The importance of stress and stressors in popular television shows such as BBC's *Sherlock* holds the public's interest, particularly because the choices Sherlock and John make to resolve their daily stressors are as important to the plot as they are to providing information about the psychology of the individuals. Episodes that incorporate stress as a major feature of the main characters' daily lives helps viewers relate to Sherlock and John and possibly to learn from their often accessible coping methods (e.g., develop closer friendships, start a blog, practice "mind palace" memory techniques). The stressors with which Sherlock and John cope also involve rich clinical concepts (i.e., attachment theory, complex trauma), advanced cognitive schemas, and empirically validated coping techniques (e.g., self-soothing behavior, narrative therapy), making *Sherlock* a fairly psychologically sophisticated television series. The characters in *Sherlock* exhibit various symptoms of PTSD yet are able to accomplish radical tasks such as solving murders, even while processing extreme stress. Not only do Sherlock and John help make Great Britain safer, but, by serving as examples of men who develop successful coping mechanisms to deal with their stress, they can help viewers deal with the stress in their own lives.

WORKS CITED

"The Abominable Bride." *Sherlock*. Writ. Mark Gatiss, Steven Moffat. Dir. Douglas Mackinnon. BBC Entertainment, 2016. DVD.

American Psychiatric Association. *Diagnostic and Statistical Manual of Mental Disorders* (5th ed., text rev.). Washington, DC: American Psychiatric Publishing, 2013. Print.

Boyd, Robert, and Peter Richardson. "Memes: Universal Acid or a Better Mousetrap?" *Darwinians Culture: The Status of Memetics as a Science*. Ed. Robert Aunger. Oxford: Oxford University Press, 2000. Print.

Corey, Gerald. *Theory and Practice of Counseling and Psychotherapy*, 9th ed. Belmont: Brooks/Cole, 2013. Print.

Creamer, Mark, Darryl Wade, Susan Fletcher, and David Forbes. "PTSD Among Military Personnel." *International Review of Psychiatry* 23 (2011): 160–165. Print.

Davis, Diana, Tracey Dietz, and Jacquelyn Pennings. "Evaluating Animal-Assisted Therapy in Group Treatment for Child Sexual Abuse." *Journal of Child Sexual Abuse* 21 (2012): 665–683. Print.

"The Empty Hearse." *Sherlock*. Writ. Mark Gatiss. Dir. Jeremy Lovering. BBC Entertainment, 2014. DVD.

"The Great Game." *Sherlock*. Writ. Mark Gatiss. Dir. Paul McGuigan. BBC Entertainment, 2010. DVD.

"His Last Vow." *Sherlock*. Writ. Steven Moffat. Dir. Nick Hurran. BBC Entertainment, 2014. DVD.

"The Hounds of Baskerville." *Sherlock*. Writ. Mark Gatiss. Dir. Paul McGuigan. BBC Entertainment, 2011. DVD.

Morris, Cynthia. "Narrative Theory: A Culturally Sensitive Counseling and Research Framework." *Narrative Therapy*. 12 Feb. 2007. Web.

Perry, Bruce, and Maria Szalavitz. *The Boy Who Was Raised as a Dog*. New York: Basic Books, 2006. Print.

"The Reichenbach Fall." *Sherlock*. Writ. Stephen Thompson. Dir. Toby Haynes. BBC Entertainment, 2011. DVD.

"A Scandal in Belgravia." *Sherlock*. Writ. Steven Moffat. Dir. Paul McGuigan. BBC Entertainment, 2011. DVD.

Siegel, J.S. *The Developing Mind*. New York: Guilford Press, 1999. Print.

"The Sign of Three." *Sherlock*. Writ. Mark Gatiss, Stephen Thompson, Steven Moffat. Dir. Colm McCarthy. BBC Entertainment, 2014. DVD.

Silva, R.R., and L. Kessler. "Resiliency and Vulnerability Factors in Childhood Post-Traumatic Stress Disorder." *Posttraumatic Stress Disorders in Children & Adolescents Handbook*. New York: W.W. Norton, 2004. 32–33. Print.

"A Study in Pink." *Sherlock*. Writ. Steven Moffat. Dir. Paul McGuigan. BBC Entertainment, 2010. DVD.

A High-Functioning Sociopath Married to His Work

On Hegemonic Masculinity in the BBC's Sherlock

Deborah M. Fratz

The explosive popularity of the BBC's hit series *Sherlock* arises in part from the long-lasting appeal of Arthur Conan Doyle's 19th-century invention and series' co-creators Steven Moffat and Mark Gatiss instinctively knowing how much of the original Sherlock Holmes should surface in their young, tech-savvy detective. Television police dramas typically support traditional gender roles, and while the BBC series operates within a conservative framework, it resists some hegemonic masculine norms, particularly its handling of non-heterosexual identities. Sherlock's ambivalent sexual status has attracted plenty of attention on the internet and other media, but at the expense of examining other qualities of masculinity, such as those associated with professional identity, physical appearance, athleticism, self-control, sociability, and affective range. What looks like eccentricity in the 21st century owes to the outright deviance of the original Holmes. The BBC's detective may resist some conventional cultural institutions and norms for men, but he does so in the same manner as the first detective to live at 221B Baker Street. Today's audiences embrace Sherlock, because our cultures more easily accept his kind of masculinity, but Holmes scholars acknowledge Conan Doyle's discomfort with his extraordinary character. The BBC's Sherlock does not present a radically different mode of masculinity as the original did, though the ambivalent sociability of both detectives marks them as exceptional.

Despite its ingenuity, *Sherlock* follows many conventions of television police and crime dramas. Rebecca Feasey describes this genre as one of "the most masculine" with its focus on "professional roles and the male world of work" (80). Looking historically at television police dramas, Feasey observes how they reflect the public's shifting attitudes toward law enforcement and masculine norms. Shows from the 1950s, such as *Dixon of Dock Green* (1955–76), feature traditionally masculine heroes fighting evil (Feasey 81). The socio-political upheavals of the 1960s and 1970s changed how television audiences viewed the police, and police shows registered their ambivalence: cops and detectives, like those on *Z-Cars* (1962–78) and *The Sweeney* (1975–78), struggled with moral and psychological conflicts, appearing to be just as flawed as criminals and even "outsiders" in their communities (Feasey 82). However fallible, they retain the image of heroism, Feasey claims, and their psychic conflicts align with masculine norms when their professional lives jeopardize their personal relationships, especially with women. James W. Maertens's description of Conan Doyle's detective fits with this representation of the television cop: "Most Victorian men's identities were defined in relationship to the women in their lives and to the male institutions to which they belonged. Holmes rejects both of these kinds of self-definition" (308–09).

Feasey's and Maertens's observations apply to the BBC's Sherlock as well. When he claims to be heartless ("The Great Game") or "married to his work" ("A Study in Pink") or says that he does not "have friends" ("The Hounds of Baskerville"), he reflects the masculine norms of the television detective. Yet his confession to being a "high-functioning sociopath" pathologizes Sherlock by suggesting that the paradigm of masculinity that privileges the professional over a personal life is unhealthy ("A Study in Pink"). Svetlana Bochman claims that Sherlock's "intense, socially detached intelligence, combined with a lack of friends, is presented as socially unacceptable … especially because it is not tempered with sexuality" (146). However, his sociability is problematic not only because he has few relationships, but rather because of his affective distance within them.

Conan Doyle also seemed disconcerted by his detective's seeming lack of affect; although his Holmes eschews romantic attachments, he must love someone—at least John Watson. Conan Doyle's dissatisfaction with the original Holmes's deviations from Victorian masculine norms led to his refashioning the detective throughout forty years, during an era of shifting ideals for gender roles (Bragg 4–5). Claudia Nelson examines Victorian discourses to follow the evolution of ideal masculinity away from introspection, independence, and androgyny toward the conforming manliness of the bluff, hearty team player. While early Victorian writers valued "the ability to conquer human nature," to the point of idealizing a kind of pious asexuality, "late Victorians and Edwardians generally agreed that to be good was to be 'normal,'" and "propriety focused less and less on the exceptional, more and more on the average" when conformity was valued as "wholesome, sound, and somehow uniquely English" (Nelson 526). Additionally, the rise of Darwinian ideas placed faith in human progress through healthy bodies and breeding, and thus favorable "[m]anliness becomes less a state of mind than a state of muscle" (Nelson 546). If "self-controlled, responsible, asexual androgyny seems newly dangerous," even "degenerate, sterile, and often homoerotic," then late Victorians might find Holmes's suspicious (Nelson 542). He is controlled, independent, uninterested in sex, and undeniably exceptional. As a soldier, doctor, and husband, Watson conforms more to late-Victorian masculine norms, but perhaps to cross purposes: on the one hand, his normality accentuates Holmes's eccentricity, but on the other, Watson's "normal" masculinity is a moral anchor for both characters, when Holmes appears most deviant next to Watson, but not when compared to clients and criminals. Both the texts and the BBC series rely on John Watson's normality, as audiences witness Holmes mainly through Watson's experience of him.

Many scholars investigate Conan Doyle's constructions of masculinity in the Sherlock Holmes stories. Tom Bragg asserts that as a "champion of traditional masculine values," Conan Doyle "found Holmes's troublesome and contradictory masculinity wearisome to maintain" (3). Holmes is "the cold scientific reasoner" and "the committed artist"; "the consummate professional" and "the gifted amateur"; and "an honorable conservative but also a 'bohemian' outsider" (Bragg 4). Most problematically, Conan Doyle "originally depicts Holmes as an effeminate and morally ambiguous character, with hints of sexual deviance" but tries, with limited success, to "reclaim his creation for the moral and masculine right" (Bragg 4). Most of Conan Doyle's first readers were middle-class men and boys, encouraged to embrace those qualities so central to Holmes: "observation, rationalism, facticity, logic, comradeship, pluck, and daring" (Kestner 77). Aware of his readership and loyal to British Imperialism, Conan Doyle refashioned the detective, but Holmes was more than just eccentric: as Bragg observes, he resisted the Victorian sites of masculine allegiance: family, God, Queen, and country. Maertens sees Holmes as an "exception to the rule of corporate masculinity," because he did not identify "with the power of the British Empire expressed in big guns or the apparatus of the police force" (312). Francesca M. Marinaro and Kayley Thomas make a similar observation about the BBC's Sherlock, identifying him as a kind of anti-hero by virtue of his "emotional detachment—from family, community, nationalism or patriotism" (74). Scholars agree that Sherlock Holmes retains conventional masculine qualities even as he rejects alliances with masculine institutions.

Conventions of the detective genre also influence the perception of Sherlock Holmes's masculinity. Leslie Haynsworth showed how detective fiction combines two diverging genres: sensation fiction, which "is typically invested in the domestic model of masculinity—and adventure fiction, which is obviously heavily invested in the imperialist model." Domestic fiction promotes older models of masculinity by valuing restraint and concern for others, whereas adventure stories feature aggressive masculine characters suited to sports, war, and capitalist enterprises. In the Holmes stories, "men who have spent time in the empire and who have been socialized according to its imperatives are shown to be discordant if not disruptive or dangerous figures when they return to settle in England," putting imperial and domestic masculine values in conflict (Haynsworth). Rather than judging Holmes as a failed domestic specimen or Imperial agent, Haynsworth acknowledges his useful liminality:

> The more actively and explicitly the Holmes stories engage the tensions and contradictions between imperialist values and domestic ones, the more welcome—and, indeed, important—Holmes's interventions become, for he, at once so keen-witted and so radically alienated from society that he appears to have no personal investments in any one particular value system, embodies the possibility of a sane, impartial, and just negotiation between the various values, beliefs, and imperatives that the stories present.

The BBC's Sherlock represents the man of our era, too, which increasingly relies on moral and cultural relativism to comprehend the global community. A central character that maintains objective neutrality appeals to today's audiences because viewers are also reluctant to swear allegiances. When Sherlock tells Moriarty, "I may be on the side of the angels, but don't think for one second that I am one of them" ("The Reichenbach Fall"), his unconventionality is less sinister because cultural consensus is that we are not angels, either.

"The precaution of a good coat and a short friend": On Appearance

In the era that invented muscular Christianity, the original Holmes diverges from hegemonic masculinity by virtue of his looks alone. In *A Study in Scarlet*, John Watson describes him as "rather over six feet, and so excessively lean that he seemed to be considerably taller." Holmes has the height of a hero, without the brawn that builds empires. According to contemporary physiognomy, his "sharp eyes" indicate mental acuity, as does the "hawk-like nose," and the "prominent chin" implies tenacity. In many respects, Benedict Cumberbatch, who plays Sherlock in the BBC series, matches Conan Doyle's description. As Moffat asserts, in addition to being the right age, "Benedict has got the look ... of a Sherlock Holmes," and casting looked no further for the title character (PBS Masterpiece Mystery!, "Sherlock: Casting the Leads"). Although Cumberbatch is only six feet tall, Sherlock's attire makes the most of "the precaution of a good coat and a short friend" ("A

Scandal in Belgravia") that create the optical illusion that this Sherlock stands taller than six feet.

However, Cumberbatch's Sherlock differs from the original in two respects: one that points back to a Victorian hero, and the other toward the 21st-century metrosexual. Cumberbatch's roles in historical dramas, such as *To the Ends of the Earth*, *The Other Boleyn Girl*, and *Parade's End*, require a man who looks not just British, but specifically English. His Sherlock looks more like an English hero than the original, whose sharp eyes and hawkish nose would suggest Eastern European heritage to Victorians. Further, Cumberbatch's detective is dashing: John Watson accuses Sherlock of being "all mysterious with [his] cheekbones and turning [his] coat collar up so [he looks] cool" ("The Hounds of Baskerville"). His cool looks are more than heroic: as Anissa M. Graham and Jennifer C. Garlen attest, he is an "icon of style, a model for the well-dressed British male, an object of emulation, admiration, and desire" (32). He matches Jeremy Kaye's description of the metrosexual, who inherits the self-disciplined performativity of the Victorian dandy. Linking the Victorian era to our own, Kaye's claims illuminate two crucial qualities of Sherlock's identity: Sherlock acknowledges the importance of a cultivated persona and the pleasures of showing off. According to Kaye, the metrosexual label belongs to a straight man benefitting from practices usually assigned to gay men. Both sexes find him attractive: Moriarty greets him with "Hello, sexy," and upon meeting him, Irene Adler declares "brainy is the new sexy" (though she has just swiped through photographs on her phone of Sherlock wearing nothing but a sheet). While Conan Doyle gave the original Holmes an asexual appearance, the modern Sherlock asserts a mysterious eroticism.

Sherlock's indeterminate sexuality contributes significantly to his appeal. More than one interview with Cumberbatch and the writers asserts that, in keeping with the original textual information, he is uninterested in sex. Yet plenty of *Sherlock* fan fiction coheres with Graham Rob's assertion that "[e]veryone already knows, instinctively, that Holmes is homosexual" (qtd. in Humble 99). Nicola Humble, however, disagrees: "It is not quite true to say that everyone knows that Holmes is gay–rather that many people suspect that he might be. Retaining that ambiguity seems to me crucial…. He sits firmly on the fence, and his ambiguities and doubleness—his queerness—are what make him both fascinating and alarming" (99). Moffat asserts that Sherlock's sexuality is neither "ambiguous [n]or mysterious," because "the books are completely clear. [Holmes] is not interested in [sex] at all. He's interested in what his brain is doing…. [P]eople say he shows no interest in women, therefore he must be gay. He shows no interest in men, either. That's just not what he does" (qtd. in Lavigne 15). "His Last Vow" complicates Sherlock's sexuality, less so in his opportunistic bedding of Charles Augustus Magnussen's personal assistant Janine, but rather in the blackmailer's assessment of Sherlock's "porn habits" as "normal." Genuine asexuality should have triggered "none," so audiences receive a baffling clue that Sherlock's sexuality might be "normal," except that, as with other physical appetites, he suppresses it. Indeed, both Cumberbatch and Moffat affirm that while Sherlock has some sexual drive, he has even more self-control. In a 2012 interview with *The Guardian*, Moffat states that Sherlock makes "the choice of a monk, not the choice of an asexual. If he was asexual, there would be no tension in that, no fun in that—it's someone who abstains who's interesting" (Jeffries). These speculations reflect our contemporary obsession with sexuality and unwillingness to accept the absence of sexual desire. The series capitalizes on the "ambiguities and doubleness" that Humble describes: by having Watson directly question Sherlock's sexuality in the first episode, the implications of an intense homosocial relationship between men are clear, as Carlen Lavigne observes (15). John's emphatic declarations that he is not gay only promote the question that Sherlock might be.

Other characters influence perceptions of Sherlock's sexuality, while affirming that queerness no longer automatically provokes social stigma: Mycroft's homosexuality is presented nonchalantly, and while Moriarty's gay persona as "IT Jim" reflects the stereotypes of the urban gay man, squeamishness about male homosexuality is largely eliminated. The fact that both Mark Gatiss (Mycroft) and Andrew Scott (Moriarty) publically acknowledge their homosexuality likewise colors the perception of the series. Even if Sherlock is gay, it is "fine," as both John and Sherlock say in "A Study in Pink." This perception of non-heterosexual people is decidedly 21st century: homosexuality no longer necessarily stigmatizes middle-class urban white men, and though it would startle Conan Doyle, Mycroft Holmes can simultaneously be referred to as the "Queen" and "the British government" ("A Scandal in Belgravia"). His sexual orientation has no bearing on his political power or profession.

The influence of a man's profession on masculine identity has changed significantly in the years following Conan Doyle's original conception of Sherlock Holmes, but the perception depends less on professional skills and more on sociability. While James Eli Adams observes that Victorian men faced doubts about the manliness of intellectual labor, history shows that those doubts were temporary: men of intellect, particularly if engaged with science and technology, never lost respect. Indeed, Holmes's chemical innovations, such as the "Sherlock Holmes's test" for detecting minuscule traces of blood, mark him as a man who contributes to the progress of his society (*A Study in Scarlet*). Nor does being a detective compromise Holmes's masculinity: his observational and analytical skills cohere with masculine ideals for rational thought. However, being the world's *only* consulting detective signals that

Holmes is not a team player, which is what makes him exceptional, and that is an issue of sociability, not intellect or professional identity. In our era of consultants and independent contractors in the field of technology, Sherlock's consultant identity is part of what makes him cool, as is his valuing the "work itself" rather than financial gains. His technological mastery props up his masculine identity, in that it supports professional independence and mobility. However, relying on technology could be problematic if it inhibits normative sociability, as it does with Sherlock. In "Detecting the Technocratic Detective," Bochman writes that "Sherlock's rationalist intelligence sometimes serves to dehumanize him until he is almost at one with the technology he so adeptly manipulates," but ultimately technology is not the issue, and once again, sociability is (152).

Other aspects of Sherlock's physicality merit examination, specifically his athleticism and capacity for action. Late Victorians rejected earlier models of manhood that privileged intellectual over physical labor, and contemporary periodicals, including those publishing Conan Doyle's work, featured idealized heroes as brave, muscular men taking charge of other men. Holmes is not that kind of hero; while he is a proficient boxer and marksman, he favors mental weapons and working alone, figuring him as a strategist rather than man of action. Sidney Paget's illustrations of Holmes frequently show him reclining, languid and contemplative: Clare Clarke notes that of the 71 illustrations of Holmes, "only 16 (less than 25 per cent) depict Holmes actually working. Twenty-six show Holmes sitting, lounging, smoking or at leisure" (87). Yet Holmes is active and energetic; in A Study in Scarlet, Watson states that "[n]othing could exceed his energy when the working fit was upon him," which is just as true for the BBC's Sherlock. Unlike the detective in Paget's illustrations, Sherlock is rarely at home. More frequently, he is out of the house—at St. Bart's Hospital, in the morgue, on a crime scene, in a cab, or on the street—where he is running, as seen in "A Study in Pink" when he sprints through two minutes of London parkour while following a suspicious cab. This Holmes is as much an athlete as the original. Enumerating Holmes's strengths in A Study in Scarlet, Watson notes the detective is an "expert singlestick player [a kind of fencing], boxer, and swordsman," activities that denote individual athleticism rather than conformity to masculine team sports. The BBC's fight scenes emphasize athletic precision and strategy as well: in "A Scandal in Belgravia," Sherlock and Irene Adler fight CIA agents using self-defense moves, like Krav Maga, which may be a nod to Conan Doyle's invocation of "baritsu," a late Victorian urban self-defense method that combined boxing and Japanese jujitsu and one that Holmes used against Moriarty at Reichenbach (Godfrey). A man and woman using the same fighting method could cast Sherlock's fighting persona as less masculine, but the method is efficient. Watson uses similar techniques in "His Last Vow."

These fights are won not through brute strength or a bad temper, but rather physical self-discipline, which is a complicated trait in both the original and modern depiction of the detective.

"Always been able to keep myself distant": On Affect and Sociability

While late Victorians began to embrace the bluff, hearty expression of manly feelings, they still valued the appearance of restraint, particularly in a man's physical bearing. Holmes's physical control remains consistent in Conan Doyle's works, even with the complication of drug use, which Victorians would have perceived as a disgraceful feminine weakness. After injecting cocaine at the beginning of *The Sign of Four*, he retains a "cool, nonchalant air" that deflates Watson's scolding; indeed, after Holmes correctly identifies the origins of Watson's watch, he apologizes, saying "I should have had more faith in your marvellous faculty." On the one hand, Holmes's physical demeanor reflects self-control; on the other, his drug use suggests the lack of it. Only the stimulation of "brain work," not his own will, curtails his use; at the end of *The Sign of Four*, he reaches for cocaine again. The BBC's Sherlock diverges from the original, both in physical restraint and how it reflects his capacity for self-control.

Though the series presents Sherlock as cool and analytical (e.g., his line "I've always been able to keep myself distant" ["The Hounds of Baskerville"]), he frequently lacks restraint. His body language betrays his impatience, and his drug use seems outside his control. As with the original Holmes, these two facets of his character are connected. Initially, "A Study in Pink" makes a joke of our fascination with his drug use: one camera angle suggests he injects himself but then reveals the nicotine patches that help him contemplate "a three-patch problem," which still insinuates that only substance use can slow him down. Even his meditative techniques are physical; in "The Hounds of Baskerville," Sherlock jerks, nods, and grimaces while retrieving information from his "mind palace." Our era might associate this brisk intensity with a masculine, Type-A personality, but Victorians would find his uncontrolled physical activity unseemly.

The Victorian Sherlock represented in "The Abominable Bride" better reflects that era's norms; he sits with the straight spine reminiscent of zazen, lightly paging through imaginary newspaper clippings floating before him. The contrast between the modern and Victorian Holmes is so striking that this episode seems to direct attention to Sherlock's struggle to control himself. Further, "The Abominable Bride" reveals a darker history for Sherlock's substance use by indicating that, without Mycroft's intervention and the help of a prepared "list" of drugs he has taken, Sherlock's addiction could be fatal.

The unaired pilot frontloads Sherlock's drug history when the murderous taxi driver asks, "Do a lot of drugs, Sherlock Holmes?" to which he answers, "Not in awhile," but because the first aired episode, "A Study in Pink," lacks this clear confession, audiences look for evidence of the original Holmes's drug use. "His Last Vow" makes his substance use explicit, but its implications are ambiguous: a urine test and his confession confirm everyone's suspicions, but the episode fails to dictate what to make of it. His agility and verbal coherence suggest that, whatever the drug (and it is never specified), it fails to slow down his mental and physical capacities: he insists he is on a case and resents the disruption. The series' depiction of his drug use is contradictory: while it makes Sherlock reckless, it simultaneously suggests that he can handle the consequences and effects, which paradoxically boosts his appearance of masculinity. The series trusts audiences to view Sherlock's drug use as it does his sociopathy: identifying as a "high-functioning sociopath" may pathologize his limited affect, yet it also acts as a shortcut to maintaining the audience's sympathies. If he seems cold, he cannot help it, as he was born that way.

The series frequently alludes to Sherlock's sociopathic tendencies, but it also acknowledges doubts about his affective range. In "A Scandal in Belgravia," Sherlock asks Mycroft, "Do you ever wonder if there is something wrong with us?" but the answer only confirms Mycroft's sociopathy: "caring is not an advantage." In "The Great Game," when John asks Sherlock if he cares about the lives at stake in their investigation, Sherlock answers, "Will caring about them help save them? ... I'll continue not to make that mistake." To establish Sherlock's limited affect, the series refers to Watson's observation from "A Scandal in Bohemia":

> All emotions ... were abhorrent to his cold, precise but admirably balanced mind ... for the trained reasoner to admit such intrusions into his own delicate and finely adjusted temperament was to introduce a distracting factor which might throw a doubt upon all his mental results. Grit in a sensitive instrument, or a crack in one of his own high-power lenses, would not be more disturbing than a strong emotion in a nature such as his.

Three episodes—"The Hounds of Baskerville," "The Sign of Three," and "The Abominable Bride"—draw attention to this crucial passage. However, upon close reading, it fails to directly state that Holmes has no emotions–only that he hates them for disrupting his ability to observe and analyze. In Maertens's examination of Conan Doyle's Holmes, he concedes that his masculine identity has room for emotion and passion, "but it is emotion aimed at the mastery of objects and the solution of logical problems, it is passion of a narcissistic kind, directed toward winning a challenging game rather that engaging with others in intimate sympathy" (310). Lacking the capacity for sympathy, however, is not the same as lacking affect. Sherlock resembles the original Holmes, but the scripts confuse audiences by invoking sociopathy and propping it up with his theatrical coldness. In the first two seasons, he shows plenty of affect: irritation, impatience, exhilaration, and occasionally righteous anger, as in "A Scandal in Belgravia" when he throws the American agent out of his window in revenge for striking Mrs. Hudson. In "His Last Vow," his hatred for Magnussen overpowers his judgment, leading him to murder the blackmailer. In fact, he displays the emotional palette of conventional television cops, thus confirming masculine norms. When asked about Sherlock's sociopathy at the 2013 Comic-Con, Moffat replied that Sherlock is "not really" sociopathic at all: "I think he finds it a convenient label. If he says he's a high-functioning sociopath, then people won't expect him to do boring things like talk. So he makes a decision to be that way" (PBS, "Comic-Con 2013 Panel with the Creators of *Sherlock*"). However, Sherlock's emotional profile gets very different treatment in the series' third season.

Expanding on Sherlock's friendships, family history, and drug use, the third season demands that audiences accept the possibility of a wider emotional range for him. What complicates comparison to Conan Doyle's creation is how little original material supports these developments. In the PBS–sponsored "Q & A with the Star and Creators" in May 2012, one audience member asked Moffat about Sherlock's "back story," to which he answered, "I don't think that's how you create a character, and I don't think that's how you know a character.... You don't bring that into the show; it's not right. There [are] some things we don't know about Sherlock Holmes ... and that's right and proper." In the same panel, he dismissed exploring Sherlock's drug use, saying, "I don't think it's the best avenue" because there are "not that many" instances of it in the canon. Either Moffat was deliberately deceiving the public, or he had not yet planned the third season, which complicates depictions of Sherlock's affective life, and thus his masculinity. "His Last Vow" is especially ambiguous: on the one hand, the outright murder of Magnussen supports sociopathy, but on the other, Sherlock kills him to protect Mary and John. The third season of *Sherlock* reaffirms Moffat's history of bewildering audiences and delivering emotional shocks. When Sherlock is called back from his four-minute exile at the end of "His Last Vow," viewers are left to speculate how Sherlock's character might be using his wider range of affect in service to England itself.

When Conan Doyle created Holmes, the most celebrated professions for young men were connected with the British Empire, which is why so many critical explorations of masculinity in Conan Doyle's work invoke imperialism. Kestner scrutinizes Conan Doyle's "adroit aligning of imperialism with the politics of masculinity" (64). Jesse Oak Taylor-Ide suggests that Holmes adeptly uses "the reason and science associated with the British masculinity" and "the intuitive, the irrational associated with the foreign and feminine" (55). Bragg does not assume that Holmes represents solidly rational English masculinity fighting the superstitious, feminized East. Contemporary with Sherlock Holmes, the British Empire ruled over 25 percent of the world's landmass and population; concerns about maintaining imperial power were linked to the young men schooled on "the playing fields of Eton." Today's Great Britain presents a highly self-aware post-imperial identity, and its global power operates far more subtly. *Sherlock* invokes only the ghosts of England's empire. John returns from Afghanistan, from a war begun by a different imperial power: the U.S. Moriarty's looks—his slender frame and dark coloring—align him with images of the colonized East, although his Irish accent invokes the colony closer to home. Whereas the Empire was a major concern for Conan Doyle, it is not for the modern detective. Sherlock openly sneers at John's anxieties about the missing Bruce-Partington missile plans by saying, "How quaint ... you are. Queen and country" ("The Great Game"). His disdain for the figureheads of Great Britain is apparent in "A Scandal in Belgravia," when he advises Mycroft to contain Irene Adler's threats by treating her "like royalty," followed by a sardonic rendering of "God Save the Queen" on his violin. Most tellingly, he offends basic British propriety by sitting naked in Buckingham Palace. His open scoffing of "Queen and country" would shock Conan Doyle, who reshaped Holmes in later narratives to align more with conventional heroes appearing in adventure stories of the *Boy's Own Paper*. Whereas loyalty to the British Empire was intrinsically tied to Victorian masculinity, it seems irrelevant to this modern man.

Perhaps *Sherlock*'s immense popularity as an international phenomenon lies in the long shadow of the British Empire, which spread English as a major global language. In the last sixty years, Great Britain's influence has changed, and instead of the Raj, the 21st century has the BBC, which uses complex, carefully crafted narratives like *Sherlock* to disseminate an image of Great Britain as cool and thoroughly modern. Sherlock Holmes survived the decline of the Empire, and his fame continues to spread; one website, Sherlocktron. com, lists 416 active Sherlock Holmes societies throughout the world, including countries outside of the former Empire, such as Paraguay and Japan. Now spanning international borders and three centuries, Sherlock Holmes is, as he says at the end of "The Abominable Bride," a "man out of his time," sometimes admirable, always exceptional, and continuing to challenge the ways we see masculine power.

Works Cited

"The Abominable Bride." *Sherlock*. Writ. Mark Gatiss, Steven Moffat. Dir. Douglas Mackinnon. PBS.org. 11 Jan. 2016. Web.

Adams, James Eli. *Dandies and Desert Saints: Styles of Victorian Masculinity*. Ithaca: Cornell University Press, 1995. Print.

Bochman, Svetlana. "Detecting the Technocratic Detective." *Sherlock Holmes for the 21st Century: Essays on New Adaptations* (pp. 144–154). Ed. Lynnette Porter. Jefferson, NC: McFarland, 2012. Print.

Bragg, Tom. "Becoming a Mere Appendix: The Rehabilitated Masculinity of Sherlock Holmes." *Victorian Newsletter* (Fall 2009): 3–26. Print.

Clarke, Clare. "Professionalism and the Cultural Politics of Work in the Sherlock Holmes Stories." *The Masculine Middlebrow, 1880–1950.* Ed. Kate Macdonald. New York: Palgrave Macmillan, 2011. Print.

Conan Doyle, Arthur. *The Adventures of Sherlock Holmes.* Prod. Jose Menendez. Apr. 2011. Project Gutenberg. Web. 14 Jan. 2016.

_____. *The Sign of Four.* Nov. 2008. Project Gutenberg. Web. 14 Jan. 2016.

_____. *A Study in Scarlet.* 1887. Prod. Roger Squires and David Widger. July 2008. Project Gutenberg. Web. 14 Jan. 2016.

Feasey, Rebecca. *Masculinity and Popular Television.* Edinburgh: Edinburgh University Press, 2008. Print.

Godfrey, Emelyne. *Masculinity, Crime, and Self-Defence in Victorian Literature.* New York: Palgrave Macmillan, 2013. Print.

Graham, Anissa M., and Jennifer C. Garlen. "Sex and the Single Sleuth." *Sherlock Holmes for the 21st Century: Essays on New Adaptations* (pp. 24–34). Ed. Lynnette Porter. Jefferson, NC: McFarland, 2012. Print.

"The Great Game." *Sherlock.* Writ. Mark Gatiss. Dir. Paul McGuigan. BBC, 2010. DVD.

Haynsworth, Leslie. "All the Detective's Men: Binary Coding of Masculine Identity in the Sherlock Holmes Stories." *VIJ Digital Annex* 38 (2010): n. p. Web. 23 June 2015.

"His Last Vow." *Sherlock.* Writ. Steven Moffat. Dir. Nick Hurran. BBC, 2014. DVD.

"The Hounds of Baskerville." *Sherlock.* Writ. Mark Gatiss. Dir. Paul McGuigan. BBC, 2012. DVD.

Humble, Nicola. "From Holmes to the Drones: Fantasies of Men Without Women in the Masculine Middlebrow." *The Masculine Middlebrow, 1880–1950.* Ed. Kate Macdonald. New York: Palgrave Macmillan, 2011. Print.

Jeffries, Stuart. "'There Is a Clue Everybody's Missed': Sherlock Writer Steven Moffat Interviewed." *The Guardian.* 20 Jan. 2012. Web. 30 June 2015.

Kaye, Jeremy. "Twenty-First Century Dandy: What Metrosexuality and the Heterosexual Matrix Reveal About Victorian Men." *Journal of Popular Culture* 42, no. 1 (2009): 103–125. Print.

Kestner, Joseph A. *Sherlock's Men: Masculinity, Conan Doyle, and Cultural History.* Aldershot: Ashgate, 1997. Print.

Lavigne, Carlen. "The Noble Bachelor and the Crooked Man: Subtext and Sexuality in the BBC's *Sherlock." Sherlock Holmes for the 21st Century: Essays on New Adaptations* (pp. 13–23). Ed. Lynnette Porter. Jefferson, NC: McFarland, 2012. Print.

Maertens, James W. "Masculine Power and the Ideal Reasoner: Sherlock Holmes, Technician-Hero." *Sherlock Holmes: Victorian Sleuth to Modern Hero.* Ed. Charles R. Putney, Joseph A. Cutshall King, and Sally Sugarman. Lanham, MD: Scarecrow Press, 1996. Print.

Marinaro, Francesca M., and Kayley Thomas. "'Don't Make People into Heroes, John': (Re/De) Constructing the Detective as Hero." *Sherlock Holmes for the 21st Century: Essays on New Adaptations* (pp. 65–80). Ed. Lynnette Porter. Jefferson, NC: McFarland, 2012. Print.

Nelson, Claudia. "Sex and the Single Boy: Ideals of Manliness and Sexuality in Victorian Literature for Boys." *Victorian Studies* 32, no. 4 (1989): 525–550. Print.

PBS. "Comic-Con 2013 Panel with the Creators of *Sherlock.*" YouTube. 16 Sep. 2013. Web. 1 Apr. 2014.

_____. "Masterpiece Mystery! Sherlock: Casting the Leads." YouTube. 8 Nov. 2010. Web. 30 June 2015.

_____. "Masterpiece *Sherlock* Series 2: A Special Q & A with the Star and Creators." YouTube. 9 May 2012. Web. 26 June 2015.

"The Reichenbach Fall." *Sherlock*. Writ. Steve Thompson. Dir. Toby Haynes. BBC, 2012. DVD.

"A Scandal in Belgravia." *Sherlock*. Writ. Steven Moffat. Dir. Paul McGuigan. BBC, 2012. DVD.

"The Sign of Three." *Sherlock*. Writ. Steven Thompson, Steven Moffat, Mark Gatiss. Dir. Colm McCarthy. BBC, 2014. DVD.

"A Study in Pink." *Sherlock*. Writ. Steven Moffat. Dir. Paul McGuigan. BBC, 2010. DVD.

Taylor-Ide, Jesse Oak. "Ritual and the Liminality of Sherlock Holmes in 'The Sign of Four' and 'The Hound of the Baskervilles.'" *English Literature in Transition, 1880–1920* 48, no. 1 (2005): 55–70. Web. 9 Feb. 2016.

The BBC's Sherlock
A *"Sociopathic" Master of the Social Game*

KATHRYN McCLAIN *and* GRACE CRIPPS

Literary figure Sherlock Holmes is known for his ingenuity as a detective, but the general public often forgets that Holmes's characterization expands beyond his genius. Indeed, contemporary readers may begin the original stories, or any adaptation for that matter, imagining Holmes as a hero-type protagonist with an incredible brain who always solves the case—and saves the day. However, Holmes is not a flat character; he is dynamic on both page and screen, and his faults, along with his intelligence, craft his presentation. Famed writer Steven Moffat (also known for *Doctor Who* and *Jekyll*) had such a shift in his view of Holmes after his initial reading of the canon:

> I do remember the genuine sense of shock when I read *A Study in Scarlet* ... realizing how unpleasant Holmes is! I had always thought that Sherlock Holmes would be like James Bond; he would be strong and brave and wise. But he wasn't—he was *horrible*, and he did all sorts of weird things, and then he started taking drugs, and I [thought]: "Oh my goodness, this is shocking!" [qtd. in Adams 3–4].

Holmes's "horrible" and "shocking" behavior certainly catches any reader's attention, and it is due to his intriguing personality that he develops from machine-like human to flawed, engrossing man. Moffat, alongside fellow writers Mark Gatiss and Stephen Thompson, vitally incorporates the reality of Sherlock's flaws and integrates those peculiarities into the BBC television series *Sherlock*, a contemporary adaptation of Sir Arthur Conan Doyle's Sherlock Holmes.

The series' interpretation blends the detective's brash and savvy wit with his penchant for odd experiments, creepy human interactions, and deficient social skills. Initial reviewers of *Sherlock* definitely noticed: Sherlock (Benedict Cumberbatch) is "part-Bond, part dark knight detective" (Jensen 92), a "cerebral, unemotional, violin-playing" character who "can seem psychologically disturbed" (Wren 31), and "a constant source of insulting ill-timed truths, a showoff who just can't help himself" (Robert). Sherlock's character evolves into a more emotionally dexterous man around certain characters as the series progresses, yet his eccentric brain remains central to his persona: "Cumberbatch's Holmes is everything we've come to expect from the character—dazzling smarts, with astounding powers of perception ... but also a near-lunatic, so lacking in interpersonal skills that others are frequently left to clean up his mess" (Lowry 39).

Once noticed, Sherlock's "unpleasantness" cannot be ignored. Sherlock keeps random body parts in the flat's refrigerator and travels on the Tube while coated in pig's blood ("The Hounds of Baskerville"), yet he sees no issue with these actions because each is "for the work." Such a claim inspires both the fictional Londoners within *Sherlock*'s universe and the real television viewers alike to obsess over Sherlock's mental state, especially as Sherlock claims to be a "high-functioning sociopath" ("A Study in Pink"). While it would be easier for *Sherlock* viewers to simply accept Sherlock's personal diagnosis, his assertion becomes less convincing the longer the series continues. The mystery to solve then becomes: why would genius detective Sherlock Holmes label himself as a sociopath, and how could such a label affect his work and lifestyle? If that case can be solved, then additional inquiries arise: how does such a label affect fictional and real viewers' interpretations of Sherlock, especially when both audiences ultimately require John to help them access Sherlock's true personality and motivations? Can either audience accept Sherlock with his unconventional behavior?

A Claim for Sociopathy

During an argument with forensic scientist Philip Anderson (Jonathan Aris) in the first episode of *Sherlock*, the detective defines *psychopath* and *sociopath* as two distinct labels. When Anderson claims Sherlock is a psychopath, Sherlock replies, "I'm not a psychopath, Anderson. I'm a high-functioning sociopath. Do your research" ("A Study in Pink"). Sherlock does not explain his diagnosis, and research, unfortunately, brings forth more confusion than answers.

The professional psychiatric community does not provide a clear-cut conception of the sociopath; it does not even recognize sociopathy or psychopathy. Though researched extensively by prominent psychologists, the *Diagnostic and Statistical Manual of Mental Disorders*, published by the

American Psychiatric Association, does not list these two descriptors as possible diagnoses. Rather, it outlines the diagnosis of antisocial personality disorder, and *sociopathy* and *psychopathy* remain unofficial terms.

Despite this lack of official recognition, so-called psychopaths and sociopaths remain an interest for many in the psychiatric community, and Sherlock does appear, at first glance, to exhibit many of the distinctive characteristics. According to Dr. David Lykken, who specialized in psychiatry and behavioral genetics, psychopaths are born, whereas sociopaths are environmentally created (113). Although both types of individuals are at higher risk for criminal activity, not all engage in such behavior (116). While Sherlock's criminal activities often are on a smaller scale (e.g., he pickpockets Detective Inspector Greg Lestrade [Rupert Graves] in "A Study in Pink"), larger incidents do occur, such as when he shoots Charles Augustus Magnussen (Lars Mikkelsen). Though Sherlock was meant to originally take responsibility for the latter crime (ironically through assistance to the British government via a suicide mission), he is instead called back to London when the image of James Moriarty (Andrew Scott) begins to appear ("His Last Vow"). Therefore, Sherlock engages in criminal behavior, and he is only saved from legal accountability by his brother Mycroft (Mark Gatiss) or the British government's need for his deductive skills.

Also important concerning Sherlock is what Lykken refers to as the appearance/utilization of intellect. Sherlock's high intelligence results in others comparing him with psychopaths who may appear more intelligent because "the unafraid, unabashed, uninhibited psychopath always has his wits about him … [and] he tends to be able to make the most of what intelligence he has" (Lykken 136). Therefore, the hyper-intelligent Sherlock, who claims that emotions create weakness ("The Hounds of Baskerville"), resembles the emotionally detached, seemingly brilliant psychopath.

His attitude toward others' intelligence further facilitates this detached persona: "This Sherlock Holmes doesn't appear to believe that everyone can do what he can do, even if they take the infinite pains that genius requires; instead, he makes disparaging remarks" about everyone he considers less intelligent than himself (Coppa 217). Additional qualities that Sherlock shares with Lykken's definition of the psychopath include outrageous behavior, desire for admiration (Lykken 138), and abuse of stimulant drugs like cocaine (142). Ultimately, the lack of moral values and conscience for psychopaths and sociopaths, whether in relation to upbringing or a "peculiarity in themselves" (134), has continually fascinated researchers.

The *Sherlock* television audience is also fascinated because the connotations of psychopathy and sociopathy still carry significant weight in the minds of the general public. This weight mostly is derived from media representation; even though the majority of the psychiatric community does not recognize these categories, the terms have a strong presence in both media and popular culture. Dr. Robert Hare, a world-renowned expert on psychopathy, claims that such individuals are "not what news media portrays them to be." While common representations portray "crazy and nuts" (Hare) characters such as Hannibal Lecter (*The Silence of the Lambs*) and Joffrey Baratheon (*Game of Thrones*), who convey "an impression of anger and implacable evil," the reality is far less emotional. A psychopath is a "relatively indifferent [person] to the probability of punishment for his actions" (Lykken 115).

Though the actual difference between *sociopath* and *psychopath* is whether a person is socially created, Sherlock specifically calls himself a "high-functioning sociopath" because of the negative baggage *psychopath* implies. Sherlock understands he cannot claim psychopathy because it is associated with psychotic behavior. As Dr. Hare elaborates, "psychopath does not equal psychotic," as psychotic individuals experience a break with reality; psychopaths understand the consequences of their actions, but psychotic individuals cannot. Despite the distinction, the public still confuses the terminology. Sherlock, undoubtedly aware of the mixed medical definitions and socially constructed connotations of *psychopath* and *sociopath*, appears to take advantage of the latter label. He considers how he presents himself at all times and intentionally constructs how others perceive him in order to gain respect and greater efficiency during his detective work. While the term *sociopath* actually engages a similar "definition" to psychopath because it is similarly regarded and feared, it creates distance from psychotic behavior. Sherlock does not want to be associated with psychotic behavior, as such behavior relates to a lack of control. The label of *sociopath* gives both fictional characters and television viewers the perception that Sherlock has a high level of control. In the fictional world, the appearance of control that Sherlock creates for himself results in greater respect and improved efficiency while he works on his cases; from the real viewers' perspectives, Sherlock's control gives him the appearance of hyperintelligence.

The self-diagnosis of sociopath, however, does not withstand close examination. Sherlock exhibits emotions throughout the show—emotions that a sociopath or psychopath could not—and this contradiction calls into question his claim. Maria Konnikova, author of *Mastermind: How to Think Like Sherlock Holmes*, puts it best in her article "Stop Calling Sherlock a Sociopath! Thanks, a Psychologist": "Sherlock Holmes is not a cold, calculating, self-gratifying machine. He cares for John Watson (Martin Freeman). He cares for Mrs. Hudson. He most certainly has a conscience…. In other words, Holmes has emotions—and attachments—like the rest of us. What he's better at is controlling them—and only letting them show under very specific circumstances." The emotional control makes Sherlock appear without feeling to those who know him casually, but the emotions he has prevent him from satisfying a sociopath's characteristics. Sherlock shows that he does emotionally attach to others—specifically, he needs John Watson. In "The Empty Hearse," Sherlock yearns for John after John refuses to forgive him for faking his death. Without John at his side, Sherlock employs Molly Hooper (Louise Brealey) to join him on a case, and she recognizes she is just John's replacement. At a crime scene, Sherlock speaks to a "John" that only exists in his head and, later in the same episode, leaps into fire to save John's life ("The Empty Hearse").

Those who do not believe Sherlock is a sociopath have suggested other possibilities to explain his peculiarities. John Watson makes the off-hand comment Sherlock has Asperger's Syndrome ("The Hounds of Baskerville"), and some viewers have suggested Sherlock has Autism Spectrum Disorder or Reactive Attachment Disorder, which are each "characterized by deficits in social interaction, limited emotional responsiveness to others, and periods of sudden moodiness or irritability" (Dondero and Pippin 6). While Jennifer Dondero and Sabrina Pippin of the Chicago School of Professional Psychology acknowledge those viewers' interpretations, they posit an alternative diagnosis: Post Traumatic Stress Disorder (PTSD). They asserted Sherlock experiences practically constant stress, which becomes a "clinically significant and character-defining trait" (3). In fact, Sherlock's constant environmental or interpersonal stress (4) creates situations where he "experiences confusion and anxiety when he sincerely wants to please someone" (3). This anxiety can be seen even early in Sherlock's relationship with John. When John first looks at the 221B Baker Street flat, he comments on how the junk needs to be cleaned out; Sherlock, at first, says he has already moved his things in, but he immediately starts to clean after John's comment in order to please his new flatmate ("A Study in Pink"). Yet, Sherlock does not let this behavior remain constant: emotional connections promote weakness in his mind. As Dondero and Pippin note, "even his self-diagnosis … is an easy excuse to remove emotional reflection from his self-concept" (4), which further proves Sherlock experiences intense emotional connection and is not a sociopath. He therefore diagnoses himself with sociopathy incorrectly for specific reasons of his own. His self-diagnosis most likely functions solely to "remove emotional reflection from his self-concept" and help him maneuver successfully in society.

Mixing Labels: The Consulting Detective's Advantageous Redefinition

During the series, other characters create several possible identifiers for Sherlock; conversely, the only label Sherlock applies to himself (besides "consulting detective") is "high-functioning sociopath." He continues to use this term to his advantage, especially while trying to oversee John's happiness prior to his marriage to Mary Morstan (Amanda Abbington) during Season Three. While fulfilling his duties as best man, Sherlock decides to confront Mary's ex-boyfriend David (Oliver Lansley) and rattles off disconcerting, personal information about him. David exclaims: "They're right about you. You're a bloody psychopath!" Deadpan, Sherlock responds, "High-functioning sociopath. With your number." A fake, exaggerated smile enhances his threatening promise ("The Sign of Three").

How the detective fits within the world around him remains a key question throughout *Sherlock*. Even when characters do not question Sherlock's self-diagnosis, they rarely hesitate to use a variety of monikers, including psychopath, freak, and hero. During John and Sherlock's first meeting, Sergeant Sally Donovan (Vinette Robinson) warns a susceptible John about the dissident detective: "He likes [crime]. He gets off on it. The weirder the crime, the more he gets off. And you know what? One day, just showing up won't be enough. One day, we'll be standing around a body, and Sherlock Holmes'll be the one that put it there." When John asks why, Donovan responds, "Because he's a psychopath. Psychopaths get bored" ("A Study in Pink"). At the start of the series, Sherlock is a potentially untrustworthy and threatening character, and his dangerous nature intrigues both the fictional characters and real-world viewers. Especially during the first episode "the viewer can't help feeling that the police [like Donovan] may have a point: with his brusque, obsessive manner and pinched, pale face, this Holmes looks as if he might someday cross over to the wrong side of sanity and the law" (Wren 31). As both audience members and fictional Londoners grapple with their confusion, other suggested terms further complicate Sherlock's representation.

How Sherlock is understood depends on who labels him. The term *freak* casts him as an incomprehensible Other, whereas *hero* appears to place Sherlock on "the side of the angels" ("The Reichenbach Fall"). As a label, *freak* captivates fictional and real-world viewers specifically because it is applied to Sherlock. As film theorist Torben Grodal explains, viewers are naturally intrigued by "deviant phenomenon" (84), and "modern mythical characters" such as James Bond, Dracula, and Sherlock Holmes increase audience interest because each is traditionally considered "bizarre" and "horrific" (85). Deviant behavior eventually becomes acceptable to viewers because the protagonist's morals take precedence, even if they are different from social norms. For example, the severed fingers and decapitated heads that Sherlock stores in the fridge appear disturbing at the start of the show. By the time viewers reach Season Three, however, Sherlock drinking tea that has an accidentally added eyeball is no longer horrific. The scene is played as comedic ("The Sign of Three"), even though the eyeball or decapitated head would be considered disturbing out of context. Within *Sherlock*, different rules can apply because real-world viewers recognize Sherlock's bizarre behavior as necessary for his work. When Donovan continues to call Sherlock a freak, or when Sebastian Wilkes (Bertie Carvel) refers to how everyone at university hated Sherlock because he was a freak even then ("The Blind Banker"), viewers do not agree with the characters' assessments. Even if the label *freak* would most likely be applied to such an individual met in reality, Sherlock dictates viewers' understanding that, within the show, *freak* is a label rejected by both Sherlock and the real-world audience.

Sherlock's quick rejection of the *hero* label further complicates his representation. While real-world viewers and fictional Londoners are ready to apply the *hero* label to Sherlock, especially in later episodes, Sherlock denies the title when he tells John not to "make people into heroes" because they "don't exist and if they did, I wouldn't be one of them" ("The Great Game"). However, in "The Reichenbach Fall," the media within *Sherlock* proclaims him to be the "Reichenbach Hero." Even though the public is eager to claim him as a hero, Sherlock understands the implications the label provides and so thusly rejects it. As with the label *freak*, characters and real-world viewers alike attempt to pin Sherlock into a specific category, and Sherlock refuses any label, even a positive one like *hero*, that has been given to him.

Even the writers were unsure how heroic Sherlock needed to be; Gatiss recounts how the writers wondered "whether it was possible to have an unlikeable hero at the heart of [a] show" (qtd. in Adams 28). In fact, the "unlikeable" nature of such a hero is what makes this label so difficult to apply to Sherlock. Even though he solves his cases and rescues others (frequently John), Sherlock's unconventionality disrupts his heroic persona. Viewers imagine a hero who "[risks his life] to save damsels in distress, thus placing fear of danger lower than loyalty and romantic attachment" (Grodal 124). Sherlock's heroism, however, transcends this narrow definition: if he has any romantic attachments, he certainly does not let them distract him, and he seems to occasionally prioritize solving a case over loyalty to others. For instance, he puts potentially poisonous sugar into John's cup as a test. This event shows how parts of "the hero and the psychopath may be twigs on the same genetic branch" (Lykken 118), and Sherlock's characteristics cannot readily coexist under one label. Sherlock's so-called psychopathic characteristics help him achieve a hero's goals; yet, he defies the definition of *hero* because of his unconventional methods. As viewers surmise Sherlock's complexity, they accept him as a "flawed [hero] who [is] still in the process of discovering who [he is]" (Dondero and Pippin 2).

In accordance with *Sherlock*'s fictional universe, Sherlock the High-Functioning Sociopath can succeed more than Sherlock the Psychopath, Sherlock the Freak, or Sherlock the Hero. Psychopaths are perceived as lacking mental control, similar to psychotic individuals; freaks are repudiated; and heroes have to follow the moral rules of society. Not one of these labels allows Sherlock the mobility needed by a consulting detective. Instead of creating problems for him, the label *sociopath* allows Sherlock to experience benefits that a socially awkward man could not.

From Sherlock's perspective, sociopathy increases his ability to solve cases—the very thing that excites and engages him. By claiming ignorance of social codes, Sherlock can focus solely on his work. Sherlock's interactions with clients and witnesses frequently illustrate this ignorance. He quickly flips between charismatic and cruel, never explaining his actions. As Cumberbatch elaborates, "I think he can be charming. It's something he turns on in order to get something!" (qtd. in Adams 29). If Sherlock needs to convince a stranger to buzz him into an apartment building ("The Blind Banker") or reassure an elderly witness that he is "friendly" ("The Reichenbach Fall"), he turns on what he calls his "charm" (Adams 44). If he needs information immediately, he may scream at a witness to quickly collect it, regardless of how his abrupt interrogation affects her ("The Reichenbach Fall"). Sociopaths do not understand social interactions, but, when Sherlock is working on a case, he simply does not care about politeness. The label *high-functioning sociopath* affords him a certain amount of critical freedom.

Refusing to build attachments also acts as a protective mechanism; Sherlock often grapples with emotions, and he shuts them out mainly in pursuit of protection because "alone protects [him]" ("The Reichenbach Fall"). In the first series, denying emotions ensures and preserves his success. When tested by his foil Jim Moriarty in "The Great Game," Sherlock views empathy for Moriarty's potential victims as a hindrance to each puzzle's effectual resolution. When John specifically asks Sherlock if he cares that there are "lives at stake … actual human lives," he adds that Sherlock needs to hurry and save them; Sherlock responds that, as long as his caring will not help those people, he will "continue not to make that mistake." Even as Sherlock bonds with John personally, he still hopes to subordinate his emotions overall. As foes discover Sherlock's attachment to John, they begin to use him to toy with Sherlock: Moriarty threatens to "burn the heart" out of Sherlock by killing John ("The Great Game"), and Charles Augustus Magnussen exploits Mary's dark past so that Sherlock will betray his own brother Mycroft and protect his best friend John ("His Last Vow"). Despite these situations that illustrate Sherlock's emotional attachments, which occur with greater frequency as the series progresses, Sherlock continually attempts to hold with his sociopathic conviction; he claims that "love [is] a dangerous disadvantage," and "sentiment is a chemical defect found on the losing side" ("A Scandal in Belgravia"). As much as Sherlock tries to remain solitary, however, he cannot do so because John Watson prevents his self-imposed emotional isolation.

John clarifies that no one label can thoroughly encapsulate Sherlock's dynamic character.

The Fundamental Need for This John Watson

Sherlock's approach to human interaction, especially toward the start of the series, has never been all that polite. Audience members and additional characters alike find fault with the consulting detective, and this reaction is unsurprising; yet, by as early as the end of Season Two, protagonist Sherlock has forged a bond with his television audience. Part of this connection develops due to distance. As Cumberbatch notes, "[t]he audience likes him because they don't have to live with him, they can just sit back and enjoy him. He's blissfully rude, entertainingly irreverent, bordering on sociopathic" (qtd. in Adams 28). The predominant link, however, is built on Sherlock and John's friendship. Sherlock's lack of emotional attachments and his personal diagnosis of sociopathy craft him as an initial Other in the show; naturally, the strange and unknowable Sherlock is consistently rejected by the majority of society in fictional London. While Sherlock is "too ruthless and uncaring of others to be the heart of the series" (Treble 86), John moves Sherlock from elevated sociopath to accessible human being through their "bromantic, crime-stopping" friendship (Jensen 92). John is that paramount connection between the viewing audience and Sherlock.

John's Counterbalancing
Friendship with Sherlock

Sherlock rarely welcomes anyone into his life; however, he is uncommonly eager to discuss his work with John and even gains John's professional (or personal) opinions. It would be easy to assert that John is "simply a decent, ordinary man" (qtd. in Adams 51), but Sherlock is able to bond with John because he and Sherlock have that basic tenet needed for solid friendships: common interests. Sherlock is undeniably unpredictable, and, frankly, John as "a military veteran who suffers from posttraumatic stress disorder after a tour in Afghanistan" is not so stable himself (Wren 31).

The trust of this bond must exist on both sides to remain successful; Sherlock has to desire friendship with John, and John with Sherlock. The best friends have a unique friendship and a certain method of working together. From their first meeting, Sherlock hesitates to leave the flat without John and instead convinces John to join him in more danger—just what he knows the military veteran craves. He may leave John to find the pink suitcase, but he immediately brings John in on his deductions ("A Study in Pink"). Their friendship escalates because Sherlock is willing to "count on Watson as a friend," and John starts to "see through some of Sherlock's ego-driven bluster" (Robert). John and Sherlock have become so close by Season Three that, when Sherlock lists off possible best man options for John at his upcoming wedding to Mary, John proclaims Sherlock and Mary as "the two people that [he loves] and [cares] about most in the world," and he asks Sherlock to be his best man ("The Sign of Three"). Inevitably, John is able to get close to Sherlock because the pair manages not only to "complete one another," but also to "fix one another" and make each other "clearly stronger" (Adams 83).

John Directs All Audiences

While the visual medium of television creates a somewhat omniscient viewpoint, *Sherlock* steadily revolves around John. He proves key to pulling viewers into the narrative so they can experience Sherlock. For instance, following Sherlock's faked suicide, viewers get little of Sherlock's story beyond his interactions with his brother Mycroft prior to his reunion with John ("The Empty Hearse"). Television viewers again engage with Sherlock once he is rescued by his brother Mycroft in Serbia, thereby allowing Sherlock to return to John's life. This event follows with *Sherlock*'s typical structure; the audience only joins Sherlock if John is at least somewhat involved. Examples include the retelling of Sherlock's death via John's therapy session ("The Reichenbach Fall") and John's discovery of Sherlock in a crack house a month after John's wedding ("His Last Vow"). It seems viewers can only follow Sherlock if John is also present.

Incredibly, even when the character of John is manifested within Sherlock's mind during "The Abominable Bride," and therefore is at the whim of the consulting detective's thoughts, Sherlock still presents the case through John: the story starts with John at war, John is the narrator for viewers and *Strand* magazine writer for Londoners, viewers meet Sherlock along with John at the start of the episode, and John, at the end of the episode, claims the official role of "a storyteller." Even within his own mind palace, Sherlock does not solely take over the main role. John is obviously not in every scene of the episode. However, he appears again before the hallucinations end in order to give Sherlock the strength to defeat Moriarty at the Reichenbach Falls, telling Moriarty that "there's always two of us—don't you read the *Strand*?" John then kicks Moriarty off the cliff to his death and gives Sherlock permission to jump off the falls himself in order to wake up from his hallucinations, showcasing again that John as storyteller is in control of the narrative ("The Abominable Bride"). Along this similar thread, writer Moffat goes farther in "Sherlock Uncovered: The Return," claiming that John Watson is actually the story's main character. He asserts that everything is "filtered through him," making it "his story."

Peter Stockwell's deictic shift theory, explained in his book *Cognitive Poetics: An Introduction,* especially illuminates how John allows television viewers to access Sherlock at all. According to deictic shift theory, "readers can see things virtually from the perspective of the character or narrator inside the text-world, and construct a rich context by resolving deictic expressions from that viewpoint" (47); therefore, readers (or, in this case viewers) interact and move within a text as presented and manipulated by the writer(s). Viewers navigate the text via characters and understand the plotlines through the continuous alterations to both the plot and the characters. One example within *Sherlock* is in "The Hounds of Baskerville," when viewers first go into Sherlock's mind palace with him. While Baskerville's Dr. Stapleton is only provided John's brief explanation, viewers see the information from Sherlock's perspective: he flips through countless possible associations to his current clues, including references to the Liberty Bell and Elvis Presley's "Hound Dog" ("The Hounds of Baskerville"). Additionally, each deictic field is typically arranged around a "relatively central" character (47–48), which further focuses the viewer's attention. In this example, John sets up the scene by explaining the mind-palace concept, but Sherlock remains the center: he is either the focus of John's conversation, or he is literally sorting through data in his mind palace. Most importantly, such elements from the series refocus viewers' attention—context tells viewers where the important information related to the narrative is stored inside the writing, as dictated by the series creator.

Even though Sherlock is shown navigating through his mind palace, John is the character directing the audience's attention. John has to introduce the concept of the mind palace *before* viewers can understand what Sherlock is doing or even follow the visual effects representing his thought process. Although John leaves during the scene, he remains the lens, the starting point; he provides the perspective so Sherlock's exploits and peculiarities at the deictic center can be known. John is the main character, and Sherlock is the exciting, incomprehensible stranger the audience may start to see.

John as the Middleman

The friendship that John and Sherlock share allows John to see through Sherlock's imposed sociopathy; when John leads audiences into Sherlock's narrative, he allows them to see past it as well. Because John represents the common man but also desires danger as much as Sherlock, he can understand both perspectives, making him, in a sense, multilingual. When humans interact, they employ theory of mind to understand each other's thoughts, desires, and goals (Boyd). Sherlock, unsurprisingly, is very difficult to understand in this way; however, John manages to employ theory of mind and understand Sherlock. He transfers his understanding to the fictional Londoners via his blog or the television viewers on screen. Only through John's insight into both Sherlock and Sherlock's potential audiences can an authentic experience of Sherlock become available.

Even Sherlock uses John as the middleman between himself and audiences. When Sherlock tells John not to "mention the unsolved ones" on his blog, John disagrees:

> John: People want to know you're human.
> Sherlock: Why?
> John: Because they're interested.
> Sherlock: No, they're not. (Pause) Why are they? ["A Scandal in Belgravia"].

In this conversation, Sherlock demonstrates his inability to fully connect with others around him. Not only does Sherlock believe that the readers of John's blog are not interested in who he is as a person beyond his ability as a consulting detective, but he admits that John could have a better idea about what others are thinking. Readers and viewers are dependent on John to illuminate Sherlock's character while Sherlock in turn relies on John to help him connect with society at large.

John Makes the Detective a Better Man

Selected as best man for John's wedding (much to his surprise), Sherlock is required to give a best man's speech (which he only gives after John's prompting, making protagonist John still the ultimate catalyst). The speech is a paramount moment within Season Three: a transition from the crime-solving duo that is Sherlock Holmes and John Watson to the married couple that is John and Mary Watson. Yet, even as this shift occurs, John and Sherlock's friendship, especially the affection Sherlock holds for John, is the undeniable emphasis. The unique blend of Sherlock's personality and intelligence, in writer Moffat's mind, could only produce one kind of speech: "I thought what Sherlock would do is he'd sit there and think, *Everyone's gonna think I'm gonna make a right cock-up of this. Everyone thinks I'm going to screw it up. So, I'm going to make them* think *that, and then of course I'm going to say something lovely.* And I always thought he'd do it well because he's a genius, and he cares about his mate—he wouldn't let his mate down" (qtd. in Martin). Moffat calls this Sherlock's "bullshitting," and it is a combination of his acerbic words and infamous charm. Though neither the wedding attendees nor the television audience is aware of his intentions at the speech's start, Sherlock clearly attempts to create a contrast between himself and John. Yet, this false dichotomy, built upon Sherlock's continued claim to sociopathy, does not hold by the speech's end.

Sherlock starts off his toast by rejecting weddings, the human experience, and love itself. Instead, he professes to prefer his sociopathic values: "All emotions, and in particular love, stand opposed to the pure, cold reason I hold above all things. A wedding is, in my considered opinion, nothing short of a celebration of all that is false and specious and irrational and sentimental in this ailing and morally compromised world" ("The Sign of Three"). He insinuates that the bridesmaids are unattractive, the vicar is stupid, and organized religion is senseless. At one point, he even implies that the only assistance John provides during their cases is his lesser, stupider mind. As Moffat indicates, all these comments are purposely vile; Sherlock wants his audience, which is gathered to celebrate John and his marriage to Mary, to recognize that Sherlock is "the most unpleasant, rude, ignorant and all-round obnoxious arsehole that anyone could possibly have the misfortune to meet." Immediately after insulting the majority of his audience, however, Sherlock then paints John as his clear opposite: Sherlock states that he "never expected to be ... the best friend of the bravest and kindest and wisest human being [he has] ever had the good fortune of knowing." In fact, Sherlock insists that he is "a ridiculous man redeemed only by the warmth and constancy of [John's] friendship" ("The Sign of Three").

Up until this point in the speech, Sherlock has planned every bit of his presentation. He knows the people present are there for John (another illustration of how John is truly the main character within the series). Sherlock realizes that most people do not like him. Yet, he is the excitement within this particular text: the deictic center that allows John to provide the forward momentum in the narrative. Sherlock's insight into his and John's relationship surprises both John and the real and fictional audiences. Additionally, Sherlock's keen perception of the roles he and John must play within that relationship astonishes all the listeners. The speech has Sherlock flipping the tone around right at the end: acting as if he botched the entire affair and then proceeding to laud John beyond measure.

The *reaction* to the speech is *not* what Sherlock expects, and this moment is when John the middleman must step in. Those at the wedding visually react to Sherlock's words, some even starting to cry, and Sherlock definitely notices. Although he initially directs his questions to the crowd, asking what is wrong and why they are "doing that," Sherlock looks quickly to the "multilingual" John for answers. He worries that he has "[done] it wrong," and John assures him that he did not. When John pulls Sherlock in for a hug, however, Sherlock remains focused on his task, noting that he has not "finished yet." He insists that he has funny stories about John to share ("The Sign of Three"), but the stories are not the true reason Sherlock wants out of this moment. Once John has "translated" for Sherlock that he has not failed, Sherlock desires to reach for his emotionless, sociopathic persona again in order to feel safe. More than perhaps any other moment in *Sherlock*, this scene encapsulates the struggle Sherlock faces in his attempts to perform sociopathy and remain distanced. Moffat addresses Sherlock's deteriorating attempts:

> He wants to think he's a high-functioning sociopath. He's not a sociopath, nor is he high-functioning.... He is at root an absolutely ordinary man with a very, very big brain. He's repressed his emotions, his passions, his desires, in order to make his brain work better—in itself, a very emotional decision, and it does suggest that he must be very emotional if he thinks emotions get in the way. I just think Sherlock Holmes must be bursting! [qtd. in Martin].

All of the emotions induced by the best man speech reveal Sherlock's character in its entirety. The emotions motivating Sherlock's pursuit of sociopathy burst out and, ironically, are shown to both the television audience and those gathered to celebrate John's wedding. Of course, those emotions are only present because of John.

Conclusion

Sherlock claims sociopathy in the very first episode of the show and fiercely clings to it at the end of Season Three. Even as Sherlock carries out arguably the most emotionally-fueled action of his life by shooting Magnussen (thereby ensuring the safety of John's future and the destruction of his own), he returns to his self-diagnosis with a slight twist. Sherlock tells Magnussen, just before he shoots him: "Oh, do your research. I'm not a hero. I'm a high-functioning sociopath" ("His Last Vow"). By now, *Sherlock*'s audience recognizes that Sherlock fits neither label.

The mystery has been solved: Sherlock simply claims sociopathy in order to successfully complete his work and divorce himself from perilous emotions. Both the audience within fictional London and the audience in the real world can accept Sherlock, regardless of his behavior, thanks to his bond with his best friend John. Indeed, John can interpret Sherlock to both audiences and support Sherlock by translating social expectations for him. What Moffat terms as the consulting detective's inherently "horrible" and "shocking" behavior is a front, one that breaks apart more with each new series of episodes. Sherlock's desperate desire for distance from emotional connection seems only to make his audiences, and John, more desperate in their desire to connect with him. Any attempts for Sherlock to "keep himself distant, divorce himself from feelings" will fail due those "interesting ... emotions" ("The Hounds of Baskerville"), and *Sherlock* viewers remain entranced by the duo of the consulting detective and his blogger, who continue to evolve inseparably.

WORKS CITED

"The Abominable Bride." *Sherlock*. Writ. Mark Gatiss, Steven Moffat. Dir. Douglas Mackinnon. PBS.org. 11 Jan. 2016. Web. 18 Jan. 2016.

Adams, Guy. *The Sherlock Files: The Official Companion to the Hit Television Series*. New York: It Books, 2013. Print.

American Psychiatric Association. *Diagnostic and Statistical Manual of Mental Disorders: DSM-5*. 5th ed. Washington, DC: American Psychiatric Publishing, 2013. Print.

"The Blind Banker." *Sherlock*. Writ. Stephen Thompson. Dir. Euros Lyn. BBC, 2010. Netflix. Web. 9 Nov. 2013.

Boyd, Brian. *On the Origin of Stories: Evolution, Cognition, and Fiction*. Cambridge: Belknap Press of Harvard University Press, 2009. Print.

Coppa, Francesca. "Sherlock as Cyborg: Bridging Mind and Body." *Sherlock and Transmedia Fandom*. Ed. Louisa Ellen Stein and Kristina Busse. Jefferson, NC: McFarland, 2012. 210–223. Print.

Dondero, Jennifer, and Sabrina Pippin. "It's Traumatic Stress, My Dear Mr. Watson: Mental Illness in the BBC's *Sherlock*." PCA/ACA. 2014, Chicago. 1–10. Print.

"The Empty Hearse." *Sherlock: Series Three*. Writ. Mark Gatiss, Steven Moffat. Dir. Jeremy Lovering. BBC, 2014. MP4 video. 11 Mar. 2014.

"The Great Game." *Sherlock*. Writ. Mark Gatiss. Dir. Paul McGuigan. BBC, 2010. Netflix. Web. 9 Nov. 2013.

Grodal, Torben. *Embodied Visions: Evolution, Emotion, Culture, and Film*. New York: Oxford University Press, 2009. Print.

Hare, Robert. Interview. "Robert Hare—Psychopath/Sociopath—The Difference." YouTube. 20 Feb. 2013. Web. 13 Apr. 2014.

"His Last Vow." *Sherlock: Series Three*. Writ. Steven Moffat. Dir. Nick Hurran. BBC, 2014. MP4 video. 11 Mar. 2014.

"The Hounds of Baskerville." *Sherlock*. Writ. Mark Gatiss. Dir. Paul McGuigan. BBC, 2012. Netflix. Web. 10 Nov. 2013.

Jensen, Jeff. "Sherlock." *Entertainment Weekly* 1296/1297 (2014): 92. Academic Search Complete. Web. 1 May 2015.

Konnikova, Maria. "Stop Calling Sherlock a Sociopath! Thanks, a Psychologist." io9. com. 8 Nov. 2012. Web. 13 Apr. 2014.

Lowry, Brian. "Surefire *Sherlock*." *Variety* 426.13 (2012): 39. OmniFile Full Text Select (H. W. Wilson). Web. 1 May 2015.

Lykken, David T. *The Antisocial Personalities*. Hillsdale, NJ: Lawrence Erlbaum Associates, 1995. Print.

Martin, Denise. "Steven Moffat Explains the Origins of *Sherlock*'s Best Man Speech." *Vulture*. 27 Jan. 2014. Web. 3 May 2015.

"The Reichenbach Fall." *Sherlock*. Writ. Stephen Thompson. Dir. Toby Haynes. BBC, 2012. Netflix. Web. 10 Nov. 2013.

Robert, Bianco. "Exemplary, My Dear Watson…." *USA Today*. Academic Search Complete. n.d. Web. 1 May 2015.

"A Scandal in Belgravia." *Sherlock*. Writ. Steven Moffat. Dir. Paul McGuigan. BBC, 2012. Netflix. Web. 10 Nov. 2013.

"Sherlock Uncovered: The Return." *Sherlock: Series Three*. BBC, 2014. MP4 video. 16 Mar. 2014.

"The Sign of Three." *Sherlock: Series Three.* Writ. Stephen Thompson, Steven Moffat, and Mark Gatiss. Dir. Colm McCarthy. BBC, 2014. MP4 video. 11 Mar. 2014.

Stockwell, Peter. *Cognitive Poetics: An Introduction.* New York: Routledge-Cavendish, 2002. Print.

"A Study in Pink." *Sherlock.* Writ. Steven Moffat. Dir. Paul McGuigan. BBC, 2010. Netflix. Web. 9 Nov. 2013.

Treble, Patricia. "The Ultimate Bromance." *Maclean's* 123.42 (2010): 86. Academic Search Complete. Web. 1 May 2015.

Wren, Celia. "The Game's On." *Commonweal* 137.18 (2010): 31. Academic Search Complete. Web. 1 May 2015.

The Evolution of
James Moriarty
How Villains Mirror Cultural Anxieties

HEATHER POWERS

The veneration of the villain is the latest craze in popular culture, perhaps because villains, as portrayed on television or film in the 2010s, are dead sexy: In *Doctor Who* (2005-present), The Master comes on to The Doctor almost as often as he or she threatens him; in the Harry Potter films (*Harry Potter and the Goblet of Fire*, 2005; *Harry Potter and the Deathly Hallows: Part 1*, 2010; and *Harry Potter and the Deathly Hallows: Part 2*, 2011), Ralph Fiennes's amazing facial structure (almost) overshadows Voldemort's lack of a nose; and in *The Dark Knight* (2008) Heath Ledger's Joker defines this generation's tragic "hero," despite his character's lack of redeeming qualities. The truly hateful villain, such as King Joffrey in *Game of Thrones*(2011-present), is the exception rather than the rule.

Moriarty, as adapted in the Guy Ritchie-directed movie *Sherlock Holmes: A Game of Shadows* (2011) and in the BBC's *Sherlock* (2010-present), provides an excellent recent example of the evolution of a villain into a handsome, charismatic character. His development clearly shows the influence of cultural change on iconic characters and the startling transformation of a villain.

Professor James Moriarty only appears twice in Sir Arthur Conan Doyle's Sherlock Holmes stories (in "The Adventure of the Final Problem" and "The Valley of Fear"), though he is retroactively placed at the center of five additional "past" cases ("The Adventure of the Empty House," "The Adventure of the Norwood Builder," "The Adventure of the Missing Three-Quarter," "The Adventure of the Illustrious Client," and "His Last Bow"). In "The Final Problem," Holmes places Moriarty at the center of many of the crimes he and

John Watson have investigated: "He is the Napoleon of crime.... He is the organizer of half that is evil and of nearly all that is undetected in this great city. He is a genius, a philosopher, an abstract thinker. He has a brain of the first order. He sits motionless, like a spider in the center of its web, but that web has a thousand radiations, and he knows well every quiver of each of them" (Conan Doyle). Holmes claims that once the police have Moriarty in custody, it will enable "the clearing up of over forty mysteries."

Through James Moriarty, Conan Doyle addresses a great fear during his time—the fear of the "criminal class." In the 1890s, middle-class citizens engaged in what we would today call "profiling" and took for granted that criminals could be identified just by looking at them. Conan Doyle plays upon these fears and gives them a twist when he has Holmes use the youngest members of the criminal class for good. In *The Sign of Four*, Holmes tells Watson about his network of street-urchin spies, known as the Baker Street Irregulars. Holmes explains, "They can go everywhere, see everything, over-hear every one." While Holmes is using his "disreputable little scarecrows" to solve crimes, they likely picked a few pockets along the way. Holmes does not try to reform the Baker Street Irregulars so much as provide some legal means of financial support to offset their other, possibly illegal means of sur-viving on London's streets.

In contrast to the Baker Street Irregulars, the adult criminal class at which Moriarty is the center is much more dangerous. Moriarty illustrates the ultimate outcome of the descent into criminality. He is far from the entic-ing figure that Moriarty will cut in future representations. Holmes describes the physical signs of Moriarty's depravity in "The Final Problem": "He is extremely tall and thin, his forehead domes out in a white curve, and his two eyes are deeply sunken in his head [which] is forever slowly oscillating from side to side in a curiously reptilian fashion." Such an image is hardly the stuff of seductive, charming television or film incarnations of Moriarty so popular in the 2010s.

Conan Doyle's Holmes stories originally appeared in periodicals with illustrations by Sidney Paget, whose illustrations for "The Final Problem" capture the physical similarities between Holmes and Moriarty. While Mori-arty is cadaverous and reptilian, Holmes resembles a bird of prey, "His eyes were sharp and piercing ... and his thin, hawk-like nose gave his whole expression an air of alertness and decision" (Conan Doyle, "A Study in Scar-let"). Both Holmes and Moriarty are tall and thin and appear to be almost consumed by their rigorous intellectual activities. The two characters' mir-roring of one another is clearly indicated by Conan Doyle, although Holmes is on the side of good, whereas Moriarty is his opposite—an evil influence on society. Neither of them possesses the charm that will characterize their later depictions on television or film.

Paget's depiction of Holmes's and Moriarty's tumble into the Reichenbach Falls in "The Final Problem" takes its cue from the physical and intellectual equality of the two men. Moriarty acknowledges, "It has been a duel between you and me ... [but] you will never beat me. If you are clever enough to bring destruction upon me, rest assured that I shall do as much to you." Holmes's response shows the heroic nature that separates him from Moriarty: "You have paid me several compliments.... Let me pay to one in return when I say that if I were assured of the former eventuality I would, in the interests of the public, cheerfully accept the latter." Moriarty's reply to Holmes's self-sacrificing threat—"I can promise you the one, but not the other"—cements his status as villain. This ultimatum also illustrates the sang-froid that later audiences would come to find so irresistible. While in Conan Doyle's time readers would be justified in their fear of "the criminal class," current viewers feel secure enough about law enforcement or national security that they relish the hint of danger represented by Moriarty.

While Conan Doyle's and Paget's Holmes and Moriarty cannot be described as physically attractive, their superior intellect and refusal to back down make them extremely compelling. While Holmes's nobility is admirable, Moriarty's cold-bloodedness is fascinating. Like the reptiles that he resembles, Moriarty holds us in his gaze. That mesmerizing power remains in later incarnations of Moriarty, although, like Holmes, he becomes sexier in *A Game of Shadows* and *Sherlock*.

Portrayals of Power in A Game of Shadows

Conan Doyle's and Paget's Moriarty represents all that was corrupt in their society. Readers were meant to admire Holmes and revile Moriarty, canon's ultimate villain. By the 2010s, however, the question of whether audiences should admire the hero or the villain became more difficult to answer, because villains, as much as heroes, had become charismatic, powerful, and seductive.

In *Sherlock Holmes: A Game of Shadows*, the physical appearance of archenemies Holmes and Moriarty are differentiated in a far different way that they were in canon. In this film, Moriarty (Jared Harris) is more outwardly and conventionally impressive than Holmes (Robert Downey, Jr.). Throughout the film Moriarty is impeccably dressed in a wardrobe ranging from Don's robes to formal tuxedos. Holmes dresses in such a bohemian style that at one point he is mistaken for a street beggar and in another he blends in perfectly with a band of gypsies. Through appearance alone, Moriarty is more stylishly eye catching and desirable.

The film's depiction of the initial meeting between the two men illustrates their physical differences in opposition to Conan Doyle's description in "The Final Problem." In Conan Doyle's version of their meeting, Moriarty catches Holmes wrong-footed by appearing in Holmes's rooms unexpectedly: "the door opened and Professor Moriarty stood before me. My nerves are fairly proof … but I must confess to a start" ("The Final Problem"). In contrast, Moriarty has a home field advantage in the film version of his initial confrontation with Holmes, and Holmes is unable to surprise or startle him.

Holmes is more prepared for his encounter with Moriarty. He seeks him out and is armed with a copy of Moriarty's latest work, *The Dynamics of an Asteroid*, which he presents for an inscription. In a publicity still that captures the scene, Moriarty and Holmes stand in front of a blackboard covered with illegible, but impressive mathematical formulas, a set-up reminiscent of the crime board on which Holmes has been tracking Moriarty's criminal activities.

Holmes is wearing a dark-colored striped velvet smoking jacket with Chinese frog fastenings. His shirt collar is undone, his hair is mussed, and he is unshaven. Moriarty looks more respectable. He is wearing a British professor's robes open over a suit jacket, waistcoat, formal dress shirt, and silk tie. His clothing is color-coordinated in shades of brown and crimson. His hair is neatly combed, and his beard is trimmed. Whereas Holmes often looks dashing in other circumstances, he looks like a ruffian in this setting and when compared with Moriarty. In this first confrontation, Moriarty is far more appealing to audiences than Holmes, and Harris's character is far more respectable and desirable than Conan Doyle's original.

In place of Conan Doyle's repulsive criminal outsider, this Moriarty is a shining example of all that is "right" with the upper class world. While audiences know that Moriarty is working for the destruction of this ideal, his flawless representation of our upwardly mobile desires is entrancing. He brandishes privilege like a walking stick. Canon Moriarty's power to entrance is built in to this portrayal, but the result is far more beguiling when an attractive, confident pillar of the community represents societal evils.

The contrast between Holmes and Moriarty, as well as Moriarty's exemplification of the suave villain, is even clearer in the film poster. Moriarty stands in semi-profile, with his right side turned away from the viewer. The mountainside resort at the Reichenbach Falls is behind him. Moriarty is dressed in formalwear, completed with a top hat. His fingers are steepled in front of his chest in the classic "plotting villain" pose. In a convention mirrored in a publicity shot of Andrew Scott as Moriarty for the BBC's *Sherlock*, Harris's face is tilted downward, and he looks up at the viewer through his eyelashes. This pose is generally used in pictures meant to portray the subject as seductive. Indeed, in addition to being well dressed and highly respected, Harris's Moriarty is charming, as Scott's Moriarty can be when he chooses, as his similarly posed publicity shot implies.

Harris's Moriarty is not only attractive and intelligent but also astute in business, a talent which creates its own allure. When *A Game of Shadows* came out, big business was frequently in the news in the United States. The American public has been mesmerized by the actions of successful business-men who are showmen with power. Like his cultural contemporaries, Mori-arty's motive is profit. As part of a shrinking U.S. middle class, many moviegoers may admire Moriarty's success while being horrified at the way he manipulates politics globally. In *A Game of Shadows,* Moriarty desires a world war, which he believes is inevitable anyway, as a way to make profit. Moriarty explains to Holmes that "hidden within the unconscious, there is an insatiable desire for conflict. So, you're not fighting me, so much as you are the human condition. All I want to do is own the bullets and bandages." Moriarty cares nothing for what he might call the "collateral damage" of human suffering in war; he simply wants to profit from the violence. In this he sees himself not as a monster, but as a successful businessman.

This variety of villainy has been all too commonly reported in the early 21st century during the time the movie was made and released. In 2009, Bernard L. Madoff admitted that his wildly successful investment funds were basically a huge Ponzi Scheme that bilked investors of millions of dollars. Before his conviction, Madoff looked like the epitome of a man who could be trusted. He has puppy dog eyes and was commonly pictured wearing a slightly rumpled dress shirt, sans jacket. He seemed like a man who would work tirelessly for his clients. *Time* described how, "for years, [Madoff] was regarded a pillar of the investment community, a taciturn superstar whose clockwork returns had clients nearly breaking down his door" ("Top Ten Crooked CEOs").

The *Wall Street Journal* quotes one of Madoff's victims, 83-year-old Jack Cutter, who was reduced to stocking shelves at Safeway when he was 79 years old because of Madoff's schemes: "He carried it off with great aplomb. He was a master of what he did…. There's a master of everything. I guess I've developed a little respect for his chicanery" (Strumpf). Contrast this image with the ugly face Madoff showed in prison. One of Madoff's most infamous quotes came from a report that *New York* magazine published in June 2010 describing his reaction to being in prison: "'Fuck my victims,' he said, loud enough for other inmates to hear. 'I carried them for twenty years, and now I'm doing 150 years'" (Fishman). Like Moriarty, Madoff cares only for profit, not for the victims of his business plan.

The Madoff scandal was merely the coup de grace in a recession that affected the middle class in the United States beginning around 2007. The housing bubble crash caused many to lose their homes and trust in bankers, while Madoff and others like him stole retirement funds. These few examples represent a much larger distrust of authority figures, ranging from local police to bankers or investors to elected officials. Many people felt that no powerful, successful man could be trusted. Within this setting, Warner Bros.' 2011 Moriarty is the perfect, timely example of a powerful, charming man working behind the scenes to destroy hardworking citizens. Like some real-world "characters" in the news, he is, indeed, the spider at the center of a very corrupt web.

In *A Game of Shadows*, Moriarty is less of a criminal mastermind and more of a corrupt businessman. As we have seen, the latter was more feared in the early 21st century. This Professor plots on the grand scale—he controls a network of plots that reaches far beyond London, all the way to the Continent, and aims to start a world war. Moriarty claims that he has no interest in the details of the conflicts he sparks. He just wants to profit from them.

Harris's Moriarty received a lot of attention in a highly popular film. *A Game of Shadows* outdid its predecessor, *Sherlock Holmes* (2009), by more than $21 million in worldwide theater receipts. It also outranked the 2009 film, reaching number nine worldwide for 2011 ("Sherlock Holmes: A Game of Shadows," *Box Office Mojo*), whereas *Sherlock Holmes*, despite two Oscar nominations, only reached number ten ("Sherlock Holmes," *Box Office Mojo*). The popularity of *A Game of Shadows* certainly had more to do with fan-baiting previews showing Downey in drag than it had to do with the promise of Harris as Moriarty, but there can be no denying that Professor James Moriarty was a well-known figure in the United States after this film, even if he may not have been before.

The Villain with Many Faces

Given the popularity of Moriarty on film in 2011 and the trend toward charismatic villains, it is fascinating to consider the fact that Jim Moriarty was not part of the very earliest game plan for the BBC's *Sherlock*. When crafting the outline for the unaired original pilot version of "A Study in Pink," series' co-creators Steven Moffat and Mark Gatiss were uncertain whether the general viewing public would recognize the name Moriarty. Following a focus testing session of the 60-minute episode, the pair received a definitive affirmative answer. Those who had seen that pilot were not only aware of Moriarty, but they wanted to see him in any future version of the show (Sherlockology, "Sherlock").

In the first episode of Season One, "A Study in Pink," audiences are introduced to the man whom Sherlock declares "could be called my arch enemy." His name, although it started with M, surprised viewers. As the writers at Sherlockology point out,

When Mark Gatiss first appears onscreen in a "Study in Pink," the first time viewer can be completely forgiven for instantly assuming that the individual we're seeing is Moriarty.... The reveal that this is actually Mycroft Holmes resets every assumption we could make. He has in his limited screen time, after all, fulfilled what we think a version of Moriarty could potentially be like in this modern adaptation, and now all bets were off [Sherlockology, "Sherlock"].

In his bespoke suit, complete with classic umbrella, pocket chain, pocket handkerchief, and tie pin, Gatiss's appearance exemplifies the kind of high-class villainy audiences have grown to expect from Moriarty. Like Harris's Moriarty, Gatiss's Moriarty presents himself as a powerful man. Later Sherlock (Benedict Cumberbatch) affirms audience's first impression when he tells John Watson (Martin Freeman) that his brother "*is* the British government."

Of course, the show's creators were simply playing with audience expectations. Their "real" Moriarty is a far different character than audiences expected. After realizing the popularity of Professor James Moriarty, Moffat explains, the creative team decided to go against expectations. They noted that Conan Doyle's Moriarty has been the model for "almost every supervillain that followed him" ("The Making of Moriarty"). He is "smug, supercilious, seemingly courteous." In contrast, Moffat and Gatiss decided to have a "genuinely mad, frightening, unpredictable psycho-Moriarty" ("The Making of Moriarty"). Despite his madness, their Moriarty is a savvy businessman, as well as a storyteller, an actor, and a thief. Moriarty's resistance to being held to one identity is what makes him so appealing to viewers. They never know what to expect next; the character remains fresh in every episode.

The audience's expectations of just what and who Moriarty is are allowed to build in the first two of three episodes in Season One. Moriarty is just a name in the first episode, and viewers do not see the man himself until episode three, "The Great Game." Jim from IT, as Moriarty is known in his first appearance on screen, is as an unlikely suspect for a supervillain: a young, nervous gay man who seems to be using Molly Hooper as a beard, or worse, as a means to meet Sherlock. (He is nothing like Conan Doyle's repellent, yet powerful Moriarty or Harris's polished gentleman.) As the BBC's Moriarty says to Sherlock during their eventual overt meeting, he enjoys hiding in plain sight ("The Great Game").

Sherlockology summarizes the way in which Scott reinvents Moriarty as "loud, wild, very funny, brilliant, knowingly insane and altogether extremely dangerous" (Sherlockology, "Sherlock"). Moriarty's charisma is closely tied to his mercurial nature. He is by turns seductive and terrifying, keeping viewers in a constant state of expectation.

The first meeting between Sherlock and Moriarty highlights Moriarty's changeable nature. While in Conan Doyle's story Moriarty accosts Holmes in his study, and in the Warner Bros.' film Holmes accosts Moriarty in his academic office, in *Sherlock* the pair meet beside a darkened swimming pool where Moriarty murdered a young man years earlier. Although Moriarty does later visit Sherlock at 221B Baker Street, this first face-to-face conversation determines the playing field for all other interactions. After Moriarty spares John's and Sherlock's lives, calling off his snipers and allowing Sherlock time to remove the bombs strapped to John's chest, he returns to threaten them again. Moriarty comments on his own about-face; he is "sooo changeable." He identifies his own lack of a stable identity and admits, "It is a weakness with me. But, to be fair to myself, it *is* my only weakness" ("The Great Game").

While this scene establishes Moriarty's madness, it also shows him as being able to present himself as conventionally powerful. Like Gatiss's Mycroft, he cuts quite a dashing figure. While Jim from IT dresses casually in a white undershirt, Moriarty cites the exclusive nature of his suit when he brushes himself off after being "held hostage" by John during an abortive attempt to allow Sherlock to escape Jim's clutches. He snarkily comments, "Westwood," to emphasize his high-end wardrobe ("The Great Game").

Sherlock costume designer Sarah Arthur describes how she paired the suit, which has a skull-and-crossbones lining, with a Spencer Hart round-collar shirt, because it had "a slightly period feel," and an Alexander McQueen tie with skull on it, because "it had a slightly sinister feel" ("Wardrobe"). As Moffat points out, Moriarty is "up against a dapper Sherlock, and since he's just as vain, he would be unlikely to let [the villains'] side down" ("The Making of Moriarty").

In *Sherlock,* Sherlock and Moriarty share more than a debonair fashion sense, yet another deviation from canon. Gatiss says, "It's a cliché to say they're two sides of the same coin but that's clearly true" ("The Making of Moriarty"). Moriarty's way of describing his job (a consulting criminal) mirrors Sherlock's self-description as "the world's only consulting detective." Like Sherlock, Moriarty is a "specialist." Moriarty tells Sherlock that he has given him a glimpse, "[j]ust a teensy glimpse of what I've got going on out there in the big bad world" ("The Great Game").

At the same time, the two men are contrasted. Moffat says, "In our series, as in the original, Sherlock is first introduced as a cold, amoral reasoner, fascinated by the game for its own sake." Moriarty enjoys the game because it allows him to play.

Scott points to this playful side of Moriarty: "Even though he's an international super-villain, I think he takes great pleasure in what he does. So it was important that I really enjoyed it and we got the sense that Moriarty is really playful about it and not serious. And then sometimes you think that he really *is* serious about it ... sometimes he's massively scary and sometimes he's just charm itself" ("The Making of Moriarty"). In contrast to Harris's poised professor or Conan Doyle's withered "reptile," Scott's Moriarty has a madcap appeal. In the 2010s, all bets are off when it comes to identifying our enemies. With the rise of social media, school shootings, and seemingly random acts of terrorism, that charming neighbor could be society's worst nightmare. Moriarty's playfulness is more terrifying than the deadly earnestness of either previous depiction.

Even his outfit during his trial at Old Bailey and his subsequent visit to 221B Baker Street epitomizes the stereotypical "wolf in sheep's clothing." Scott says that he "kind of like[d] the idea of him wearing a light suit, not something that you would necessarily see on a stereotypical villain—the big black cloak and the black hat—and I just wanted to do sort of the opposite of the stuff I may have imagined Moriarty to wear" ("The Making of Moriarty").

Moriarty's grey suit and grey shoes blur the line between black and white, representing his mixed persona. Whereas Jim from IT and, later, Richard Brook, "The Storyteller," are harmless and rather shy, Moriarty is completely terrifying. His round-collared shirt mirrors his earlier appearance in the thoroughly wicked Westwood, and his wolf's-head pin shows the true nature of his villainy. As Moriarty says, "Every fairy tale needs a good, old-fashioned villain" ("The Reichenbach Fall"). Moriarty's identities may shift in a kaleidoscopic manner, but he is always the villain.

While he plays the villain in the stories he weaves around his interactions with Sherlock, Moriarty paints Sherlock as the "hero" in "The Reichenbach Fall." Moriarty realizes that he and Sherlock are two sides of the same coin, and he takes this opportunity to flip sides.

Moriarty frames Sherlock for kidnapping two children a la Hansel and Gretel and as the criminal mastermind who hired Richard Brook (whose name is a loose German translation from "Reichenbach") to carry out his criminal plans. Moriarty calls Sherlock "Sir Boast-a-Lot" as he tells Sherlock the true story of his unavoidable fall from grace. Moriarty uses his chameleon-like qualities to erase himself out of each tale, leaving Sherlock looking incredibly guilty.

Sherlock's Jim is a master actor who does indeed "hide in plain sight." The difference between this Moriarty and previous portrayals is that he plays many roles simultaneously. He is not content to pose as a respected professor. Instead, Moriarty, whom Mycroft Holmes calls "the most dangerous criminal mind the world has ever seen" ("The Reichenbach Fall"), portrays many characters. Sherlock, however, can see the man himself.

"I am you"

Perhaps the reason that the BBC's Sherlock can see Moriarty so clearly is that Sherlock's identity is the mirror of Moriarty's. While Moriarty plays many roles that obfuscate his true identity, Sherlock plays one role that hides the many facets of his personality. Sherlock's chosen identity is that he is unfeeling, supremely logical, and detached. However, audiences can see through his interactions with John Watson, Mycroft, Irene Adler, and others that he is actually a fallible but passionate man. In the Season Three finale, the parallels between Moriarty and Sherlock become clear.

In BBC's "The Reichenbach Fall," during their confrontation on the roof of St. Bartholomew's Hospital, Sherlock says to Moriarty, "I am you," and Moriarty agrees, "You're me. You're me." Sherlock may be, as Moriarty claims, "on the side of the angels," but, as Sherlock asserts, he is not one of them. However, this confrontation also illustrates that both men are often intellectually bored because they are smarter than their peers, enjoy playing games, and often act outside legal boundaries. Their motives may differ, but they recognize in each other great similarities in personality. As a result, this modernized Moriarty is more memorable than Conan Doyle's original character.

Moriarty was originally created to be Sherlock's perfect foil and a way for Conan Doyle to nobly kill off Sherlock Holmes. However, Moriarty, instead of ending the story as he was designed to do, took on a life of his own.

Because Moriarty's backstory in canon is limited, he has been largely created by the imaginations of audiences and adaptors. He is a perfect "blank slate" upon whom audiences (and film and television series' creators) can write their greatest fears and secret desires. Of course, Sherlock Holmes also changes to reflect the culture represented by an adaptation, but his identity is so firmly established in canon that he cannot be completely rewritten without risking the loss of an audience. Moriarty, on the other hand, is simply a canon villain who is Sherlock's foil. What manner of villain he can become is left to interpretation—and the interpretations in *A Game of Shadows* and *Sherlock* ably illustrate society's fears of the powerful, successful, charming businessmen who are perceived to manipulate the world.

Works Cited

Conan Doyle, Arthur. "A Study in Scarlet." Project Gutenberg. 12 July 2008. Web. 11 May 2015.

_____. "The Final Problem." *Memoirs of Sherlock Holmes*. Project Gutenberg. Mar. 1997. Web. 11 May 2015.

_____. "The Man with the Twisted Lip." *The Adventures of Sherlock Holmes*. Project Gutenberg. 18 Apr. 2011. Web. 11 May 2015.

_____. "The Sign of Four." *The Adventures of Sherlock Holmes*. Project Gutenberg. 19 Nov. 2008. Web. 11 May 2015.

Fishman, Steve. "Bernie Madoff: Free at Last." *New York*. 6 June 2010. n.d. Web. 11 May 2015.

"The Great Game." *Sherlock*. BBC. 8 Aug. 2010. Television.

"Illustrations of Arthur Conan Doyle's Sherlock Holmes Stories by Sidney Paget." The Victorian Web. 18 Dec. 2013. Web. 11 May 2015.

"The Making of Moriarty." PBS Masterpiece. n.d. Web. 11 May 2015.

"The Reichenbach Fall." *Sherlock*. BBC. 20 May 2012. Television.

"Sherlock Holmes." Box Office Mojo. n.d. Web. 11 May 2015.

"Sherlock Holmes: A Game of Shadows." Box Office Mojo. Web. 11 May 2015.

Sherlock Holmes: A Game of Shadows. Dir. Guy Ritchie. Perf. Robert Downey, Jr., Jude Law, Jared Harris. Warner Bros., 2011. Film.

Sherlockology. "Sherlock: Jim Moriarty, Redefining the Original Supervillain." *Metro UK*. 19 Nov. 2013. Web. 11 May 2015.

_____. "Wardrobe: Jim Moriarty Suit." n.d. Web. 11 May 2015.

Strumpf, Dan. "Madoff Scandal Still Haunts Victims." *Wall Street Journal*. 10 Dec. 2012. Web. 11 May 2015.

"A Study in Pink." *Sherlock*. BBC. 25 July 2010. Television.

"Top 10 Crooked CEOs." *Time*. n.d. Web. 11 May 2015.

God, Grace and Sherlock

Religious Narrative and Identity in BBC's Sherlock

FELECIA MCDUFFIE

The BBC's modern take on the story of Sherlock Holmes and John Watson has become a wildly popular worldwide phenomenon in part because the architecture of the show stands on a foundation of spiritual and theological tropes of love, sacrifice, and personal transformation that touch people on a deep level. These spiritual themes have traditionally been linked to religious narratives, but those narratives have become increasingly hollowed out, vacuous, remote, and intellectually unavailable to many people in the rabidly secularizing cultures of the first world.

Sherlock can be interpreted as a religious narrative for the irreligious. Visual and verbal images of grace, salvation, sacrifice, and redemption abound in *Sherlock*. It matters little whether the showrunners intend them explicitly or whether they are drawing on the submerged power of the Judeo-Christian narratives that form the deep structure of the Western imagination. That deep structure exists and draws people in.

Because an ever-increasing number of people in the West no longer consider themselves religious in any traditional sense, they may only encounter religion when the deep structure exerts its power in popular culture. In works such as *God Without Being* and *Prolegomena to Charity*, Catholic theologian Jean-Luc Marion has suggested that there is a need for theological narratives that are hidden and for a God who can be approached only as love and through love. *Sherlock* is a prime example of this sort of narrative.

What Is Religion, and Why Is Popular Culture a Fertile Ground for New Religious Narratives?

The word *religion* is notoriously hard to define, but it is fair to say that, in the field of religious studies, understanding of the term has gradually shifted from a definition focusing on supernatural deities, rituals, and perhaps narrow belief systems to a much broader understanding of religions as symbolic systems of beliefs, narratives, and practices through which human beings seek meaning and transformation. Through these symbol systems, people relate themselves to the things they judge to be of transcendent or ultimate value. One scholar of religion has defined it as "human transformation in response to perceived ultimacy" (Young 4).

Two interrelated accounts of this *ultimacy* formed the bedrock of the Western understanding of both cosmic reality and human identity for hundreds of years. The first understood God as the Ground of Being, the First Cause. That "God" of metaphysics dominated philosophy and theology. Friedrich Nietzsche declared "God" dead, and modern science and secularism have continued to pound nails in His coffin ever since.

The second account, just as ancient, speaks of God as Love, Dante's "love which moves the sun and other stars" (*Paradiso*, Canto XXXIII, lines 142–5). This God has haunted the visions of the mystics of Western tradition and has proved more difficult to kill. Although that Love has been associated with the Judeo-Christian God throughout the history of the West, post-modern thinkers like French Catholic theologian Marion and Jewish philosopher Emmanuel Levinas posit a more radical understanding of that God. Instead of God as love, they suggest that Love is God. They do not argue for the non-existence of "God" in the sense of modern secular atheism. They argue, rather, that God (as transcendent ground of being) can now be seen (experienced/named) and can *only* be seen (experienced/named), in our seemingly secularized world, as self-giving Love. Human identity forms in the encounter with that Love, with the Other, the "not-me." Marion (*Prolegomena to Charity* 61, 78) wrote that religious conversion consists of surrendering to love, not surrendering to evidence. This conversion forms and transforms human identity at the deepest level. Like Marion, Levinas turned away from philosophical speculation on a transcendent God "conceived of outside the world" (94) to the task of finding an immanent God, and an authentic self, in loving encounters with other people. Levinas reverses the traditional commandments (first love God, then love the neighbor) and insists that love of others "takes place neither on a side-street nor a detour" (95) and that the face of the Other is the direct route to God. For both Marion and Levinas, the heart of religious experience lies in the risky business of moving from the "tranquility of egoism," through the painful realization that the self "fails to be sufficient unto itself" (Levinas 97), into the possibilities of transformative love (Levinas 97; Marion, *Erotic Phenomenon* 95–99).

Some forms of post-modern theology embrace the idea of transformative love as God, rejecting the God of modernity. There are many and diverse accounts of the origins and characteristics of modernity and postmodernity as well as their relationship to religion and theology (or to the secular and the sacred). Modernity is the worldview arising as early as the late Middle Ages that viewed human rationality as the measure of all things and increasingly emphasized human freedom and individual autonomy. It gradually grew with the development of empirical philosophy, science, and humanism until it overshadowed the earlier worldview that God's glory and rationality were the measure and goal of all things. This process took several centuries to play out in the West (and some, such as theologian Graham Ward, would argue that it plays out still).

Post-modernism developed in the 20th century, associated with various strands of a critique of the underpinnings of the "modern" in art, architecture, critical theory, philosophy, and theology. For this chapter, the significant points of the post-modern worldview are a skepticism regarding the idea of the universal in anthropology, metaphysics, and ethics as well as skepticism toward assumptions about the primacy of human rationality and autonomy established during the Enlightenment. Some post-modernists, including theologian Ward, credit Nietzsche as the founder of the movement with his announcement of the death of the God of modernity. Ward argued that "[w]ith the death of God Nietzsche announces the overcoming of metaphysics, for he announces that there is no foundation, no ground, no origin that ultimately is not governed by a perspective.... In an act of Titanic iconoclasm he announces a nihilism in which there is no truth, goodness, reality, reason, origin which is not contingent, ephemeral, and the effect of the human will" (xxix).

The death of "God," however, does not mean the death of God. Marion employs the term *God* to refer to the "God" of modernity and metaphysics, the Ground of Being, the literal universal placeholder in the great game of philosophy. According to Marion, God was "assimilated" into "God" and reduced to a useful abstraction. Marion's project is to liberate God from his confinement and rediscover him, through phenomenology, as the "Being-as-given." While "God" is no longer thinkable, God is available to experience as the "being who is completely given (*l'étant-abandonné*) ... given without restriction, without reservation, without restraint" ("Metaphysics and Phenomenology" 291–292). This is the God of the mystics, the God of the crucifixion, the God of overwhelming, self-giving love. This is the God encountered in and through love of any sort, through the abandonment of the self, through sacrifice. This definition, of course, leads to Sherlock and *Sherlock.*

How Does Sherlock *Fit the Category of Religious Narrative?*

The narrative heart of *Sherlock* is not the hop, skip, and jump from one puzzle to another to the accompaniment of clever graphics and exciting chase scenes punctuated by cups of tea. In the first episode, the writers lay out what has proved to be the central narrative arc of the show through Detective Inspector Lestrade's comment that Sherlock Holmes is a great man who someday may become a good one ("A Study in Pink"). The *Sherlock* showrunners have made it clear that their central story concerns Sherlock's "gradual humanization" (Jacobsen). In the DVD commentary on "A Study in Pink," series co-creator Mark Gatiss gave audiences a large hint about how this transformation is to take place when he said that "you need to see [the story] through John Watson's eyes. We pick up the story where this unbearable man becomes not just bearable, but loveable" (Gatiss).

Religions concern themselves with the good life, and they tend to be quite realistic in their recognition that actual human life often tends to be, as John Watson says, "a bit not good" ("A Study in Pink"). Because people "fall short of well-being and well-doing," religions are in the transformation business, and some of their most effective tools are sacred stories (Brown 113). Because religions seek to help people relate to transcendent reality, that which often cannot be named or spoken of directly, they often operate with most effect and potency through narratives. Stories sketch out a vision of what human life can be. Religious narratives have traditionally asked and tried to answer big questions: What does it mean to be human? What is worth living for? What is worth dying for? Where do we find meaning in our lives? For many people in our increasingly secularized world, however, explicitly religious narratives have become vacuous, remote, and intellectually unavailable. One of the founders of post-modern theology, Mark Taylor, argued that theology "must learn to speak of God godlessly and of the self selflessly" (87). Themes of love, sacrifice, grace, and human transformation continue to resonate, but they have gone underground into implicit religious narratives found in popular culture instead of in scriptures and stained glass windows.

Sherlock tells the story of one man's transformation into a good man through the grace of unmerited love and through his own response of love and sacrifice. Of course, there is mystery and mayhem aplenty along the way. Clues and carnage abound. The overarching narrative, however, of the first nine episodes and one special (2010–2016), especially during the Season Three episodes (2013), concerns a man who becomes truly human through love. He becomes loveable because he is loved. Because he is loved, he learns to love. Because he loves, he learns what is worth living for and what is worth dying for. He sacrifices himself for his friends.

How Do These Themes Play Out in Sherlock?

If *Sherlock* is, at its core, a story about a great man becoming a good one, that journey has not been a straightforward trajectory. The story of Sherlock's transformation instead forms a spiral. Each season recapitulates Sherlock's journey into spiritual growth and change and takes him deeper into his own heart and identity. In a broad outline, the movements might be described as the statement of the problem (self-centeredness), the challenge to identity (the call to love), and rejection or acceptance of transformation (the call to sacrifice). The main movements of the spiral take place during the first two seasons, with the themes reaching a dramatic climax in Season Three and the closely-related 2016 special episode.

At least one crucial scene in the first episodes of each of the three seasons (i.e., "A Study in Pink," "A Scandal in Belgravia," "The Empty Hearse") emphasizes or re-emphasizes Sherlock's essential self-centeredness, independence, and unwillingness to understand or care for other people. In "A Study in Pink," Sherlock's inability to recognize that a stillborn child might result in grief for a woman years later underscores his disassociation from normal human connections. This attitude is, as John points out, "a bit not good." In Season Two, the story of Sherlock and Irene Adler revolves around Mycroft Holmes's assertion that "caring is not an advantage," a reminder he feels obligated to make as a weird sort of brotherly comfort when Sherlock seems to be upset at the woman's apparent death ("A Scandal in Belgravia"). Sherlock, in turn, seems to adopt and amplify that lesson in a blistering confrontation with his brother and Irene Adler toward the end of the episode. Sherlock (again, apparently) sends the woman who fascinated him to her death with the bitter assertion that "sentiment is a defect found in the losing side" and the advice that she should never let her heart rule her head. However, in an unexpected final scene, Sherlock appears in the masked guise of a silent film hero to rescue the damsel in the distress into which he sent her. This reversal follows the pattern of the overall narrative so far as Sherlock vacillates between the call of ego and emotional regression and the demands of love and emotional growth. In the first episode of Season Three, "The Empty Hearse," the Sherlock who comes back from the "dead" seems to have heeded his brother's advice from the previous season about the disadvantages of caring. In many scenes, the detective seems as acerbic and heartless as ever. He makes a hash of his reunion with John, complete with disguise and mangled French accent; insults his friend's facial hair; treats his parents rudely; and, at first, fails to reckon with the emotional fallout of his "death" on those around him. As the more detailed discussion of "The Empty Hearse" later in this chapter reveals, however, in spite of the recapitulation of some of his worst qualities, Sherlock has not remained static. There are, with each episode, increasing chinks in his armored self-absorption.

The second episode in each series (i.e., "The Blind Banker," "The Hounds of Baskerville," "The Sign of Three") highlights the tug of war between Sherlock's self-absorption and his desire for connection. Circumstances increasingly require that he probe the gap between his self-understanding and his increasing interest in relationships. This probing deepens with each season. The second episode of Season One, "The Blind Banker," consists of a series of almost tragi-comic episodes in which Sherlock ventures further out of his self-imposed isolation, drawn toward a relationship with John Watson, only to withdraw again into his shell like a sensitive and misunderstood snail. When Sherlock introduces John as his friend to banker Sebastian Wilkes, John quickly corrects that term to "colleague." Sherlock, obviously hurt, retreats back into himself and draws his armor around him. That turns out to be a good thing, because Wilkes proceeds to trot out his previous history with Sherlock at university, asserting that he used to "wind up everybody. We hated him." Sherlock's overtures of friendship have been too subtle for John Watson. John sees but does not observe, focusing on Sherlock's admittedly still-problematic behaviors. Later in the episode, Sherlock gets the life almost strangled out of him in an apartment he is investigating, while John focuses on the fact that Sherlock will not let him into said apartment. John yells his take on his "colleague's" identity through the letter drop in the door, mocking Sherlock's desire to "always work alone because no one else can compete with [his] massive intellect." John has somehow missed the fact that Sherlock, in fact, no longer works alone. Sherlock, for his part, lets his hurt and pride rule him. He does not, and will not, explain himself. Like all second episodes in the series, the path leads one step forward and two steps back.

In the second episode of Season Two, "The Hounds of Baskerville," this pattern of challenge and identity-formation continues and deepens. The heart of the episode comes when Sherlock sees what seems to be a giant, supernatural hound. He sees something he could not have seen. His senses and his reason disagree, and the bottom drops out of his self-understanding as a rational, unemotional observer. He fears that both his mind and body have betrayed him. His hands shake as he tries to take a drink of whiskey, and he tries to talk to John about his fears. He loathes himself at that moment and excoriates himself for his inability to keep his usual distance from the emotions that he despises, "the grit on the lens, the fly in the ointment." This questioning of identity is much deeper than that in Season One, and Sherlock reacts furiously, lashing out instead of feeling quietly hurt. In a reversal of the "friends/colleagues" moment in Season One, John tries to comfort Sherlock and remind him that they are friends and that John is there for him. Sherlock snarls, "I don't have friends." This time, however, instead of walling himself up with his pride, fear, and hurt, Sherlock reaches out to John the next day. He humbles himself and assures John that not only is he Sherlock's friend, but his only friend. That declaration foreshadows Sherlock's deeper challenge and call to love in the second episode of Season Three, "The Sign of Three."

The third and final episode of each season (i.e., "The Great Game," "The Reichenbach Fall," "His Last Vow") calls for increasingly difficult choices, leading to further breakthroughs in Sherlock's journey to goodness. The 2016 special episode, "The Abominable Bride," serves as a fascinating and extended "edition" of "His Last Vow" and will be discussed as part of the analysis of that episode. These episodes call for increasing levels of self-sacrifice and recognition of the claims of love, the claims of the Other on the self. In the final episode of Season One, the claim is subtle. The irony of the title "The Great Game" is John's attempt to make Sherlock realize that his puzzles are not games at all and the pawns on the chessboard are living, suffering human beings. As Sherlock tells viewers explicitly in "The Hounds of Baskerville," he believes objective distance is crucial to what he does.

It turns out that he and John have different ideas of what it means to be good and to do good. For the Sherlock of "The Great Game," a good state of being consists of excitement, engagement, lack of boredom, and excellence at what he does, which is solving puzzles. This sort of "goodness" requires objectivity and the honing of his razor-sharp intellect. As far as viewers can tell, "doing good" for Sherlock simply means getting to the truth of a particular situation and letting the chips fall where they may. The episode emphasizes, time and time again, that he does not operate out of empathy with the plight of others. John Watson, however, has a different standard of being and doing good. He believes that compassion and kindness should be part of the equation. When Sherlock deduces that Molly's latest boyfriend is gay and informs her of this fact, John accuses him of being unkind. Sherlock replies that it is kinder to give her the truth. For John, kindness is compassion, putting oneself in the place of another. John wants Sherlock to sacrifice the distance that keeps him from feeling, from hurting with those who are hurt. Sherlock implies that Moriarty's motivation for the "game" is a simple desire not to be bored. This hits too close to home for John, because he lives with a man who also seems to live for distraction. John reminds Sherlock that there are actual lives at stake in this particular game. Sherlock, in turn, asks whether caring will help save them. When John says no, Sherlock replies that he will continue not to make the mistake of caring and actually finds it easy not to make that mistake. John is, obviously, disappointed in Sherlock. On the surface, Sherlock's reaction to John's disappointment is snidely dismissive. "Don't make people into heroes, John," he says. "Heroes don't exist, and if they did, I wouldn't be one of them" ("The Great Game"). This conversation holds the key to Sherlock's transformation of identity. Sherlock and John start with different concepts of what makes a good person and a good deed. Sherlock, at first, takes a utilitarian approach. Feelings do not matter; motives do not matter. What matters is the outcome, the greatest good. John believes that, no matter the outcome, caring matters most. He asks Sherlock to be something other than he understands himself to be. He asks Sherlock to give up the distance and the objectivity that are crucial to his identity. He asks for kindness and compassion. He implicitly asks for a hero. Although Sherlock apparently rejects the call to love in this conversation, John plants a seed that flowers in Seasons Two and Three.

The last episode of Season Two, "The Reichenbach Fall," and the last episode of Season Three, "His Last Vow," are Sherlock's response to that conversation. He was not deaf to the demands of love, the possibilities of sacrifice, and the glories and vulnerabilities of fairy-tale heroes after all. In "The Reichenbach Fall," Sherlock's archenemy Moriarty tries to take everything from him: his reputation and his identity as the heroic detective who has solved a series of high-profile cases. Moriarty even promises to "burn the heart" out of him. The Satanic snake visits Sherlock in the little Eden that is Baker Street and plays with a blatantly symbolic apple while he promises Sherlock a fall.

What, exactly, is the temptation? Moriarty carefully sets up his continuing game with Sherlock in the context of a fairy story. He assures Sherlock that "every fairy tale needs a good old-fashioned villain" and does everything in his power, including a children's cartoon, to mock and undermine the fact that every fairy tale needs a good old-fashioned hero. This scene clearly resonates with the story of Adam and Eve in the garden, as much as the fairy-story context the writers have just as clearly introduced. Bruno Bettelheim, a scholar of fairy tales, said that they are "for children growing into maturity" (8–9), stories which recognize a clear duality of the good and evil present in every person and give children the inspiration and tools to solve the moral duality within themselves, the tools to reject the attractions of evil. The story of Adam and Eve is just such a fairy tale, and the apple represents the choice to leave childhood and to take on the task of moral adulthood, the knowledge of good and evil. "The Reichenbach Fall" is a recapitulation of Sherlock's journey from moral childhood to moral maturity, from the fascination of the games of childhood to the difficult choices of love and sacrifice. The temptation faced is the choice, always possible, to remain a self-centered egoist.

In the final confrontation of good and evil in this episode, Sherlock makes a leap of faith. He chooses the side of the angels, even while assuring the Tempter that he is not really one of them. He sacrifices his life for the safety of three people he has come to love. The iconography of his final stance on the ledge at St. Bart's is unmistakable. Arms straight out, he is crucified against the air and his own inconvenient love. Although he does not literally die, he does sacrifice his identity, reputation, and the life he has come to know and value. His willingness to sacrifice goes deeper in the final episode of Season Three.

"The Empty Hearse," Crucifixion and Resurrection

In the first episode of Season Three, "The Empty Hearse," Sherlock returns from the "dead," having spent two years disassembling the pieces of Moriarty's network which threaten the lives of the people he has come to love. The most significant iconographic link from the final episode of Season Two to the first episode of Season Three is the clear visual references to the crucifixion of Jesus, the gold standard of self-sacrificing love in the historical consciousness of the West. The fulfillment of this theme of sacrifice comes early in "The Empty Hearse" with a striking scene of Sherlock undergoing torture in a fetid dungeon somewhere in Eastern Europe. Backlit by a halo of light from a high window, stripped to the waist and shackled, Sherlock's arms are stretched out in a cruciform position. His hair is unusually long, wavy, and tinted an atypical light reddish-brown. Naked to the waist, a latticework of bleeding wounds cover his arms and torso. Anyone who misses the Christological reference has not looked at enough flagellation and crucifixion paintings.

Interested readers might wish to compare a freeze frame of the scene on the DVD at the point the interrogator says "you broke in here for a reason" with a painting called *Flagellazione di Cristo* (*The Flagellation of Christ*) from the early 1590s that is sometimes attributed to Ludovico Carracci. Although not exactly the same pose, some elements are strikingly similar and are found in similar positions: a flame/light to the left; the hunched over figure with the long, light-red-blond, curly hair and bare torso in the center; an archway behind; and a torturer in an identical shade of grey to the right. Whether this particular painting served as a reference point in creating the scene, similar conventions in religious paintings make the Christological and sacrificial elements in the scene clear. As one art historian has pointed out, traditional paintings of the crucifixion "were usually intended to foster meditation on Christ's self-sacrifice, and they thus indicate his suffering by showing him hanging heavily with bowed head and bleeding wounds" (Sorabelle). Similar iconography occurs in Cornelis Engebrechtsz's *The Crucifixion with Donors and Saints Peter and Margaret* (c. 1525–1527), Rogier van der Wyden's *Crucifixion Diptych* (c. 1460), Matthias Grünewald's *Isenheim Altarpiece* (1512–1516), and Diego Velázquez's *Christ Crucified* (1632). This is precisely the image of Sherlock offered to viewers early in "The Empty Hearse."

Another painting intentionally referenced in the scene gives viewers even more insight into the themes of identity and sacrifice in this episode. Tumblr blogger Mid0nz interviewed *Sherlock* cinematographer Steve Lawes and talked to him about the torture scene. Lawes revealed that his inspiration was the 1768 painting by Joseph Wright, *An Experiment on a Bird in an Air Pump*. Art historians often interpret this painting as a celebration of the Enlightenment. Wright was known for treating industrial and scientific subjects with the composition and lighting traditionally employed in religious paintings. This particular painting shows an 18th-century natural philosopher, a proto-scientist, in the process of replicating one of Robert Boyle's experiments. Air is pumped out of a glass container holding a bird, creating a vacuum. The bird loses consciousness, neatly proving both the properties of a vacuum and the need of living creatures for oxygen. If the experiment is not stopped soon enough, the bird dies.

Significantly, the scientist in the painting "stands in" for the inventor of the experiment, Robert Boyle. As a famous alchemist and one of the founders of modern chemistry, he was concerned with the transformation of substances. If one were choosing the most obvious parallel for Sherlock Holmes in this painting, it would be with the scientist, the chemist, the one in control of the "magic trick" being demonstrated to the onlookers. The scientist in this painting is, however, displaced to the viewer's left. The true center of the painting, the center of the light, the parallel to most traditional crucifixion paintings, is a vertical axis that runs from a mysterious skull resting on a table in a light-emitting vessel up to another glass vessel that contains the dead or dying bird, the "sacrifice" to science. The mostly indifferent, objective spectators look away from both the dying bird and the mysterious *memento mori* of a skull in the center of the painting. If this painting is the inspiration for the torture scene, Sherlock as the central figure is not the scientist, or even the rational observers, but the sacrificial victim. The Sherlock who leaps from the ledge at St. Bart's only lands, finally, in shackles in the dungeon in Serbia. In the interim, he has lost his identity as the always-in-control scientist basking in the light of reason. Love has brought him into the dark underground of pain and death, suspended by the will of others, out of control, his life sacrificed for the lives of others. This foreshadows another turn of the downward spiral viewers see more clearly in "The Sign of Three," where, in the course of his best man speech, Sherlock undergoes a rhetorical transformation that recapitulates the journey of the first three seasons.

When viewers next see Sherlock in "The Empty Hearse," he seems jarringly at odds with the man in the dungeon. Once back in London, he appears to have regressed to the self-centered, tone-deaf, self-proclaimed sociopath of Season One. He expresses no gratitude whatsoever to his brother for "wading in" and rescuing him from a dungeon in Serbia and no concern for the death of one of Mycroft's agents. He expresses incredulity at the idea that John Watson might have had a life apart from him and engages in a singularly heartless and ill-timed "reveal" to John. All of these actions make sense in the context of a narrative of grace. If Sherlock was being transformed because of the love of his friends, he has been cut off from that influence for two years.

The Sherlock of earlier seasons presents himself as a "high-functioning sociopath," a heartless deduction machine who sees love and involvement as weaknesses. There are ample hints in the first two seasons, of course, that this is (as his insightful enemy Moriarty realizes) "not quite true" ("The Great Game"). Surrounded by people who inexplicably love him and seem to expect to be loved in return, he begins to question the identity he has constructed. The Sherlock who returns in "The Empty Hearse" demonstrates, along with his usual egotism and tone deafness, a new sensitivity and vulnerability.

In "The Empty Hearse," viewers see further awakening of compassion and a new realization of the need for connection. Sherlock turns the tables on Mycroft with a reference to a scene in "A Scandal in Belgravia" in which Mycroft accuses him of knowing nothing about sex. He accuses Mycroft of knowing nothing about loneliness and emotional need. Sherlock himself is now well aware of both. Mixed with episodes of emotional tone deafness in this episode, he also shows hints of much greater sensitivity to others, empathy, and the ability to detect emotional nuance. He holds the hand of a client and seems empathetic to her disappointment in love. He picks up emotional cues in his dealings with Molly that he would have missed earlier. The Sherlock depicted in this episode is in process; he is fragmented, his armor fissured.

"The Sign of Three" and the Mystical Marriage

In "The Sign of Three," Sherlock, bemused but increasingly game to respond to the claims of the Other and to venture upon the life of an actual human being, spirals further down the treacherous slope of love when he becomes the best man at John and Mary's wedding. Although he assures a dubious Mycroft that he is "not involved," he is, of course. On the surface, the tone of this episode is light and delightful up until almost the end. Viewers are offered a series of treats: Sherlock as wedding planner, Sherlock actually interacting successfully with a small boy, sunny cinematography, champagne, waltzes, touching speeches, and declarations of love all around. Beneath the surface, things are not quite so sunny. This episode is a complex set of nested stories: the wedding, the run-up to the wedding, Sherlock's narration of highlights of his and John's story together, the Mayfly man mystery, and Sholto's story. It is a story about stories, all centered in the best man's speech which is literally at the center of the episode and Season Three. Sherlock attempts to make a surprisingly sensitive handoff in stories, from his and John's story "of two men and their frankly ridiculous adventures" to the "new story," the "bigger adventure" of John and Mary's life together.

In the speech, Sherlock openly acknowledges that he has been "redeemed" by John's loyal friendship, refers to himself as the man that John has "saved," and declares that he and Mary are the two people who love John "most in all this world." These terms reveal a profound transformation of identity. Love, redemption, and salvation are all keywords of religious transformation and a deep, far-reaching identity re-formation. The narrative of "great to good" fully claims Sherlock in "The Sign of Three," but he does not quite realize it until he is in the middle of his speech. The speech is not just at the center of the story arc so far; it is a microcosm of the key component of the narrative arc: the transition of Sherlock from great to good. Just as the Sherlock of "A Study in Pink" is not the Sherlock of "His Last Vow," the Sherlock who starts the speech is not the Sherlock who finishes it. The modern (Enlightenment) account of the self, going back at least to Plato, is that the self is a difficult balance of reason and desire "with the primary function of reason being to control desire. It is further assumed that desire or passion can give no clues to the nature of the good, for the good can only be determined in accordance with 'reason'" (Hauerwass and Burrell 171). The Sherlock of Season One would wholeheartedly agree with this definition; the Sherlock of Season Three, not so much.

Right before the speech, Sherlock assures Mycroft that he is not emotionally involved in the proceedings. He starts the speech as (or at least projecting) the "old" Sherlock, offended by and dismissing the sentiments of the telegrams, self-centered, and egotistical. A flashback to the scene in which he agrees to be John's best man gives viewers insight into the nature of Sherlock's ethical thinking. When John brings up the topic of "the best man," Sherlock responds as if John is asking him for his general opinion on what makes the "best" person. Sherlock immediately offers his opinion that Billy Kincaid, the Camden garrotter, is the best man he has ever known because he made "vast contributions to charity, never disclosed" ("The Sign of Three"). This is a revealing choice within the context of the "great to good" story arc. Sherlock chooses Kincaid, a serial killer who also made lives better through contributions to hospitals and children's homes, because the lives saved outweighed the occasional victim of strangulation. His explanation places him within the rational, utilitarian moral calculus of the greatest good for the greatest number. This scene forms a narrative link with the key scene in "The Great Game" in which Sherlock asserts that it is saving lives that matters, not whether he cares about them. He carries this familiar rejection of emotion into his best man's speech, claiming that "all emotions are opposed to the pure, cold reason that I hold above all things." He rapidly offends as many constituencies as possible. He condemns weddings, sentiment, and beauty. For good measure, he takes a gratuitous shot at God as a ludicrous fantasy and career opportunity for those too stupid to handle reality. He presents himself as a modern, scientific rationalist.

That may be what he was, but that is no longer exactly who he is becoming. Somewhere along the way, and the where and when are ambiguous, Sherlock realizes that he is loved and that he loves. He has been transformed by subjection to the Other in the person of John Watson. John's virtues of kindness, bravery, wisdom, and love have called Sherlock out of what he thought was himself. In terms of traditional Christian theology, grace can be understood as unmerited love, freely given. This gift enables flawed persons to "reach above" their flawed nature to grow and develop. Only John has both loved Sherlock for what he is and has faith that he can be more. Through this grace, Sherlock transcends himself. The egotistical atheist sociopath is moved, by love, to humility, to re-thinking the foundations of his life, to speaking in terms of salvation and redemption.

Toward the end of "The Sign of Three," Sherlock makes a vow to always care for and protect John, Mary, and their unexpected child. A vow is a binding promise, but the word is usually associated with promises made to or before God. In this case Sherlock takes his vow before the community of people present. The episode ends with another, more painful, sacrifice on Sherlock's part. When he realizes that Mary is pregnant, he literally takes a step back from the pair and symbolically takes a step back from their lives, the lives he has just vowed to protect. He relinquishes whatever claim he has on John's attention and affection, recognizing that he is, suddenly, peripheral. While the sight of Sherlock "leaving the wedding early" and alone broke many viewers' hearts, another way to view the ending is as a mystical marriage. Traditionally, marriages in literature, Christian mysticism, alchemy, and fairy tales alike symbolize "an integration of different aspects of the personality," achieving transformation and a harmony of disparate elements (Bettelheim 146). No one ever said the journey to the good was not sometimes (perhaps often) a painful one.

"His Last Vow," "The Abominable Bride" and the Fairy Tale Gospel

Most canny fans realized that Steven Moffat titled the final episode of Season Three "His Last Vow." They may have reveled in the wedding festivities and the increasing humanization of Sherlock, but they were wary. They expected that the writers would shortly pluck out their hearts, and Sherlock's, and stomp those suckers flat. That, of course, is exactly what they did. Sherlock's vow was to protect John, Mary, and the surprise Watson baby, no matter what happened, no matter what it took. In the last episode of the season, Charles Augustus Magnussen, a truly vile piece of work, threatens their future, their happiness, and even their lives.

At one point in "The Sign of Three," Mycroft says somewhat sarcastically, albeit prophetically, that Sherlock thinks of himself as Saint George, the slayer of dragons. Magnussen, it turns out, is a dragon, and Sherlock slays him— shoots him dead. In committing murder, Sherlock again offers to sacrifice his life for his friends. Sherlock's decision to kill Magnussen in "His Last Vow" has been the occasion of heated arguments within *Sherlock* fandom. What did the act reveal about Sherlock's moral character and his progress along the story arc of "great to good"? The 2016 special episode, "The Abominable Bride," sheds light on that question and on the spiritual themes of Sherlock's development. This episode, billed as a Victorian-themed one-off, turned out to be a direct follow-on from "His Last Vow." Sherlock takes a potent cocktail of illegal drugs either before or soon after he boards the plane taking him to Eastern Europe at the end of Season Three. The special takes place almost exclusively within Sherlock's mind palace and links directly to the mind-palace scene in "His Last Vow." Taken together, these two mind-palace scenes take viewers into the heart of Sherlock's ongoing spiritual transformation.

Like all good sacred stories, Sherlock faces temptations along his path to love and wholeness. When he is shot and technically dies in "His Last Vow," he enters his mind palace. There in the depths he encounters the Tempter in the form of Moriarty. The choice he faces there is a transcendent question of identity. Will he choose the peace of death or the pain and difficulty of life? Moriarty tells Sherlock that he is going to love being dead, because "no one ever bothers you." Just "one little push," and there will be no more pain, heartbreak, or loss. The Sherlock of Season One might have chosen death. The Sherlock of Season Three chooses the pain of life, love, and subjection to the Other. In "His Last Vow," Sherlock chooses life because of his love for John Watson. Unfortunately, that love leads him to murder. He gives up the life he has known with no hope or expectation of return. "The

Abominable Bride" takes Sherlock, and viewers, through some emotional and spiritual consequences of that decision.

Sherlock says explicitly several times in "The Abominable Bride" that he is required to go deep to solve the mystery. The story does, indeed, take Sherlock deep into the labyrinth of his own heart and soul in what is essentially spiritual psycho-drama. He is an unreliable narrator, even of his own story, so when says he has taken drugs in order to revisit a case from the past to illuminate the problem of Moriarty's return, viewers should be wary. The story contains ample clues that the mystery of Moriarty's return is only the surface narrative. At the deepest level, the narrative in this episode points to the return of the repressed in Sherlock's soul. An exploration of all the clues would require a separate chapter, but the heart of the matter is, as always, the question of whether Sherlock will become a good man. Throughout the episode, Sherlock probes layer after layer of his own identity and self-understanding. Is he the self-described sociopath who murdered Magnussen, or is he St. George who slew a dragon? Is he the Sherlock Holmes of Watson's narrative, the reasoning machine who always wears the deerstalker? Is he the stupid little brother always humiliated by Mycroft? Is he the "unprincipled drug addict" or the "gentleman hero" ("The Abominable Bride")?

The critical questions of this episode are those asked by the Victorian John Watson to a visibly resistant Victorian Sherlock: "Why are you so determined to be alone?" "Why do you *need* to be alone?" "What made you like this?" Sherlock trots out the stock answers about emotion being abhorrent, the grit in the lens. These phrases harken back tellingly to his emotional meltdown in "The Hounds of Baskerville." After three seasons of gradual humanization, they are even more jarring in this context. Here he insists that nothing made him this way. "Oh, Watson," he says, "nothing made me. I made me" ("The Abominable Bride"). The whole episode, however, implies that this is only partly true. There are things in the depths, things still to be revealed throughout the whole story arc of the series, that shaped this largely false self-concept. His sarcastic rejection of Watson's questions in this scene as more appropriate to an "alienist" is much more than a throwaway line. An alienist is a somewhat archaic term now used to describe "a psychiatrist who specializes in the legal aspects of psychiatry as determining sanity or capacity to stand trial" ("Alienist"). One possible interpretation of the entire episode is that Sherlock has put himself on trial for the murder of Magnussen. There are ample clues throughout the episode that the subject of the trial also includes his treatment of others, especially women, as well as more deeply buried traumas that may be the subject of future episodes. Who or what is he? Is he truly a sociopath? Is he unworthy of the love of those that he loves? The focus of Sherlock's spiritual journey in "His Last Vow" is whether he could love and sacrifice for those he loves. The focus of his spiritual journey in "The Abominable Bride" is whether he can accept the gift of grace for himself. Is he worthy of forgiveness? Is he worthy of love or death?

Throughout the episode, Sherlock gradually distances himself from the public thinking-machine persona, the sociopath without emotions. If that is not to be his identity, the mind-palace sequences in "His Last Vow" and "The Abominable Bride" suggest that the struggle for a new identity must be in confronting the Other, the twin. In the depths of his soul, is he the Monster at the heart of the labyrinth, twinned with Moriarty, or is he the beloved willing to be rescued by the people who love him, personified in this case by John Watson? Will he embrace death or life?

Sherlock's ongoing transformation is the stuff of the best fairy tales. In a telling detail, viewers discover in "His Last Vow" that Mycroft has given his little brother the codename "Ugly Duckling" to use in intelligence tracking. That is Sherlock's story in a nutshell, and it is the story not only of Hans Christian Andersen's confused duckling but a universal and sacred story about the human hope of transformation. Theologian Frederick Buechner pointed out that, above all, fairy tales "are tales about transformation where all creatures are revealed in the end as what they truly are. The ugly duckling becomes a great white swan, the frog is revealed to be a prince" (79). He links the transformations of fairy tales to the sacred story of religious transformation in which the angel of the Book of Revelation gives to every person a white stone with a new name, the name that was theirs from the beginnings of the world (Buechner 80). That is the story that draws so many people to *Sherlock*. The story is ongoing, and fans eagerly anticipate where it goes. Perhaps Sherlock's story is the story of the great white swan. The fall that his enemy promised him may turn out, just as in the story of Genesis, to be a fortunate fall, the fall into Love. Sherlock's joyful leap from the Reichenbach cliff face after Moriarty is defeated in "The Abominable Bride" certainly indicates that that is where the story is heading. In that scene, he throws away the "Sherlock Holmes" hat with his old identity. The man who leaps is not only one who loves but one who will allow himself to be loved. *Sherlock* evokes intense interest, involvement, and loyalty from viewers because it tells a deeply religious story for the religious and the irreligious alike. Like all great religious narratives and the best fairy tales, *Sherlock* tells the story of human transformation through love.

WORKS CITED

"The Abominable Bride." *Sherlock*. Writ. Mark Gatiss, Steven Moffat. Dir. Douglas Mackinnon. BBC, 2016. Television.

"Alienist." *Findlaw Legal Dictionary*. 6 Jan. 2016. Web. http://dictionary.findlaw.com/definition/alienist.html.

Bettelheim, Bruno. *The Uses of Enchantment: The Meaning and Importance of Fairy Tales*. New York: Vintage, 1977. Print.

"The Blind Banker." *Sherlock: Season One*. Writ. Steve Thompson. Dir. Euros Lyn. Hartswood Films, 2010. DVD.

Brown, Frank Burch. *Religious Aesthetics: A Theological Study of Making and Meaning*. Princeton: Princeton University Press, 1989. Print.

Buechner, Frederick. *Telling the Truth: The Gospel as Tragedy, Comedy and Fairy Tale*. San Francisco: Harper & Row, 1977. Print.

Carracci, Ludovico (by/after). *Flagellazione di Cristo*. c. 1590–1592. Wikigallery.org. n.d. Web. 9 Sep. 2014.

Dante Aligheri. *The Divine Comedy*. Trans. C. H. Sisson. New York: Oxford University Press, 1993. Print.

"The Empty Hearse." *Sherlock: Season Three*. Writ. Mark Gatiss. Dir. Jeremy Lovering. BBC Worldwide Ltd., a Hartswood Film Production for BBC, 2014. DVD.

Engebrechtsz, Cornelis. *The Crucifixion with Donors and Saints Peter and Margaret*. c. 1525–1527. Oil on wood. Metropolitan Museum of Art. New York.

Gatiss, Mark. Audio commentary to "A Study in Pink." *Sherlock: Season One*. Writ. Steven Moffat. Dir. Paul McGuigan. Hartswood Films, 2010. DVD.

"The Great Game." *Sherlock: Season One*. Writ. Mark Gatiss. Dir. Paul McGuigan. Hartswood Films, 2010. DVD.

Grünewald, Matthias. *The Isenheim Altarpiece*. 1512–1516. Oil on wood. Unterlinden Museum. Colmar, France.

Hauerwas, Stanley, and David Burrell. "From System to Story: An Alternative Pattern for Rationality in Ethics." *Why Narrative? Readings in Narrative Theology*. Ed. Stanley Hauerwas and L. Gregory Jones. Grand Rapids: William B. Eerdmans, 1989. 1–20. Print.

"His Last Vow." *Sherlock: Season Three*. Writ. Steven Moffat. Dir. Nick Hurran. BBC Worldwide Ltd., a Hartswood Film Production for BBC, 2014. DVD.

"The Hounds of Baskerville." *Sherlock: Season Two*. Writ. Mark Gatiss. Dir. Paul McGuigan. BBC Worldwide Ltd., a Hartswood Film Production for BBC, 2012. DVD.

Jacobsen, Kevin. "*Sherlock* Season 4 Promises Holmes to Grow More 'Human' in New 2016 Episodes?" *EnStars*. 6 Mar. 2014. Web. 24 Sep. 2014.

Levinas, Emmanuel. *Alterity & Transcendence*. Trans. Michael B. Smith. New York: Columbia University Press, 1999. Print.

_____. *The Erotic Phenomenon*. Trans. Stephen E. Lewis. Chicago: University of Chicago Press, 2003. Print.

_____. *God Without Being*. Trans. Thomas A. Carlson. Chicago: University of Chicago Press, 1991. Print.

_____. "Metaphysics and Phenomenology: A Summary for Theologians." *The Post-Modern God: A Theological Reader*. Ed. Graham Ward. Oxford: Blackwell, 1997. Print.

_____. *Prolegomena to Charity*. Trans. Stephen Lewis. New York: Fordham University Press, 2002. Print.

Mid0nz. Untitled post. Mid0nz.tumblr.com. Tumblr. 5 Aug. 2014. Web. 28 Sep. 2014.

"The Reichenbach Fall." *Sherlock: Season Two*. Writ. Steve Thompson. Dir. Toby Haynes. BBC Worldwide Ltd., a Hartswood Film Production for BBC, 2012. DVD.

"A Scandal in Belgravia." *Sherlock: Season Two*. Writ. Steven Moffat. Dir. Paul McGuigan. BBC Worldwide Ltd., a Hartswood Film Production for BBC, 2012. DVD.

"The Sign of Three." *Sherlock: Season Three*. Writ. Steve Thompson, Steven Moffat, and Mark Gatiss. Dir. Colm McCarthy. BBC Worldwide Ltd., a Hartswood Film Production for BBC, 2014. DVD.

Sorabelle, Jean. "The Crucifixion and Passion of Christ in Italian Painting." *Heilbrunn Timeline of Art History*. New York: The Metropolitan Museum of Art, 2000-. n.d. Web. 6 July 2015.

"A Study in Pink." *Sherlock: Season One*. Writ. Steven Moffat. Dir. Paul McGuigan. Hartswood Films, 2010. DVD.

Taylor, Mark C. *De-constructing Theology*. New York: The Crossroads Publishing Company and Scholars Press, 1982. Print.

Van der Weyden, Rogier. *Crucifixion Diptych*. c. 1460. Oil on wood. Philadelphia Museum of Art. Philadelphia.

Velázquez, Diego. *Christ Crucified*. 1632. Oil on canvas. Prado Museum. Madrid.

Ward, Graham. "Introduction, or, a Guide to Theological Thinking in Cyberspace." *The Post-Modern God: A Theological Reader*. Ed. Graham Ward. Oxford: Blackwell, 1997. xv-xlvii. Print.

Wright, Joseph. *An Experiment on a Bird in an Air Pump*. 1768. Oil on canvas. National Gallery. London.

Young, William A. *The World's Religions: Worldviews and Contemporary Issues*. Boston: Pearson, 2013. Print.

Chosen Families, TV and Tradition

Queering Relations
in the BBC's Sherlock

LINDA J. JENCSON

"It's a disgrace, sending your little brother into danger like
that. Family is all we have in the end, Mycroft Holmes!"
—Mrs. Hudson ("A Scandal in Belgravia")

Sherlock co-creators Steven Moffat and Mark Gatiss have described their
series as a love story (Rosenberg). Fans often interpret this to mean sexual
love, but an equally intriguing interpretation can investigate it as a series
exploring familial love. The series can represent family with all its ramifications: function, dysfunction, love, hate, rivalry, nurturance, coupling, parenting—every aspect of the rapidly shifting societal fragment we call family.
The series, however, does not depict a traditional, normative family, nor does
it repeat tired familial stereotypes. Moffat and Gatiss build a fictitious chosen
family centered on 221B Baker Street while simultaneously deconstructing
"the Family" in Western society.

Deconstruction is the creative, often playful repositioning of the components of a social institution (such as the family or the state) in order to see those
component parts better; to bring to full awareness old unconscious assumptions;
to allow one, or whole societal groups, to be able to rethink that institution.
While it involves a mental picking apart, the goal is not destruction but a
re-envisioning. To follow up on the architectural metaphor implied by the
term, it is a way to clear out the dry rot, reinforce foundations, fix roof leaks; to
install new beauty and comfort in societal structures in need of repair. Deconstruction calls social structures into question in order to make well-thought out

improvements. The goal is to allow participants in the deconstruction to make better choices about enhancing the quality of their lives (Ludemann).

The emerging family at 221B is decidedly *queer*. This is meant in the vernacular sense of being outside of normative parameters, although not in any negative sense. It is also meant in the scholarly sense that its unusualness is meant to draw viewers' attention to its creativity and uniqueness of form, thus assisting the process of deconstruction by helping the audience see all families in a new light as a result of observing the family at 221B. *Queer* once referred to intentional deconstructions of sexuality and gender, but I use it in the broader sense, borrowed from popular culture scholar and sociologist of the family, Jes Battis, "to signify multiple and overlapping forms of ambivalence: physical, sexual, psychic, philosophical, mystical and moral" (Battis 12). Ambivalencies expressed in narratives such as *Sherlock* can be consciously utilized to question traditional constructions of social categories and boundaries, such as "the family." Deconstruction of social institutions through engagement with queered narratives can be utilized to form new social identities and relationships which may have greater adaptive value than those traditional forms which the queered ambivalencies question (Bedore).

Televised families were once the antithesis of anything deconstructive. They originally served as idealized loci of narrow domestic "normalcy." This function was carefully maintained by government and industry censors. Although many other family forms existed at the time, only families composed of mom, dad, and the kids, isolated from extended family (but sometimes including a domestic servant), were praised and supported by government, medical establishments, churches—and therefore, by television. In America, social scientists called this the *nuclear family*, while in England, the term preferred by those engaged in debating appropriate family forms was the *elementary family* (Bott). Normative families in the 1950s were patriarchal, headed by a controlling male in the role of father and husband.

Televised series and film broadcasts of various versions of Sherlock Holmes appeared during the early days of television, as early, in fact, as 1939 (Steward 135). Produced when television genres were first forming their distinctive separateness (and were therefore rarely creatively combined), no one would have recognized a mystery program as having anything to do with families as yet. Holmes stories were conceptualized as who-done-its, period, although there were comedic adaptations as political satire in England in the 1970s (Steward 137). There was no commercially produced depiction of Holmes and Watson forming a couple, a chosen family, or any other form of family until Billy Wilder's 1970 comic production, *The Private Life of Sherlock Holmes*. It became the first cinematic interrogation of Holmes and Watson's relationship—and presented it under the influence of a troop of gay Russian ballet dancers. Although the Russians were gay and clearly attracted to

Watson, Holmes and Watson's sexuality was only examined inconclusively, and there was no interrogation of their family roles within the 221B household. Still, Gatiss and Moffat cite it as a significant influence on their version of the detective duo (Adams 138–139).

Chosen families, those where familial roles of support and nurturance are filled by non-kin, have become common in television series. For example, in the 1990s the demon-fighting companions of *Buffy the Vampire Slayer* became a chosen family. At the same time that the series experimented with crossing multiple simultaneous genres (horror, coming-of-age, romance, dramedy [a narrative with serious themes punctuated by frequent comic relief]), *Buffy* evolved into a series about non-relatives taking on familial roles in a shared household. In later seasons major characters gave one another personal strength to fight inner demons, at the same time organizing to repair broken pipes and windows in the house they all shared. They took turns filling a variety of familial roles—surrogate father, big sister-turned-mom, protective big brother, and confidante sister, among others (Battis). *Buffy the Vampire Slayer* has had quite a lot of influence on subsequent developments in television. Fans and scholars can recognize it as a precursor for *Sherlock's* crime-fighting, nation-protecting, meal-getting, housecleaning family of non-relatives at 221B.

Over time, televised chosen families increasingly have taken on the duties of blood- and marriage-based kin. It is a matter of relevance and familiarity, as partial kin, blended, extended, and non-kin households have replaced nuclear/elementary, patriarchal families in the real world throughout most of Europe and America. By 1970, only 40 percent of households in the United States were nuclear/elementary families; in the 2010s nuclear/elementary households make up only 19% of households. Thirty-four percent of U.S. households today are made up of non-relatives, just like the household at 221B, and 27 percent of households are people living alone (U. S. Census), as had John, Sherlock, and Mrs. Hudson prior to finding one another.

While traditional "defense of family" groups denounce the new majority household as both a symptom and a cause of the decline of morality in Western civilization, research suggests that alternative family forms, because they are more flexible, can be better adapted to deal with the emotional and practical needs symptomatic of the chaotic modern world (Battis; Douglas). As an example of what is meant by this flexibility, imagine having to marry before being allowed to leave the natal family to attend university or take a distant job, if roommate-based households were culturally or legally unacceptable for university students or adult employees. Such an idea may sound strange, yet in the past, government restrictions on household composition have been common. Most popular television series have taken the practical, adaptive approach, role-modeling solutions whereby chosen families, composite families, single-parent families, extended families, and all sorts of family combinations can take over the functions of the 1950s nuclear/patriarchal family, aided by a wider range of participants, while helping individuals heal from its faults. Chosen families such as the one depicted on *Sherlock* can fulfill material, emotional, and social needs—essential functions to keep Western Civilization going, not lead it to its doom.

Sherlock Holmes (Benedict Cumberbatch), John Watson (Martin Freeman), Mrs. Hudson (Una Stubbs), and even characters dwelling outside the 221B household such as Greg Lestrade (Rupert Graves) and Molly Hooper (Louise Brealey) whom viewers might recognize as Sherlock's extended chosen family, come from traditional families that have in many ways failed them. When the audience first meets John Watson (pre–Sherlock) he is isolated, lonely, bored, and suffering from nightmares and a psychosomatic limp. Yet he is unwilling to reach out to family, especially shunning his sister, an alcoholic in the process of divorce ("A Study in Pink"). Mrs. Hudson had attempted marriage, but her husband turned out to be heavily involved in drug trafficking and organized crime ("A Study in Pink"). He killed people and, perhaps more significant to Mrs. H, cheated on her—a lot ("The Sign of Three"). Molly Hooper longs for a traditional relationship but consistently fails to find one, attracting "sociopaths" such as Moriarty (Andrew Scott), instead. When she finally attracts a more stable man, they break up. When Greg Lestrade thinks things are better with his estranged wife ("We're back together. It's all sorted"), Sherlock reveals, to Lestrade's dismay, "no, she's seeing a PE teacher" ("A Scandal in Belgravia").

Sherlock Holmes's natal family raised him in isolation from other children (with the exception of his older brother, Mycroft—who cruelly convinced the genius Sherlock that he was stupid) ("The Empty Hearse"). Mycroft is a friendless, loveless man who is mad for political power, manipulates everyone, and is verbally abusive. Insults between the two brothers reveal that Mycroft not only filled the role of brother but had a significant role in parenting young Sherlock. When Mycroft grabs a tea pot at Buckingham Palace and offers to pour with the words, "I'll be mother," Sherlock interjects, "there is a whole childhood in a nutshell" ("A Scandal in Belgravia"). More troubling, Mycroft is willing to send Sherlock to his death to dispose of him for the British government. Furthermore, the conversation about that plan between Mycroft and certain high officials implies that Mycroft has already had a hand in the elimination of another Holmes sibling, referred to mysteriously as "the other one" ("His Last Vow"). Mycroft's influence on Sherlock has been significant, and if not for the counter-influences of John, Mrs. Hudson, Lestrade, Molly, and others, Sherlock might have spent his lonely life believing Mycroft's dictum that "all lives end. All hearts are broken. Caring is not an advantage, Sherlock" ("A Scandal in Belgravia").

Sherlock's upbringing leaves him with the personal identity of a high-functioning sociopath, either through formal diagnosis or general consensus, although some of those with whom he works, including Anderson (Jonathan Aris) and Sally Donovan (Vinette Robinson) of Scotland Yard attribute to him an identity even worse—that of a criminal psychopath. He does exhibit some symptoms. His upbringing failed to socialize him in many ways. He is often unable to express emotion (perhaps not even to recognize his own feelings). Nor can he relate easily to others, or even understand basic social conventions and values, a condition depicted and explored in depth in every episode.

Family psychologists Monisha Pasupathi and Marya Schechtman define identity as consistency, the idea that a person's self-concept and projection of self remain recognizable and predictable in regards to a number of core factors, including beliefs, values, social roles, occupation, moral stances, and group commitments. This identity has long been recognized by social scientists and psychologists as being powerfully influenced by family of origin (Pasupathi; Schechtman; Wainryb and Recchia). Because constancy is a key factor in identity, that identity is going to be difficult to change. Yet one of the great draws for *Sherlock* fans is watching major characters (especially Sherlock) grow and change through contact and interaction with one another within their chosen family.

Household Chores, Household Spaces

What are the common functions of families (whether nuclear/elementary, extended, patriarchal, matrilineal, matrifocal, arranged, adopted, or chosen)? Anthropologists have established that, around the world, an incredible variety of family forms first and foremost establish households to provide for material needs (Medick and Sabean). Families organize production and consumption so everyone has food, shelter, clothing, warmth, enough showy possessions not to be laughed out of town by the neighbors, and maybe transportation or entertainment. Are these essential functions really being fulfilled by *Sherlock*'s residents at 221B?

John Watson and Sherlock Holmes maintain a consulting detective business out of their shared flat. John's blog effectively advertises Sherlock's detective skills. John also has better money sense, accepting checks for services when Sherlock would have worked unpaid ("The Blind Banker"). Sherlock's apparent unconcern about payment is established early in the series. In the first episode, New Scotland Yard detective Sally Donovan explains Sherlock's detective work to John: "He doesn't get paid or anything. He gets off on [solving crimes]" ("A Study in Pink"). Sergeant Donovan perceives Sherlock's interest in crime as an unhealthy attachment to bloody murder. As Sherlock admits, he solves crimes "to keep from getting bored" and "to keep from getting high" ("His Last Vow"). Despite Sherlock's lack of monetary motivation, John ensures that their combined skills can support them. They spend a significant amount of their income on rent, which provides income for Mrs. Hudson, the third member of the chosen family. She lives in a downstairs flat, yet she comes and goes as she pleases from John and Sherlock's unsecured rooms, bringing sustenance, tidying up, and having her say on every topic of conversation.

Even the layout of 221B is conducive to the consulting business, as well as an "open door" policy to this extended family. Viewers cannot help but notice that the room layout at 221B is rather queer. It requires viewers to think about what rooms do for those who live in them. Not one, but two doors, next to one another from the hall, access adjacent rooms in the main flat shared by Sherlock and John, who never seem to keep the doors locked. Not only Mrs. Hudson but a variety of clients, government agents, and villains come and go freely. Perhaps this is because the odd little flat is discontinuous; John's bedroom lies outside the two doors, down the hall and up the stairs. His required access to kitchen and bathroom may have something to do with why they never lock and rarely close any doors. Mrs. Hudson's rooms sit two floors below John's and one floor below Sherlock's bedroom, the kitchen, and the sitting room, where most scenes take place. From her open door below the stairs, Mrs. Hudson can dart out to engage with John and Sherlock as they pass by, as well as conduct many of their visitors up the stairs. The flat is one, yet three. The physical layout of the household allows very fluid, only partially bounded, and often unpredictable interactions among the householders living within it. It works for Sherlock, John, and Mrs. Hudson because their interpersonal roles are equally fluid and unpredictable.

Family scholars have concluded that cross-cultural families accomplish consumption and production through the organization of gendered and age-based labor—families get chores done by assigning certain of them to certain categories of people. The 221B household divides tasks among John, Sherlock, and Mrs. Hudson, with John doing most of the shopping (normatively perceived as an adult feminine role in Western society). Sherlock messes up the flat with scattered research material and kitchen experiments on human remains. His messy (mis)behavior provides a lot of humor, as in the scene where Mrs. Hudson enters the flat one early morning and detects a foul smell. She follows her nose to the refrigerator and begins tossing stinky containers into the trash, finally lifting one ziplock bag for closer inspection and suddenly exclaiming, "Oh, dear! Thumbs!" ("A Scandal in Belgravia"). Sherlock's disgusting research habits ambiguously mix stereotypical income-producing (adult masculine) and unruly child roles. John and Mrs. Hudson share the (traditionally adult feminine) cleaning. Mrs. Hudson brings tea, biscuits, and other sustenance, because Sherlock's kitchen is too un-hygienic for cooking.

Mrs. Hudson also fills a maternal role (normatively that of elder females). This is reflected in caring behavior as well as word choice, such as calling John and Sherlock her "boys." She adamantly states she is "not your housekeeper" ("A Study in Pink"), yet she does not nurture the boys for pay, but out of love. Pointedly, the otherwise ice-cold Sherlock warmly hugs Mrs. Hudson in his first scene with her in the first episode and responds to maternal hugs and kisses from her ("A Study in Pink"). As evidenced by their already-comfortable relationship at the series' beginning, Mrs. Hudson was already contributing to considerable emotional growth for Sherlock, even before the advent of John.

When John and Sherlock disappear for two years following "The Reichenbach Fall," Mrs. Hudson grieves like many an empty-nester; she keeps their rooms as they left them. When John returns, her pain is apparent. She tells John, "I know I'm not your mother, but ...," clearly expressing that she thought it understood by all that she has indeed become their chosen mother ("The Empty Hearse"). Her character is stereotypic of televised elder females most of the time, but in "A Scandal in Belgravia" she breaks free of normative age and gender constraints when she conceals an electronic device holding classified information from thugs who break in, tie her up, and beat her to get the device. In this scene, her courage and stoicism are atypical of most depictions of an older woman and instead include actions normatively coded young and masculine. She also defies the normative stereotypes of domesticated older women because of her past. It is revealed in Season Three that Mrs. Hudson used to help Mr. Hudson run a drug cartel. Furthermore, she accuses Sherlock of watching readily available YouTube videos of her exotic dancing days ("His Last Vow"). Much to their credit, the writers of *Sherlock* have created a far more interesting Mrs. Hudson than any Holmesian predecessors. Nevertheless, she still fills a "mother" role for her "boys."

At times, Mrs. Hudson overtly critiques Sherlock's natal mother as well as his brother on their familial inadequacies. When she discovers that Sherlock has accepted morning tea from her for years without realizing it was she who brought it every day, she tells him, "Your mother has a lot to answer for." He responds, "I have a list. Mycroft has a file." Later, in response to Sherlock's selfish inattention, she tells Sherlock, "I need to have a talk with your mother." Sherlock responds, "You can try. She understands very little" ("The Sign of Three").

Overall, the series' depiction of traditional, elementary/nuclear/patriarchal/hetero-normative families, like the one in which Sherlock and his less-than-loving brother were raised, is extremely negative. Perhaps surprisingly, this is nothing new to Sherlock Holmes. Many cases in the original Conan

Doyle canon revolve around crimes rooted in the failures of the traditional family: domestic violence, divorce, infidelity, shame, and secrecy. In "Black Peter," the family patriarch "has been known to drive his wife and daughter out of doors in the middle of the night and flog them through the park until the whole village outside the gates was aroused by their screams" (Conan Doyle 149). Tom Ue discusses story lines in the normative detective story which end with weddings and happily restored families, contrasting Conan Doyle's Holmes plotlines for "the antithesis that they pose to the restoration of genealogical and social order" (Ue 11). Conan Doyle's happy endings often see traditional families torn asunder.

Sherlock continues Conan Doyle's Holmesian tradition. The primary victim in "A Study in Pink" neglects to clean her wedding ring; Sherlock deduces that her marriage is unhappy, and she removes the ring to conceal her marriage from "a string of lovers." He finds this quite clever of her. Infidelity and the associated heartbreak appear so frequently that Sherlock has a standard, curt reply: "Get a lawyer." The serial killer cabbie of "A Study in Pink" is divorced from his wife, who does not let him see the children, a situation that contributes to his killing spree.

As demonstrated by Sherlock's ongoing need for remedial mothering from Mrs. Hudson, all is not well in the nuclear/elementary families of main characters. However, their emotional wounds and struggles to overcome stunted social development are part of what endears them to fans. Sherlock and Mycroft's genius is explained in "His Last Vow" as an inherited trait from their mathematical genius mother. As her husband (clearly no genius himself) explains to John's wife Mary, "she gave it all up for children." This decision appropriate for the normative 1950s family is not very successful for the brilliant mathematician who must have made this life-changing decision in the late 1970s (in order to be the mother of the 40ish Mycroft and late 30s Sherlock). One son, Sherlock, is a "high-functioning sociopath," often perceived as a psychopath, and Mycroft exhibits far more symptoms of both illnesses. Both sons have histories of reclusive, highly anti-social behavior. Sherlock is often at a loss when it comes to basic responses to everyday social situations.

Raising Sherlock: Age-Role Ambiguity

Perhaps the most important function of families cross-culturally is the support and socialization of children, a function obviously done *dysfunc*tionally in the Holmes brothers' family history. It needs a re-do within the chosen family at 221B. Childhood and parenting issues take center stage, as Season Three introduces John's impending fatherhood, Archie the ring-bearer at John and Mary's wedding, and flashbacks to a child Sherlock. Although

John and Sherlock are physically adults, Sherlock in particular acts and thinks in ways appropriate to a broad range of developmental levels; he is the family child. His efforts to get Archie to do the ring-bearer role in the wedding provide an excellent example of the way that he sees himself in this role. "Why do I have to wear the outfit?" asks Archie. "Grownups like that sort of thing," explains Sherlock. "Why?" asks Archie. Sherlock admits, "I don't know. I'll ask one." Sherlock wins the boy's affection by showing him pictures of decapitations, to the chagrin of grown-ups at the wedding ("The Sign of Three"). Also in "The Sign of Three," Sherlock vocalizes his inner identity as the family child when he tells the newly pregnant Mary and John, "Well, you're hardly going to be needing me around, now that you've got a real baby on the way."

Whereas Sherlock's social age is decidedly queered, sometimes John's is, too. John usually takes the parental role; however, the series plays with audience expectations. For example, "A Scandal in Belgravia" begins with Sherlock not wanting to leave the flat. He sits at his laptop, wrapped in a bed sheet. Government agents barge in, demanding he come to Buckingham Palace. Like a petulant five-year-old, Sherlock presses his case for staying by refusing to get dressed. Cut to a scene with Sherlock, still in the sheet, seated on a fine Empire sofa, now at the palace. John enters and asks if Sherlock is wearing pants. "Nope," he replies. Instead of John delivering the usual lecture on appropriate behavior, both of them giggle like children, and John tells Sherlock he is fighting the urge to steal an ashtray. A subsequent camera cut reveals that Sherlock finally gets dressed, probably to conceal the ashtray he has stolen for John. These scenes demonstrate that, on the one hand, Sherlock is such a competent adult that royalty call upon him, yet his immature unpreparedness for the case ahead is established in the same scenes. Sherlock's royal assignment is to stop a professional dominatrix who has embarrassing images of a royal family member, and Sherlock is about to experience his first school-boy crush—on the dominatrix. It gives John and Mrs. Hudson opportunities to share concerned parenting, recasting John from the role of her son into the role of Mrs. Hudson's adult partner, a co-parent of "tween" Sherlock. Despite his personal identity as a brilliant detective and "high-functioning sociopath," Sherlock also sees himself (by the end of Season Three) as a child.

"Whatever it is you are": Queering Gender and Sexuality

Families teach, construct, and regulate gender roles in every culture; they also construct and restrict sexuality. John and Sherlock's gender and sexual identities are decidedly boundary-blurring. Although the stereotypical detective is hyper-hetero-masculine (Bedore), nearly everyone John and Sherlock encounter (e.g., waiters, motel clerks, police, friends, enemies, villains) assume they are gay. Despite this, virgin Sherlock behaves asexually, while John tries to chase every woman he meets, eventually marrying Mary Morstan. Despite these non-homosexual actions, the duo's constant gazes, touching, joking, and not-so-masculine bonding can remind viewers of one of the tenets of contemporary queer theory: sexual orientation need not be a fixed fact of biology but a socially constructed, interactive, fluid role. So, if not gay, then what exactly are John and Sherlock?

From the start, Mrs. Hudson assumes her two boys are lovers, asking John if they need to rent one or two bedrooms. In a favorite line among fans, immortalized on tee-shirts and posters, she tells them, "we've got all sorts 'round here. Mrs. Turner next door's got married ones!" After years of sharing the oddly interconnecting flats at 221B, when John announces he has found someone he hopes to marry, Mrs. Hudson exclaims, "so soon after Sherlock? What's his name?" John informs her his partner is a woman, and Mrs. Hudson gasps in surprise, "you really have moved on!" ("The Empty Hearse").

In the scene fans fondly call Sherlock and John's "first date," awkwardness ensues as the prospective flat mates get to know one another in a restaurant. The waiter calls John Sherlock's date, bringing them a romantic candle, which leads John to ask Sherlock, "So, do you have a girlfriend to feed you up?" Sherlock replies, "Not my area." John's eyes widen in realization, and he asks if Sherlock has a boyfriend. Sherlock's eyes widen as he assumes John is coming on to him ("A Study in Pink"). In the longer version of the scene from the original Pilot, Sherlock asks, "Is that what girlfriends do? They feed you up?" This sets the stage for John's chronic effort (coded as girlfriend) to get Sherlock to eat. It also colors interpretations of Sherlock's habit of feeding John at restaurants while Sherlock eats nothing. It is sexually ambiguous, but also age-ambiguous, as feeding can also be interpreted as parental.

Some fans are dismayed that John and Sherlock are not openly homosexual in the series, but perhaps something even more queer than gay is going on. In a study of the gay classic, *Brokeback Mountain*, James Keller and Amy Goodwyn Jones (22–30) describe the stereotypical "masculine" as angry, in denial about emotions, violent, stoic, and neglectful/sacrificing of self. Bedore adds that masculine detectives also isolate themselves. Sherlock enacts these descriptors. He gets angry and is in denial about emotions to the point of mental illness. "I'm a high-functioning sociopath," he proclaims repeatedly. He throws Mrs. Hudson's attacker out a window, shoots the walls when he is bored, crushes the dying cab driver's wound under his shoe, and apparently kills Jim Moriarty's entire criminal network. He stoically goes without food when he is thinking and lives on the street during some case investigations. Sherlock denies himself close human companionship, addressing most of his thoughts to a human skull prior to John's arrival, and accepts his brother Mycroft's pronouncements that "sentiment" benefits no one. Villains project masculinity onto Sherlock and try to manipulate him by attacking John, whom they perceive as his "damsel in distress." This is exactly what the villain Charles Augustus Magnuson calls John, as he explains that kidnapping and nearly immolating John was his way of discovering Sherlock's "weakness" ("His Last Vow"). The action mirrors an earlier use of John when Moriarty kidnaps him and wires him with explosives, another villainous attempt to gain power over Sherlock ("The Great Game").

These events would make Sherlock stereotypically masculine (and John quite feminine, with his deeper emotionality, nurturing side, and recurring need of rescue) if not for several complications. Sherlock is quite affectionate with Mrs. Hudson. His efforts to "feed John up" are more successful in this feminine endeavor than John's efforts to feed him. Compared to former soldier and expert marksman John, Sherlock's fight scenes include too many pratfalls accompanied by silly music to earn any macho points ("The Blind Banker"). John, the post-traumatic stress disordered soldier, never goes anywhere without a gun (in heavily gun-controlled England). This codes John *very* masculine. Unlike John, who coolly kills the cab driver without remorse to rescue Sherlock in "A Study in Pink," when Sherlock shoots Charles Augustus Magnuson in "His Last Vow," viewers see Sherlock's inner self regress to a sobbing child.

Other gender stereotypes examined and queered in *Sherlock* involve the question of domestic violence, where gender stereotypes predict the male to be the most likely batterer. Unfortunately, the family at 221B is dysfunctional enough to experience domestic violence. Yet it is the feminine-labeled John who hits Sherlock most often. In "A Scandal in Belgravia," John punches, pounces on, and chokes Sherlock, albeit initially at the detective's request while on a case. John simply loses control. Later, in "The Empty Hearse," John reacts angrily to Sherlock's "return from the dead." He knocks Sherlock to the ground, chokes him, punches him, and head-butts his face. In each incident Sherlock takes the "feminine" role of apologizing, makes no attempt at self-defense, and allows the battering to go on until John's stereotypically masculine anger is spent. Is it truly masculine anger, however? John's heart breaks when Sherlock fakes his death and does not bother for two years to tell John he is still alive. Is anger, if prompted by a broken heart, strictly perceived as masculine? A man repeatedly hitting a woman who does nothing but apologize is judged as wrong by most people in the modern Western world. Male-to-male fisticuffs are perhaps more acceptable. Does that make the interpersonal violence okay because John and Sherlock are both men? Is it okay because of specific circumstances (e.g., Sherlock's insensitivity/John's broken heart)? By queering identities and relationships in their narrative, *Sherlock's* writers lead viewers to see these violent actions in new ways, without the familiarity of gendered stereotypes. This can allow viewers to consciously question relational categories and social norms, perhaps coming to more aware and refined conclusions in the process.

Popular narratives can contribute to changes in societal norms and values. For example, the film *Brokeback Mountain* is recognized for influencing greater acceptance of homosexuality, by helping heterosexual viewers identify with homosexual characters. However, Keller and Jones make the case that the screenwriters did so at the expense of reinforcing masculine, patriarchal gender stereotypes, progressing one step forward for sexuality, but two steps back for gender equality. Both gay men in *Brokeback* are emotionally out of touch, violent, stoic, self-neglectful masculine cowboys. Sexuality is queer, but gender is decidedly stereotypic. Perhaps the writers of *Sherlock* lack the queer *chutzpah* to make John and Sherlock a gay couple, or perhaps the series' creators are bolder than writers who queer their characters merely by making them gay mirrors of heterosexual norms. *Sherlock* presents two men in a domestic, chosen family relationship, who love one another and swap gender roles as easily as Sherlock utilizes his cell phone.

A poignant scene in "A Scandal in Belgravia" asks viewers to reconsider John's continuing denial of couplehood. In this episode Sherlock gets flirtatious texts from the dominatrix Irene Adler. Both man and child, Sherlock experiences his first crush. When Irene fakes her death, Sherlock is devastated. John finds her alive and begs her to save the emotionally fragile Sherlock by letting him know she is alive. "Are you jealous?" she asks. John responds, "We're not a couple." "Yes you *are*," she insists. John angrily replies, "Who the hell knows about Sherlock Holmes, but if anyone out there still cares, I'm not gay." "Well, I am," she says. Sherlock overhears this conversation and becomes aware of the complex sexualities in their apparent "triangle." Tragically, none of them can "have" the one they love, because their bounded, either/or sexual identities get in the way.

Sherlock always tells John that he sees but does not observe; this scene asks viewers to observe, to mentally and emotionally rethink categories of sexuality and love, to question the very concept of "couple." No traditional categories of gender or sexuality apply in this scene. Viewers are led to ask what makes a couple. Is it sex? Is it a cluster of experiences: shared housekeeping, changing one another's lives, healing one another's wounds, saving one another from loneliness, loving one another deeply, making a commitment? Could the sum of these activities be more important than sex? Millions of fans have an opportunity to change their definition of *couple* to a more flexible, inclusive concept, one which incorporates love and sexuality as independent variables.

In Western civilization, the ultimate rite of the family is the wedding, and as Bedore points out, detective novels often end in weddings to demonstrate that patriarchal, hetero-normalcy has been restored (28). Season Three's "The Sign of Three" provides a deconstructive wedding. Sherlock, the best man, keeps slipping into wedding photos with the groom. His speech at the reception becomes a toast to his and John's mutual love, which Sherlock proclaims in no uncertain terms, lovingly narrating their years together. The bride never tosses a bouquet; Sherlock tosses his boutonniere. Sherlock makes a public vow of lifelong commitment—to John and Mary, but Sherlock only includes Mary because she means so much to John.

The *couple* question arises again. As Bedore explains in her analysis of queered detective novels, this is an example where television writers "distort that marriage plot in ways that undermine rather than reify dominant norms" (24). Because a couple is normatively the building block of a family, can a family have two overlapping couples with one person—John—in each? Viewers who may wonder how overlapping couples could possibly work in the real world are encouraged to watch the Franklin and Eleanor Roosevelt segments of Ken Burns' documentary, *The Roosevelts: An Intimate History* (2014), to see how multiple overlapping couples (sexual and asexual) gave one another the strength to preserve the free world during global economic depression and Nazi threat, much as John and Sherlock (and Mary) work together to save a fictitious England. Although *Sherlock's* dual couple hinges on John, these couples (e.g., John and Mary, Sherlock and John) are made possible because of Sherlock's extreme sexual, gender, and age ambiguity. The wedding's maid of honor, frustrated by her inability to strike up a normative heterosexual flirtation with Sherlock, verbalizes it succinctly: "I wish you weren't … whatever it is you are." She may be dismayed, but fans of the series delight in that ambiguity.

The Power of Popular Culture: Reflecting Families, Deconstructing Families, Changing Families

Sherlock is a product of the 2010s, thus reflecting contemporary societal questioning, and participating in the renegotiation of the social norms of its era. In the dawning era of television, families were narrowly defined nuclear/elementary units with restrictive gender roles, as the industry carefully cooperated with government censors. Yet even in the 1950s, television was already pushing social boundaries, already contributing to changes in its host cultures. In that period, some of the most popular fictional families were real families. *Ozzie and Harriet* (1952–1966) were a real husband and wife, raising sons who played their sons in the series named for the parents. The married couple Desi Arnaz and Lucille Ball played Ricky and Lucy Ricardo in the much-beloved *I Love Lucy* (1951–1957).

That series in particular contributed to some significant shifts in societal norms. In fact, *I Love Lucy* nearly never made it onto the small screen. It had to stand up to charges of illegal race-mixing because of its European-American leading lady and Hispanic husband. Had the couple in question not been real husband and wife, the producers would simply have made a casting switch. Because the couple was a real husband and wife, the network chose instead to take a stand against industry regulators, thereby making a significant contribution to positive changes in the social acceptance of Hispanics, as well as broadening the societal range of acceptable marriages. The series fostered another step in America's norms of social acceptance when Lucille became pregnant. It had been considered unacceptable for pregnant women to appear on television; series writers never would have written in such a story line, had reality not required it. Rather than cancel or temporarily retire the series until the baby had come, the producers made the bold move to push the boundaries of societal norms once again. The pregnancy season became a fan favorite, and the birth episode made viewership history (Adir 13–14). Most significantly, it was not only television that was changed. The acceptability of pregnant women to appear at will in public, and the popularity of attractive fashions for pregnant women, as role modeled by Lucille Ball in the series, became a new societal norm.

Sherlock, too, utilizes real families portraying fictional families, and it seems to intensify fans' emotional engagement, just as *Lucy* did sixty years ago. Benedict Cumberbatch plays Sherlock; his parents (Wanda Ventham and Timothy Carlton) play Sherlock's parents. Martin Freeman plays John Watson, and the mother of Freeman's children, Amanda Abbington, plays his expectant wife Mary. Una Stubbs is an old friend of the Cumberbatches, present during Benedict's childhood; now she co-mothers his character on television. Steven Moffat's son Louis portrays young Sherlock in flashbacks. Promotional interviews highlight the real familial relationships in the context of the series' "family," a promotional strategy which encourages fans to focus on family while watching and contemplating the program. It appears that, just as *I Love Lucy* did sixty years ago, *Sherlock's* portrayal of chosen familial relationships has the same potential to move society toward increased acceptance of new familial behaviors and forms. One could say that televised families increasingly allow the deconstruction of "the Family" in the hearts and minds of viewers.

Family roles are organized at 221B, but they are not constants. They are fluid and situational; each person freely takes or rejects a role as needed for the mutual benefit of participants. *Sherlock's* family is one of the queerest, free-form TV families yet to appear on television. The family at 221B challenges old norms and stereotypical assumptions about gender roles, age norms, couplehood, and more. Depiction of such innovative, flexible role models on television can encourage creative solutions to human needs that once were addressed acceptably by one kind of family only, in a world where everyone had to remain frozen into one familial role, and one role only. Series such as *Sherlock* anticipate an evolving society where material and emotional human needs may be taken care of by far more creatively constructed relationships, identities and households.

WORKS CITED

"The Abominable Bride." *Sherlock:* New Year's Special. Writ. Mark Gatiss, Steven Moffat. Dir. Douglas MacKinnon. BBC Home Entertainment, 2016. DVD.

Adams, Guy. *The Sherlock Files: The Official Companion to the Hit Television Series.* London: BBC Books, 2012. Print.

Adir, Karin. *The Great Clowns of Television.* Jefferson, NC: McFarland, 2002. Reprint.

The Adventures of Ozzie and Harriet: The Complete Series. Mill Creek Entertainment, 2014. DVD.

Battis, Jes. *Blood Relations: Chosen Families in* Buffy the Vampire Slayer *and* Angel. Jefferson, NC: McFarland, 2005. Print.

Bedore, Pamela. "Queer Investigations: Foxy Ladies and Dandy Detectives in American Dime Novels." *Studies in Popular Culture* 31, no. 1 (2008): 19–38. Print.

"The Blind Banker." *Sherlock*: Season One. Writ. Mark Gatiss. Dir. Euros Lyn. BBC Home Entertainment, 2010. DVD.

Bott, Elizabeth. *Family and Social Network: Roles, Norms, and External Relationships in Ordinary Urban Families*, 2d ed. New York: The Free Press, 1971. Print.

Buffy the Vampire Slayer: The Complete Series. Twentieth Century Fox Home Entertainment, 2010. DVD.

Burns, Ken. *The Roosevelts: An Intimate History.* PBS, 2014. DVD.

Conan Doyle, Sir Arthur. *The Return of Sherlock Holmes.* London: Arcturus, 2011.

Douglas, William. *Television Families: Is Something Wrong in Suburbia?* Mahwah, NJ: Lawrence Erlbaum Associates, 2003. Print.

"The Empty Hearse." *Sherlock*: Season Three. Writ. Mark Gatiss. Dir. Jeremy Lovering. BBC Home Entertainment, 2014. DVD.

"The Great Game." *Sherlock*: Season One. Writ. Mark Gatiss. Dir. Paul McGuigan. BBC Home Entertainment, 2010. DVD.

"His Last Vow." *Sherlock*: Season Three. Writ. Steven Moffat. Dir. Nick Hurran. BBC Home Entertainment, 2014. DVD.

Keller, James R., and Anne Goodwyn Jones. "*Brokeback Mountain*: Masculinity and Manhood." *Studies in Popular Culture* 30, no. 2 (2008): 21–36. Print.

Ludemann, Susanne. *Politics of Deconstruction: A New Introduction to Jacques Derrida.* Stanford: Stanford University Press, 2014. Print.

Medick, Hans, and David Warren Sabean. "Interest and Emotion in Family and Kinship Studies: A Critique of Social History and Anthropology." *Interest and Emotion: Essays on the Study of Family and Kinship.* Ed. Hans Medick and David Warren Sabean. Cambridge: Cambridge University Press, 1984. 9–27. Print.

Pasupathi, Monisha. "Constricting the Good Enough Self: Parent-child Conversations and Moral Development from an Identity Framework." *Talking About Right and Wrong: Parent-child Conversations as Contexts for Moral Development.* Ed. Cecelia Wainryb and Holly E. Recchia. Cambridge: Cambridge University Press, 2014. 389–415. Print.

"Pilot." *Sherlock: Season One.* Writ. Steven Moffat. Dir. Coky Giedroyc. BBC Entertainment, 2010. DVD.

The Private Life of Sherlock Holmes. Writ. Billy Wilder and Itek A. L. Diamond. Dir. Billy Wilder. United Artists, 1970. DVD.

"The Reichenbach Fall." *Sherlock.* Writ. Stephen Thompson. Dir. Toby Haynes. BBC Home Entertainment, 2012. DVD.

Rosenberg, Alyssa. "Sherlock's Return, the Holmes-Watson Love Story, and Updating the First Supervillain." Think Progress. 7 May 2012. Web. 25 Aug. 2015.

"A Scandal in Belgravia." *Sherlock: Season Two.* Writ. Mark Gatiss. Dir. Paul McGuigan. BBC Home Entertainment, 2012. DVD.

Schechtman, Marya. "Empathic Access: The Missing Ingredient in Personal Identity." *Personal Identity.* Ed. Raymond Martin and John Barresi. Malden, MA: Blackwell, 2003. 238–259. Print.

"The Sign of Three." *Sherlock: Season Three.* Writ. Stephen Thompson, Steven Moffat, and Mark Gatiss. Dir. Colm McCarthy. BBC Home Entertainment, 2014. DVD.

Steward, Tom. "Holmes in the Small Screen: The Television Context of *Sherlock.*" *Sherlock and Transmedia Fandom: Essays on the BBC Series.* Ed. Louisa Ellen Stein and Kristina Busse. Jefferson, NC: McFarland, 2012. 133–147. Print.

"A Study in Pink." *Sherlock:* Season One. Writ. Steven Moffat. Dir. Paul McGuigan. BBC Home Entertainment, 2010. DVD.

Ue, Tom. "Sherlock Holmes and Shakespeare." *Fan Phenomena: Sherlock Holmes.* Ed. Tom Ue and Jonathan Cranford. Bristol: Intellect Books, 2014. 8–27. Print.

United States Census Bureau. United States Families and Living Arrangements: 2013. Web. 25 Aug. 2015.

Wainryb, Cecelia, and Holly E. Recchia, eds. *Talking About Right and Wrong: Parent-Child Conversations as Contexts for Moral Development.* Cambridge: Cambridge University Press, 2014.

Fan Fiction as an Argument

Arguing for Johnlock through the Roles of Women and Explicit Sex Scenes in Sherlock Fan Fiction

ALYXIS SMITH

The Urban Dictionary defines *fan fiction* as "when someone takes either the story or characters (or both) of a certain piece of work, whether it be a novel, television show, movie, etc., and creates their own story based on it." Although this is a fantastic definition for those unfamiliar with fan fiction or struggling to explain it to someone else, the definition does not stop there. The entry adds that "most people who bash fan fiction are not willing to look past the fact that it's based on something else [in order] to see that it could be worth reading." This defensive addition represents two common reactions to fan fiction: the misunderstanding and distrust of fan fiction often felt by those unfamiliar with it and an anxiety felt by those who engage in fan fiction either as readers or writers as to the overall purpose of fan fiction itself. Fans in general often are criticized in the media for their "crazy" behavior. Fan fiction writers may worry about this reputation or the additional perception that what they write is not "original" or "creative" because their stories are based on, in the case of *Sherlock*, a popular television series.

One genre that most often invokes this mixture of anxiety and misunderstanding is also one of the most popular: slash, or homoerotic, fan fiction. This is largely because many slash works center around relationships between characters who are not queer in their mainstream incarnations but have had a queer identity structured for them by fan fiction writers. By giving these well-known fictional characters a new, queer identity, fan fiction authors create a space to explore these queer identities and share these new narratives with other fans.

Fan fiction, specifically slash fan fiction, may be read as an argument. Popular works of fan fiction inspired by the wildly successful BBC television series *Sherlock* form the basis of the following case study, which is focused on Johnlock (i.e., the slash relationship between John Watson and Sherlock Holmes) from both before and after the third season of *Sherlock* (the episodes when John is engaged or married to Mary Morstan). This study illustrates how *Sherlock* fan fiction works as an argument for the queer interpretation of Sherlock Holmes and John Watson, based primarily on the reoccurring roles of women as catalysts and the use of explicit sex scenes.

The Argument

According to the fan fiction website Archive of Our Own, BBC *Sherlock* fan fiction is the third most prolific genre of fan fiction based off a television show, while "Sherlock Holmes and Related Fandoms" is the most prolific genre of fan fiction based on books, even beating out the *Harry Potter* series of books and films. The fan fiction tag for "Sherlock Holmes & Related Fandoms" has more than 86,000 works, and the tag "Sherlock (TV)" has more than 79,000 works as of January 2016. Out of these works in the BBC *Sherlock* fandom, more than 40,000 are specifically designated as "Sherlock Holmes/ John Watson," a ship (i.e., a way of writing about a relationship) more commonly known as Johnlock.

These are peculiar statistics, considering that the co-creators of *Sherlock*, Mark Gatiss and Steven Moffat, along with the show's other writers and its actors, have all gone on record multiple times denying the possibility of a queer sexual identity for Sherlock Holmes or John Watson. It is clear to anyone who has watched *Sherlock* that "Sherlock Holmes is an easily-fetishized cyborg whose sexuality … [is] questioned within the text" right from the start, with Mrs. Hudson asking if John and Sherlock will even need two bedrooms, and John asking Sherlock if he has a girlfriend and, then, if he has a boyfriend (Coppa). However, any mention of Sherlock or John as a romantic couple is always written off as outlandish and humorous by those outside of the *Sherlock* fandom. An infamous example of this happened in 2013, when "controversial U.K. writer Caitlin Moran humiliated the show's largest audience" by coercing "stars Benedict Cumberbatch and Martin Freeman into reading aloud an explicit work of erotic Johnlock fanfic that Moran had gleaned from the fan-run Archive of Our Own," turning those fan works, and by extension their creators and others who enjoy them, into the butt of a very public joke (Romano).

This sentiment is reflected, to a degree, by those involved with the show as well. For example, in a 2012 article in the *London Sunday Times*, Gatiss said, "It's very much a men's thing—they're just friends. You can't really quantify it. I'm sure that you could never explain it. Except that John Watson is gradually making Sherlock Holmes more human, and Sherlock Holmes has given John Watson his mojo back. They form a unit" (Wilson).

The unit Gatiss mentions, however, is not sexual. Moffat similarly has stated that Sherlock Holmes, in the canon of *Sherlock*, is not gay (Hibberd). What the 40,000 works of Johnlock fan fiction on Archive of Our Own inherently do, then, is argue against Moffat's and Gatiss' readings of the show as a text. This is reflected in the high number of slash stories in this archive alone and the number of hits each story receives. Sherlock fan fiction indicates that an audience clearly exists for these stories—dozens of new stories are added daily. Such a vibrant fan fiction community shows that Sherlock and John's relationship in the show can be read as a romantic and sexual relationship, not just a homosocial friendship.

Much research already conducted about slash fan fiction has also looked at the psychological implications of reading and writing explicit slash fan fiction—for example, what the writers and readers get out of it. However, an anthropological or a psychological look into fan fiction also tends to cause an uproar from fan fiction readers and writers, particularly of slash, who do not believe that one approach or idea—or any—can encompass why they do or do not read or write explicit slash fan fiction.

In light of this divergence, the goal of this analysis is not to question the validity of a queer reading of Sherlock Holmes, John Watson, or their relationship as represented in BBC *Sherlock*. Instead, a close reading is used to examine the ways in which those fan fiction authors who do choose to argue for a queer reading of John and Sherlock's relationship execute that argument within their fan fiction. This analysis is focused first on three of the most popular works of fan fiction from the *Sherlock* fandom: "Performance in a Leading Role," by Mad_Lori, "A Cure for Boredom," by emmagrant01, and "The Progress of Sherlock Holmes," by ivyblossom. This case study involves a literature studies approach to two recurring themes in *Sherlock*-based Johnlock fan fiction: the roles of women as a catalyst to get John and Sherlock together romantically and sexually, as well as the explicit sex scenes between John and Sherlock. These three fan fictions establish a baseline of the most common arguments for Johnlock.

Women as Catalysts

Critics as well as fans know that one of the most important aspects of fan fiction, regardless of genre, is a fan fiction's verisimilitude to the source material. "The highest praise in feedback or recommendation" that a fan fiction author can receive "is that the reader was really moved, or the story was really convincing" (Driscoll 88). Convincing, of course, means that the story adds to the source material, so that fan fiction readers may easily believe that the characters they are reading about are the same ones they know already from the source material (i.e., *Sherlock* episodes).

However, when fan fiction is analyzed as an argument, the word *convincing* takes on new meaning. The fact that readers may praise a fan fiction by claiming that the events of the story felt convincing in relation to the source material also acts as a testament to the fan fiction's argumentative power. If a fan fiction about Sherlock and John working at a coffee shop, for example, is convincing to readers, that fan fiction author has successfully argued how and why two men *Sherlock* viewers know to be a detective and a doctor would logically be working at a coffee shop. The argument for a queer interpretation should convince readers that a queer reading of the source material as the basis for a character's queer identity is not so farfetched that it strips the story of its verisimilitude to the source material.

This quest for verisimilitude offers one reason why, in each of the three popular works of Johnlock fan fiction on Archive of Our Own on which this study is focused, the works commence when Sherlock and John are not already in a romantic or sexual relationship, only a homosocial one—in essence, picking up the characters where the show left them. In each of these three works of fan fiction, female characters act as the catalyst for the start of a romantic and sexual relationship between Sherlock and John. Women often help Sherlock and John get together and stay together, as in "Performance in a Leading Role" and "A Cure for Boredom."

"Performance in a Leading Role" explores an alternative universe (AU) where Sherlock and John are actors cast in a new movie as each other's love interest. Their on-screen romance eventually leads to a romantic and sexual relationship outside of the context of the movie. In this story, Molly Hooper writes the movie script that brings Sherlock and John together, Sally Donovan and Harry Watson are, respectively, Sherlock's and John's personal assistants, who plan to put the two in a position to confess their feelings, and Irene Adler is a publicist who helps the two keep their eventually blossoming romantic relationship a secret until they are ready to come out to the public. Women, then, are essential to the Johnlock relationship in "Performance."

The roles of Molly, Sally, Harry, and Irene in "Performance in a Leading Role" are similar to the role of an important but nameless original female character in "A Cure for Boredom" by emmagrant01. This story begins with John walking in on Sherlock attempting to masturbate and follows the two as they then frequent a sex club, where Sherlock orchestrates and then watches John participate in sexual relationships with first women and then men. During these sessions, Sherlock tells the third parties that he and John are dating.

The lie about their relationship starts off as purely pragmatic, until Sherlock arranges for John to sleep with an unnamed woman, who, during the encounter, uses Sherlock and John's fake relationship as fodder for her dirty talk. She assumes that Sherlock enjoys dominating John, tying him up and hurting him, and these speculations "[threaten] to send [John] over the edge" (emmagrant01). "He'd never even considered anything like that," at this point in the narrative, "but she made it sound sexy" (emmagrant01). This encounter starts John thinking about sex with Sherlock and eventually leads to John and Sherlock developing a relationship that might not have happened otherwise.

Of course, those familiar with the canon know that, traditionally, Stamford introduces Sherlock and Watson, and in fan fictions such as "A Cure for Boredom," where Sherlock and John already live together at the start of the narrative, this may still be the case. However, while in the canon Stamford does help Sherlock and John meet, his efforts only result in them living together as friends until John moves out to live with his bride, although he moves back in with Sherlock once he returns in "The Empty House." While many fans choose to increase the importance of Stamford's role in their fan fiction through such tropes as Cupidford, he is never seen as a potentially-negative factor in regards to Johnlock in the way that women are. (*Cupidford* is a portmanteau of Cupid and Stamford, used when discussing fan works that equate Stamford's role to that of the ancient Greek god of love.) Stamford, for example, never presents himself as a potential partner for either John or Sherlock; his goal is always just to get the two of them together.

Because of this, instead of having Stamford set Sherlock and John up only to have women tear them apart, many fan fiction authors choose to have their female characters play Stamford's positive role in facilitating Johnlock. This positions the women, like Stamford, as being in favor of Sherlock and John getting together. The women are no longer possible romantic interests for Sherlock or John, despite clues in the source material that they may want to be, such as Molly Hooper's *Sherlock*-canonical romantic interest in Sherlock.

However, not all fan fictions use women as catalysts for the development of a romantic and sexual relationship between John and Sherlock. "The Progress of Sherlock Holmes," by ivyblossom, is a first-person fan fiction that explores, from Sherlock's point of view, John meeting and marrying his canonical wife, Mary Morstan. However, in "Progress" Mary is portrayed as a serial cheater, compulsive liar, and generally awful person whose flaws and infidelities eventually drive John into Sherlock's arms. Once again a woman (Mary) is the catalyst for Johnlock, but in a different and much more negative way.

This treatment of Mary Morstan is not unique to "The Progress of Sherlock Holmes." As John's canonical wife, she clearly presents the biggest threat to Johnlock, when fan fiction authors choose to include her in the narrative. Although her presence in the canon does not prevent Sherlock and John from going on adventures, John being in a monogamous and heterosexual relationship prevents him ending up romantically with Sherlock. To overcome this obstacle, fans often transform Mary Morstan into a woman that John Watson does not want to marry, or at least not one to whom he wants to stay married, as is the case in "The Progress of Sherlock Holmes."

The roles of women as catalysts seem to have two main purposes in developing the argument that a queer reading of *Sherlock* is reasonable: to reinforce the verisimilitude to the source material, as well as to eliminate women as romantic threats to either man so that John and Sherlock may come together in a romantic and sexual relationship. This narrative need to eliminate a threat or require a catalyst, as in the works previously discussed, indicates the ease in which a queer reading may be applied to Sherlock and John in *Sherlock*. This reoccurring trope seems to answer the ultimate question about the series: If Sherlock and John are so perfect for each other, why can't they be together romantically? Using women as either a catalyst to spur the relationship forward or a hurdle that must be overcome allows fan fiction authors to answer this question in a way that still rings true to the source material.

Explicit Sex Scenes

Not only does the elimination of women as romantic threats to John or Sherlock allow the fan fiction to keep its verisimilitude by keeping women in the story while removing them as a threat, but it also illustrates holes in the source material that may be addressed in the fan fiction. As Ika Willis poetically states in her article "Keeping Promises to Queer Children," the goal of fan fiction "is not simply adding the final piece of a jigsaw" (158). If fan fictions' point were as simple as adding the last piece, they would complement, not argue, the source material. Instead, as with the repurposing of female characters in *Sherlock* fan fiction as catalysts for a homosexual relationship, "fan fiction first of all *makes* gaps in a text" only to "supplement these gaps with intertexts" (Willis 158). By arguing that women can facilitate homosexual relationships, fan fiction argues for the creation of a gap in the source material that permits such intervention and then inserts the argument that a homosexual relationship may fill the position left open by the lack of a heterosexual one.

None of the previously discussed three works of fan fiction ends with

Sherlock and John becoming a couple; they show John and Sherlock navigating life as a couple, both in and out of the bedroom. Exploring how Sherlock and John operate as a couple engaged in a romantic and sexual relationship often is manifested in the form of explicit sexual content that is not only titillating but also helps to strengthen the argument for a queer reading of the source material. As Mafalda Stasi correctly states in her article, "The Toy Solider from Leeds," looking at fan fiction from the angle of the author's feelings and intentions only allows "a view of slash limited to the anthropological perspective, or confined to the reader's or writer's psychology" (117). An anthropological or a psychological look into fan fiction also causes an uproar among the fandom's readers or writers of fan fiction, particularly slash, who do not believe that any one approach or idea can accurately summarize why they do or do not read or write explicit slash fan fiction.

Explicit sex scenes may be read as parts of the overall argument for a queer reading of the source text; they are not simply pornography and help develop an argument for queer texts' literary merits. As Catherine Driscoll asserts, pornography "would be anathema to fiction because only by characterization, setting, and plot can a story enter the web of canon and become part of the community that will circulate it" (89). This is not to say that there are not pornographic elements in erotic fan fiction; however, traditional pornography creates characters as vehicles for erotic content. Fan fiction, on the other hand, involves characters who have a history not only with each other, but with readers as well. The character's specific history, along with the setting and plot of the fan fiction, encourages readers to have an emotional connection to the pornographic elements of fan fiction that is often not present in traditional pornography.

For example, in "Performance in a Leading Role," readers must follow seven chapters of sexual tension between Sherlock and John before encountering any sort of erotic content beyond the two kissing and filming a sex scene. This build-up places the erotic elements in a larger context of characterization, plot, and setting that connects the erotic content to the characters, and thus the fandom at large. Unlike in traditional pornography, an understanding of the characters, as well as the narrative build up, is necessary for a successful explicit sex scene in a fan fiction that not only furthers the plot of the fan fiction, but also enhances its strength as an argument.

In the previously discussed most popular three *Sherlock* slash stories, Sherlock and John's relationship must demonstrate that the pairing is romantically and sexually gratifying to both. Such gratification is implied to continue after the fan fiction ends, which enhances the story's believability and furthers readers' confidence in a queer reading of the source text. A prime example of a fulfilling sexual encounter between John and Sherlock may be found in the sequel to "Performance in a Leading Role," "Lifetime

Achievement," when Sherlock and John take a brief detour between their wedding and the reception to enjoy steamy sex in the back seat of the car.

Sex in these example stories is always written as physically and emotionally gratifying to both John and Sherlock. The sexual gratification, not to readers but to the characters, argues for the validity of their coupling and, in turn, for the validity of an interpretation that would lead to such a coupling. The nature of sexual gratification being designed for the characters, and not only for readers' pleasure, separates explicit fan fiction from pornography.

This gratification also argues against interpretations of Sherlock and John's relationship as purely homosocial, with anything beyond that as just silly, as the series' writers and actors have stated in the media. In his article "Holmes and the Small Screen," Tom Steward states that "the references to a romance between the couple [in *Sherlock*] are often played for comic effect" (134). In order to argue against the skeptical brushing off of the possibility of a realistic sexual relationship between Sherlock and John, fan fiction must include serious sex scenes. The presence of explicit sex scenes in fan fiction, according to Francesca Coppa, "[tears] down the false barrier between sex and the rest of human experience" (211) so that the physical and emotional connections evident in explicit scenes between John and Sherlock equal the non-sexual physical and emotional connections between them. Tearing down the barrier between sex and every other aspect of life furthers the argument that a queer interpretation of *Sherlock* is valid. By graphically explaining how and why the relationship is romantically and sexually gratifying to both John and Sherlock on a daily basis, not just during intercourse, slash fan fiction authors make Johnlock believable and illustrative of real-world sexual relationships.

The Complications for Johnlock in Season Three

The most common way that the authors of the top three slash stories argue for Johnlock is by using women as catalysts to get John and Sherlock together and by including explicit sex scenes. However, these are not the only ways to argue for Johnlock, or any slash fan fiction's authenticity, in relation to its source text. The third season of *Sherlock*, as well as the information leaked about episodes before they were broadcast, posed questions and potential threats to the viability of a queer reading. For example, in Season Three, John meets, marries, and impregnates Mary Morstan—who turns out to be a trained assassin. While these new revelations do not affect works such as "Performance in a Leading Role" and "A Cure for Boredom" as much as other stories, because they posit Johnlock in AUs, one may argue that the verisimilitude of ivyblossom's "The Progress of Sherlock Holmes," written after the release of Season One and relying far more on television canon, is called into question in light of developments in Season Three. Arguing for Johnlock since Season Three has become problematic, but not insurmountably so, for fans invested in asserting a queer identity for Sherlock or John.

Three more recent fan fictions, published right before, during, or just after the release of Season Three, present new facets of Johnlock, the argument for it, and a more complex negotiation between the source material and fans' reading of it. As of January 2016, a new fan fiction took over the number one spot on Archive of Our Own, the spot that used to belong to Mad_Lori's "Performance in a Leading Role." "Nature and Nurture," by earlgreytea68, is about 50,000 words longer than "Performance" and offers a unique Johnlock argument: parentlock.

Parentlock is the term for any fan fiction involving John and Sherlock raising a child together. This is the main trope in "Nature and Nurture," a fan fiction in which John and Sherlock find out that, while Sherlock was away after faking his death, his brother Mycroft used Sherlock's hair to create an infant clone of the Great Detective. Sherlock and John then decide to raise the child together. Although not an unheard of genre before either Season Three or "Nature and Nurture," the unprecedented mass popularity of this type of fan fiction at this particular time in the source text's development is worth noting. Especially because of Season Three's depiction of heavily pregnant Mary in "His Last Vow," fans who ship Johnlock are more likely to consider the inclusion of a Watson baby within the parentlock narrative of Sherlock and John. On Archive of Our Own, for example, more than one thousand works tagged "Alternative Universe—Parents" have been posted since Season Three aired.

This genre is significate because it addresses many readers' anxiety about Season Three, even before the episodes were broadcast. Verisimilitude to the source material in a Johnlock argument would suffer if John's relationship with Mary was not addressed. However, some popular fan fictions take another direction: they ignore Mary altogether and deviate entirely from the series' canon. Nowhere in "Nature and Nurture" does John even meet her. Because of this choice to ignore Mary Morstan—or, indeed, to suggest that a wife/mother is unnecessary to rearing a child—"Nature and Nurture" differs from the three fan fictions discussed previously. In this story, women are *not* the catalyst for Johnlock—a baby is.

The first major example of the baby being a catalyst for Johnlock happens when John and Sherlock name their baby:

> There was something about the idea of naming the baby after John. Something more. Something terrifyingly more. It was the same more that was sometimes in Sherlock's smiles, sometimes lurking in the looks they gave each other after a successful session of sleuthing, sometimes rising suddenly in the space between them in the back of a cab, or in the space not between them when they collided in the crowded kitchen in the midst of experiments and tea [earlgreytea68].

Although the name they end up choosing for the baby is Oliver, the most common name in the country, according to Sherlock, the baby's surname is Watson-Holmes. Whereas Sherlock and John's relationship has not turned romantic yet, their child's hypothetical surname reflects the way that they are already "married" in all but the legal sense. This idea of there being more to John and Sherlock's relationship than friendship comes up many times, such as when the three go to the park and John watches Sherlock and Oliver feed the ducks: "It was not the first time John had thought about this, of course…. He told himself not to, but he'd stopped denying they were a couple, subconsciously, and subconsciously was where the thoughts happened. Sometimes the dreams were fevered and filthy, but sometimes the dreams were also casual and sweet, a cuddle on the sofa, a snog in the kitchen while John was making tea" (earlgreytea68). Baby Oliver causes John to more seriously consider his desire for Sherlock, based on the bond the men share from their agreement to raise a child together.

This shift from something heteronormative (e.g., John having a baby with Mary) to something queer (e.g., John raising a child with another man) is interestingly reminiscent of the scene in "A Cure for Boredom," while, in having sex with a woman, John finds himself desiring to have sex with Sherlock. In both stories, John says it is not the first time he has thought of Sherlock in a sexual or romantic way, but, unlike in "A Cure for Boredom," baby Oliver leads John to this revelation.

This continued need for a catalyst, even in a story with such far-out elements as clones, reflects the deeply-imbedded nature of the question brought up earlier: Why, if Sherlock and John are perfect for each other and by almost all accounts married, aren't they in a romantic relationship? Whereas "Nature and Nurture" uses a baby instead of a female character as a way to get past this question, the fact that each of these top-rated works of *Sherlock* fan fiction comes up with an answer to this question reflects not only fans' continuing confusion as to why Sherlock and John are not together, but also the multitude of different ways in which this question may be answered. This question represents a dissonance between the way the text presents itself and the way the fans read it, allowing Johnlock fan fiction to act as an argument for the validity of a queer reading of *Sherlock*. The validity of a queer reading is particularly important in relation to Season Three, when Mary Morstan poses a threat to the verisimilitude and stability of Johnlock.

Johnlockary

In writing fan fiction before Season Three of *Sherlock*, many fan fiction writers could and did simply ignore John's canonical wife, Mary Morstan.

However, in the wake of the second episode of Season Three, "The Sign of Three," which shows not only John's wedding to Mary but Mary's interactions with Sherlock, many fans instead chose to embrace her in a new type of pairing: Johnlockary (i.e., a sexual and romantic polyamory relationship among John, Sherlock, and Mary).

Although there are only about 400 Johnlockary works on Archive of Our Own as of January 2016, compared to the approximately 40,000 Johnlock works, Johnlockary offers a radically different way of reading *Sherlock*, especially in light of Season Three. For example, "The Sign of Three" offers an extended look at how John, Sherlock, and Mary interact, as well as how Sherlock plays an integral role in John and Mary's wedding. Whereas the idea of a polyamorous Johnlockary relationship did not arise from the airing of Season Three, that season is responsible for its increased popularity in fan fiction.

The most popular Johnlockary work on Archive of Our Own, "Orange" by emmagrant01, offers a succinct, but not sexually explicit, argument of how a polyamorous relationship would work among John, Mary, and Sherlock. Set just after John and Mary's wedding, the Watsons come to Baker Street to say goodbye to Sherlock as they leave on their honeymoon, but also to invite him to be a part of their marriage. Because a conversation between John and Mary allows this idea, one may argue that once again a woman is the catalyst for John and Sherlock getting together.

However, unlike in "The Progress of Sherlock Holmes," this getting together does not exclude Mary. She kisses Sherlock goodbye first, giving him a chaste kiss on the lips before she leaves. His kiss with John, however, is described in language reminiscent of many Johnlock works, even without becoming explicit: "all [Sherlock] could do was feel and breathe and moan softly at the sensation of John's tongue sweeping across his lips" (emmagrant01). This type of scene allows perhaps the most radical interpretation of Season Three, that Mary does not negate Johnlock but instead has a place within Johnlock. Mary transcends being a hurdle that must be overcome and becomes more than a catalyst to get Sherlock and John together. Instead, she becomes an equal part in their relationship. This interpretation of Johnlock as Johnlockary suggests polyamory as a way to reconcile the tension between John and Sherlock with verisimilitude to the source text, including as opposed to excluding Mary Morstan.

The most popular explicit Johnlockary work on Archive of Our Own complicates the idea of queerness, polyamory, and Johnlock(ary) even further. In the Johnlockary fan fiction "Round" by Songlin, Mary is again the catalyst for John and Sherlock getting together. Through conversations with John, she eases him into the idea of bisexuality, both his and her own. This allows her to broach the topic of inviting Sherlock to be a part of their relationship.

Mary then tells Sherlock exactly when to come over for this planned sexual encounter. Once Sherlock arrives, Mary tells each man when to do what and ultimately is in charge of the scene.

This story complicates the role of female characters as catalysts. Instead of being absent during the erotic sex scenes, Mary is instead in charge of them and takes part in them. Mary may be the catalyst, this work argues, but that does not mean she has to disappear after that. Additionally, instead of showing a kiss between just John and Sherlock, the sexual acts in "Round" actively involve all three participants. Even with Mary's involvement with John and Sherlock, the language used to describe their pleasure does not change or downplay Mary's role. She is an active participant in the sexual encounter, as are both Sherlock and John.

Mary's presence, Johnlockary fan fiction argues, does not negate the queer relationship between John and Sherlock. Instead, she allows a blurring of the often oversimplified gay/straight dichotomy, bringing into the conversation ideas of bisexuality and polyamory that are not only still queer, but also true to the source material. Although Johnlock is certainly the most prolific argument for a queer reading of the relationship between John and Sherlock, Johnlockary argues that there is more than one queer interpretation of the text, and the inclusion of a woman in the Johnlock relationship does not make it any less queer. Mary does not have to destroy or even impede Johnlock, "Round" argues. In fact, she may even make it better.

Of course, the fact that there are only 400 Johnlockary works on Archive of Our Own shows that fans, as a whole, prefer to read and write fan fiction that deals with Mary in a way that does not include her in the relationship. The possible ways of doing this are only limited by the author's imagination, and the options expand infinitely when the author chooses to write an AU fan fiction. In the wake of Season Three as well as "The Abominable Bride" special episode, fan fiction authors continue to argue for Johnlock. The lasting popularity of "Performance in a Leading Role," "The Progress of Sherlock Holmes," and "A Cure for Boredom" shows that, even as the television canon develops, women and explicit sex scenes are the standard way to argue for Johnlock, even though, as "Nature and Nurture" proves, that is not the only way to successfully make that argument.

As the BBC *Sherlock* canon slowly grows, so too does the argument for a queer reading of the show. Fans of *Sherlock* continue to use the space offered by Johnlock fan fiction to argue for their queer interpretation of *Sherlock*. Even with the addition of new source material, this argument continues to draw on the trope of women as catalysts for the formation of a sexual relationship as well as the inclusion of explicit sex scenes to show how the show's homosocial dynamic transfers easily into a homosexual dynamic. While these are not the only ways to argue for Johnlock, or even Johnlockary, these argumentative elements appear to be the most established in *Sherlock*-based Johnlock fan fiction and to make the most convincing argument for the validity of a queer reading of *Sherlock*. The popularity of these Johnlock works of fan fiction represents just how committed fans are to this queer reading of *Sherlock*, both because and in spite of the source material.

WORKS CITED

"The Abominable Bride." *Sherlock*. BBC, 1 Jan. 2016. Television.

Coppa, Francesca. "Sherlock as Cyborg: Bridging Mind and Body." *Sherlock and Transmedia Fandom*. Ed. Louisa Ellen Stein and Kristina Busse. Jefferson, NC: McFarland, 2012. 210–223. Print.

Driscoll, Catherine. "One True Pairing: The Romance of Pornography and the Pornography of Romance." *Fan Fiction and Fan Communities in the Age of the Internet*. Ed. Karen Hellekson and Kristina Busse. Jefferson, NC: McFarland, 2006. 79–96. Print.

earlgreytea68. "Nature and Nurture." Archive of Our Own. Mar. 2013. Web. 12 June 2015.

emmagrant01. "A Cure for Boredom." Archive of Our Own. Feb. 2012. Web. 22 Nov. 2013.

_____. "Orange." Archive of Our Own. Jan. 2014. Web. 14 June 2015.

"Fanfiction." Urban Dictionary. 7 Aug. 2006. Web. 28 Jan. 2016.

Hibberd, James. "Sherlock Co-Creator: For the Last Time, Holmes Is Not Gay!" *Entertainment Weekly*. 30 Mar. 2015. Web. 10 Mar. 2016.

ivyblossom. "The Progress of Sherlock Holmes." Archive of Our Own. Mar. 2011. Web. 22 Nov. 2013.

Mad_Lori. "Performance in a Leading Role." Archive of Our Own. July 2011. Web. 22 Nov. 2013.

Romano, Aja. "Why Fans Are Outraged at Sherlock and Watson Reading Sexy Fanfic." *The Daily Dot*. 16 Dec. 2013. Web. 10 Mar. 2016.

Songlin. "Round." Archive of Our Own. Jan. 2014. Web. 17 June 2015.

Stasi, Mafalda. "The Toy Soldier from Leeds: The Slash Palimpsest." *Fan Fiction and Fan Communities in the Age of the Internet*. Ed. Karen Hellekson and Kristina Busse. Jefferson, NC: McFarland, 2006. 115–133. Print.

Steward, Tom. "Holmes in the Small Screen." *Sherlock and Transmedia Fandom*. Ed. Louisa Ellen Stein and Kristina Busse. Jefferson, NC: McFarland, 2012. 133–147. Print.

"The Sign of Three." *Sherlock*. BBC, 5 Jan. 2014. Television.

Willis, Ika. "Keeping Promises to Queer Children: Making Space (for Mary Sue) at Hogwarts." *Fan Fiction and Fan Communities in the Age of the Internet*. Ed. Karen Hellekson and Kristina Busse. Jefferson, NC: McFarland, 2006. 153–170. Print.

Wilson, Benji. "Watching the Detectives; The Nation's Favourite Sleuths Are Back. Benedict Cumberbatch and Martin Freeman Tell Benji Wilson Why Their Holmes and Watson Partnership Is Such a Success." *Sunday Times* [London] 1 Jan. 2012: 12. Academic OneFile. Web. 22 Nov. 2013.

(No) Sex and Sherlock
Asexuality, Victorian Abstinence and the Art of Ambiguity

Amber Botts

Both the BBC television series *Sherlock* and the character Sherlock have fans who can be euphemistically called "enthusiastic." This exuberance has paid off with record-breaking numbers of viewers, as well as box office receipts. For example, the 2016 Victorian-set special episode, "The Abominable Bride," was released to U.S. and U.K. movie theaters within days after it appeared free on PBS and BBC on January 1. Revenues topped $30 million worldwide, with the limited-release episode hitting fifth in the U.S. box office earnings and first in China, where it raised $20 million (Sweney). This lucrative box office balanced the episode's audience appeal. "The Abominable Bride" had excellent U.K. ratings, with 8.4 million viewers, making the special the most-watched program during the holidays (Tartaglione). The program has a global audience, with 98 million viewers watching Season Three episodes in China alone (Tartaglione). This popularity has spelled additional success for actors Martin Freeman (who plays John Watson) and Benedict Cumberbatch (who plays Sherlock Holmes); since starring in *Sherlock*, they have attained A-list star status in such high-profile roles, respectively, as Bilbo Baggins in *The Hobbit* trilogy and as Dr. Strange in the Marvel film franchise. Their *Sherlock* characters are so popular that fans eagerly await any news about forthcoming episodes.

Cumberbatch's ascension as a sex symbol has somewhat mystified the self-deprecating actor, but Sherlock's sex appeal has encouraged fans to read the character in a variety of ways, most notably through fan fiction but also by personally identifying with the character's sexual orientation. Because series' co-creators Steven Moffat and Mark Gatiss have left Sherlock's sexual orientation in question, fans have filled the gap with their own interpretations.

In interviews, Moffat has addressed Sherlock's sexual ambiguity by stating that he has based his writing on the Arthur Conan Doyle works, with occasional nods to other film and television Holmeses, including the Basil Rathbone films, the Jeremy Brett television show (Frankel 10), and even U.S. television series *House* (2007–2012), with its "very, very grumpy protagonist," according to Gatiss (Frankel 36). The showrunners consider all these influences canonical, although their primary focus is to pay tribute to Conan Doyle, and Moffat and Gatiss are self-professed Conan Doyle super-fans. Moffat has said, "Our own fanboyness about Sherlock Holmes means there are absolute limits to what we do. Ours is an authentic version of Sherlock Holmes" (Jeffries). Moffat, in particular, has spoken often of the desire to honor the source material and to adhere to the spirit of Conan Doyle's work, even if he is modernizing Sherlock Holmes.

Moffat once called Sherlock one of "the two most asexual characters on television" (Mavity) when asked about fan fiction in which the Doctor from *Doctor Who* and Sherlock run away to be together. This story reflects fans' interest in Sherlock as a sex symbol, although he has not had a single sex scene in the *Sherlock*, despite being pursued by adoring coroner Molly Hooper (Louise Brealey), deceptive dominatrix Irene Adler (Lara Pulver), and (fake) fiancée Janine (Yasmine Akram), as well as sharing an emotionally intense bond with best friend John Watson. Both Moffat and Cumberbatch have offered theories to explain Sherlock's sexless state. While Moffat has used the term *asexual*, he seems to employ it more as a reference to Sherlock's chosen repressed sexuality (literally meaning "not sexual"), rather than the Asexuality Visibility and Education Network's (AVEN's) definition of *asexuality* as a sexual orientation rather than a lifestyle choice. In fact, Moffat and Cumberbatch have both stated that Sherlock has the capacity for sexual desire but channels it into his work. This, according to Moffat, is a Victorian concept pulled from the text of Conan Doyle's novels, in which the capacity for sexual desire exists, but Sherlock represses it. While either of these two interpretations—asexuality or abstinence originating from channeled sexual energy—explains Sherlock's disinterest in sex, the question is if there should be a definitive interpretation of Sherlock's sexual identity or if this very sexual ambiguity contributes to *Sherlock* fans' obsession with the character.

Sherlock and Asexuality

Despite Moffat's statements in interviews that Sherlock is not interested in sex because it is a distraction, the episodes are artfully ambiguous and can be interpreted in multiple ways. Instead of a consistent emphasis on a Victorian-esque repression that leads to Sherlock's suppression of all emotion and sexuality, thereby resulting in (a possibly life-long) abstinence, Moffat has offered several potential interpretations within the episodes, sometimes directly through dialogue, which could lead viewers, particularly asexual ones, to conclude the character also is asexual. In fact, Cumberbatch's portrayal speaks to certain viewers and reflects their own sexuality. "I was stopped on the street," Cumberbatch says, "and thanked on behalf of asexuals everywhere" (Adams, *The Sherlock Files* 29).

Asexuality is a sexual orientation, one which asexuals have been working to have acknowledged within the LGBTQ+ community. While some asexuals have used the LGBTQA designation, others see the A as not inclusive of all variations within the asexual community, thereby preferring the +. The asexual community is relatively small, yet diverse. "About 1% of adults have no interest in sex," according to a study by Anthony Bogaert, psychologist and human sexuality expert at Brock University ("Study: One in 100 Adults Asexual"). Thus, it is a more common orientation than the public may realize, particularly as some people may be on the asexual spectrum but do not self-identify as asexual. This, at least partially, may be due to the diversity within the asexual spectrum. Asexuals display a variety of behaviors, although the basic definition of *asexual* is "a person who does not experience sexual attraction" (AVEN). (*Asexuality* is not an interchangeable term with *celibacy*, which is a choice not to have sex rather than lacking a physical drive for sex.)

The asexual spectrum (Whatisasexuality.com) includes descriptions of demisexuals, or people who can form strong emotional but not necessarily romantic bonds; gray asexuals, or "gray-As," people who feel physical attraction but only in few circumstances; non-libidoists, who have no sexual feelings; the sex-repulsed, who find the idea and act of sex repulsive; and aromantics, people of any sexual orientation who do not experience romantic attachments (AVEN) but may identify as sexual (Doctor Azo). (*Sexual* is the term asexual organizations use to differentiate between those with sexual urges and those without.) In a more limited usage on Tumblr, though one which some *Sherlock* fans use to self-identify, is also the "aego/auto sexual or chorissexual, who are people who are aroused by sexual content, fantasize about celebrities or characters and are neutral or repulsed by sex with someone else" (mogai_library). Thus, the asexual spectrum encompasses more than the simplest definition of no sex drive. Though the physical drive may be non-existent or extremely selective, asexuals can choose to have sex to show affection and, according to AVEN, might enjoy it, particularly as a means of feeling close to a loved one. Many asexuals also can "get crushes and fall in love" because emotional and romantic attraction can be separate from sexual attraction. Asexuals may also be intellectually attracted to someone (AVEN), and bonds between people can be formed, but the relationship never includes sex.

Asexuals watching *Sherlock* can easily read Sherlock's behavior as asexual. In "A Study in Pink," John and Sherlock have a conversation about Sherlock's orientation. John asks if Sherlock has a girlfriend, to which he replies, "Not my area." John assumes this means he is gay, but Sherlock says, "I think you should know I consider myself married to my work, and while I'm flattered, I'm really not looking for any...." ("A Study in Pink"). This dialogue establishes early in the series Sherlock's disinterest in sex or romantic relationships, which would make Sherlock potentially both asexual and aromantic. In the next episode, "The Blind Banker," Sherlock does not understand why John is upset at his tagging along on John's date and "Sherlock-blocking" him by making it quite unlikely that "three continents" John will have sex with his girlfriend, as he is clearly planning. Sherlock does not seem to be aware that John has sexual needs, which could be due to Sherlock's lack of needs. His potential asexuality would not prevent his friendships or a deeper intellectual connection to John [or Irene Adler, Molly Hooper, Lestrade (Rupert Graves), or Mrs. Hudson (Una Stubbs)], but it would dictate his lack of interest in sexual contact. For example, in Season Three, bridesmaid Janine is sad at John's wedding to Mary Morstan (Amanda Abbington) that Sherlock is not a viable hook-up: "I wish you weren't ... whatever you are" ("The Sign of Three"). This ambiguous bit of dialogue leaves Sherlock's orientation open to interpretation, because Janine is incapable of identifying it. She is not upset that he may be gay or repressed but is confused that he is something different than either of those. Although these examples can most specifically be interpreted as evidence that Sherlock is asexual and aromantic, Season Three complicates the issue.

This season is potentially the most romantic season for Sherlock, who returns from a two-year hiatus spent dismantling Moriarty's criminal network and is finally reunited with those closest to him. However, Sherlock's sexual ambiguity increases, and viewers can still read Sherlock's behavior as asexual, though perhaps as more gray-A than in Season One. In "A Scandal in Belgravia," Sherlock says, "Sex doesn't alarm me," to which his brother Mycroft (Mark Gatiss) replies, "How would you know?" The dialogue implies that Sherlock has not had sex and therefore would not know how he would react. Later in this episode, John also discusses Sherlock's orientation with Mycroft; he asks if Sherlock has ever had a girlfriend or boyfriend or been in any type of a relationship, and Mycroft does not know. Irene Adler also reports that Moriarty (Andrew Scott) calls Sherlock the Virgin. Although Sherlock has neither confirmed nor denied his virginity, several characters' speculation provides evidence to support Sherlock's lack of sexual experience. Adler specifically asks Sherlock, "Have you ever had anyone?" Sherlock answers, "I don't understand." She puts her hand on his and asks Sherlock to have "dinner." Sherlock asks why he should have dinner if he is not hungry. Certainly, viewers can interpret Sherlock's comments literally. He has previously stated that he does not eat while on a case ("A Study in Pink"), and a dinner could actually be dinner (though no doubt Freud would disagree). However, with the addition of Cumberbatch's voice, which *The Times'* Caitlin Moran describes as "like a jaguar hiding in a cello" (likeaghostlyballet), "dinner" could be interpreted as double entendre. In this scene between Adler and Sherlock, he is intellectually intrigued. Gatiss calls what happens between Sherlock and Irene "intellectual flirting" (Frankel 65). However, without any insight into Sherlock's physical reactions, his emotional response is left up to viewers' interpretation.

In "A Scandal in Belgravia," Sherlock could be euphemistically telling Adler that he lacks a sex drive. (In other words, why have sex if he does not feel the urge?) His attraction to her can still fit within the asexual spectrum; Sherlock's attraction to Adler could be an intellectual one he does not feel the need to act upon (i.e., he is a non-libidoist). Sherlock could be a gray-A, and his response to Adler is one of the few limited instances in which he is physically attracted to someone, but he does not trust her enough to move forward with a sexual encounter. Viewers could also make a quite strong case for Sherlock as aromantic. He repeatedly emphasizes that he does not understand emotion and eventually tells Adler that "Sentiment is a chemical defect found in the losing side." Asexual fans or viewers who think of Sherlock as an asexual character might interpret Sherlock's dialogue and actions in a variety of ways that reflect the asexuality spectrum of behaviors in relationships.

Artful ambiguity plays in this relationship as the audience is never specifically told what Sherlock feels for Adler, other than a respect for her as an admirable foe. For example, in the final scene in "A Scandal in Belgravia," Sherlock feels an allegiance that leads him to rescue her, which potentially negates his being aromantic. (Infiltrating an international terrorist organization in time to save Adler from a beheading would be a lot of trouble to go to for someone for whom he has merely intellectual respect.) Additionally, sentiment is indicated in "The Abominable Bride," as Victorian Watson states that he has seen Irene Adler's picture in Holmes's watch. Carrying an image of Adler could also negate Holmes's orientation as aromantic, although it would not eliminate him being asexual or gray-A. On the other hand, Holmes replies to Watson that "as I have often explained before, all emotion is abhorrent to me. It is the grit in a sensitive instrument." This statement could be interpreted as support for Holmes being aromantic. He does not specifically refer to sexual involvement but rather to love and relationships. In fact, calling emotion "grit" in a machine goes well beyond what *aromantic* means, as aromantics feel emotion and can love, just not romantically. To further complicate matters, Holmes's comment could be intended to encompass all emotion and be less about repulsion to romantic love specifically than a fear of love and other emotional connections that could interrupt his work.

The latter appears to be the interpretation that Moffat favors. Interviewers frequently ask him about Sherlock's sexuality, and Moffat has answered, "There's no indication in the original stories that he was asexual or gay. He actually says he declines the attention of women because he doesn't want the distraction" (Jeffries). Moffat concludes that if Sherlock found men attractive, he would not live with John, and he directly disputes that Sherlock is asexual. "It's the choice of a monk, not the choice of an asexual. If he was asexual, there would be no tension in that…. It's someone who abstains who's interesting. There's no guarantee that he'll stay that way in the end" (Jeffries). While the word *choice* in this statement is not an accurate description of an orientation and the sentiment is not politically correct, Moffat does clarify that, from a writing and character-development standpoint, asexuality is not his intended interpretation of Sherlock's sexuality as it would eliminate too many potential dramatic conflicts if Sherlock were aromantic or non-libidoist. (Sherlock being gray-A, however, would not affect the series one way or the other, except that the narrative would require dialogue to explain *gray-A,* as many viewers may not know what the term means. Whether this dialogue would be welcomed is a separate issue.)

One fan writer researching Victorian crime novels agreed (although not happily) with Moffat's assessment: "I can imagine that [an asexual Sherlock wouldn't be popular] to be true. As long as readers/viewers can imagine sexual tension between Holmes and whatever character, they'll keep reading/viewing. If that is simply wiped away, this tension would be gone, too. At least in the eyes of a sexual person, whoch [sic] 99% of people are" (Annelie). Moffat has likely considered the hazards of declaring Sherlock asexual and has decided that, with the majority of his audience being sexual and the diversity of cultures viewing *Sherlock* (China, for instance, is one of the largest audiences), losing potential romantic and sexual conflict is not worth the potential risk of definitively stating Sherlock's sexual orientation, much less confirming his asexuality.

From an acting perspective, Cumberbatch agrees, echoing Moffat's stated intent. "[Sherlock is] asexual for a purpose, not because he doesn't have a sex drive, but because it's suppressed to do his work" (Jaworski). Some fans who are asexual have taken exception to the wording of this comment, just as they did to Moffat's misuse of *asexual.* gwydions wrote:

> Because a person doesn't choose one's sexuality, one only chooses to identify oneself as such, the thing is, it doesn't matter whether Sherlock has a sex drive or acts on it. The problem is whether he feels sexual attraction. And Benedict doesn't state this clearly…. For me, as Benedict puts it, Sherlock chooses to be celibate because of his work. And that's something completely different [from asexuality] [Jaworski].

Therefore, Cumberbatch plays Sherlock as repressed, though the ambiguity of the text is that Sherlock has not stated anything about his sex drive.

For some fans, Sherlock represents a character who lives life in a way similar to their own, as he does not have sex and seemingly does not need it. He also repudiates relationships, which is counter to most television series; thus, he speaks for the aromantic, even if that is not Moffat's intent.

Sherlock and Celibacy

Moffat's answer to the question of Sherlock's sexuality is that he focuses his sexual energy in the same way that monks do. Generally, Moffat does draw as much from Conan Doyle as possible, and he cites the original novels for his inspiration for Sherlock's sexuality: "It's a funny thing when a character for over 100 years has been saying, 'I don't do that at all. He's been saying it for over 100 years. He's not interested in [sex]. He's willfully staying away from that to keep his brain pure—a Victorian belief, that" (Hibbert). The idea of focusing sexual energy into something else actually is an even older idea. "For centuries, man has tried to channel this [sexual] energy into more fulfilling areas and higher states of consciousness," including Tantric and Taoist sexual energy practices. Many creative people have seen sex as a distraction from their creativity, including Homer, Ludwig von Beethoven, Gandhi, Henry David Thoreau, Leonardo da Vinci, Dante, and Nikola Tesla (Sol). They may have been asexuals or gray-A in practice, even before the vocabulary to describe their sexual orientation existed, but the idea of channeling sexual energy does have a long history that can explain someone's lack of sexual activity. Although, as Moffat has noted, monks have channeled their sexual drive into other outlets long before many Victorians did, the Victorians no doubt came up with inventive approaches to circumventing sexual urges.

The ideal Victorian viewed sexual urges as problems to be solved. Victorians engaged in educational or political campaigns to "encourage chastity, to eliminate prostitution, and to discourage masturbation" (Rubin 100). This attitude came both from Christian doctrine and the Enlightenment, which "stated that sexual passion should be tamed and controlled" (Anand 109). Thus, Victorians saw sex as "inherently sinful. It may be redeemed if performed within marriage for procreative purposes and if the pleasurable aspects are not enjoyed too much ... the genitalia are an intrinsically inferior part of the body, much lower and less holy than the mind, the soul, or the heart" (Rubin 107). With this attitude in mind, Conan Doyle's Sherlock represents the purest of the Victorian ideals, the elevation of the mind over body. Exerting that control was evidence of the highest degree of accomplishment. This attitude is the one to which Moffat refers as Victorian repression.

William Acton, Victorian writer of *The Functions and Disorders of the Reproductive Organs*, both epitomized and immortalized this attitude within his work. He famously claimed that "the majority of women (happily for them) are not very much troubled by sexual feelings of any kind" (Furneaux). One presumes that they are "happily" not having to fight to rise above an "inherently sinful" sexual nature, but the description sounds like non-libidoist asexuals. On the other hand, Victorian men were then considered the "sole bearers of sexuality" (Anand 110) and thus had to apply themselves to caging their animal natures, beginning in youth. "All its [the mind's] vital energy should be employed in building up the growing frame, in storing up external impressions, and educating the brain to receive them" (Marcus 13), and Acton warned that if young men started masturbating, it would lead to acne, clammy hands, stunted growth, and the inability to look others in the face (19). While most critics agree that even Acton likely did not believe that boys could be entirely prevented from masturbating, he suggested, with general Victorian optimism, that they could at least make an attempt. For gentlemen, the key to the heights of masculine identity was to be the "incarnation of ascetic discipline" with a "strenuous regimen … a charismatic self-mastery" (Adams, *Dandies* 7). This means practicing abstention and self-control, which applied to all activities, including sexual ones.

To achieve this self-mastery, Acton recommended continence, which involves not only sexual abstinence, "but in controlling all sexual excitement," which "drives him with unwavering energy along his course of purity" (Acton qtd. in Marcus 23). This very much sounds like what Moffat describes as the way Conan Doyle portrays Holmes's sexual repression as focusing his energy into observation and retention. This also sounds much like Sherlock's comment on being married to his work ("A Study in Pink"). While this statement can be seen as evidence of Sherlock's asexuality, it can also be interpreted as Victorian repression; Sherlock's first priority is to the exclusion of romance and sex. This can then be interpreted as the Victorian ideal of elevating mind over body, with work, achievement, and accomplishment as his goals.

Sherlock, in Season One, sees no test to his focus; however, Moffat, in Season Two, introduces Irene Adler specifically as a challenge to Sherlock's repression, one drawn from the books. Moffat says Sherlock "encounters the only woman in the original stories that he really pays any attention to at all" ("Sherlock Uncovered"). Adler is a challenge to Sherlock in all arenas, which is a conscious choice in the writing and acting. Guy Adams, author of *The Sherlock Files,* adds that "A Scandal in Belgravia" is "the closest *Sherlock* is ever likely to get to a love story for its titular hero. A love story with betrayal, sexual violence, assassins, and a plane full of corpses" (104). Cumberbatch has also described the way he played his adversarial relationship with Adler as "love, horror, and thriller" ("Sherlock Uncovered"), so he portrays a relationship with romantic connotations, at least. Similarly, Lara Pulver states that Adler's relationship with Sherlock is "like they're looking in a mirror at each other. They're just in tune. They get each other. They see through each other's masks…. It's an infatuation, a mutual infatuation" (Adams, *The Sherlock Files* 105). She plays Adler with an intent to show connection and chemistry, regardless of whether her character gets any "dinner."

Cumberbatch also plays Sherlock as attracted to Irene, but actively repressing that sexual and emotional attraction. Cumberbatch further explains that relationships are "a negative in his [Sherlock's] book; it's something that is basically going to undermine his ability to do his job, to concentrate and focus and apply logic" ("Sherlock Uncovered"). The actor believes Sherlock is capable of emotion and desire but wills them away. In an interview with *Elle UK*, Cumberbatch adds that he believes that Sherlock likely had sex with Adler and is quite capable of pleasing a woman. Then, he goes into detail about Sherlock's potential prowess, regardless of his level of experience (Brog). Cumberbatch believes Sherlock would do some extensive research with porn and sex manuals, then employ his powerful mind to pleasure. The actor clearly has thought about Sherlock's amorous abilities but, by the end of the interview, reminds viewers that regardless of what could happen if he uncaged the beast, *Sherlock* is not the kind of series to show Sherlock's sexual adventures.

Thus, from the production end, an abstinence due to repression is the interpretation that the writers, producers, and actors have in mind. Sherlock avoids sex and relationships as they would lead to emotional attachments and thus distractions from his work. Nevertheless, his ability to keep emotional distance is not perfect; Sherlock comes to love John as his best friend, to care enough for Mary to kill Charles Augustus Magnussen (Lars Mikkelsen) in order to protect her, and to trust Molly enough to ask for her help, for example. In all of these situations, Sherlock has tried to maintain an emotional distance that could allow his total focus on work, but he has failed. He cannot repress his emotions, despite his best efforts.

This Victorian repression is most explicitly expressed in the Victorian setting. In "The Abominable Bride," Holmes quotes Watson's words back to him: he is "the brain without a heart, the calculating machine," but Watson says that that is only the image in the stories he writes, not the reality. As much as Sherlock wants to be all brain, he does care, and caring does affect his work. It makes him vulnerable, first when Moriarty threatens Sherlock's friends' lives to force his fall ("The Reichenbach Fall") and later when Magnussen does the same ("The Empty Hearse"; "His Last Vow"). Regardless of how much Sherlock states his dedication to logic, he does have emotional ties. Ultimately, Watson asks Holmes, "What made you like this?" Holmes answers, "Nothing made me. I made me" ("The Abominable Bride"). This statement implies the Victorian idea of focused repression: *I made me*. This is not being born with an innate orientation but making a specific choice, which tracks with the idea of repressing his sexuality as well as a means of staying focused on the job and not being distracted by love and relationships.

Conclusion

Sherlock as a program is ambiguous enough to allow fans to interpret it (including its title character's sexual orientation) in a way that best suits them. The quagmire that Moffat perhaps is avoiding is that, once any definitive self-identification occurs, it would alienate those viewers who want to see what they wish to see, whether that be a romantic relationship between Sherlock and John, Sherlock and Molly, or Sherlock and no one. The other hazard is more of a problem on the writing end, as it would require expository dialogue to explain whatever type of sexual orientation applies to Sherlock, and if Moffat were to change his mind and decide to have Sherlock fall in love or to pursue a sexual affair, he would have to meet the audience's expectations of that orientation. To be done well, Sherlock's sexual orientation would have to be portrayed realistically and sensitively.

Moffat's main goal is to entertain. The audience may be preoccupied with Sherlock's sexual identity, but Moffat clearly is not. Episodes provide enough ambiguity so that people can see what they want, which is as it should be. As long as the ambiguity exists, asexual viewers looking for asexual characters can see one in Sherlock; other viewers, including some asexual viewers, can see emotional connections that may someday become romantic or sexual but are currently being repressed. Depending on the lens with which the viewer watches, either interpretation could be considered valid. The show does not have to promote either asexuality or celibacy, as long as the fans are satisfied with the artful ambiguity.

WORKS CITED

"The Abominable Bride." *Sherlock*. Writ. Mark Gatiss, Steven Moffat. Dir. Douglas Mackinnon. BBC Entertainment, 2016. DVD.

Adams, Guy. *The Sherlock Files: The Official Companion to the Hit Television Series.* New York: It Books, 2013. Print.

Adams, James Eli. *Dandies and Desert Saints: Styles of Victorian Masculinity.* Ithaca: Cornell University Press, 1995. Print.

Anand, Natasha Rupkatha. "Theorizing Men and Men's Theorizing: Mapping X." *Journal on Interdisciplinary Studies in Humanities* 7, no. 3 (2015): 107–117. Web.

Annelie. "Was Sherlock Holmes Asexual?" The Mystery, Crime, and Thriller Group Discussion. Goodreads. 19 Jan. 2013, 12 July 2013. Web. 8 Mar. 2016.

Asexuality Visibility and Education Network (AVEN). "Overview." Asexuality.org. 2001–2012. Web. 19 Sep. 2015.

"The Blind Banker." *Sherlock*. Writ. Stephen Thompson. Dir. Euros Lyn. BBC Entertainment, 2010. DVD.

Brog, Annabel. "Benedict Cumberbatch Talks Sherlock & Sex." *Elle UK*. 29 Oct. 2014. Web. 5 Nov. 2014.

Doctor Azo. "The Aromantic Thread." AVEN. 7 Aug. 2010. Web. 6 Mar. 2016.

"The Empty Hearse." *Sherlock*. Writ. Mark Gatiss. Dir. Jeremy Lovering. BBC Entertainment, 2014. DVD.

Frankel, Valerie Estelle. *Sherlock: Every Canon Reference You May Have Missed in BBC's Series 1–3*. Sunnyvale, CA: LitCrit Press, 2014. Print.

Furneaux, Holly. "Victorian Sexualities." Discovering Literature: Romantics and Victorians. 2016. Web. 17 Feb. 2016.

Hibberd, James. "*Sherlock* Co-Creator: For the Last Time, Holmes is Not Gay." *Entertainment Weekly*. 30 Mar. 2015. Web. 15 Sep. 2015.

"His Last Vow." *Sherlock*. Writ. Steven Moffat. Dir. Nick Hurran. BBC Entertainment, 2014. DVD.

Jaworski, Michelle. "Benedict Cumberbatch: Sherlock Knows How to Please a Woman." *The Daily Dot*. 2 Nov. 2014. Web. 5 Nov. 2014.

Jeffries, Stuart. "There is a Clue Everybody's Missed: Sherlock Writer Steven Moffatt Interviewed." *The Guardian*. 20 Jan 2012. Web. 15 Sep. 2015.

likeaghostlyballet. "Benedict Cumberbatch." Urban Dictionary. 6 Dec. 2010. Web. 20 Jan. 2016.

Marcus, Steven. *The Other Victorians: A Study of Sexuality and Pornography in Mid-Nineteenth Century England*. Piscataway, NJ: Transaction, 2009. Print.

Mavity, Anne. "*Sherlock*: Cast Interview." YouTube. 7 Sep. 2015.

mogai_library. "Characteristics." Tumblr. 2016. Web. 23 Feb. 2016.

"The Reichenbach Fall." *Sherlock*. Writ. Steve Thompson. Dir. Toby Haynes. BBC Entertainment, 2012. DVD.

Rubin, Gayle S. "Thinking Sex: Notes for a Radical Theory of the Politics of Sexuality." *The Lesbian and Gay Studies Reader*. New York: Routledge, 1983. 100–133. Print.

"A Scandal in Belgravia." Writ. Steven Moffat. Dir. Paul McGuigan. BBC Entertainment, 2012. DVD.

"Sherlock Uncovered." *Sherlock: Season 2*. BBC Entertainment, 2012. DVD.

"The Sign of Three." *Sherlock*. Writ. Stephen Thompson, Mark Gatiss, Steven Moffat. Dir. Colm McCarthy. BBC Entertainment, 2014. DVD.

Sol, Mateo. "Transforming Sexual Energy into Spiritual Energy." Loner Wolf. 2015. Web. 29 Dec. 2015.

"A Study in Pink." *Sherlock*. Writ. Steven Moffat. Dir. Paul McGuigan. BBC Entertainment, 2010. DVD.

"Study: One in 100 Adults Asexual." Science & Space. CNN. 14 Oct. 2004. Web. 14 Mar. 2016.

Sweney, Mark. "*Sherlock*: The Abominable Bride Cinema Sales Top £21m Worldwide." *The Guardian*.14 Jan. 2016. Web. 7 Mar. 2016.

Tartaglione, Nancy. "'Sherlock' Returns to BBC1 with 8.4 Million Viewers; Tops UK New Year's Day Ratings." *Deadline Hollywood*. 2 Jan. 2016. Web. 10 Jan. 2016.

Whatisasexuality.com. "What is Asexuality?" 2015. Web. 10 Sep. 2016.

Sherlock and the Case
of the Feminist Fans

CHARLA R. STROSSER

"He used to make merry over the cleverness of women, but
I have not heard him do it of late."
   —John Watson ("A Scandal in Bohemia")

The Sherlock Holmes canon is no stranger to engaged and outspoken fans. When Sir Arthur Conan Doyle killed off Sherlock Holmes in 1893 so that he could focus on his more serious writing, fans all over the world took to the streets in black arm bands. *The Strand* lost thousands of readers. Newspapers published obituaries (Klimchyskaya). Eventually, Conan Doyle resurrected Sherlock Holmes, largely because he needed the money and partly to keep his unruly fans from overtaking the character. In the vacuum of Conan Doyle's stories, fans had begun writing their own stories in what modern audiences would refer to as fan fiction (Harrington). Conan Doyle was even able to purchase one of these stories for ten pounds and adapt the idea (Harrington). Steven Moffat and Mark Gatiss, the creators of the BBC's *Sherlock* (2010-present), one of the most recent and popular adaptations of the Holmes canon, face similar, if not even more robust criticism and input from their fans, especially their female fans. Although Conan Doyle may have experienced occasional backlash over character decisions, writers and co-creators Moffat and Gatiss are inundated with fan response and reaction from all sides. Moffat (in particular) and Gatiss have been sharply criticized by fans for their portrayal of female characters. Although it is true that the Mrs. Hudson (Una Stubbs), Molly Hooper (Louise Brealey), Irene Adler (Lara Pulver), and Mary Morstan (Amanda Abbington) found in the television adaptation offer a change from the original characters that Moffat describes as "a bit boring," it is short-sighted to pretend that simply adding more female characters makes a show feminist (Radish). Although these women obviously offer more interesting backstories, in Season One they seldom display any real agency and frequently claim the role of the damsel in distress. In the last episode of Season Two and in Season Three as a whole, there are major changes made to the portrayal of female characters. In fact, Molly (in "The Reichenbach Fall") and Mary (in "His Last Vow") are credited with saving Sherlock's life, and John is identified as the "damsel in distress" ("His Last Vow"). The *Sherlock* special episode, "The Abominable Bride," stumbles in its feminist aims when the Victorian victims of male abuse are revealed to be a secret cabal of murderous suffragettes. Although Moffat and Gatiss do adapt their female characters to a more contemporary worldview, just as they are contemporizing other aspects of the show, these character adaptations are sometimes shallow attempts at feminism. Nevertheless, the creators do at least seem to be aware of feminist fans' desire to see more dynamic and powerful women on the show, indicating that this series is ultimately a case where the voices of feminist fans are being heard.

Sherlock Holmes and His Fans: Who They Are and Why They Matter

Traditionally, most Sherlock Holmes fans were fans of the books first. Even iconic screen representations of the character, like that provided by Basil Rathbone in the 1940s, did not create the robust fan reaction created by Benedict Cumberbatch's portrayal of the character in the 2010s. Because fans most frequently connect to the stories on a literary level, Roberta Pearson argues that these fans may even prefer to categorize themselves as "aficionados" or "connoisseurs" (98). The transition of the character to television and the show's overwhelming popularity has changed this identification, at least for part of the audience. Although *Sherlock* airs on the BBC, hardly considered mainstream by American audiences who watch the imported episodes on PBS, the popularity of the show has transcended the broadcast channel. *Sherlock* is popular with college students, their parents, and their grandparents. In *Sherlock and Transmedia Fandom*, Louisa Ellen Stein and Kristina Busse attributed some of this popularity to the fact that "The series unites participants in the highly active traditions of Sherlock Holmes fandom with long-time fans of Holmes who have not acted on that fandom in community contexts…. The series has also capitalized on its close association with the fan/cult favorite *Doctor Who*" (14) because of Moffat's simultaneous role as showrunner/writer of both BBC series. Fans flocking to *Sherlock* might previously have never had more than a passing encounter with the original canon.

Although the range of Sherlock fans is broader, the appeal of the character is not. As Anastasia Klimchynskaya points out in "Sherlock Holmes: The Original Fandom," "The kind of hype surrounding *Sherlock* today very much resembles the hysteria around the time the stories were originally published." For example, when Conan Doyle resurrected Holmes for *The Hound of the Baskervilles, The Strand's* readership increased by 30,000 subscriptions (Willis). *Sherlock* can also claim a significant increase in viewership, moving from 3.2 million for the Season Two premiere to almost 4 million for the Season Three premiere (De Moraes), which is particularly notable because of the long hiatus between seasons.

Growing fan numbers are only strengthened by modern marketing techniques and consumer culture. Pearson's fan article also acknowledges artifacts as a strong component of the fan experience and claims that "Sherlockians … can acquire an endless array of artifacts in addition to the core television shows and Conan Doyle works" (104). Since the onset of *Sherlock*, the opportunity for more fans to gain these artifacts has increased drastically. Now fans can use a "Sher-locked" phone case while wearing a *Sherlock* t-shirt and playing a *Sherlock*-themed game of Cluedo. They can have ownership, literally, of the stories in a way that has not been possible before. Once fans can begin to feel ownership, whether of a phone case or a fan fiction story, they are much more likely to engage with showrunners and writers. They are more likely to vocalize criticism or expect to have a say in the direction of the characters.

The increased number of viewers and the fan base in general may be attributed to the show's ability to reach fans through other channels and narratives. Fan studies critic Henry Jenkins defines these additional narratives beyond the primary text as *transmedia* (Stein and Busse). In many ways, *Sherlock* is a perfect example of a transmedia show. It is, after all, a show that announced its third season with a hearse driving around London, a sight that encouraged fans using Twitter and other social networks to help with the marketing by posting images or video (Stein and Busse). It is also a show that publishes John Watson's blog and Sherlock's *Science of Deduction* website. Stein and Busse acknowledge that "these official transmedia extensions do not encourage (or actually even allow) fan engagement with the characters or story directly," but there are fan forums and fan fiction sites that do (13). Stein and Busse posit that Jenkins' definition is too narrow and that "a looser definition of transmedia would suggest that audiences as well as official authors co-construct transmedia narratives, storyworlds, and frames for engagement," which would acknowledge the input of fans in the evolution and creation of characters and plot lines (14). Fans connect to the show through multiple channels, such as fan fiction, Twitter, and Tumblr. Not only do Gatiss and Moffat understand these connections and channels, they engage in them. They encourage them.

Gatiss and Moffat: Fan[boy]s and Aficionados

In many ways, Gatiss and Moffat's own identity as fans is what opens the showrunners up to the idea that fans can, and possibly even should, contribute to the direction of a show like *Sherlock* with such a rich history and canon. In fact, in the case of *Sherlock*, they acknowledge on the DVD commentary of "A Study in Pink" that they are "fanboys" of the canon and that other "fanboys" may be excited about the more obscure references to the canon throughout the show (Gatiss, Moffat, and Vertue). Matt Hills addresses what he refers to as the "heretical fidelity" of *Sherlock*, arguing that "the show's parameters are, to an extent, suggested by Moffat and Gatiss' own status as Sherlock Holmes fanboys, with this gendered identity being (problematically) extended to those assumed to be listening to the DVD commentary. Fan and producer identities are knowingly represented as mirrored, offering up the 'fidelity dimension'" (34). This fidelity dimension is important to create a common ground with fans, and the producers use this first DVD commentary to address the issue with their potential fans. Although it is true that they seem to identify those fans as primarily male or "boys," like themselves, it is important to point out that they are identifying with fans of the show from the very beginning. Gatiss and Moffat are certainly not dismissive of fans. They don't ignore them or treat them as silly because, to an extent, they identify with them. Ultimately, this ability to identify with all fans, not just the boys, is what will help the show grow in new directions, particularly in ways that acknowledge the contributions of the women in the series.

Gatiss and Moffat's acknowledgement of fans is most apparent in the first episode of Season Three, "The Empty Hearse," in which fictional fans of Sherlock have meetings at which many of them are wearing the infamous deerstalker hats. They present arguments through Twitter regarding how Sherlock could have staged his own death (shown in the previous season's finale). The scene quite possibly references Moffat's tongue-in-cheek reaction to the show's actual fans and, during a long hiatus between seasons, their great investment of time and energy in theorizing how Sherlock survived. Benedict Cumberbatch acknowledges that the first episode of Season Three "toyed with that sort of fictional world, that fan-fiction" ("Sherlock Uncovered: The Return"). In the casting for this scene, the fans are not solely "fan boys." There is a fairly equal representation of male and female, indicating that the showrunners are trying to appeal to, and acknowledge, a broader audience. Gatiss and Moffat explain that they wanted to create a strong fan reaction to Sherlock's death, although, unlike Conan Doyle, they showed him alive in the last shot of "The Reichenbach Fall." Part of this approach, they acknowledge, was to keep the fans from suffering unnecessarily between seasons, implying the showrunners' affection and possibly respect for their vocal fans (*Unlocking Sherlock*).

Clearly, Moffat does not want to alienate the series' fan base. Gatiss refers to the fan reaction after Season Two as "astonishing" and "breathtaking," and producer Sue Vertue even mentions that fans offered her money to reveal how Sherlock survived ("Sherlock Uncovered: The Return"). Both the creators and the actors are aware of and appreciative of fans and their dedication to the show. Martin Freeman (John Watson) has said about the fan reaction: "That's exactly what you want from an audience, and most of the time you don't have that response. So yeah, you cherish it when you get it" ("Sherlock Uncovered: The Return"). The fact that the writers and actors for this show understand and "cherish" the audience's engagement in their show and their characters is an indication that they are likely to take legitimate criticism seriously. Some of the most vocal criticism has come from feminist fans.

Sherlock Holmes and Feminism

Feminism—the advocacy of women's rights on the grounds of political, social, and economic equality to men—and feminists have been more vocal in their criticism of sexism in the entertainment sector since around 2014. Not only have actresses, such as Jennifer Lawrence and Charlize Theron, pushed for equal pay in Hollywood, but audiences are demanding stronger roles for women in television and film. Directors and producers who ignore these demands can expect to be held accountable in the press.

Accusations of misogyny against Moffat, and by extension *Sherlock*, have appeared everywhere from *Jezebel* to *The Guardian*. The show, and Moffat in particular because of his connection with both *Sherlock* and *Doctor Who*, has been criticized for depicting women as secondary characters, damsels in distress, or sidekicks. Despite the sometimes ineffectual female characters in *Sherlock*, Moffat is correct in his claims that he has made these female characters more interesting than they were in Conan Doyle's works. Conan Doyle was writing books with two male protagonists, one of whom was stridently anti-marriage. Holmes, for example, tells Watson, on the occasion of his engagement, that "I really cannot congratulate you.... [L]ove is an emotional thing, and whatever is emotional is opposed to that true cold reason which I place above all things. I should never marry myself, lest I bias my judgment" (Conan Doyle, *The Sign of Four*). Even Watson's wife, Mary Morstan, is barely mentioned in the canon. Watson marries her and becomes a widower in the space of one novel and three short stories before moving back to Baker Street with Holmes. Mrs. Hudson appears in the Conan Doyle canon primarily as window dressing. She is Holmes's long suffering landlady, nothing more. The only other notable woman in the Holmes canon is "The Woman," Irene Adler. Despite Adler's popularity among Holmes fans, she only appears in one story, "A Scandal in Bohemia." So Conan Doyle can hardly be acknowledged as a great feminist champion.

Showrunners Gatiss and Moffat acknowledge these differences most directly through "The Abominable Bride," the special episode between Seasons Three and Four, in which Sherlock romps through a Victorian version of his mind palace brought about by a formidable pharmaceutical cocktail. In this hallucination, he and Watson are trying to solve the mystery of Emelia Ricoletti. The Victorian versions of Mrs. Hudson, Molly, and Mary all strain at the gender conventions inflicted on their characters, with Mrs. Hudson criticizing John's characterization of her in *The Strand*, saying, "I'm your landlady, not a plot device." Even in the Victorian version of events, Mary works as a spy as well as being a suffragette. Despite these positive steps, however, not all choices made by the showrunners demonstrate a clear understanding of the feminist goals they espouse, for example, when they dress the suffragettes in purple KKK robes. Sherlock admits that the "women I, we, have lied to, the women we have ignored, disparaged" have a right to be angry, and Mycroft (Mark Gatiss) tells him that "this is a war we must lose," demonstrating that the writers' intentions are good, even if their execution is sometimes poor.

In *Collider*, Moffat argues that the female characters of *Sherlock* are better equipped to understand and manage Sherlock (Radish). Specifically, he notes that, despite the writers' desire to "stick very close to the original style," they are challenged by the fact that "there are no women, and what women do turn up are not that great. They're a bit boring. Not all of them, but most of them are not very interesting" (Radish). Moffat even suggests that Conan Doyle "didn't seem that comfortable with women." However, he insinuates that this is not a problem for the new *Sherlock* because the women as they are written for this show "see through [Sherlock] much faster. John is still pretty much enthralled with [Sherlock's] act. All the women he meets decode him so fast" (Radish). Moffat clearly feels that the show has made steps in the direction of feminism. He believes the female characters' ability to understand and "handle" Sherlock, when the male characters, such as John Watson and Greg Lestrade (Rupert Graves), cannot, is a testament to their emotional stability, intellect, and agency.

One thing is clear—the portrayal of women changes drastically over three seasons and a special episode. This transformation can be seen in the growth of characters such as Mrs. Hudson and Molly Hooper, as well as with later additions of characters such as Irene Adler and Mary Morstan.

Mrs. Hudson: "Not your housekeeper, dear"

Mrs. Hudson's progression throughout three seasons is perhaps the most subtle. She repeatedly tells both Sherlock and John that she is "not your housekeeper, dear" in the first episode of Season One, despite the fact that she sometimes behaves like one ("A Study in Pink"). In addition to this fact, Mrs. Hudson has the decidedly dubious honor of not being addressed by her first name. In large part, this seems to be because of a motherly affection and respect that both John and Sherlock have for her rather than any actual affiliation to her late husband. However, the audience discovers by late in Season Three that the Mrs. Hudson of *Sherlock* has a rather sordid past (e.g., exotic dancer with substance abuse issues; "His Last Vow") and knows how to handle herself. Although Sherlock helped get her drug-lord ex-husband convicted in Florida and has, in a way, rescued her ("A Study in Pink"), she also is a strong character who is not merely a damsel in distress.

The relationship between Mrs. Hudson and Sherlock is much closer than in the books, establishing a stronger female perspective in the show from the beginning. Una Stubbs, who plays Mrs. Hudson, explains that because Sherlock and John are cast as younger characters in this show and because she has sons of her own, it is natural for her to take on a more maternal role as Mrs. Hudson ("Sherlock Uncovered: The Women"). Sherlock is incredibly protective of Mrs. Hudson and reacts violently during "A Scandal in Belgravia" when she is physically injured by a CIA agent. He tells Lestrade that he "lost count" of how many times her assailant "fell" out of the window. However, Mrs. Hudson is hardly a shrinking violet. She also protects Sherlock by guarding his secrets (and his phone) in that episode. Although she portrays herself as a delicate and frightened old woman to the attackers, viewers see that this is not the whole story. She even grins when Sherlock later asks her about the experience. When John suggests that she stay with her sister to recover from the trauma, Sherlock protests: "Mrs. Hudson leave Baker Street? England would fall!" ("A Scandal in Belgravia").

By the end of Season Two, in "The Reichenbach Fall," Mrs. Hudson is identified by criminal mastermind Jim Moriarty as one of Sherlock's three friends, along with Lestrade and John, marked for death if Sherlock does not comply with Moriarty's demands. In *Sherlock*, a woman has made it into the boys' club. Essentially, Mrs. Hudson has progressed from a character who, quite literally, does not have a voice in the original Conan Doyle stories to a major influence in Sherlock's life with a backstory and personality all her own. Mrs. Hudson is nobody's grandma. She is tougher than she appears, and although Sherlock does sometimes come to her rescue, he does the same for his male friends John and Lestrade. Arguing that a show is anti-feminist because a female character is rescued by a male character who is also the titular hero of that show misses the point. The point of the show is that Sherlock, at least the modern iteration, is loyal and protective of his friends, regardless of whether those friends are men or women.

Molly Hooper: The Friend

The evolution of Sherlock and his friendships can be seen even more clearly through the character of Molly Hooper, a character invented for the show. While Molly starts out as a timid, waif-like character with a bit of a school-girl crush on Sherlock, her transition throughout three seasons is significant. Initially the character was only meant to appear in "A Study in Pink" (Gatiss, Moffat, and Vertue). The mere fact that Molly makes it out of the first episode and all the way through the third season and special is a testament to the creators' willingness to adapt the character and Sherlock's relationship with women.

Even in the first season, Molly becomes a stronger character. Early in the series, Sherlock easily manipulates her into showing him the bodies in the morgue in "The Blind Banker" by complimenting her hairstyle. By the beginning of the second season, Molly stands up to Sherlock after he humiliates her by drawing attention to her crush on him by saying: "You always say such horrible things. Every time. Always." Her response elicits Sherlock's first apology, at least as far as the show is concerned ("A Scandal in Belgravia"). By the end of Season Two, in "The Reichenbach Fall," Molly's friendship with Sherlock allows him to successfully fake his own death. In fact, Molly is the only character in this episode who can see that Sherlock is in trouble. He says that Moriarty (Andrew Scott) made a mistake in identifying the three people closest to Sherlock, because "the one person he thought didn't matter" is "the one person who mattered the most" ("The Empty Hearse"). Ultimately, Molly, as much as Mycroft, saves Sherlock from Moriarty.

By the end of the third season, Molly's relationship with Sherlock has changed significantly, and Molly is a much stronger, more self-assured character. When she fears Sherlock has returned to drug addiction, she slaps him three times and chastises him, exclaiming, "How dare you betray the love of your friends? Say you're sorry!" ("His Last Vow"). It is telling, as well, that when John is angry with Sherlock, and Sherlock is trying to find a fitting replacement for a sidekick, Molly is his choice, not Lestrade or some other male character. When Molly asks Sherlock why he chose her, he acknowledges it is out of gratitude for everything she has done for him. In the Season Three finale, when Sherlock is shot, Molly is the first person to appear in his mind palace, indicating her importance to him; she helps him decide to fall backward, thereby saving his life a second time ("His Last Vow").

Of all female characters, Molly is the most enamored of Sherlock. Like John, Molly loves Sherlock. However, in many ways, she is also the character who exerts the most influence on him and his behavior. She is willing to address his problematic behavior head on. While Mrs. Hudson is amused by Sherlock and Irene Adler sees their relationship as a game, Molly takes Sherlock seriously and expects him to take her seriously. She is one of the few characters he ever thanks and one of the fewer characters that he trusts with his secrets.

Irene Adler: "The Woman"

While feminists may be annoyed by Molly's initial passivity (which she overcomes as the series progresses), their greatest ire is directed at Gatiss and Moffat's treatment of Irene Adler. On the surface, perhaps, Adler should not be so upsetting to feminists. She is strong and independent. Rather than an opera singer with compromising letters from former lovers, as in the canon, this version of Irene Adler is a dominatrix who stores compromising photos of her conquests on her phone. She may not defeat Sherlock, but she comes closer than anyone else, except possibly Moriarty, and is still "The Woman."

However, despite these strong characteristics, feminist fans such as Jane Clare Jones of *The Guardian* argued that the creators ruin Adler's feminist credibility by having Sherlock rescue her at the end of the episode. Despite Adler's job as a dominatrix, *Sherlock* makes her a "damsel in distress," suggesting that her role as a dominatrix has nothing to do with strength and everything to do with female objectification (Jones). These feminists argue that because the original Conan Doyle stories simply end with Adler defeating Holmes and leaving him a note explaining how she defeated him, these stories are more feminist than *Sherlock's* depiction. It is true that Sherlock rescues her at the end of the episode, but if any character in *Sherlock* plays the damsel in distress, it is John. He is rescued by Sherlock no fewer than three times, at least once a season, and even Charles Augustus Magnussen (Lars Mikkelsen) and Jim Moriarty see him as the primary target to motivate Sherlock's behavior.

In "A Scandal in Belgravia," Adler has named herself, at least professionally, as The Woman. In the canon, Sherlock Holmes gives her this moniker, and she accepts it, much as a wife taking on her husband's name. In *Sherlock*, however, he simply acknowledges a name she has already chosen for herself. This ability to name herself, rather than accepting an identity from a man, is an indicator of her independence. As Lara Pulver, who portrays her, explains, "She is a strong, powerful woman. Instinctive. She's educated.

She's a lot of fun" (*Unlocking Sherlock*). She is also on much more even footing than the original character. Critics also fail to note that the Irene Adler of the original stories does not even get to keep the name Adler because she gets married and becomes Irene Simmons. Her marriage and her promise not to use the compromising letters are enough to convince the men in the story that she is no longer a threat. The threat she poses in the story is one of personal embarrassment for the King of Bohemia, not national security for all of England. Moffat and Gatiss may take the win from Adler, but they give her more teeth as well.

In the canon, Adler disappears after one story. Conan Doyle uses a female opponent as more of a party trick to entertain fans or an exception that proves the rule about women and their usefulness. The original Holmes is amused and surprised by Adler's ability to outsmart him. In *Sherlock*, Adler's character takes on a much more important role. She is set up as (almost) Sherlock's equal. Cumberbatch explains, "She's the same as [Sherlock]. She has a capacity for a very calculated use of love, sexuality, charm, and intellect" and she "hoodwinks" him (*Unlocking Sherlock*). The only man in the series given this same status in regard to Sherlock is Moriarty, who, through several episodes, is established as the "consulting criminal" to rival the consulting detective. Even Magnussen never really seems to take on the appearance of an equal adversary; Sherlock despises but is not intrigued by him. In contrast, Sherlock's emotions for "The Woman" are tied much more closely to respect and admiration. Because of this, she has a far more lasting effect on Sherlock and presents herself as a far more interesting adversary than the original. While it is true that, as characters go, she is not a great feminist icon, she is certainly stronger, more interesting, and more admirable than her predecessor.

Mary Morstan: The Liar

Like Irene Adler, Mary Morstan takes on a more active role in *Sherlock* than she ever did in the canon. Her courtship with John Watson in the books is stilted and awkward and primarily takes place over the course of one novel, *The Sign of Four*. Watson falls in love with her because she is physically attractive and essentially passive. In *Sherlock*, Mary's appearance on and integration into the show is almost as quick, but this Mary has more personality. Mary Morstan is the most obvious response by creators Moffat and Gatiss to complaints regarding misogyny in previous seasons.

She appears for the first time in Season Three's "The Empty Hearse," as John's fiancée. Sherlock doesn't notice Mary at first because he is too focused on surprising John and playing dress up as a French waiter. Then he is busy dodging punches from an understandably angry John. Once Sherlock really looks at Mary as she and John are leaving, viewers are allowed to see Sherlock's thoughts about Mary superimposed on the screen. In a camera shot representing Sherlock's deductions about Mary, lasting less than ten seconds, viewers learn about her character for the first time. She is a cat lover, a size 12, and a liar. The first two indicators are traditional female markers, perhaps a sign that Sherlock is overlooking more important clues because Mary is another in a long string of John's dates. Unlike many of John's previous romantic distractions, Mary is fun. She is clever. Mary's ability not only to "manage" but also care for John and Sherlock distracts audiences, as well as Sherlock, from her tenuous relationship with the truth early in the season. By the end of the season, despite her impending motherhood ("The Sign of Three"), she is presented as an action hero of sorts. Fans are led to believe that she is a former assassin and CIA agent. She shoots Sherlock, but so skillfully that she knows he will live long enough to receive medical attention, a skill Sherlock refers to as "surgery" ("His Last Vow"). Sherlock points out that John is attracted to Mary because of, not in spite of, her danger and unpredictability. If anyone could potentially replace Sherlock in John's life, it would have to be a person like Mary. She is female, visibly so in the most elemental of ways, and she is strong. She cares desperately for John, but she is not willing to sacrifice her identity for him.

It would be easy for the show to set Mary and Sherlock up as adversaries, but instead they are written as equals or potential teammates. In fact, when they are planning Mary and John's wedding, she tells Sherlock, "I'm not John. I can tell when you're fibbing" ("The Sign of Three"). The creators intentionally did not make Mary a "drag" or a "ball and chain" ("Sherlock Uncovered: The Women"). While their word choice is not likely to appeal to feminist fans of the show, their intentions should. She is not one of the boys, but she likes to be around them and is able to participate in their adventures. At the wedding, for example, when John tells Mary to "Stay here" while he and Sherlock rescue John's former commanding officer, James Sholto (Alistair Petrie), she waits about three seconds before following to help. She is the one who remembers Sholto's room number and who keeps John from breaking in the door, which would ultimately have resulted in Sholto's death. More importantly, she does not allow herself to be sidelined. She is part of the team.

Mary also genuinely seems to understand the relationships between John and Sherlock, convincing both of them to "run" the other on a case before the wedding as a way of assuring them both that while things are changing, they will still get to solve cases together ("The Sign of Three"). When Sherlock returns from the "dead," Mary convinces John to take Sherlock back ("The Empty Hearse"), and, in turn, Sherlock convinces John to take Mary back after he discovers the truth about her past ("His Last Vow"), something that never would have happened in the original stories. When John says, "But she wasn't supposed to be like that. Why is she like that?" Sherlock knowingly responds, "Because you chose her" ("His Last Vow"). While Mary desperately fights to hide her past from John so that he will still love her, when he eventually learns about it and confronts her, she is unapologetic about what she has done, saying "People like Magnussen should be killed. That's why there are people like me" ("His Last Vow"). This version of Mary is a far cry from Conan Doyle's creation, who is introduced as a client, becomes a wife, and dies soon after so that Watson can get back to Baker Street.

Adaptation and Fan Response

Should a television adaptation like *Sherlock* attempt to correct cultural or historical wrongs? Should it give fans what they want, especially when it comes to feminist characters? There is not likely to be any adaptation that can please everyone–fans of the canon, fans of *Sherlock*, feminists, and critics. Ashley D. Polasek acknowledged this problem:

> Rarely does a Sherlock Holmes adaptation appear that does not cause some fans to bemoan, for one reason or another, that the screenwriter, director, and/or actors were not familiar enough with the literary source, that if only the canon had been consulted more often and more assiduously, the adaptation would not have contained so many errors or committed so many violations. The result is that instead of being judged on their inherent quality, adaptations are put on trial and often found guilty of criminal infraction against the Canon, regardless of how entertaining or insightful they may be [45].

Gatiss and Moffat make *Sherlock* because they are both fans of the original Conan Doyle stories, but they also have a clear understanding that setting the stories in modern-day London requires them to make some significant changes to the behaviors of both Sherlock and John as well as the women with whom they interact. In this way, they engage in what Hills refers to as a "heretical fidelity," meaning "Gatiss both acknowledges that creative decisions may be 'heretical' to Sherlockians, but suggests that those self-same decisions can also display fidelity to Conan Doyle by highlighting the limitations, and textual inauthenticities, of previous adaptations" (36). Hills also notes that "Television authorship is discursively produced as a matter of creative autonomy: fan expectations are disregarded, as are previous versions of Holmes, but fidelity to 'the famous stories' is preserved" (36). While it is certainly possible that television can ignore fans as it chooses, this approach to adaptation does not actually seem to be the case with *Sherlock*.

It may have taken the creators longer to realize that they have to modernize more than the technology and clothing, but *Sherlock* addresses the concerns of its fans, and its feminist fans in particular. Perhaps the most apt example of this approach can be seen in an exchange between John and Mary in "The Abominable Bride" when, in a fit of frustration, John says, "I'm taking Mary home!" to which she responds, "You're what?" John then rephrases his exit by saying "Mary's taking me home," and Mary responds, "Better." Much like John, Gatiss and Moffat may need to try harder to move beyond their paternalistic first instincts, and although it is not always a perfect example of feminism, as the seasons continue to unfold, it is most certainly "better."

WORKS CITED

"The Abominable Bride." *Sherlock*. Writ. Mark Gatiss, Steven Moffat. Dir. Douglas McKinnon. PBS. KUED, Salt Lake City, Utah. 1 Jan. 2016. Television.

"The Blind Banker." *Sherlock: Season 1*. Writ. Mark Gatiss, Steven Moffat. Dir. Euros Lyn. BBC Home Entertainment, 2010. DVD.

De Moraes, Lisa. "UPDATE: Benedict Cumberbatch Sentimental About 'Sherlock' But Mum About More Seasons After Season 3 Premiere Scores in Ratings." Deadline.com. 20 Jan. 2014. Web. 3 Oct. 2014.

Conan Doyle, Arthur. "A Scandal in Bohemia." Oak Park, IL: Prologue Publishing Services, 2012. Kindle.

_____. *The Sign of Four*. Oak Park, IL: Prologue, 2012. Kindle.

"The Empty Hearse." *Sherlock*. Writ. Mark Gatiss, Steven Moffat. Dir. Jeremy Lovering. BBC, 2014. Netflix. Web. 19 June 2015.

Gatiss, Mark, Steven Moffat, and Sue Vertue. Audio Commentary: "A Study in Pink." *Sherlock: Season 1*. Writ. Mark Gatiss, Steven Moffat. Dir. Paul McGuigan. BBC Home Entertainment, 2010. DVD.

Harrington, Jo. "The Victorian Dawn of Fandom Through Sherlock Holmes Fanfiction." *Fans and Fandoms*. n.p. n.d. Web. 17 Sep. 2014.

Hills, Matt. "*Sherlock's* Epistemological Economy and the Value of 'Fan' Knowledge: How Producer-Fans Play the (Great) Game of Fandom." *Sherlock and Transmedia Fandom: Essays on the BBC Series*. Ed. Louisa Ellen Stein and Kristina Busse. Jefferson, NC: McFarland, 2012. Kindle.

"His Last Vow." *Sherlock*. Writ. Steven Moffat, Mark Gatiss. Dir. Nick Hurran. BBC. Netflix. Web. 19 June 2015.

Jones, Jane Clare. "Is Sherlock Sexist: Moffat's Wanton Women." *The Guardian*. 3 Jan. 2012. Web. 17 Sep. 2014.

Klimchynskaya, Anastasia. "Sherlock Holmes: The Original Fandom." Den of Geek. 2014. Web. 17 Sep. 2014.

Pearson, Roberta. "Bachies, Bardies, Trekkies, and Sherlockians." *Fandom: Identities and Communities in a Mediated World*. Ed. Jonathan Gray. New York: New York University Press, 2007. 98–109. Print.

Polasek, Ashley D. "Winning 'The Grand Game': *Sherlock* and the Fragmentation of Fan Discourse." *Sherlock and Transmedia Fandom: Essays on the BBC Series*. Ed. Louisa Ellen Stein and Kristina Busse. Jefferson, NC: McFarland, 2012. Kindle.

Radish, Christina. "Executive Producer Steven Moffat Talks SHERLOCK, His Plans for Moriarty, Adding a Female Perspective to the Character, Other Villains, and More." *Collider*. n.p. 3 Feb. 2014. Web. 5 Oct. 2014.

"The Reichenbach Fall." *Sherlock: Season 2*. Writ. Steve Thompson, Mark Gatiss, Steven Moffat. Dir. Toby Haynes. BBC Home Entertainment, 2012. DVD.

"A Scandal in Belgravia." *Sherlock*: *Season 2*. Writ. Steve Thompson, Mark Gatiss, Steven Moffat. Dir. Paul McGuigan. BBC Home Entertainment, 2012. DVD.

"Sherlock Uncovered: The Return." *Sherlock*. BBC. Netflix. Web. 19 June 2015.

"Sherlock Uncovered: The Women." *Sherlock*. BBC. Netflix. Web. 19 June 2015.

"The Sign of Three." *Sherlock*. Writ. Steve Thompson, Steven Moffat, Mark Gatiss. Dir. Colm McCarthy. BBC. Netflix. Web. 19 June 2015.

Stein, Louisa Ellen, and Kristina Busse. "Introduction: The Literary, Televisual, and Digital Adventures of the Beloved Detective." *Sherlock and Transmedia Fandom: Essays on the BBC Series*. Jefferson, NC: McFarland, 2012. Kindle.

"A Study in Pink." *Sherlock*: *Season 1*. Writ. Mark Gatiss, Steven Moffat. Dir. Paul McGuigan. BBC Home Entertainment, 2010. DVD.

Unlocking Sherlock. BBC. Netflix. Web. 19 June 2015.

Willis, Chris. "The Story of *The Strand*." *Strand Magazine*. 2006. Web. 2 Feb. 2014.

#Setlock and the
Power of Fandom

JENNIFER WOJTON

Since its debut on BBC television in July 2010, *Sherlock* has become an international fan phenomenon. When the cast and crew filmed outdoor, on-location scenes for Season Two episodes, fans shared information about the series' production and showed up, whenever and wherever possible, to watch the actors at work. During filming for Season Three in 2013 and especially for the *Sherlock* special, "The Abominable Bride," filmed early in 2015, fans organized their on-location visits and shared news of on-site filming via Twitter. As the result of fans' extensive searches into upcoming filming locations and casting decisions, as well as reports from residents being made aware of filming in their town in preparation for the shoot, the hashtag #Setlock became an effective way to alert fans to the latest news about the series' on-location filming, episodes' character development, and plot.

#Setlock has become so popular that even U.K. newspapers follow the Tweets and debate the propriety of fan behavior regarding *Sherlock* filming. In 2015 in particular, #Setlock, like the object of its affection *Sherlock,* has gained media attention. *The Daily Dot* defined #Setlock participation by stage:

> The first stage of [#Setlock] addiction is following *Sherlock*'s actors, writers, and behind-the-scenes crew members on social media. But let's be honest here, that's amateur hour. A more dedicated setlocker also keeps track of public casting calls and potential location rumors, just in case someone connected with the episode accidentally shares something—*anything*—that might contain some clues about the next episode. The top tier is for those who actually visit the set in person [Baker-Whitelaw].

This acknowledgment by the mainstream media is significant as it lends credibility to fan-created knowledge systems because these systems have been historically ostracized and promulgated in print or via word of mouth in subcultural settings, like fan conventions.

However, digital media allow ephemeral, topical information and images to be captured in real time. This immediacy has raised the bar for the extent to which fan activity may influence a show. In addition, the affordances of digital media have the potential to empower fans and raise the bar for how fan culture is often perceived by the public. Perhaps not surprisingly, given so much media and fan attention, #Setlock has begun to more significantly influence three areas related to *Sherlock* and its media-savvy fandom: the series' production and official relationship with fandom, mainstream media's use of fan sources and commentary about fandom, and the creation of an ever-larger "safe space" in which fans can creatively express themselves in relation to the series, leading to "alternative" interpretations of the characters' identities, most notably, that John and Sherlock may be in a homosexual relationship.

#Setlock and the Series' Production

Sherlock co-creator Mark Gatiss explained to the *Radio Times* in late 2014 that #Setlock, which often results in hundreds of fans watching on-location filming, has changed the nature of the series. "When we were filming Baker Street exteriors last time, the fact you've got about 300 people behind crash barriers is … interesting, [so] we have factored in trying to minimise large scenes outside…. If you're just drawing up in a taxi and running through a door, it's easier but large dialogue scenes outside are quite tough." Gatiss, who also plays Mycroft Holmes, added that "in terms of concentration it's hard when you feel like you're being observed by more than just the crew" (Jones, "Sherlock Fans").

Series' co-lead Martin Freeman (John Watson) was more outspoken in his opinion of #Setlock a few months later, during the filming of the *Sherlock* special: "It's like trying to act at a premiere…. When we're [filming at] our stand-in for Baker Street, it is hard to do your job. And I don't love it" (Gill). Although entertainment media might be expected to emphasize the #Setlock story, it also was covered by highly respected mainstream newspaper *The Guardian*, which reported additional comments by Freeman. The actor could only compare it to Beatles fandom: "I wasn't in The Beatles. But I've never seen anything like it. There's such a heightened sense of excitement, so every time we come out there's applauding…. Or, if we do anything –'Cut!'— applause…. It's like, 'No, this isn't a gig.' There are hundreds of people taking pictures of you and holding up placards" ("What Does Martin Freeman Think of #Setlock?"). Freeman's comments instigated an online public debate among fans and critics whether #Setlock should be discouraged or more drastic measures taken on location to end it.

The *Radio Times* polled fans online, asking Is it acceptable for fans to attend #Setlock? More than three-quarters of the 5,000 fans responding to the poll (76.87 percent) answered No; only 23.13 percent voted Yes (Jones, "Should #Setlock Continue?"). A follow-up article included criticism of #Setlock by two *Sherlock* fans:

> Actors and crew should have the freedom to work without people spying on them and spreading spoilers about what and how and when and where they do it.... You don't spy on people working on the streets, do you? Nor tweet about how their job is done, right? If you did, they would also ask you to step back in order to get some privacy.
>
> I don't know why people can't let the actors and crew get on with filming.... They're distracting the actors from their job just by being there. They're spoiling upcoming episodes of *Sherlock* not just for themselves, but for everyone else as well [Jones, "Sherlock Fans Say No to #Setlock"].

The article also includes an anecdote from Gatiss that #Setlock fans once "broke into wild cheering when Martin Freeman opened a package of crisps on set," yet another piece of evidence to the public that not only does #Setlock influence the ways that *Sherlock* can best be filmed but indicates the nature of #Setlock fandom. Overly enthusiastic fans—also perceived as self-centered or selfish fans—are portrayed as giving a bad reputation in the media to *Sherlock* fans in general.

At last, co-creator and showrunner Steven Moffat concluded the 2015 debate by spinning Freeman's comment more positively and "making nice" with the series' fans. "Martin just made a very innocuous remark.... He doesn't mind [#Setlock].... We're all genuinely—including Martin, including grumpy old me—very appreciative that people love our show so much, we're thrilled by it in fact" (Holmes). Moffat emphasized that his comments, which included calling fans "incredibly well behaved and polite and sweet and nice," was not spin but only the truth. Nevertheless, his comments seemed like official damage control of public criticism of fans, coupled with the understanding that likely the most vociferous *Sherlock* fans participate in some way with #Setlock. Those who cannot or do not choose to visit filming locations nonetheless may follow the tweets and share information with other fans. Moffat does not want to alienate a large percentage of *Sherlock* fans, especially when the series takes months- or years-long hiatuses between seasons.

In-person positive interactions with #Setlock fans during on-location filming (e.g., the actors chatting with or signing autographs for fans between scenes or as they leave the location) can help promote the series within fandom and make fans feel that they have a larger personal stake in the production. As well, shared photos or news tweeted via #Setlock generates interest in new episodes long before they are broadcast and keeps *Sherlock* in the news throughout the year.

However, according to an increasing number of media and fan reports—

many of them tweeted via #Setlock—not everyone among cast, crew, or fandom is happy (no matter what Moffat says) about the amount of influence #Setlock increasingly has on the way the series is filmed. If more scenes are filmed on closed interior sets, the series' "look" will change, as will the types of action scenes that can be filmed. The "flavor" of real locations throughout the U.K. has been one reason for *Sherlock*'s success; international fans in particular enjoy vicariously visiting U.K. locations lovingly filmed for episodes. If filming delays or increased security results in a higher budget for on-location filming, the budget-conscious BBC, as well as production company Hartswood Films, may decide that #Setlock warrants fundamental changes in where and how the series has traditionally been scripted and filmed.

Furthermore, Gatiss notes that the "insider information" tweeted by fans watching a scene being filmed also "gives a lot away, which is a shame" (Jones, "Sherlock Fans"). Fans often share information about who is on set each day, indicating which characters are in a scene, what they are wearing, and what they are doing during a filmed scene. However, fans' interpretations of what is revealed during location filming may be misleading, and, at best, #Setlock provides only part of the larger picture of the entire episode. Nevertheless, astute fans may be "spoiled" about aspects of plot or character development because of information shared via #Setlock. The surprise elements of a new episode may not be quite so surprising if they are revealed months before an episode is broadcast, and the potential exists for audiences not being as excited about new episodes as they would have been if they had not been "spoiled" by #Setlock news or images.

Not only may fans accidentally or intentionally publish spoilers about upcoming episodes, but the mere presence of so many fans showing up in a public place to watch filming can pose logistical problems as well. During outdoor filming of "The Empty Hearse," the camera could not avoid every fan standing in the background of the shot. As one entertainment news writer explains, "The crowds of onlookers were so difficult to avoid that the first episode of season three includes some accidental cameos from fans who were caught in the shot" (Baker-Whitelaw). Although being captured for posterity within a *Sherlock* episode may make some fans feel special or make others jealous, the presence of people who are not characters, or not even extras providing background actions appropriate for the scene, can destroy the illusion being created by the *Sherlock* cast and crew. Fans who are not dressed appropriately for the scene or who are obviously watching the lead actors instead of reacting to the fictitious drama taking place can break the fourth wall just as surely as an actor turning to the camera and addressing the audience directly. For better or worse, #Setlock is changing the way that *Sherlock* is made and the way that fans or even casual viewers perceive characters' identity.

Mainstream Media's Use of #Setlock Information

Publications such as the *Radio Times, Daily Dot, Den of Geek,* and *Wales Online* follow #Setlock and use information gathered by fans as the basis of their own highly clickable articles. Because *Sherlock* is often a hot topic in entertainment news, the media becomes influenced by #Setlock when writers rely on second-hand information from fans visiting *Sherlock* filming locations. Instead of doing their own reporting, they scan Twitter and other social media sites for the latest #Setlock news. This legitimizing of an internet community as a source for critical information about the show demonstrates the extent to which a web-born community can gain both recognition and status, re-positioning fan culture and its spoils from the fringes to the mainstream.

As #Setlock has become more controversial—in part, because stories about this phenomenon have been published in mainstream media—these media outlets editorialize about #Setlock fandom and the potential harm that #Setlock could be doing to the production of *Sherlock* episodes. In 2015, more than 50 articles, many repeating information from #Setlock tweets or actor interviews, alerted the general public to #Setlock and earned money for their publications from each click to an online article about it. From *The Guardian* to *The Hollywood Reporter,* with tabloid coverage in between, #Setlock was both promoted by mainstream media but also criticized by it.

Nonetheless, #Setlock had become a newsworthy topic, one associated with a highly popular international television series. Fans who were quoted within articles or had their tweets republished or followed by mainstream media writers thus could gain status (or notoriety) within the #Setlock community specifically or more generally within *Sherlock* fandom. They had been recognized as "experts" with a strong opinion—either for or against #Setlock. Their interest in this series had been publicized to a mass online audience, giving them "authority" status when it comes to *Sherlock*. This evolution of such a ready-made audience for one's exploits and a social capital-based hierarchy is indicative of how expertise is built and wielded in online communities such as #Setlock and the kind of shaping force that they can exert when it comes to perceptions about the show and its characters, but also about how the show itself is produced. Since computer-mediated communication has made possible the creation and dissemination of texts by talented individuals with access to digital media and the inclination to create and post their work, traditional author(ity) is being de-centered. #Setlock community members are gaining credibility within *Sherlock* fandom for their insights into plot or character development in upcoming episodes.

#Setlock as a "Safe Space" for Fans

Perhaps the most notable influence of #Setlock is on the fans themselves. Those who participate in #Setlock—at whatever "stage" as described by mainstream media—are expressing themselves creatively and sharing their interpretation of the series with other fans. In the early days of TV fandom, fans consumed and collected products and texts to support their favorite show(s). Fans eagerly awaited the publication of their favorite fanzine or the yearly gathering at conventions. A small number of fans were also producers of content, like fan fiction or the keepers of fan club archives. Fans were most often recognized by mainstream media for their raucous behavior, following their heroes around—screaming, fainting. Beatlemania, at its height, is an example of extreme fan behavior captured on film by mainstream media outlets. Perhaps not surprisingly, *Sherlock* fandom through #Setlock has been dubbed a modern version of Beatlemania. Freeman explains in an interview with *Empire Magazine*, "I've got some great reactions to things I'm very proud of, but I don't think any surpass *Sherlock* in terms of critical acclaim and number of people watching—and just a general feeling that you're in a mini Beatlemania." However, perceiving #Setlock as only like Beatlemania is to miss an important difference.

Today, with the affordances of digital media, fans can more easily consume media *and* create it. This low threshold for entrance into the world of producer, rather than passive consumer has opened up fan culture like never before. Instead of being background noise, the voices of fans are being heard loud and clear by mainstream media and the objects of their affection. While Freeman may think of them as background noise and Moffat may not want to alienate them, through #Setlock, fans are affecting the show but also using it to make some creative work of their own to be consumed and catalogued by their fellow fans and a much wider audience. #Setlock features creative works such as real photos, creative manipulation of photos, all sorts of visual art, and video production. These works, without the affordances of digital media, would likely be kept in envelopes and passed from fan to fan at a convention, but now these creative works can gain recognition and generate discussion on a much larger scale. #Setlock has inspired fan fiction which will often be demarcated with a #Setlock tag and which reference particular posts.

This is particularly important because the content of fan musings regarding *Sherlock* characters often takes the form of "play" in which Sherlock and John are imagined to be in a gay relationship. These musings can range from perceptions regarding the characters' true romantic feelings for each other to the erotic/pornographic entanglements expressed in popular Johnlock fan fiction. Henry Jenkins, in *Confronting the Challenges of Participatory Culture*, defines "play" as the "the ability to experiment with one's surroundings as a form of problem solving," and because "appropriation" is such a part of participatory culture, the type of play that fans enact should prove unsurprising, when their attachment to source materials is considered as the impetus for their works. What may be surprising is the extent to which this "play" has the capacity to create alternate epistemologies within fan communities. Fans may be attempting to "solve the problem" of how to feel closer and to continue their investment in *Sherlock* during the show's long hiatus, and the solution that the digital environment allows is their appropriation of their beloved characters to be used in service of their own creative works.

Although #Setlock creates a viable international fan community that makes the most of Twitter, Tumblr, and Pinterest, for example, the narratives, photos, and videos linked by the #Setlock tag do far more than share potential spoilers. The #Setlock texts also affect the way that fans perceive the characters and the episode's plot months before the next new episode arrives. Especially because the *Sherlock* special, "The Abominable Bride," was broadcast in January 2016, two years after the previous episode, fans became eager for any information about this new episode. However, speculation derived from #Setlock accounts of the episode's scenes or glimpses of cast members in costumes set up expectations for character or plot development that were not always met when the episode was broadcast. Because "The Abominable Bride" takes the usually-modern adaptation back to Victorian times and introduces "new" versions of familiar characters, the most ardent fans were more likely to create and share their own television-canon stories based on information from #Setlock, at least until the episode was broadcast and fans had an "official" source in which to base their creative works. Because #Setlock requires fans to construct their own context based on the limited number of images and descriptions captured and shared during on-location filming, what fans observe and share about an episode, including which characters are included, what they wear, and what they are observed doing, probably is not what the series' creators, writer, director, and cast ultimately end up creating for commercial broadcast. This was true for "The Abominable Bride" and likely will be true for other episodes, because #Setlock seems to be a continuing phenomenon. Thus, #Setlock helps create, at least within fandom, two sets of characters—#Setlock-context characters and official *Sherlock* characters—based on different interpretations of what takes place during on-location filming.

Fans' Creation of Characters' Identity

Two images shared via #Setlock in January and early February 2015, at the height of the special episode's filming, illustrate the ways that a character's identity, especially sexual identity, may be "created" by fans who use a limited number of shared images to support their interpretation of a character or relationship. This interpretation may differ greatly from the series' official interpretation of that character or relationship.

One #Setlock image from 2015 is a photograph taken by a fan watching filming take place on a city street-turned-set. Because the "set" was a public space, fans only had to respect barriers put in place to contain people who were not involved with filming. Unless fans became disruptive or went outside the barriers, they could not be prevented from watching what was taking place on the other side. Fans' view, however, was often restricted by cameras, extras, or sheer distance from the main characters, Sherlock Holmes (played by Benedict Cumberbatch) and John Watson. One of the most shared #Setlock photos captures Sherlock and John, attired as Victorian gentlemen, walking together into the Diogenes Club. Although the image may seem unremarkable—two friends walking together toward a building—fans' interpretation provides a different context for the image than is likely to be promoted in the official series.

The photo shows Sherlock to the left of John as they walk together. John's arm appears to be linked in Sherlock's, which prompted tweets endorsing this image as the series' recognition of John and Sherlock as more than good friends. Almost as soon as the image was tweeted via #Setlock, a fan asked, "Were they walking arm in arm like in Sidney Paget's illustrations?" This comment references not only the original illustrations for Arthur Conan Doyle's stories but also Victorian mores that allowed close male friends to link arms in public. In this context, Holmes and Watson in *Sherlock* are merely following precedent for an acknowledged Victorian male friendship, and nothing more should be thought about the image. It is within *Sherlock*'s canon that Sherlock and John are only good friends.

What is more interesting is the interpretation by the majority of fans who retweeted the image via #Setlock that day. Meg, also known on Twitter as @Setlockegg, tweeted "arm in arm?!" as she retweeted the photo, and Anastasis made the comment emphatic by posting all in capital letters "ARE THEY ARM IN ARM." Almost immediately, #Setlock became inundated with comments such as "It looks like they are arm in arm!" and "THIS IS MY HEART" (Collins). Within minutes of sharing the twitpic via #Setlock, the photo had been retweeted 65 times and was "favorited" 116; other users who copied the photo or posted and retweeted it from their accounts distributed the image far more widely among the #Setlock community.

The photo had been taken by Redbeard221B, a moniker derived from the name of Sherlock's dog and the detective's Baker Street address. Redbeard221B's Twitter profile describes her as "21-year-old tv show obsessed laura," whose favorite shows include *Sherlock*. She also notes that she is a "johnlock shipper," or someone who promotes the idea that the relationship between John and Sherlock is sexual. From this perspective then, which seems to strike a chord among other fans in the #Setlock community, Redbeard221B captured a moment on film that resonates with her (and other fans') belief that Johnlock is a viable way to read the series.

Finally, Redbeard221B admitted in a follow-up tweet that "i think this might just be the angle of my camera, couldn't tell if they were in arm and arm but even if not it's cute :)." Despite its questionable perspective, a photo of something as simple and straightforward as two men walking into a building became an illustration (or, to some fans, proof) that John Watson and Sherlock Holmes share a far more intimate relationship than the homosocial friendship depicted in the BBC's *Sherlock* or the close male friendship described in canon Victorian stories.

It does not seem to matter to fans that the broadcast episode is unlikely to include such an image, whether because the camera angle provides a different perspective than that from the fan's viewpoint behind a barrier or because the scene is eventually cut. (An arm-in-arm shot did not appear in the broadcast episode.) Johnlock shippers or #Setlock community members who first viewed Redbeard221B's photo in early February 2015 encourage the "reality" that John and Sherlock are so comfortable with their relationship that they can walk arm in arm on a public street without worry of censure. By touching each other in this way, they signal to #Setlock fans who approve of a Johnlock reading that they are a homosexual couple comfortable with even fairly platonic, public displays of affection. This single photo, which seems to provide "evidence" to the #Setlock community because a fan snapped it during the filming of a television-canon scene, allows fans to validate Johnlock as a sanctioned reading of the series. To these #Setlock fans or Johnlock shippers, it no longer matters whether the television episode includes a scene in which John and Sherlock walk arm-in-arm into the Diogenes Club; it only matters that a real photograph is perceived as validating fans' queer identity for Sherlock and John.

Sometimes the photo does not even have to be real in order to be perceived as real, simply because it is shared through the #Setlock hashtag and is retweeted just like any other photo or description among community members. An image of John and Sherlock distributed through #Setlock around the same time mimics a scene from the modern adaptation's first season, in "The Blind Banker," when John is apprehended by police while he holds a spray can of paint. To the police, it looks like John is the artist behind the illegal graffiti, although he is merely holding the paint for an informant Sherlock has been questioning before they run off, leaving John behind. In the #Setlock-distributed image, John and Sherlock, in Victorian garb showing the characters as they appear in "The Abominable Bride," are standing before a brick wall, and John holds a can of spray paint. He seems to be writing "Sherlock is gay" while Sherlock looks on.

The image turned out to be a photo manipulation from images of John and Sherlock dressed as Victorian gentlemen—as they are in dozens of other #Setlock photos as well as official BBC publicity photos and the later San Diego Comic-Con teaser video. However, the red spray-painted graffiti, which reads "Sherlock is Ga ...," has been added as one fan's representation of what John should be writing about Sherlock.

Some #Setlock followers assumed that Freeman and Cumberbatch were kidding around between takes but that the photo captured a real behind-the-scenes moment. Internationally, the #Setlock photo was retweeted with the description "imagem atual de setlock" (Jess). The rough translation from Portuguese is "actual image from Setlock," which only added perceived authenticity to the increasingly shared photo. When fan Rashmika Ramlall pinned to her Pinterest site a similar image of John drawing a heart under the label "Sherlock + John," she entitled the image "Johnlock graffiti while filming Series 4 (setlock)." The #Setlock hashtag gave credence to images of John creating graffiti indicating a sexual relationship between Sherlock and John or revealing Sherlock's sexual identity. Only when some fans began seeing multiple variations on this photo—"Sherlock + John," "Sherlock is gay," or a Not Safe for Work (NSFW) image of John drawing a huge penis—did #Setlock followers begin to question the authenticity of the original photo. By then, the photo had been retweeted dozens of times, as well as shared on Pinterest and Tumblr.

The originally #Setlock-tagged image was later proclaimed to be a photomanip, created by Johnlock fan Bluebellglowinginthedark (another name reflecting specifically *Sherlock* television fandom. Bluebell is the experimented-upon, glow-in-the-dark rabbit in "The Hounds of Baskerville.") Bluebellglowinginthedark's Tumblr entry "John felt creative" was posted in late January 2015, at the height of #Setlock for "The Abominable Bride." This manipulated photo's origin could easily have been misread as actually having been generated by the show, and this may be proof of the challenge to traditional credibility when content goes digital. In addition, though it would have been possible for any number of the fans who endorsed and shared the image to check the authenticity of it, many lack the inclination or the digital literacy to do so. In the online environment where information can be spread so quickly without it having been vetted, there are often challenges to credibility. However, even after the image was revealed to be a manipulated photo, it continued to be popular because this fan-generated "knowledge" is meant to be part of some very serious play in which fans must have sufficient knowledge of the game and the players to be taken seriously, but just enough creativity to keep things interesting. The "truth" of the characters' sexual identities is less important than fans' participation in creating alternate character identities that are lauded within the #Setlock community. Within a year of the original posting, this photomanip had generated more than 3860 notes of "like this" or "reblogged this" from Bluebellglowinginthedark's Tumblr site alone, attesting to the image's enduring popularity (even after the episode's broadcast) among Johnlock fans in particular. It is only in the digital environment that viewers can so easily quantify the veracity of an image. As the number of notes increases, regardless of what those notes are likely to say, the image's popularity increases, as well. To the fans who believe that a queer reading of the series' modern episodes is supported by innuendo in dialogue among the series' regular characters, the photomanip initially shared through #Setlock is validation—this time through popularity within the #Setlock community—that such a reading is not only viable but highly desirable. This desirability is particularly important when a reading of characters' sexual identities goes against traditional, heteronormative interpretations. Valorizing alternative readings that venerate non-traditional identity groups can be empowering for fans, who may revel in the illicit nature of those representations, but also for those underrepresented groups, as well. For example, whereas individual photos of Sherlock or John taken during #Setlock focus on details of Victorian costume and compare the *Sherlock* version with canon illustrations or other adaptations set in the Victorian era, the most often-shared photos of John-and-Sherlock as a unit emphasize the pair's close physical proximity. In one photo, for example, the friends ride together in the back of a carriage, their faces appearing even more closely together because they are photographed through the carriage window, which foreshortens the perspective and makes it suitable for a two-shot close-up (Ashley). Another photo focuses on John and Sherlock as they walk in step closely together (bumblebee-cuttlefish). Such photos, even without overt sexual overtones, remind fans, especially those with an interest in Johnlock, of the characters' emotional and physical closeness.

Fan art picks up this theme as well. In the days following the 2015 San Diego Comic-Con and the release of the first teaser video for "The Abominable Bride," a drawing of John and Sherlock, dressed as Victorian gentlemen, became popular on Tumblr (Cupidford). The drawing was posted on a site entitled "I Blog About It—He Forgets His Pants," John's lines from "A Scandal in Belgravia." Above the site name are silhouettes of John and Sherlock. John's cartoon bubble says, "O, God, yes!," yet another *Sherlock* line, this time taken out of context from "A Study in Pink." Sherlock's dialogue bubble replies, "Racy!" Using episode dialogue out of context to indicate a Johnlock relationship suggests that the fan who posted the drawing and those who follow this site are at least interested and likely heavily invested in a Johnlock reading of the series and are using formidable knowledge of the show to create a plausible alternative to mainstream interpretations of John and Sherlock. Fan-generated texts and fan-maintained communities, as Matt Hills explains in "Virtually Out There," rely on *affect* (emotion), and fans' highly affective attachment to the objects of their affection and their devotion to them are key elements in understanding why/how fans and fan communities generate such a wide variety of texts. These texts are often found to be worthy of other fan attention if they are able to establish their credibility by flaunting their knowledge of the show/characters and then using that knowledge to "play." These affective attachments, when cultivated in online affective spaces, lead to the creation of new knowledge systems based on particularly fannish ways of interacting and meaning making. According to Hills, "The fans' oppositional subculture must always precede and culturally support fan interpretation and affect, rather than vice versa. Taking this view ... means considering affect as playful, as capable of creating culture as well as being caught up in it" (1143). This symbiotic relationship governs much of what fans have come to appreciate about creative works distributed via the cultural "setting" of #Setlock.

For example, the fan's drawing of Victorian-era Sherlock and John is chaste, depicting two fully-dressed men standing next to each other, but the oval frame surrounding them makes the complete picture seem more Victorian-era appropriate and romantic. Sherlock is turned toward John, as if they are in conversation, and John looks toward the audience (or artist/"camera") as if suddenly aware the pair are being captured for posterity. What is notable about this "Victorian" image is that John is clean shaven, instead of having the mustache shown in #Setlock photos, official photos, and the Comic-Con video (as well as, eventually, the broadcast episode). The missing mustache indicates that, although the characters are dressed for the Victorian era, they are very much the modern John and Sherlock familiar to *Sherlock* audiences. Only a true fan would notice, let alone read so much into a missing mustache.

Such #Setlock posts or Johnlock interpretations go against the "official" sexuality of Sherlock Holmes as interpreted by *Sherlock* co-creator Moffat. He reiterated during San Diego Comic-Con 2015 that "It's a funny thing when a character for over 100 years has been saying 'I don't do that [that is, have sex] at all.... He's willfully staying away from [sex] to keep his brain pure— a Victorian belief, that. But everyone wants to believe he's gay" (Hibberd). Moffat may be correct in his assessment of many fans who participate in #Setlock and create their own queered "head canon" for the series, whenever it is set. It does not seem to matter to 21st-century fans that homosexuality was illegal and hidden within Victorian society or that the close male friendship depicted in Conan Doyle's canon was platonic and intellectual, not sexual. Although novel and possibly titillating, the characters' outward appearance, such as Sherlock and John wearing Victorian costumes, does not change #Setlock fans' understanding of the characters "inside," and for many fans, the characters' emotions and relationships will always reflect Johnlock. #Setlock gives fans the opportunity to embrace this reading of the series and to validate it through shared tweets and images.

Conclusion

Ultimately, the power of *Sherlock* fandom realized via #Setlock is significant enough to garner national attention—attention in which the "work," both practical and creative, of #Setlock fans has been appropriated by mainstream media, even as that media debates the ethics of a fandom that may, in turn, interfere with or enhance the show in various ways. Whether #Setlock enhances or interferes with the show depends on one's perspective: showrunners and actors must balance their reactions such that they do not alienate their fan base, while clearly being frustrated with fan interference, and those who create and consume #Setlock feel the show is enhanced by their "detective work" on set and their creative endeavors online. #Setlock affects the way the show may be produced and alters the way that the characters may be perceived, and because of the affordances of digital media, alternative interpretations of characters' identities, even those that contradict Conan Doyle and Gatiss/Moffat canon, are gaining significant traction both inside and outside of the insular, online communities in which they traditionally exist. This validates fans' readings of the characters, lending them power traditionally reserved for a text's original creator. Through #Setlock, fans have the opportunity to contribute to the body of knowledge and creative works regarding the object of their affection in unprecedented and empowering ways.

WORKS CITED

Anastasis. Twitter. 8 Feb. 2015. Web. 8 Feb. 2015.
Ashley. "allfandoms5ever." Pinsta.me. 4 Feb. 2015. Web. 1 Aug. 2015.
Baker-Whitelaw, Gavin. "#Setlock: The Fans Who Stalk the 'Sherlock' Film Set." *The Daily Dot*. 15 Jan. 2015. Web. 17 Jan. 2015.
"The Blind Banker." *Sherlock: Season One*. Writ. Steve Thompson. Dir. Euros Lyn. BBC Home Entertainment, 2010. DVD.
Bluebellglowinginthedark. "John felt creative." Tumblr. Jan. 2015. Web. 1 Feb. 2015.
bumblebee-cuttlefish. Tumblr. n.d. Web. 1 Aug. 2015.
Collins, Valerie. Twitter. 8 Feb. 2015. Web. 8 Feb. 2015.
Cupidford. "I Blog About It and He Forgets His Pants." Tumblr. 12 July 2015. Web. 1 Aug. 2015.
Gill, James. "Martin Freeman—'I Don't Love #Setlock. It Makes It Hard to Do Your Job.'" *Radio Times*. 18 Jan. 2015. Web. 20 Jan. 2015.
Hibberd, James. "Sherlock Co-Creator: For the Last Time, Holmes Is Not Gay!" *Entertainment Weekly*. 30 Mar. 2015. Web. 30 Mar. 2015.

Hills, Matthew. "Virtually Out There: Strategies, Tactics, and Affective Spaces in On-line Fandom." *Technospaces: Inside the New Media.* Ed. Sally Munt. London: Continuum, 2001. Print.

Holmes, Jonathan. "Steven Moffat on Setlock: 'We're All Genuinely Very Appreciative That People Love Our Show So Much.'" *Radio Times.* 29 Jan. 2015. Web. 1 Feb. 2015.

Jenkins, Henry. Ed. *Confronting the Challenges of Participatory Culture.* MacArthur Foundation, 2006. Web.

Jess. "Atual Imagen de Setlock." Twitter. 23 Jan. 2015. Web. 23 Jan. 2015.

Jones, Paul. "Sherlock Fans Have Changed the Way We Make the Show, Says Mark Gatiss." *Radio Times.* 25 Nov. 2014. Web. 19 Sep. 2015.

_____. "Sherlock Fans Say No to #Setlock." *Radio Times.* 22 Jan. 2015. Web. 24 Jan. 2015.

_____. "Should #Setlock Continue?" *Radio Times.* 18 Jan. 2015. Web. 20 Jan. 2015.

Meg. Twitter. 8 Feb. 2015. Web. 8 Feb. 2015

Ramlall, Rashmika. "Johnlock graffiti while filming Series 4." Pinterest. n.d. Web. 8 Feb. 2015.

Redbeard221B. Twitter. 8 Feb. 2015. Web. 8 Feb. 2015.

"A Study in Pink." *Sherlock: Season One.* Writ. Steven Moffat. Dir. Paul McGuigan. BBC Home Entertainment, 2010. DVD.

"What Does Martin Freeman Think of #Setlock?" *The Guardian.* 19 Jan. 2015. Web. 19 Sep. 2015.

About the Contributors

Amber **Botts** has taught language arts at Neodesha High School in Neodesha, Kansas, for nearly 20 years. She teaches American literature and composition to juniors and British literature and composition concurrent credit through Independence Community College to seniors.

Grace **Cripps** is pursuing master's degrees in education and English at Truman State University in Kirksville, Missouri. Her research interests include cognitive literary theory, code-switching, disability studies and gender studies.

Jennifer **Dondero** is a staff member at the Chicago School Forensic Center, an outpatient mental health facility. Her research interests include humanistic/existential approaches to mental health treatment, traumatic stress, juvenile delinquency, community mental health interventions and media psychology.

Deborah M. **Fratz** teaches 19th-century British literature at the University of Wisconsin–Whitewater, where she is an associate professor. Her research focuses on Gothic and Victorian literature, with an emphasis on gender and disability studies.

Linda J. **Jencson** is a senior lecturer in the Department of Anthropology at Appalachian State University in Boone, North Carolina. Her interests center on the use of symbolic communication and narrative to motivate social action. She has written on new religions, organizational aspects of disaster response and popular culture.

Clare Douglass **Little** is an assistant professor of humanities and communication at Embry-Riddle Aeronautical University in Daytona Beach, Florida. Her research interests include pedagogy and composition instruction; serialized, illustrated fiction and Victorian art and literature.

Kathryn **McClain** teaches English at John Wood Community College in Quincy, Illinois. Her theoretical interests include cognitive literary theory, men's studies and fan studies.

Felecia **McDuffie** is an associate professor of religion at Georgia Gwinnett College in Lawrenceville, Georgia. Her main areas of interest are the intersections of religion and literature, religion and embodiment, and religion and popular culture.

Sabrina J. **Pippin** is the manager of the Business Psychology Department at the Chicago School of Professional Psychology. Her research interests include classical literature adaptation, especially *Sherlock Holmes* and *The Three Musketeers*.

Lynnette **Porter** is a professor in the Humanities and Communication Department at Embry-Riddle Aeronautical University in Daytona Beach, Florida. This is the second collection of Sherlock Holmes-themed essays she has edited; the first was *Sherlock Holmes for the 21st Century: Essays on New Adaptations* (McFarland, 2012).

Heather **Powers** is an associate professor of English at Indiana University of Pennsylvania. She teaches everything from basic writing to 18th-century British literature to Harry Potter and is working on a book on the history of shaming fans of popular culture.

Alyxis **Smith** teaches English as an adjunct at Wenatchee Valley College in Wenatchee, Washington. She presented on deconstructing the idea of Hogwarts as a safe space for LGBT students and readers at a recent PCA/ACA national conference.

Charla R. **Strosser** is an assistant professor of English at Southern Utah University in Cedar City, where she teaches composition, business writing and introductory literature courses. Her research interests include detective fiction, fairy tales, gender studies and southwestern literature.

Jennifer **Wojton** is an instructor at Embry-Riddle Aeronautical University in Daytona Beach, Florida. Her interests in popular culture are broad, although her work tends to focus on LGBTQ culture and digital culture, sometimes both at the same time.

Index